The DANGER OF DESIRE

The DANGER OF DESIRE

ELIZABETH ESSEX

BRAVA

KENSINGTON PUBLISHING CORP.

www.kensingtonbooks.com

BRAVA BOOKS are published by

Kensington Publishing Corp.
119 West 40th Street
New York, NY 10018

All Kensington titles, imprints and distributed lines are available at special quantity discounts for bulk purchases for sales promotion, premiums, fund-raising, educational or institutional use.

Special book excerpts or customized printings can also be created to fit specific needs. For details, write or phone the office of the Kensington Special Sales Manager: Kensington Publishing Corp., 119 West 40th Street, New York, NY 10018. Attn. Special Sales Department. Phone: 1-800-221-2647.

Brava and the B logo are Reg. U.S. Pat. & TM Off.

ISBN-13: 978-0-7582-5158-9
ISBN-10: 0-7582-5158-0

First Kensington Trade Paperback Printing: December 2011

10 9 8 7 6 5 4 3 2 1

Printed in the United States of America

For my parents, for love, education, and support.
But most especially, for my mother, Carol Craven Robinson,
for her lifelong dedication to books and the fine art of reading.

ACKNOWLEDGMENTS

Thanks are due to many people, but most especially: to my delightful editor, Megan Records, for her careful stewardship of all of my books for Kensington Brava; to Kristine Mills-Noble and Franco Accerno for three absolutely magnificent, gorgeous, lush covers; to my agent, Barbara Poelle, for convincing me that writing on a deadline was simple; to Anna Campbell, for her generosity in reading the manuscript and providing a smashing cover quote; and last, but never least, to my brilliant critique partner, Joanne Lockyer, for always finding the right words to encourage me to do my best—three hearty and heartfelt *huzzahs!*

CHAPTER 1

London, November 1799

Lord, but it was cold and raw as a St. Giles curse. Nothing kept out the aching damp. Meggs hugged her arms closer to her sides, tucked her bare fingers up in fists, and quickened her pace along the deserted sidewalk as she and her brother slipped their way through St. James's dripping streets toward the Strand, looking for a few more likely culls. But drunken lords had been thin on the ground this morning. The icy drizzle had been falling in fits and starts since dawn, and the sky remained an ominous, bone-cold gray.

She hated it. Hated it all—the insidious cold, the incessant rain, the petty larceny—but hunger had a way of sorting out priorities. There was thievery to be done.

"Tell me again." At her side, Timmy swiped at his cold nose with the back of his sleeve.

For her brother, Meggs pushed the bleak feeling of unease aside.

"We'll be rich, we will. And we'll live in a lovely house, a stout cottage, you and me, my lucky Tanner, just the two of us. Someplace warm, like Dorset."

She had no idea if Dorset really was a warm place. Perhaps

she had heard it said once, or perhaps she had been told palm trees grew there. And even she knew palm trees grew only in warm places. But wherever it was they went, she was determined it be warm. They had been cold for far too long.

Almost forever. And today, when London's creeping, yellow fog was thick with ice, she felt as though it would be winter forever. Days like this, she despaired of ever being dry and warm again. Or full. Her stomach growled in empty resentment.

And so, in the face of such barren grayness, she lied. "We'll have a house with lots of fireplaces with warm cozy fires, all snug and toasty. And in the summer, a rose garden so the air will always smell nice, not like coal. We'll have a big garden with an orchard at one end with apples and pears for you to eat whenever you like, and trees for you to climb. And a tree with a rope swing for you to play on."

Her brother was too young to remember what it had been like before. He'd been barely four years old when they'd been packed off to London. And eight years under old Nan's deft tutelage couldn't help but leave its mark.

"When?" he asked with the cynical straightforwardness of a child who was well used to hearing Banbury tales.

"Soon, I think." Her eyes never stopped combing the pavement, even as her mouth spun fantasy out of the chill air. "There. They'll do. Look sharp."

Three rich, sotted culls were ahead, weaving their way homeward from their club. Drunk as lords. Young toffs with more hair and money than wits. Never notice the lowly housemaid they'd barreled into had relieved them of their purses, would they? In their pleasant stupor, buffered from the cares of the world by wealth and copious amounts of good liquor, they would not even see Timmy, the small, whip-quick crossing guard to whom she would pass the take as he chanced by.

Timmy nodded once, then melted across the street, made silent and invisible by the fog. Meggs resisted the urge to give him more instruction, or follow his progress to make sure he was well positioned. It wouldn't do. Her Tanner was getting old enough to know their business as well as she. If they wanted to eat, they needed to steal.

The men lurched closer, in and then out of the small circles of lamplight, laughing loudly and singing some bawdy tune. *"There was a young girl from Crupp, whose pleasure it was for to tup . . ."*

Meggs let the lewd lyrics slide past and echo down the street. The one on the left was tallest. Tall Boy's arms and hands were completely engaged in holding up his drunken comrade, who was draped over his shoulder like a drunk sailor. Tall Boy was happy. His coat flapped open to reveal a bounteous, bulging waistcoat pocket. Tall Boy had been the winner.

And so would she be. Meggs flexed her hands on the handle of her basket and wiped her fingers dry on the inside of her apron, swallowing the jitters that crawled up her throat. It would work. It always worked. Drunks were easy. Easy as taking gin from a dead whore. She gauged the distance and picked up speed, keeping even pace with the rising hammer of her heart, aiming to reach them just as they left the watery circle of lamplight. She'd be in the dark, and they'd never see her until it was too late.

Three yards to go. Two. Eyes and ears stretched open, blind to everything but the waistcoat pocket and deaf from the roaring of her blood, she put her head down and plowed right into them.

And it was dead easy. A turn of her body, a firm shove with the prickly reed basket, and the culls were separated and falling. And there she was, patient as the saints, waiting for the precise moment when his purse eased into her waiting hand, like a ripe plum plucked from a tree.

Then she was racing past and beyond, into the safety of the dark before they had even registered her presence. "Come back, darling," one of them called. "I'll make it worth your while."

He'd already made it worth her while, thank you very much. Meggs dismissed the drunk young culls from her mind as she passed Timmy the take and moved on swiftly into the rising dawn.

But she was wrong. Two blocks later, when they met up, Timmy had already discarded the purse and counted the money. "Flimsies," he sighed, "and small change."

Banknotes. Not so good as ready coin. They'd not get full value if they tried to fence them, and they couldn't very well waltz up Poultry Lane to the Bank of England to exchange them, could they? Get shoulder clapped right there in the lobby, they would. "How much in coin?"

"Two quid, three crowns, six pence."

She couldn't look at the disappointment scraped across his pinched face. It was not enough. Why was it never enough?

"We need one more this morning. One good one." It was always the hardest—that last purse of the morning. After nearly four hours she and Timmy were getting tired, but the toffs were waking up. So much easier to dip them when they were still half-muzzied with drink. "So look sharp, my little Tanner. You clap your peepers on a likely greenhead, and we'll get a meat pie, after."

"Each?"

She hated that hopeful tone. The one she always had to disappoint. "To split. But only if we spy a likely toff to tip. So look sharp. Mind the traps." The last thing they needed was to run afoul of the Constabulary, who were always about in this part of town protecting the deserving rich from the undeserving poor, the criminal element. From thieves like them.

Hugh McAlden's leg had begun to ache. The cold, wet walk up from Chelsea, all the way to the Admiralty Building in Whitehall, had taken more out of him than he had anticipated.

He ought to have taken a walking stick, or gone down river by boat with a waterman, but the morning had promised to be fine. So much for his weather eye.

Normally, the leg only pained him like this when it rained. But this was England. The only place wetter was the bilge of his ship.

His *former* ship. And the only way he was going to regain command of *Dangerous* was by currying the favor of the Admiralty. Thus, gimpy and out of sorts, he presented himself to the porter in the cavernous Admiralty Building in Whitehall and wound his way through the warren of rooms to his appointment.

"Captain McAlden?" the clerk inquired as soon as he found the room. "Admiral Middleton will see you immediately. Please come this way."

Sir Charles Middleton, recently promoted to Admiral of the Blue, greeted Hugh like an old friend, which they were if giving Hugh dangerous, unsavory assignments and rewarding him heartily with advancement counted as friendship.

"Captain McAlden." The admiral came though the doorway and held out his hand. "Good to see you, my boy. You're looking fit. I expected to find you much the worse for wear after hearing of your injuries."

"I'm improving, sir, I thank you."

"Good, good." The admiral refrained from clapping Hugh on the back, but his smile was full of relief. "I was pleased to hear such things of you at Aboukir Bay—how you took *Dangerous* to cut the line to engage the French from behind. Well done, sir, well done, but I expected nothing less from you. The dispatches were full of it. And at Acre. Hell of a thing for a sailor to be wounded in a battle on land, what?" He glanced down. "How's the leg?"

"Still attached."

"Ha! We'll have you back to the fleet in no time. Come walk with me."

Hugh kept his grimace to himself and limped after Sir Charles, back down the echoing staircase and out the rear of the building toward the parkland beyond. "It's damnable to be so hobbled and unfit for command," he said to cover his awkwardness on the stairs. "I don't know what bothers me more—the leg or being so damn useless."

"Ah, but that is where you are wrong, Captain. I have every expectation you will be very useful to me—even in your present state."

"Admiral?"

"I have another interesting assignment for you."

Hugh found his leg began not to pain him so very much with such a prospect before him. And the weather was improving as well. The damned iced drizzle had at last begun to give way to snow. "More interesting than the last?"

It had been over four years since Sir Charles, who at the time had been an influential member of the Admiralty Board, had sent him off on an *interesting* special assignment. Special meaning unofficial and unacknowledged—at least publicly. But Sir Charles had seen to it Hugh was rewarded with command of *Dangerous*. Which had led to his success at Aboukir Bay and then Acre. And ultimately, his damn wound. But caution had never brought him success or advancement. Completing Admiral Sir Charles Middleton's unsavory tasks had. "Admiral, I am completely at your disposal."

The admiral nodded once with sharp satisfaction. "Good. I think you should also know there is talk of putting you up— well, you've already been put up—for a knighthood. Your name is on the list for His Majesty's consideration. Nelson, in particular, has been fulsome in his praise for your valor, though he was certainly not the only one to note it."

Hugh could not stop the warm feeling of pleasure brewing in his chest from becoming a smile. He was more than surprised, and even a little chagrined. His Scots grandfather would be turning over in his grave to hear he'd been made into an English version of a gentleman, though he would be proud of all Hugh had accomplished for himself. But Sir Charles intended him to understand something else as well—that a preferment, as well as this knighthood, would be advanced only by his accomplishing whatever unsavory task Sir Charles was about to assign him. Hugh could feel his smile broaden across his face. Here was work, at last.

As they walked out over the newly frozen ground, Sir Charles's tone became more firm, though also more quiet in the hush of the lightly falling snow. "You will have noted my need to assure our solitude"—he gestured to their empty surroundings—"and concluded I do not want our conversation overheard by anyone."

"Anyone?" Hugh glanced back at the building, a bastion of staunch patriotism. "In the Admiralty?"

Sir Charles shook his head, and in that instant, he looked care-worn and old. "With the country embroiled in the war with France, one would like to think the Admiralty, of all places, would be safe. But it is, I fear, not. We will take only a short turn, for your leg is no doubt cramped, and then we will go back inside to meet with a . . . staff officer of the army."

"Sir?" Unease tightened Hugh's spine. He was a straightforward man. He took orders and accomplished them. But the admiral's hesitation indicated some unpleasant odor was in the breeze. It smelled like the sort of army staff officer who never seemed to have an official function. The kind who dealt in dark alleys and informants. And Hugh would rather navigate his ship through a harbor full of mines than tangle with the likes of them.

The admiral was nodding his head in apparent agreement. "This is a navy matter, unquestionably. However, it gives our colleagues in the army . . . comfort to be involved. They have sent a representative."

Hugh expected the *representative*'s involvement had not eventuated without serious resistance. He kept his mouth shut and listened.

"Since I took up the Blue, I left the Admiralty Board. Earl Spencer is First Lord of the Admiralty now, and he has his Cambridge cronies in as Lord Commissioners. However, Spencer has appealed to me, since I am not directly involved with the board at present, to intervene and stop a serious leak of information."

Hugh's blood got colder by degrees. The ramifications were immense.

"Valuable information, sensitive, secret, or what ought to be secret information, has gone missing. Here, from this building, where every man's loyalty and honor ought not be questioned!" The admiral's face grew ruddy with frustrated, suppressed rage. "It's intolerable."

"My God." Hugh let out a low expletive. "That's treason. Do you have a suspect?"

Admiral Middleton fixed Hugh with a bleak stare. "I obtained a list of the intercepted communications from Military Intelligence along with the dates they were intercepted. I could immediately correlate the missing information with dates of meetings of the Board of Admiralty."

"God's balls. One of the Lords Commissioners."

"Yes. And there are seven Lords Commissioners on this Board of Admiralty. All very high up, both in the government and in society."

This was why Sir Charles had asked him. He knew Hugh didn't care two farthings for society or rank. The navy had taught him merit and character were all that mattered. "Surely it can't be one of the Naval Lords?"

Sir Charles gave a grim negative. "I should like to deny the possibility it is one of the Naval Lords—they know the consequences as well as you or I. Much as I would like to, it would be beyond foolish to assume it could only be one of the civilian politicians instead."

"You want me to find out which one is responsible."

"Yes. Before the next formal meeting of the board, you will rout out this traitor and serve him up to Earl Spencer trussed and ready for hanging. I want this handled quietly, within the navy, before any other part of the government becomes involved. Or notified."

Hugh could easily understand the ramifications of treason of such magnitude. Governments had fallen for less. "This representative of the army knows of my involvement?"

"Unfortunately, yes. I would wish I could leave this solely within navy hands, but ministers must be appeased. Special staff officers must be catered to. But I've told them nothing of what I suspect regarding the Admiralty Board." They had arrived back at the steps. "They've sent a Major Rawsthorne. Twenty years in. India service for the most part. We'll see him now."

Major Rawsthorne proved to be a pale, solid man in his middle years with an air of callous importance. If India had left a mark on him, he hid it well. He looked like any soft, well-connected, government-posted officer, not the hardened, sun-baked veteran Hugh had expected. There was shrewdness but no understanding in his eyes. A political man. Hugh always got a pain from political sorts, but he knew enough to keep both his feelings and his opinions to himself.

"Major Rawsthorne," Middleton introduced them, "Captain McAlden. Captain McAlden will be handling this matter for the Admiralty."

Rawsthorne lifted his eyebrow for a leisurely inspection. Hugh let him look, preferring to keep his gaze level on Admiral Middleton. He was a navy man. Rawsthorne would do well to learn where his loyalties lay.

"And Captain McAlden is experienced in these sort of . . . subtleties?"

Pompous bastard.

"Yes." The admiral did not deign to qualify his statement. He knew well enough how to play these games. "You will appreciate that from your reading of the reports from Acre."

"Making use of Arab street rats born into a life of crime? London isn't a walled, besieged city with a captive populace of heathen children."

A pompous man with his own ways of getting information, if he already knew Hugh's record. Yet the major must not look about him in the streets of London. God knew the sidewalks and alleys here were crawling with the same kind of children, crafty and quick, their lives full of meanness and want.

The admiral felt as Hugh did. "Heathen or not, there are plenty of street rats in London. Damned if one of those cheeky young devils didn't relieve me of no less than six silver buttons as I was getting into my carriage last evening. Cut them off my cuff with one swipe of a knife before I knew it."

And there it was. Hugh knew exactly what he was going to do. He would have laughed at the lunacy of it not five minutes ago, but now it made unaccountable sense.

"No," Rawsthorne was insisting. "While I'm sure Captain McAlden is a competent enough and courageous commander of a fighting ship, you need to leave this sort of thing to us. We have all the experience necessary to deal with the problem. My men—"

"Admiral Middleton, I have my assignment." Hugh bowed to his admiral and turned, bland and obedient, to give the same honor to Rawsthorne, though Hugh was the higher ranking officer. "Major."

The major was too full of his own importance to notice the courtesy. "Now see here. I don't want to have to make a fuss, but this is our jurisdiction. We cannot tolerate any further breach or compromise of information."

"I understand you perfectly, Major. You may consider the matter taken care of. Admiral Middleton."

"Captain McAlden." The admiral gave his hand in a firm grasp. "I'll see you out." They left the major sputtering objections in their wake.

As soon as they had reached the outer doors, Hugh asked, "The Lords Commissioners—your clerk will furnish me with a list?"

"I have it here. I have sealed it personally." Middleton handed over a missive. "All the information I have to hand on each man."

"Thank you. Will you want to be kept up to date on details of my plans and progress?"

Middleton held up a hand to forestall him. "No, no. Whatever you feel necessary. I don't want to hear the particulars—because this conversation has not taken place." His lips curved in a wry smile. "Not until you are successful, of course."

"How much time do I have?"

"As little as possible. Two weeks at most. We need this done, Hugh."

Sir Charles had never called him by his Christian name before. He'd no idea the man even knew it. He gave his admiral his hand. "You have my word, sir. I'll begin at once."

Hugh took his leave and stiff-legged his way back down the echoing marble stairs and out onto the streets, heedless of the aching cold and blowing snow. He was thinking of Acre, of heat and meanness, and the faces of children.

CHAPTER 2

The toff limping out of Spring Gardens onto Cockspur Street was just the sort she liked, if she couldn't have a drunk. Big man, but tired he was, weariness stewing from his bones like the cold steam of his breath in the frigid, snowy air. And he was a gimp—heavily favoring his left leg—but without a cane or walking stick. So far so good. It paid to stay well clear of walking sticks. But he was a gentleman, all right, with a well enough set of togs, though he looked none too comfortable in them. Too new. Country man recently come up to town was her guess.

Meggs took a deep breath, hitched the basket of sewing higher onto her hip, tipped Timmy the wink, and headed along the pavement in the man's direction.

She kept her eyes on the mark. On his hands and his face. Definitely a country man, though he was younger than she had first thought. Pain and injury did that to a man—aged him. His face, as he looked up and down Cockspur Street for his direction, was weathered and rugged like the granite hills of Derbyshire. A walking tor, that's what he was.

There it was again, that same strange pang of dread, that feeling that was half memory and half longing for something just out of reach. She tried to mentally push the nebulous sensation away, but it was like swatting at a cobweb—invisible, tenuous bits of feeling clung stubbornly to her brain.

But there was no room for mooning about. She needed to keep her wits about her and concentrate on the flat ahead. On the gleaming watch he'd just pulled from his pocket to consult the time.

And then, he looked up and Meggs saw his eyes. So pale a blue, they were shocking in a face so tan. Chips of ice held greater warmth, and yet there was a fire, a force that sparked so strongly, so powerfully within the frozen wasteland of his gaze, she had to turn away for fear of being singed.

She knew that look. A zealot. Moon eyed. Dicked in the nob. Whatever it was, every instinct she possessed screamed *danger*. And clever girl that she was, she minded quick-like, keeping her head down and scurrying across the street to stay well clear of his path, away from all that steely awareness. She had no desire to receive another blast from the furnace that was his eyes, thank you very much.

But that was a mistake, too.

For while she was minding the dangerous, sharp-eyed cove, she smashed headlong into another body and down they went, for real.

It was generally *not* the sagest of ideas to frisk a toff without having ever clapped peepers on him to see if he were a likely chum, but her clever fingers were already making professional-like, cataloging his portable chattels before she could have a look-see and come to a prudent decision.

Merino wool, good quality. Waistcoat, brocade silk. Belly of considerable girth. Scent of expensive cigars and brandy. Toff. Watch, fob, and purse, quick and easy as you please as she fell down, and the top button of her loosely pinned bodice obligingly popped open to fill his eyes with the sight and feel of her padded, upthrust breasts as they brushed against him. And to finish the business, a spill of white petticoat and a breathless, helpless display of calf.

It was all as familiar as a Drury Lane play, and twice as well rehearsed.

"Lawks," she cawed on top of him, "me basket!"

Then she snatched at the fallen bits of fabric and sewing, an embroidered bodice piece having fallen, quite by design, in the gentleman's considerable lap. Her fingers brushed mercifully fleetingly across his cods so his blood would keep well away from his brain.

It was just as old Nan always said—a man couldn't think and fill his rod at the same time. Keep him doing the one, and he'd never be able to do the other.

And it was done. She was up and fussing with her basket and moving away muttering, "Don't care who they knock over. Missus'll have my head, if— Ere, gimme that!" she called as Timmy darted by pretending to grab at the lacy underthings she carried in her basket.

"Here now! Leave off there!"

Meggs turned back, thinking for some ungodly reason of the pale-eyed man. But no, it was worse—a constable. How had she missed seeing him? Cripes, that was all they needed—the Law barging his way toward her, waving his cosh at Timmy.

But Timmy scarpered right quick, the heavy purse she passed him already surreptitiously down his shirt. "I saw her bottom, I saw her bottom!" he yelled gleefully as he went running through the foot traffic.

Meggs stepped into the trap's line of sight to divert his attention. "Oh, Constable!"

"You all right, miss?" the constable asked.

The constable was young, and thankfully, someone she had never crossed before. Meggs let her real fear and apprehension color her voice. "Brazen it out," old Nan would have said, "but make it real, dearie."

"Thank you. Knocked me off my feet, he did." She cut her eyes toward the fat toff still righting himself and fanned her hand demurely across her half-revealed décolleté. Lovely word that, one of Nan's favorites. "Have to be rich to have dé-colleté," she used to say. "The poor just have titties." Rich or poor, the young constable's gaze had dropped six inches to what one hand revealed, while under the basket, her other hand concealed the liberated watch deep within the folds of her skirts.

It was a risk to draw such attention to herself, but she needed to make sure Timmy was clean away, and with the constable's eyes glued to her bumped up titties, she'd earned herself some running room. Speaking of which.

"Lawks, the time! My missus'll have my head. Much obliged, Constable." And she was off, muttering and fussing, turning from the pavement and heading into the sea of people moving through Charing Cross.

And then she felt it—the icy blast from the devil's own fur-nace. Meggs turned to find the eyes of the pale-eyed country man slicing into her like cold, sharp steel. That was when she abandoned all play acting and ran like hell was opening up be-hind her.

This time, she kept her eyes wide open.

McAlden had to admire the ploy at the very least. It was smartly done. Quick and devilishly efficient, yet seemingly spontaneous. And completely unexpected.

He had barely noticed the nondescript maidservant in her cap and apron as she scurried out of his way. He was used to women, even housemaids, avoiding him. His mother said it was because he didn't trouble himself to smile. But he knew it was because he exuded discomfort around the fairer sex. Not that he didn't like them; he did, but after sixteen years at sea in the almost exclusive company of men, he was deucedly un-easy around them. Even housemaids.

The poor girl had appeared as common as a housefly and just as harmless, but there was no doubt in his mind, the agile pickpocket with the shapely ankles had just relieved the Honorable Member of Parliament for Lower Wherever of his watch and purse. What was more, the stupid bastard had no idea. For all that she had landed herself right atop his crotch, the fat MP had neither *seen* her nor credited her with the brains and nerve to leave him without so much as a farthing.

And in the middle of all the textbook commotion, all Hugh could think of was something else his widowed mother had said several years ago on the occasion of her remarriage.

His mother had been more than flattered Viscount Balfour had asked for her hand—she had been astounded. "I really had no idea that he should want to marry me at my age, let alone have noticed me to begin with. A man, any man, but especially a man as handsome as Balfour can always find a younger woman. Women my age are largely invisible to the world."

And so had that girl been—invisible even as she scrambled off the rich man's lap. Just a maidservant or a shop girl. A nobody. Just an inconvenience in the aristocrat's busy day.

Whoever she was, she was almost a sign from a helpful God. If he believed in God, which after sixteen years of death and destruction in His Majesty's Royal Navy, he did not.

By his reckoning, life was a matter of happenstance and things only turned out the best for those who were prepared to make the best of the way things turned out. His was a singularly un-English philosophy, but then again he was Scots, a more fatalistic breed than these English, who like the Member for Lower Bagshot, saw only what they wanted to and thought about even less.

What Hugh thought was that the girl would do very well for him. Very well. She was clearly just as clever as any other street rat, but potentially more adaptable to his needs. Indeed, he could use her as the maidservant she was dressed up to be, planted within the traitor's house to steal all of his secrets, not just the ones he happened to carry out of the Admiralty in his coat pockets.

All he had to do was catch her.

She was already moving quickly down the sidewalk, away from the constable. Hugh immediately crossed between traffic at Charing Cross and followed her onto the Strand, weaving his way around shoppers, beggars, and tradesmen. He was forced to pick up his pace to keep her in his sights. It was a hell of a strain on his already fatigued leg, but he was a bloody officer of the navy—the senior service—he'd be damned if he couldn't keep up with some light-fingered slip of a girl.

She kept on, purposeful and steady, without a hint of urgency, until she glanced back at him. He instinctively tried to hide himself, shying into the doorway of a building before he was seen, but he saw the knowledge he was on to her darken her eye before she ducked immediately between buildings and disappeared into the Kings Mews.

Hugh was forced to an awkward jog to the entryway of the mews. But she was easy to spot here, and her face, pale with terror as she turned round to watch for him, was like a beacon amid the darker sea of hats and horses. He jostled his uneven way after her, dodging hoofs and weaving his way across the open yard to where she again disappeared into the back of a building.

It was a linen drapers warehouse. Bolts of cloth, arranged on racks and piled high on countertops, obscured his view and hid her from him. Hugh stopped, wary lest he should pass her by, or she should try to double back into the pell-mell of the mews. So he did what he had learned to do at sea, and searched for stillness. By concentrating on the stillness, his eye was drawn to the contrast of the least flicker of movement. And there she went, a silent wisp of worn, dark fabric, stealing swiftly down an aisle toward the front of the building. He damned his aching leg and clawed upwind after her.

He was almost at full sail now, pushing the limit of his ability, chasing after her, but she was quick as a running tide, flowing in and out of doors and around corners as surely as water racing downstream. Out onto St. Martin's Lane and across, swinging around the far side of the church building, rushing toward the warren of streets and alleys that ran between Long Acre and Covent Garden. The strident ache in his leg intensified into a sharp, digging pain as he abandoned all caution to pelt across the churchyard and turn round the back of St. Martin's Church just in time to see the foam of her skirts whip behind the wall of Moors Court. He accelerated and gained some ground, closing enough distance to watch her head down for New Round Court.

She, too, had abandoned all pretense and was running flat out. She must have had the bloody map of London in her head for she flitted through every narrow, obscure alley and passageway and knew every unlocked gate and twisted path, leading him on a goose chase that had him panting for breath to keep up.

But still he pushed on. She was too good a find, too perfect a match for his needs, to give up now—his bird-almost-in-hand, if he could stay with her. He was a grown man, a hardened veteran of the French Wars, a captain of His Majesty's Navy, in the prime of his life, and even with a stiff, shrapnel-filled leg, surely he could outrun a malnourished slip of a rapscallion girl.

Damn it all to hell. He clenched his jaw over the pain throbbing from his leg and flung himself up another blind alley. And thanked his lucky stars she had finally made a mistake.

The door she had counted on at the back of the narrow alley was locked. She was trapped. Hugh slowed to a walk and began to close the remaining distance between them. She was breathing hard from the exertion, and her exhalation rose and frosted the air above her head like a net. The brick of the next building ran four stories straight up on one side, while a tall stone wall, topped with inset shards of broken glass, penned her in from the other.

The passageway was narrow—so narrow he could run his

hands along both walls as he advanced on her—and eerily quiet. The only sound was the panting of their breaths, white clouds steaming into the fetid, back alley air. Her face—for some strange reason he wanted to see her face. He needed to *see* her. To make sure she became something other than just another maidservant in his mind. To fix her in his memory.

She was older than he would have guessed for one so swift. Her face, pale with animal fear, was unlined, although her dirty cheeks were hollowed with the hard look of a street rat— or perhaps hunger. She ought to have been able to feed herself off what she'd just stolen, but he had to consider it probably all went to her kidman. Or her pimp. The girl would be lucky to get cold soup.

By God, when she was with him, he would feed her.

No, her face was not particularly dirty—the smudge was a dusting of freckles across her nose. The darker shadows were circles the color of a bruise under her eyes—glittering, dark and huge, in her ashen face. The mobcap on her head obscured the color of her hair, but it looked to be dark brown from the tendrils fallen loose down her neck.

Her gaze darted around him, scanning the alley frantically and looking in vain for an escape.

"You won't find it. You're trapped." The queer rush of triumphal pleasure took him mildly by surprise. It shouldn't gratify him so to defeat this feral, scrawny, half-starved lass. But it did. She'd made him work for his little victory. She was a worthy opponent. She would be a valuable asset.

"You're very good," he continued more diplomatically. "That was a neat piece of work."

She didn't respond but gripped the ridiculous basket in front of her with tight, whitened knuckles, as if it alone could ward him off. No farcical, false denials. Hugh felt his mouth curve into a half smile. It pleased him he would not have to teach her the value of silence. Another decided mark in her favor.

She had backed up hard into the end of the passage, the impassable door flat at her back.

"I have a proposition for you."

"I'm not a whore."

The blunt assertion surprised him. "No, you're a pickpocket. A clever one. And as it happens, I am in need of a clever pickpocket. I'd like you to steal for me."

She shook her head, a frightened refusal creasing her brow with the perfect touch of false bewilderment. "I'm a seamstress. I take in sewing." She pushed the basket out just a fraction to show him. Oh, she was good.

Hugh smiled and shook his head. "I'll wager," he said in the low, calm voice he employed with frightened midshipmen, "you carry that basket around all day long, and not a bit of that sewing ever gets finished. I'll wager"—he took another step toward her—"you've a soft little pouch on the bottom, where you've stashed the gold watch of the Member of Parliament for Lower Sudbury."

She widened her eyes in puzzlement, opened her plum lips in astonishment, and tipped the basket carefully toward her chest so the bottom was completely visible to him, and then felt along the lower rim as if afraid to find what he had just described.

There was nothing. Hugh's head swam for a moment. Perhaps he was wrong. Perhaps, like the Honorable Member for Lower Hayrick, he had been swayed by what *he* had wanted to see. He had been looking for a thief, and for some unaccountable reason he wanted it to be this comely, if scrawny, wench.

No, it could not be. His instinct, well honed by years of service, told him otherwise. So she hadn't hidden her take on the bottom of the basket. There were plenty of other, more *personal*, places for concealing stolen bits and bobs.

The grin that hatched on his cheeks was probably not pretty. It was certainly unfamiliar. *Dangerous* had been blasting the French to splinters the last time he had felt such unbridled, unholy glee. Yet, his gaze had already swept over her body, cataloging all the likely spots. On a frame so spare, there were really only two choices.

Her bosom, with its cleverly burst pin, and rounded little breasts pushed high and visible by her stays, was his first choice. Her display of affronted modesty notwithstanding, the current rapidity of her breath, either in fear or anticipation, was serving to offer her breasts up for breakfast. In his mind's eye, he was already delving his fingers down into the warm vee between the improbably soft-looking mounds, sliding the back of his hand against the slight pillow of her skin, slowly pulling the gold watch chain, still warm from the heat of her body, out of the crevasse.

The unwarranted base lust coursing into his veins must have communicated itself to her plainly. She thrust out a hand to forestall him.

"No!" Her voice held a real edge of panic. "I'm not a whore," she cried again.

"Maybe not, but you're not above using your body for your means. But I don't need to search you—though we both know I can, and will, if I want to. I don't need to search you for actual evidence of your light-fingered guilt. My word alone—that I saw you relieve the Honorable Mr. Penton-Thornbraith, Member of Parliament for Lower Sudbury"—he made up the name out of thin air for effect—"of his watch and purse would be enough to get you hung by your scrawny neck. Or if you were very lucky, and either the judge or the jailor decided to avail himself of your very visible offerings, you just might be kept alive in the hulks for transportation. But my experience is most convicts die on the voyage to Botany Bay."

He let that sink into her pale face. "Or, you could work for me."

"I'm not a whore," she repeated stubbornly.

"So you've said. Repeatedly. Which I begin to find tiresome. I think the *lady* protests too much." He took a deep breath to stave off his annoyance. He was trying to convince her of the benefits of employment, wasn't he? Showing her the hot end of his temper wasn't going to help negotiations. Not that she really had a choice, but it would all go so much easier if she thought she did.

"I need a thief, and you, to all appearances, fit the bill quite nicely. Now, who do you work for?"

"You got this all wrong, mister. I don't work for no one, like that. I take in sewing."

"Talented lass like you? Hardly likely. Some kidman must have trained you up for it. I'll buy you off him." Lease her was nearer to the truth, but she'd work that out, clever girl that she was. "And I'll pay you as well. One hundred pounds." It was a bloody fortune to someone like her, provided she didn't drink it away, but her face didn't bear any of the telltale signs of over-fondness for the gin.

But not even the mention of so much money changed her tune. "You got this all wrong," she insisted with a frustrated little stamp of her foot. Her eyes began to brim with tears. "I'm a seamstress. Look." And again she proffered her basket of sewing, thrusting it forward for his inspection.

And damn his eyes, he looked.

He looked down only for a moment, long enough for an embroidered "T" on one of the pieces of fabric to catch his eye and make him pause at the improbability of such a personal, intimate touch to her disguise. Maybe he really *did* have this all wrong.

And in that instant, she upended the whole bloody basket onto his lowered head.

He threw up his arms to cast the damned thing off and scatter the clinging, obscuring bits of cloth that fell over his head. When he did, she darted to his right. But when he turned to grab her, she bounded off the wall with her left foot, and with her right, came down with infuriatingly accurate force upon the weak spot on his thigh.

Pain exploded up his leg, hot and cutting. He crumpled to his knees from the force of her blow, even as she pushed off from his leg with a dazzling display of agility to bound back to the right upon a windowsill set high into the building, and then back again, flinging herself across the air above his head to scramble up over the top of the wall.

Slumped to the ground beneath, Hugh could only look up at the empty space into which she had so neatly and so completely disappeared. He couldn't quite believe it. She had zigzagged her way up and over him as easily as if she had been scaling a ladder.

But there, at the top of the wall, was a shiny patch of fresh blood. She must have cut herself on the glass. And she had done so without a sound. She was gone, as quiet and lethal as a Mohawk Indian.

Even as he damned the desperate determination that allowed her to injure herself in order to escape, he admired it. Oh, she was good. Damn him for being bested by her, but she was very good.

At his feet, the scattered linens fallen from the overturned basket were getting soiled, absorbing the damp grime of the alley. He rummaged through them, half expecting to find her abandoned booty amongst them, and half knowing she had well and truly bested him.

There was no watch, nor fob. No purse, either. Nothing. But there, there among the linens, was that beautifully and carefully embroidered letter "T," in flowing, flourished script. And something, some bizarrely insistent remnant of his clearly malfunctioning instinct, told him she had actually done it— embroidered it with her own dexterous hands.

If he had not seen her with his own eyes bound over the wall like the feral cat she was, he could almost have believed she really was the impoverished seamstress she so brilliantly claimed to be. Almost.

Hugh heaved himself to his clumsy feet, rubbed his aching

thigh, and set his rumpled clothing to rights. And that was when he felt it. The empty space in his pocket where his own watch had lately been.

The cloud of his hollow laugh echoed off the brick walls and evaporated slowly into the frigid air.

Oh, God, yes. She was very, very good. And he wanted her more than ever.

CHAPTER 3

Jesus, God in heaven, that had been cutting it far too fine. And she'd gone and lost the bleeding laundry and the basket. Well, she could send Timmy back later, long after the pale-eyed toff should have cleared off. Gave her the jim-jams, that one. Meggs twitched her shoulders to shake off the shivers at the thought of his eerily hot, pale blue gaze.

In the meantime, she had to do something about the ferociously stinging cut across the palm of her hand. Nearly lost her hold on the blighter's watch when she'd hit the jagged glass. Meggs fisted her fingers tight over the pain and held the hand well away from her body. On top of everything else, she didn't want to ruin the damned shop dress with bloodstains. At least she still had all the take. Timmy had the money from the other purses, but she had the two thimbles.

The first watch was tucked close in the hidden pocket along the inside of her leg, and the other she had hastily slid down her bodice on the run. She could feel the chain all the way down, pressed in by the busk of her stays, warm and strangely liquid against her skin, like a slithery metal serpent.

Hopefully, they'd fetch decent change at a pawnshop, and they would make enough on the day despite the loss of the basket and linen, or God forbid, the lost days if her hand were too badly cut to work. Her right hand, too. It hurt like the very devil.

Damn the man all the way down to hell. She should have known he was more than trouble the minute she'd clapped peepers on him.

Meggs ducked into a doorway to catch her breath and make sure there was still no sign of pursuit from the icy-eyed cove. She was nearly to Covent Garden—she'd be safe as a dove there.

She leaned her head back against the wall and eased open her hand. She couldn't stop the hiss of pain escaping through her tightly clenched teeth any more than she could stop the sluggish flow of blood seeping through her fingers.

It was bad. From the lowest joint of her index finger, all the way across the palm, as if a fortune teller had traced her future in blood. Fie and damn and—oh, she couldn't even come up with curse words bad enough to express the well of fear and anguish and frustration that opened up within her.

But she bloody well wasn't going to go all soft and bawling like a bantling. Old Nan had taught her better. She would make do. She would get a potato from a stall in the market and put a raw slice across her hand. Potatoes were brilliant for that. Old Nan had bound one up over a burn on her arm once, and it had healed up twice as fast.

In the market, Meggs paid for the tattie instead of stealing it, mostly because she didn't think she had the nerve or skill for it at the moment, but she *did* have the devil-eyed toff's purse to hand. She fished out a couple of pennies and, without looking, palmed the rest down into her pockets before she tossed the incriminating evidence of the sueded purse into the refuse underfoot for some other sharp-eyed street arab to find and take to a fence or ragwoman. She pulled her disarrayed kerchief from around her neck and wrapped it carefully around the wound.

"Meggs!" Timmy ranged alongside. "Wot happened? Took so long I thought you'd been boned by the trap."

For safety's sake, Meggs made no objection to Timmy speaking the thieves slang when they were on the street. "It wasn't the trap tried to shoulder-clap me." She shook her head and nodded forward, out of the market, pushing east toward Great Russell Street. She felt an implacable, itchy need to keep moving. "That bloody swell was flash, but I finally tipped him the double. Lost him back near the Old Round Court."

"The fat geezer? Didn't think he could run without wheezing."

"No, the other cove—the gimp."

"Never. That gimp chased you? Why? Didn't bung *his* pockets, did we?"

"Dunno," she lied. "Chased me all the way from Cockspur. Nearly got me, the bloody bastard. And I've done for my hand."

Timmy's laugh was half shock, half glee. Normally, she tried to watch her language around him. Not that he couldn't hear worse on the streets any day of the week. But still. She wanted to set a better example.

"Lemme see," he demanded, all gory curiosity.

She shrugged him off. "I'm all right. Let's keep moving." Meggs had them turn south again toward the east end of the Strand, making sure they stayed well clear of both Seven Dials to the north and St. Giles to the east, especially with the lour still in their pockets. If they ventured into those areas, they'd be sure to fun afoul of some well-honed sharp who wanted her to strap for him.

Make that *another* well-honed sharp. Out-running the pale-eyed cove was more than enough for one day.

Because since the sad day old Nan had met her astonishingly swift end with the drop of the rope, Meggs had sworn to steal only for herself. And Timmy. After all those years of living hand to mouth, she vowed to do anything she could to keep from giving the lion's share of the cut to someone else. Today, and every day since last Eastertide, all the lovely, golden meggs in their pockets were for her and Timmy alone.

Once she was more than sure they had not been followed, Meggs found a quiet spot near the entrance to St. Clement's Church to fish out the take. With her back turned into a wall, she dug down into the hidden pocket and let her clever fingers sort out the coinage. She'd known it was heavy, the cold-eyed toff's purse, but weight alone proved nothing. She'd come up with a load of pennies before. But the coins felt right, heavy and warm in her palm, so she pulled one out.

Golden guineas. She let her fingers count—four and change. Thank God. She didn't want to think what she would have felt if she'd gone through all of that for mere pennies. But guineas—meggs they called them—were always well worth the trouble of a chase. It should be as fine a haul as they'd ever had. They would come through just fine for a while, even if she were caw handed.

"Right. What's the take, then?" She kept her voice pitched low. No need to attract unnecessary and unwanted attention.

Timmy was quicker than a Change Alley clerk. "Five quid in flimsies." He handed over the banknotes. "Two, three and six from the first, and"—he counted out the remaining coins—"eighteen meggs, six and four from the fat man. You do know how to pick 'em, Meggs. Regular goldfinch, he were, pockets lined with gold."

"And I've another four. A grand total of—"

"Thirty-one, three and ten. Thirty-one quid, Meggs! Damn, that's prime."

"Shh." She shot an uneasy glance around the empty space. No one appeared to have been listening. Still. A body couldn't be too careful. "Save your breath to cool your porridge. It's too much to have about."

Too much money was always, always a mistake. So much money tempted a body to spend it recklessly. When a body had so much, it was too easy to piss it away on pies and shoes, blankets and coal. But they'd done without for so long, they could do without for a bit longer.

She'd get rid of it—put it safely beyond their immediate reach. Beyond immediate temptation. "I'll off to Threadneedle Street."

"What about the pie?"

Lord, he was always hungry. And he was too thin. His eyes looked huge in his face. Surely out of thirty pounds they could spare a decent meal. At least for him.

"I gave you my word, didn't I?" She counted out the coppers. "You can get a whole pie for yourself over Temple Bar way."

Timmy let out a yelp of delight and bounded to his feet, eager to be off. She didn't follow. "What about you?"

Meggs shook her head. "Threadneedle Street for me. And then fence the goldfinch's thimble. You double back down Strand and see if you can find the basket down behind that derelict lot down Vine Street. The one leads to that passage to Chandos."

"Got it!" Timmy wasn't even listening anymore, and he scarpered right off to find his breakfast.

"Mind yourself, Tanner," she called after him, though he was already gone. She finished the rest under her breath. "And for fuck's sake, look sharp."

Look sharp. That was bloody ironical wasn't it? Now he was gone, Meggs peeled back the crimsoning bandage covering her hand. She could no longer deny it—it was more than bad. It was worse. The burning misery was making her clench her teeth and suck in air through her nose. A raw tattie wasn't going to fix this. Nothing was.

She hadn't looked sharp and now her hand was ruined. She'd be lucky if she stole so much as a pie ever again.

Threadneedle Street was in the heart of the old city and the home of the firm of Levy and Levy, Brokers and Men of Business. *Her* men of business. Meggs was proud of the fact that what had always set her apart from the rest of the nypers and foysters was that she could add two plus two and come up with five.

She had early on understood the value of economy and had practiced it from the beginnings of her career as a cutpurse. She'd palmed a penny here and a tanner there from what she brought to old Nan, until she'd had five pounds of her own stuffed under the sole of her worn-out, too-small shoe and persuaded Mr. Michael Levy, the younger, to take her account.

And along with economy, she had diligence. The amount had slowly, but steadily, increased with the years, and in the little under the eight-month since old Nan had been put to bed with a shovel, she had made sure she and Timmy relieved the unworthy gentry of at least thirty-two shillings per day, or no less than eleven pounds, four shillings per week.

Some days were better than others, but in trying diligently to meet their daily goal, they had provided themselves with a fortune of close to four hundred quid, three hundred of which was currently invested in the safe and sound "cent-per-cent" funds.

It was very nearly enough. Meggs had her heart set on a fortune of five hundred pounds to get them out of London for good. Get them back to the life she had longed for, but now had very nearly forgot.

Today she was thirty pounds closer. And still a world away. She cupped her burning, maimed hand and kept moving past St. Paul's and into Cheapside. Kept thinking. It was more than thirty pounds, she reminded herself. There was not only the fat goldfinch's watch to pawn but the sharp-eyed cove's as well.

But that's why she'd got rid of Timmy, because she hadn't told him about the second watch, had she? Nor where the extra four meggs came from. Nor anything about their encounter in the passageway behind Chandos Street.

Nor about the temptation he made her feel.

"Steal for *me*," he had said.

Right. Hadn't she heard that before? But never in that way, with that voice that sounded like whiskey and moonlight. A voice that soothed even as it lured her deeper into his net.

She'd sworn off kidmen, but he didn't look like any kidman she'd ever seen. All that country bumpkin she thought she'd seen in him on Cockspur Street had disappeared when he'd come after her like a hangman with an empty noose. He had been all smooth agility, even with that leg. She'd tried all her best dodges on him. Hate to think what might have happened if he'd been fit. Or had a stick. Man like that was bound to know how to handle a weapon. Man like that looked solid and hard, as though he'd never been scared a day in his life.

But he didn't have that meanness, that surly pleasure all the greasy sharps had in giving others pain. He hadn't tried to hurt her to bring her in line, quick-like. And he hadn't pawed her at all. Of course, she put paid to him before he'd had any chance, but something told her he wouldn't have cut up rough even if she hadn't.

And he didn't stink of gin or stale ale, either. He didn't smell at all.

Meggs searched her memory and stretched out her senses. She had a nose for that sort of thing, a knack for sorting scents out from one another—the lavender seller on the corner, the coffeehouse across the road, the pungent odor of horse droppings on the slick cobbles—but all she could come up with from this morning was the damp, heavy whiff of coal in the cold air and the acrid-sweet vapor of urine in the alley. Of him, she had nothing.

Fancy that.

Never met with a cove who didn't have some smell, bacon or brandy, offal or gin. Half of St. Giles smelled like they'd never met with bathwater in their life, but he must bathe regular. Lord, what must that be like?

Meggs stumbled to a complete stop at the unlikely and entirely unfamiliar vision of him, of that man she'd only laid eyes on for the first time that morning, rising out of a steaming bath, all wet, gleaming skin and pale, intent eyes. She blinked her eyes hard to clear her head. Devil take her—she'd never thought of a cove like *that* before, naked as God made him.

Maybe he *was* the devil himself, come down with his fiery looks and icy eyes to tempt her into hell.

She palmed his thimble deep inside her pocket. Heavy it was, and far thicker than the goldfinch's. She ducked into a doorway along Poultry Lane and fished it out. The gold was warm and solid in her palm. She turned it over slowly, examining it as if it could yield clues to his character, as if it could tell her what she wanted to know. Like, what did he really want with her? And why would a man like that want, or need, her to steal anything?

The fine script on the front of the dial read *Thos. Earnshaw, London.* She consulted the always present catalog and map in her head. Earnshaw's was up on High Holburn. Back in the other direction. Still, she was going north a bit for Threadneedle Street. And she did want to visit the rag traders after that. Another glance down at her hand and she made up her mind. She was completely done for at present. What could it hurt to find out more about the pale-eyed cove and his hundred pounds? Now, before she lost her courage, as well as her hand.

*   *   *

After Levy's, where Mr. Levy the younger clucked and tutted over her hand but thankfully didn't ask too many questions, her next stop was Ruby the Ragwoman in Black Swan Alley.

Meggs loved the rag traders. To her, Ruby's yard was like an enormous wardrobe for the theater of her imagination. She rotated her patronage between no less than four establishments so that she rarely had to turn over so much as a crown in the exchange of goods. She swapped out her clothing to suit whatever character she was attempting to play. Most dippers just went out day after day without any mind to their appearance. But Meggs had seen too many kiddies get the shoulder clap because someone eye-bolted them. "That's him! I recognize him, the boy in the red cap," some biddy would bawl, and that would be the last of Red Cap.

Meggs changed her appearance as often as she changed the part of the city she worked. Always one step ahead of the law and the sharps. If they couldn't recognize her, they couldn't stop her. This morning she had been the seamstress, this afternoon, she would be the down-on-her-luck lady. The Relative. The Companion. The togs cost her a few extra pennies, but she'd needed the bonnet and the shawl, both good quality, but a few years out of date and faded, to give her just the right touch of genteel poverty, and the dark gray gloves, to cover the ruin that was her hand.

Her second stop, dressed as neat and respectable as an old pin, was Thomas Earnshaw and Co., Watchmakers, at Number One Hundred and Nineteen High Holborn. The door rang out its discreet warning as she stepped tentatively into the quiet interior and was enveloped in the pleasantly industrious smell of lubricating oils and solder.

The clerk, a long, sallow piece of unpleasantness with a beak of a nose, unfolded from behind a counter and condescended to ask, "May I help you?"

She countered with a rush of breathless temerity. "Oh, I do hope so. I was wondering if you might help me return this watch to its rightful owner, sir. I believe it comes from your establishment?"

The beak was all superiority and suspicion. He looked over his spectacles and down his long bill of a nose at her. "That is not a mere 'watch.' That is a pocket chronometer. To be exact, a gold, pair case, openface, pocket chronometer. One of the finest instruments we make."

She widened her eyes and strove to look suitably impressed. "Oh, my. A chronometer is it? It doesn't belong to me, you see, but I feel I ought to try and get it back to its rightful owner. I thought perhaps *you* might have a record of its owner, so I might be able to return it to him."

The clerk pursed his already thin lips and considered her timid reply. He must have decided she presented no harm, as he took up the watch and his loupe to look at the markings on the dial and the case. "Number two hundred and fifty-six." He turned his eye from her only long enough to consult a book of records on the desk behind the felt-topped counter. "Ah, yes. That would be Captain Hugh McAlden, of the navy."

"Ooh, a *captain*. That would make sense, with it being, as you say, a pocket *chronometer*, not just an ordinary watch, and as I found it near the Admiralty Building."

So that's where he'd come from, Himself, down Spring Gardens, from the back of the Admiralty. She should have seen it—the weathered tan and the granite jaw. Bloody naval captain.

"Might you have his direction? Or—" Seeing the suspicious disapproval seep back into the beak's face, she swiftly adapted her plan. "Perhaps you might be so kind as to send a message directly to Captain McAlden that his watch has been found and he may come here to pick it up? I hate to have a thing so valuable in my possession. Makes me nervous, it does." She fluttered her hands away from the thimble.

The beak's mouth softened just enough. It was as good as done.

CHAPTER 4

He came.

Another sleepless, cold night had her second-guessing herself, rubbing her throbbing head and wondering if she'd done the right thing. But there he was, the captain. Captain Hugh McAlden. Meggs rolled his name around in her mouth as if it were a stone she could smooth down into a pebble. McAlden. Hugh.

He appeared at the corner of Newton Street and turned up High Holborn. Had a cane with him today. He leaned on it more heavily as he crossed over through thick traffic to fetch up at the watchmakers. Meggs had to smile. She had served him a thorough basting, hadn't she?

He looked more like a seafaring captain this morning, wearing a dark, double cape over a blue merino coat, buff-colored breeches, and heavy boots. His tricorn hat was pulled down low on his brow, so she couldn't see his eyes. But it was him, no doubt about it. He wasn't burnished with the gloss of town bronze, but now she had more than a few seconds to size him up, and now that she knew better, he moved with what she could only call command.

Captain, the clerk had said. Used to having things his way.

Used to telling people what to do. Used to having the fate of people resting solely in his hands.

What in blue blazes did he want with her?

Meggs hid herself well out of his sight, across the street and down a ways in New Turnstile Lane. She was unrecognizable in shapeless boys clothes this morning, her hair shoved under a worn tweed cap and her body hidden in loose, woolen folds. He would never see her here, let alone know it was her even if he did see her.

Once the captain was safely under the watch shop's bells, Meggs took a chance and sidled nearer—still across the street but so she had a clearer look through the window. Her head was pounding as she squinted in the unfamiliar sunlight pouring into the street and tried to get a sense of what was going on behind the watchmaker's glossy windows. And tried to figure out what she ought to do.

But before she could figure her way clear through the muddle, he reappeared through the door of the shop and slowly, carefully looked around.

She hitched herself back into the shadow of a doorway, but the canny bastard had seen her. And he waved. Right there on the High Holborn, where God and every sharp within a mile could see—he held up his watch to her and waved.

Jesus God. In the first place, how the hell had he seen her, and in the second, did he want to get bunged all over again? Was he dim?

She couldn't help herself. After all the trouble she'd gone to, to get the damned thimble back to him, so he wouldn't pursue her. She skidded herself across the street and fetched up close enough to talk to him, but not so near he'd be able to shoulder-clap her. She was mindful of that stick.

"Take it easy there, Gov'nor. You want to put that away afore someone flips you for it."

"Again, you mean?"

She felt rather than heard his exhalation of satisfaction. He gave her a crooked hitch of a smile and buried the "gold, double case, openfaced pocket chronometer" away on the inside of his waistcoat. Safe enough, but not impossible. But she was *not* here to bung him again. She turned up the pavement without looking to see if he followed. He did.

"Ain't here to argue with you. The old beak give it to you *gratis*, the way he was meant?" She tossed her head back in the direction of the watch shop.

"Yes. He returned my watch to me. May I know why?" His accent was pure toff, all polished address, but his voice was low and rough. He sounded like solid oak beams and creaking spars. He sounded, even though he spoke to her quietly, like he could be heard above a cannon's roar.

And he smelled like soap. No perfume, no flowers. Just like pure soap. Clean. God Almighty.

"Just don't want no trouble with you, see?"

Meggs crossed behind a dray and skirted down a convenient alley into a timber yard. The air was full of sunshine and sawdust, all pungent, golden, and lovely. Like his bleeding watch. She sidled away from Himself, just far enough, so she was on one side of a three-foot-high brick wall dividing the yard while he was on the other. It gave her some measure of security, however flimsy. She already knew she could outrun him. Barely. But the lumberyard gave her the advantage, as it was full of objects and pitfalls, ready to trap the less than nimble.

The captain nodded at her answer and looked ahead, mindful of his unsteady pegs. "I see. I was hoping we might have a chance to meet again." He glanced at her and held out his hand. "This is for you."

When she made no move to accept the shining coin, he tossed it over and she caught it reflexively, with her left hand. Her right, she kept hidden deep in her coat pocket. The long, sleepless night had not improved the hot, miserable ache that had spread from her palm upward, throughout her whole arm.

She held the guinea gingerly, in plain sight, so no one could accuse her of having stolen it. "Why?"

He smiled, but there was little enough warmth, just shrewd calculation. "Why don't we call it a reward. For the return of the watch."

She glanced around, wary of the traps. "Why?"

"A token of my faith. And because you look hungry." His voice sounded almost angry. "Buy yourself a decent meal."

She held silent. And skated a glance up at him. Faith? There was a word she hadn't heard much of in a very, very long time. He was looking away, out over the lumberyard, not at her, and his face was silhouetted against the clear blue of the sky. He looked solid and unmovable. Reliable even. He looked as though he meant it.

"D'you mean it? Wot you said?"

"Yes, I did. I have a . . . business proposition for you."

She made a scornful sound of temper and disbelief. "We been over this. I'm not a whore, mister. Whatever you think about shop girls is wrong."

"Ah, but you're not a shop girl, are you? Not dressed like that. Although you did fool both the Member of Parliament for Lower Sudbury and the watchmaker's assistant yesterday. Neither of them took you for a thief."

And then, quick as a mortal shyster, he reached over and grasped her hand in his. She twisted and braced one foot against the wall to break his implacable hold, but it proved impossible without both hands. Her strength had deserted her.

"Be still. I'm not going to hurt you. And I'm not going to call the constables."

"Lemme go."

He didn't. He turned her left hand palm upward and traced his bare hand over her fingers. Her other hand clenched reflexively in her pocket, and she clamped her jaw down over the wince of pain.

"They're strong and nimble enough, but you've not got the callouses I would expect to find on a girl who plied her needle all day long." He dusted his finger over the top edge of her pointer.

His touch made her all quivery, like the inside of a pie. She must have a fever to be so weak and foolish as to let this man get ahold of her. Old Nan had taught her better.

"I'm not a whore." She twisted within his grip.

"Yes." He acknowledged her insistence with a nod of his head. "I can see that. As it happens, I am not interested in working you on your back. Your business, if I'm not mistaken, and I seldom am, is conducted with nimble, sure fingers and a distracting display of ankle. Very fine ankle if I may say so, but as I said, your physical attributes are not of primary interest to me."

He saw too bloody much, this cove. "I don't strap for no one but myself."

"Really? Very well. That leaves you free to come work for me."

"You the law, then?"

"In a manner of speaking."

"What's 'at mean?"

"It means I work for the government. And I am in a position of authority. I can either treat you well, or treat you badly. It all depends. Upon you."

She was about to refuse again and opened her mouth to do so, when he spoke.

"You think about it. Can you read?" He gave her back her hand, and then a card.

Meggs squinted at the small engraved piece of stationery as if she hadn't a clue in the world. The flummery gave her a whisper of advantage. It was always helpful to get sharps to underestimate you, and she needed all the advantage she could get with this cove. "What's it say?"

"It says I'm McAlden, and it has my direction. Number Eighteen Cheyne Walk in Chelsea. Do you know where that is?"

"Yeah, up the river, innit? But I don't care where you come from. I don't work for no one."

"But you'll work for me." He smiled and turned his face up to the watery wintry sunshine as if her will—her wishes—didn't matter a plug farthing.

"I don't think so."

"Oh, you will." He leaned down close to her ear so she could feel him towering over her, and he spoke so very quietly, it whispered inside her. "I've got what you want."

Meggs swallowed down the queer feeling fluttering inside in her chest. "And what do you think that is?"

"Amnesty. Freedom. If you steal for me, you can't get arrested for it."

Temporary freedom, that, not an amnesty. Still, it was something—they might be safe for a while, at least while her hand healed. If her hand healed. It was almost too good to be true. A hundred pounds would make their fortune.

"Can't get nicked for it, no matter what? Even if I flub?"

"You can't get nicked for it. But they'll be no 'flubbing.' Do it right and we'll pay you for your services."

" 'Oo's 'we.' I don't see no one else 'ere?"

He looked away from her a moment and moved his lower lip a little, as if he had to chew on the words before he spit them out. "We are the government. A private, anonymous part of the government."

"Navy part of the government?"

His eyes, with their probing cold steel, sliced back to her. "Very good. How did you know that?"

She refrained from telling him the obvious—that she'd had

it from the watchmaker's clerk. "I got eyes. Come out of Spring Gardens back o' the Admiralty, big man, all commanding. A gentleman but tanned like a navvy. So that's what you are, navy. What does the navy want stolen it can't get for itself?"

His eyes crinkled up a little at the corners, as if he might be thinking about being amused.

"You're to be congratulated. And that's a very good disguise, you know. I wouldn't have realized you were a girl myself, except for the fact I was looking for you. A boy's well enough, I suppose, but you're more in the line of what I was looking for."

"An' what's that?"

He did smile then, strangely pleased in the middle of a lumberyard. "Clever, quick, adaptable. Attractive. And female." He flicked a glance down over her disguise before he looked back up at her. She felt as if he had seen straight through her clothes, as if he were the one having a vision of her standing in front of him, naked as God made her. "You. You've got spark."

Meggs ducked around the parked dray and ran. But she held on to his card.

Trinity Street had little to recommend it. Squeezed in between Cheapside and the docks, the neighborhood and its residents were crooked, bawling, and abysmally dirty. It didn't matter that it was home. Meggs knew it for what it was: the bare bones of existence, plain and simple. Trinity Street wasn't living, it was merely existing.

She and Timmy had been rooming out of this particular house for nearly a month, and their one small room hadn't improved at all upon closer acquaintance. The floor was bare and creaky, and it was covered with a dust so fine that sweeping seemed to do no good. The grate was filthy and would probably smoke incessantly when the cold drove them to spend precious money on a coal fire. The grime-coated garret window gave out only onto a view of other grime-covered, empty windows that stared back like blank, open eyes.

Meggs had spared tuppence for a candle, but now even that small light pierced her head like a pole-axe. The pain seemed to spread everywhere in her body until all she wanted to do was close her eyes, curl up into a ball, and rest.

But she needed to see to Timmy. Make sure he would be all right.

"Why?" he was demanding. "Why I gotta read? No one else does."

"I do. And it's important. You'll need to know when we retire and move to our cottage. Don't you remember?"

"'Member wot?"

"What it was like, before. Before we came to London."

He thought about that for a moment before he shrugged. "It was green. And it smelled good."

"Yes, it was very green. And it smelled very, very good." A memory of baking bread filled her head, but she couldn't conjure up the smell or the warmth. Not when icy rain pattered against the single, drafty window.

That was all she wanted—warmth and a home—a real home, not a drafty unfurnished room in a garret. And she wanted more for Timmy than being a sneak thief who was one false step away from the gallows every day. She had tried, really she had, but despite her best attempts, her brother was very nearly illiterate. He could read a little, of course, but all they ever had to read were street signs, shop names, and posted bills. Or, like this morning, the occasional scrounged newspaper that still stank of whatever fish it had been wrapping.

Even if they did manage to accumulate enough money to leave London before they got their necks stretched, what was he going to do with the rest of his life? He needed a real education, which she couldn't give him. Her own formal education had been all too brief, and the past eight years had been devoted to an entirely different field of education—a School of Misfortune, if you will.

That man, the captain, had been educated, sharp or no. Meggs turned his card over in her fingers. No sharp ever had an engraved card. No sharp was ever a captain in the Royal Navy.

And she was sick, as sick as she had ever been. Her skin felt hot and tight, and her hand had settled into a dull, aching throb, except for when she moved it. Then, it shot lances of pain up her arm into her bruised elbow. Made it too hard to think straight.

"Meggs, you don't look so good."

"I know." But she couldn't just lie there on the cold floorboards and wish it all better, could she? She had to choose—between the bear and the bull—but she had to choose. She heaved herself vertical. "Timmy, you've got to listen to me. I'm going to go and see this cove."

"What cove? I thought we weren't gonna foyst for no one but ourselves?"

"You're not going to have to foyst at all anymore. But you have to listen to me."

"I like foysting. We're good at it. We could do more house-breaking. I—"

"No. No more. Listen to me." She grasped his arm, hard. "Give me your word."

"Meggs!"

"Just listen. I'm going to go see this Captain McAlden, but you're going to go to Levy's in Threadneedle Street."

"Why? I wanna go with you."

"Listen! I need you to go to Levy's to make sure the deal goes through. You're to stay there until a deposit comes in for our account."

He was predictably diverted by the mention of money. "How much?"

God, she hadn't thought of that yet. Her head was pounding with the effort to hold on to one track of thought at a time. "Don't know, but a lot. At least a hundred pounds."

Timmy's mouth rounded in astonishment. "Meggs"—his voice was going shaky with apprehension—"*what* are you gonna do?"

"I'm going to strike a bargain, that's all. But you're to stay there until the money comes in, all right? And wait for my word." She was going to strike the bargain with the devil and then—*what*? She shut her eyes to keep the heavy pain in and think. Planning out a caper had always come easy-like, as simple as breathing. Why could she not plan her way out of this?

"Right. If for some reason I can't send word, or . . . Well then, you're to take that money, that just came in, in cash as traveling money. But first you're going to make sure you have a full accounting from Mr. Levy as to what's in the accounts. It should be four hundred pounds at least, nearer to five with the special deposit that's going to come in. Have you got that?" She ought to have the exact number. Hadn't she just checked it yesterday? But the figures were swimming in her head.

Timmy nodded, but his eyes had begun to gloss. "Four hundred quid. Meggs, you're starting to scare me." He swiped at his nose with his dirty sleeve. But she couldn't give in to him. She couldn't.

"You have to listen to me. Get the accounting and all the information for Mr. Levy's direction and then take the money that comes in, in cash. Got it?" And then where? An image of a huge house on Grosvenor Square ghosted into her mind, before she rejected it. No, he had to leave London. "Then, you're to go north on the post, to Tissington. In Derbyshire. Do you remember?"

"Tissington." He was crying now, fat tears plopping down his hollow cheeks. "But I want to stay with you."

"I don't know. I don't know what's going to happen. I'm

sick. We both know that. And if I can't get better, then you have to go. There's nothing left for us here. Not with my hand."

"Meggie." He pitched himself at her, trying to hold on to her, but every bone in her body ached with protest. She pried him off.

"Go to Mr. Mackey, the steward at the hall. He'll help you. And I'll come find you in Tissington. I will. When I'm done here. I promise." She shook him a little, a rough, desperate sort of love. "I need you to do this for me. I need to know you'll be safe, do you understand?" She thumbed the tears off his face, and all she could think was, salty as they were, they were likely the only warm water they would have.

"All right, Meggs." He wiped his nose and nodded. He knew their business as well as she. "I understand. Let's get on with it."

CHAPTER 5

It was a very, very long walk. And she was so very, very tired. Her head pounded and her hand felt as if it were on fire. She stopped to rest twice, and each time she'd been tempted to turn back, or not move at all. So in the end, she just kept herself moving south. Toward Chelsea.

The row of houses making up Cheyne Walk faced the riverfront, where the embankment was dotted with trees, post fences, and steps leading down to the water. The house at number eighteen looked plain, neat, and orderly. Nothing to mark it apart from its neat and orderly neighbors. Nothing to tell her what she'd find within. Houses were like that.

She'd stood like this, outside, looking up at fine houses before. Standing on the cold side of the door, wondering, praying she'd be admitted. She never had been.

But she couldn't afford to wait another minute, dithering like a debutante on his doorstep. Himself might have already found someone else, and now that she'd warmed to the idea, well, she'd already counted the money, hadn't she? Best to get on with it.

No matter her resolve, she still stood there, hidden in the shadow of a tree for a full ten minutes before she gathered up enough strength and nerve to do it. Then she took a deep breath, wiped her cold nose on her sleeve, and marched herself up the front steps of number eighteen. She had a job to do.

She hammered the knocker down twice. Hard. Decisive.

A strange little man, with a flattened nose and mashed-up ears that blossomed away from his skull like fairy leaves, answered the door. And promptly tried to shut it.

"Not hirin'."

But Meggs had come too far to be turned back now. She summoned the last of her strength, got her foot in the door, darted under his arm and across the threshold by stomping wickedly on his instep. She'd slid well into the hallway, past the little table with the candle branch and the small silver plate, before he could recover himself enough to grab her coat up in a surprisingly tenacious grip.

"Whot in bloody blazes do ya think yer doin'?"

Irish and mean. That explained the fairy ears. She raised both her eyebrows and her chin. She wasn't about to be intimidated by any Irishman, fairy or no.

"Come to see your gov'nor, the captain, haven't I? Got 'is card, wot he give me."

The fairy man swiped it out of her cold fingers and was displeased to discover it was authentic.

"Wait 'ere." He moved across the hall to a door and cracked it open. "Boy to see you, sir. Got your card, 'e has. Probably stole it," he finished, cutting a sharp, suspicious gaze back at her.

"A boy?"

Then the door was opened wide, and she could see Himself striding his uneven way across the deep, quiet rug with the singular concentration of a silent hawk swooping down on its prey. The ghost of a smile creased the edges of his mouth and lit the corners of his eyes before he hid whatever amusement he had not meant to share. She was struck again by the eerie, incandescent light of his ice blue eyes. Her stomach did a nasty little flip that made the floor tilt underfoot. Gave her the jim-jams bad, this one. Coming here was a mistake.

"Well, well. It seems good things do come to those who wait. Please, come in."

He gestured toward two armchairs in front of the glowing hearth. Lord help her, but it was warm. She took a hesitant, half step forward, turning as she did so to check behind. The wiry fairy man stood across the door, his arms folded across his chest, glaring at her with a look as black and mean as a bog. Another mistake. Never box yourself in. Always have an escape planned. There were two windows in the side wall, but they were barred against burglars.

Now she was here, she would just have to face it. Face him. Brazen it out.

"Thank you, Jinks. I'll see to our guest." The captain held his arm out to show her farther into the room and closed the door behind her. "I'm impressed. Jinks clearly didn't recognize you. I see you've decided to accept my offer."

So he'd had the fairy man with him before, at the watchmakers. Stupid of her not to have seen him. This cove was too flash by half.

"Ain't decided nofink. Yet." She didn't like being inside, all caged up with nowhere to run. Though it was nice and warm.

"I see. So you've come to negotiate, have you?" He seated himself behind his desk, leaned back in the leather-bound chair, and steepled his fingers across his chest. All to show her he was in charge. "You're hardly in a position to ask for a pot to piss in. I could see you in jail or transported on the strength of my word alone. I could see you hung."

He meant to frighten her. Good thing she was already scared shite-less. It saved them both time. "You could see me do what you want, nice 'n easy-like. For the right price."

He considered that for a long moment. "All right," he said

mildly. "Why don't you make yourself more comfortable. A drink, or some food perhaps, to help our negotiation. You look like you could use a decent meal."

He thought to muddy her mind with drink. He couldn't be half smart if he thought her stupid enough for that gambit. She felt a little flash of hope in her chest but let it die out. She'd have to see, wouldn't she? Himself reached behind his desk for a bell pull, and in another moment the fairy man was back, suspicion bristling from him like hedgehogs' spines.

"Make up a plate of dinner for our guest, will you?"

"Right, sir." Another peat-black look and he slipped back out.

The captain had followed her gaze. "That was Mr. Clarence Jinks who is in charge of the household here. Mr. Jinks is a former prizefighter and navy man, and he takes great pride in the efficient running of the household. He does not care for slackers."

So there'd be two of them to play the bully back. They were scaring her more by the minute.

"I'm a hard worker."

"I'm very glad to hear it because then we shall all get on very well." Himself rose, crossed to the fireplace, and gestured to the two wing-backed leather armchairs flanking the fire. "Shall we?" He sat, leaned back into the warm copper-colored leather, and crossed his ankles out in front of him. "Come, do have a seat while we discuss the particulars of your employment."

He meant to look all hospitable and gentleman-like, but it was impossible. He was about as civil and harmless as a hanging judge. But he was in his shirtsleeves, his cuffs turned back to expose his forearms, and his collar was unbuttoned and lacking a cravat. Much more navvy than gentleman. Even with that limp, he was all raw, cagey power.

And he was very much a man. A handsome man, if a girl liked that rough-hewn, strong type. Which she didn't. She didn't like men at all. Had no use for them, except in providing ready money for her to take. Speaking of which.

"What'd I hafta do, if I was to work for you?"

"Just what you do now—steal things."

"What kinda things?"

"Any thing I choose. You will conduct yourself, and these thefts in a manner approved by me, under my supervision. We will get the information I am seeking at any cost, by any means possible."

Any means? Hadn't she heard that before. "I told you, I won't whore."

"That remains to be seen."

That was it. She was done here. Even if she had ruined her hand, she wasn't going to whore. No matter what. There was just some things a body couldn't do. She had skills, she had standing. She could housebreak, even if she couldn't dip. Much riskier, but more profitable, even if she had to deal with fences. That was how Nan had got taken—fences ratting her out to thief-takers. But she was letting her mind wander too far down the street. She had to concentrate on the money.

"We got to come to a right agreement about the blunt."

"You will be adequately remunerated in compensation for your time."

She supposed she was expected to be impressed by all that taradiddle. Remuneration, indeed. " 'Ow much?"

"How much time? It depends on you, and how willing you are to work, and how well you do the tasks assigned to you."

"No. 'Ow much blunt?"

He looked over the top of his steepled fingers. "One hundred pounds."

"A thousand," she countered.

He made a dismissive sound and lowered his eyebrows at such an outrageous sum. She forestalled his automatic refusal. "And fer how long, anyways?"

"An unspecified amount of time of my choosing. Until the job is done."

"How many marks? Or jobs?" she added, to clarify.

He hesitated and eyeballed her, as if he was trying to reckon how much he could tell her. "Initially, seven, but then I assume we'll have to narrow it down for further . . . investigation."

"Any housebreaking, or just the dipping?"

"Perhaps. Probably. We'll have to see."

"Then I'll need my cut 'o the take."

"There's no 'take.' The things you'll steal have no monetary value. No value to anyone but me."

"Everything's got monetary value, even paper. To you, an' to whoever wants to keep it away from you."

"Don't think you can play one hand against the other, lass. I'll make you—"

"Then don't make me dicker. A thousand," she repeated firmly.

He shook his head. But there was warmth, perhaps even amusement, in his voice. And his eyes had the barest crinkles at the corners. "Three hundred."

Now they were getting somewhere. Relief trickled into her and warmed her in a way the fire never could. "I make that working free an' easy in a few months." When he looked dubious, raising one eyebrow at her, she smiled blithely back and removed the silver salver, formerly housed on his hall table, from the inside of her coat. It gleamed in the light as she turned it in her hand. "Recon'ize this?"

Clearly he did. His eyes narrowed as he leaned forward to retrieve it.

"If you want my expertise, see, you gotta pay fer it."

"Five hundred."

"For 'an unspecified amount of time,' " she echoed his words. "I don't fink so."

"Seven hundred and fifty, and that's my final offer."

"Done." But she didn't spit in her hand, nor did she extend her palm to shake on the deal. She kept her ruined hand well hidden in the deep pocket of her coat. And besides, she would never shake on something on which she planned to renege. But she didn't want him noticing any of that. " 'Ow do I know you won't turn me in to the traps, when yer done wiff me?"

"It wouldn't make sense. But if it makes you feel better, you have my word on it."

"Don't know you well e-nuff to take your word. I wanna contract."

"A contract?" His voice was laced with disbelief.

He doubted she could even read. Let him think what he wanted. "Yeah. All proper and legal-like. I knows a fella what'll look at it fer me." Mr. Levy would be counted upon to see to the thing right and proper. He'd see to her interests. "An' I want 'alf of it up front."

He made the same dismissive sound.

"In a 'count. Like what you nobs call security. You puts it all int' a 'count and I gets half now and the rest paid me as I do yer jobs."

He looked away, into the fire in contemplation, as if he were turning the idea over in his mind trying to come up with the snags.

"Show yer on the up 'n up, it will," she prodded.

"How do *I* know you won't take the half and run? Where's *my* security? I already know you well enough *not* to take your word."

"I stay. *Habeas corpus* as the traps would have it. 'You shall have the corpse.' "

"The 'body,' " he corrected. "You shall have the body." But his eyes were smiling.

"Yeah, well, when I gets word the money's safe where I want it, I'll do your jobs." A body could get itself lost working a job. Nothing so easy as to walk away once they'd begun. Providing she was able to work. Or walk for that matter. Her head was still pounding away like a blacksmith's anvil. "So what's it to be?"

"Where do you want the money sent?" His dismissive grin told her he had no expectation of an answer.

"Levy and Levy, Threadneedle Street. Number twenty-four. You'll go now?"

"No." He recovered his astonishment quickly. "As you so keenly pointed out, I have to stay *with the body*. I'll send my man with the money."

She didn't like the way he said that—stay with the body. "How do you know he won't pocket the whole and give you the slip?"

That turned his mind away from "the body" and amused him. The little chewed-up smile threatened to warm one side of his face as he took out a ledger of some kind and wrote out the paper. "Three hundred and fifty pounds, to be paid into your account now. And the remaining four hundred to be paid in increments as the jobs, as you call them, are accomplished."

She watched him limp to the door and call for the fairy man to make away for Threadneedle Street. "Take a wherry downriver," Himself instructed. "The tide's right."

And then the sound of the door closing. Meggs crossed toward the window to watch him go, to make sure the hedgehog fairy man was obeying, but her head swam and made little points of light dance between her eyes.

She held still and closed her eyes until they went away, but by the time she'd made it to the window, there was nothing to see.

With luck, the money was away. She sat weakly in the nearest chair. That was all that mattered. With the three hundred fifty pounds, Timmy would have well over seven hundred to start. That was more than enough. Wasn't it? And there'd be more, maybe, if she could pull this off.

The captain trolled slowly back into the room. He sent a long glance her way and went over to a tray with bottles of spirits on it. She could see he was pleased with himself. He had relaxed a bit, his shoulders settling down as he poured himself a healthy splash of something brown from a tray near the desk.

"Shall we drink to our bargain?" He came over and handed her an exquisitely delicate, cut-glass snifter with a small amount of liquid amber swirling at the bottom.

French brandy. Maybe even smuggled on Royal Navy ships. The world was full of all sorts of bloody ironies, wasn't it? But she had her part to play, so she sniffed at the drink and took a tentative sip. It nearly blistered her lips. "Gor! Whacher' call this stuff?"

"Cognac. Very old. From before the present wars. It was my grandfather's."

"He a toff then, your grandfather?"

"No, he was not a toff. He was Scots."

Which seemed to amuse him to no end, because he smiled full out, and it made him look happy, and harmless and maybe even a little silly, that grin.

Lord, but he was handsome, even with the silly grin. His lethal, wide-set blue eyes had nothing in them to frighten when the corners were all crinkled up like that. And his straight, blunt nose and the stack of granite boulders that were his jaw looked softer in the haze of warm firelight. The severe haircut, cropped so close as to make her think he might have left off his wig, except she had never seen him wearing one, now looked merely tousled, soft and golden in the afternoon light.

When the golden silence stretched between them, he chuckled. "Cat got your tongue?"

"Lot's wife, that's me. Gone all pillar o' salt at the sight of so much gov'amint iniquity."

"Iniquity, is it? So you don't want the money? You'll work for free? For the chance to serve your country?"

It was her turn to laugh. "Not bloody likely. I'm in it strictly for the money."

"Right." He nodded, as if in agreement, and took his first sip before he crouched down on his haunches in front of her and reached out a hand to stroke her face. "Now, let's have a look at you under that disgrace of a cap. I'd like to see what my three hundred fifty pounds have bought me."

He had forgotten how feral she was. The moment he surrendered to the impulse and touched her, she bolted, wreaking havoc like a cannon blown loose across a deck.

She had the drink out of his hand and dashed into his eyes before he could think to stop her. And when he put his hands up to wipe the stinging alcohol from his streaming eyes, she threw all her weight against him, tipping him over backward and sending him crashing to the floor before she streaked toward the door.

By God, she was fast. Faster than any scrawny, ill-fed guttersnipe like her ought to be, but her speed was undoubtedly what made her successful. Or at least kept her from the noose. Stupid of him to have tossed back the drink like that, but he had been unaccountably elated she had finally agreed to his plan. And he had, in his stupid happiness, simply wanted to touch her. Stupid. She was shyer of personal contact than any wild animal.

Hugh had to launch himself off the floor to keep her from reaching the door. He caught her hard about the waist, sending them both crashing into the back of the panel. He hadn't even had time to turn his body to take the force of the blow. Christ, he hoped she wasn't hurt. That was the last thing he needed—to break her scrawny arm before they'd even had a chance to get properly started. He pulled back off her.

"Are you all right?"

He got a vicious elbow in his ribs for his pains, and while his body was registering that sharp insult, her boot connected with his jaw with an unholy thud. Pain cleaved through his skull.

That was it! All bets were bloody, fucking well *off*. He cursed fluently and loudly, just managing to hold on to the squirming bundle of rags while his vision cleared enough to find the salient parts. And just in time, too. He caught her left hand in his, just before her fist was about to connect with his face. He gave it a savage twist that ought to have had her groveling before him in pain, but she held grimly on, turning to sink her sharp teeth into his wrist. Hugh gritted his own jaw and rammed her back hard against the wall, once, to knock the wind out of her, and wrenched his wrist free. Still she came at him, lowering her head to butt him hard in the abdomen.

He made an animal sound in the back of his throat that was distinctly like a roar as they went down hard with her beneath, crashing her head into the floorboards and overturning a chair. She gave up the fight for a moment then, just long enough for him to pin her down with his own body weight and shove her damn pugilistic hands high over her head in an iron grip.

"Don't trifle with me," he growled through gritted teeth. "If you ever, ever try that crap again, I'll blister your arse so hard, you won't sit down for a month!"

But she was limp—out cold. Stunned, he loosened and transferred his grip to one hand and placed the other on her chest to make sure she was still breathing. God's balls, what a scrapper. She must get into fights often. One of her hands was already bound up in bloody, filthy rags, wrapped around what was obviously a grievous injury.

No, not a fight. The wall. The wall with the glass shards and the shine of blood. She had hurt herself. Badly. Her fingers looked swollen. He touched them, and she cried out.

She came to fast enough, still fighting, still refusing to yield. Her body bucked and twisted beneath him. And then, for some reason, some strange, unholy reason, Hugh looked down. He looked down at her chest and saw, through the none too clean linen of her shirt, the unmistakable pink, pebbled shape of a nipple. His eyes automatically slid across to the other, but he could see that breast was still covered in the heavy cotton banding with which she had bound her chest. It must have slipped during their tussle. His gaze snaked back of its own volition, to dwell on the rounded bud pressing up impudently against the soft, worn fabric.

A jolt of pure lust, hot and unadulterated by thought, shot through him like a pistol. Christ almighty! He had obviously remained celibate for far too long, to be even so much as thinking, let alone feeling, erotic impulses for the scrap of rags and vitriol writhing beneath him. But that was the problem, wasn't it? She was writhing. Beneath him. The bones of her pelvis were jutting up against his arse. And unmistakably, he found it highly erotic. He was as stiff as a cannon.

He flung himself off her with another foul curse and came to his feet. It took several long gulps of air before Hugh could get a complete grip upon himself and his extremely wayward thoughts. And his wayward body.

He was inconveniently and undeniably attracted to her. There was no getting around it. It was something he had not foreseen when Admiral Middleton had given him his instructions, nor had he thought about it when he had first noticed her in the street.

Now, that was a bloody lie. He had noticed her precisely because she had been attractive, or at least her ankle had been. But only God knew why he was attracted physically to the dirty ragamuffin that Jinks had shown into the study. She smelled. He ought to be repulsed. But he was not. He was drawn to her.

She tried to rise. Her head wobbled weakly before she curled onto her side, drawing her injured hand closer to cradle against her chest. And then she went still.

Before he could check himself, or caution himself that it might be another one of her foul tricks, he was back down on the floor, kneeling at her side. Hugh touched the girl's shoulder, and she rolled onto her back, limply unconscious. He put his fingers to the side of her neck—she was devilishly hot. Flushed with fever, no doubt because of the putrid hand.

"Jinks!" he called through the door. "Are you still here?"

His man appeared, hauling in air with his hands on his knees. "I was coming, sir. Could hear you all the way across the street. Thought you was being murdered."

"I was. She's out cold. And ill, it would seem. I'm going to need hot water and salts. And a strong soap."

"Right y'are, sir."

"And Jinks, do be careful. The little bitch bites." He'd need lye soap for his own arm as well.

But instead of shifting her over his shoulder like a sack of mealy potatoes, as would be prudent, he scooped her up and cradled her snug against his chest. Damned if he knew why. She was nearly insubstantial in his arms. He could hardly credit the fight she'd put up earlier.

"Biter, is she now?" Jinks eyed her cautiously as he held open the door. "Best wash tha' out, then." He nodded at Hugh's forearm. "She's like to give you the rabies. She be mangier than a rabid dog at any rate. Where to?"

"The kitchen. We can tie her to the table if we have to. Damn her eyes, she's no good to me if she loses her hand."

"That bad, sir?"

"I don't know, Jinks. I just don't know. Just get the water heated and we'll find out."

Once down the kitchen stairs, he laid her carefully on the deal table and set to pulling off the threadbare jacket that enveloped her spare frame. He told himself it was to see if she had any other injuries, and to be able to treat her hand as best he could, but he knew there was another reason when he found his hands straying to the buttons of her tattered shirt. He forced himself to step back.

Hugh busied himself with practicalities. He lit a lantern

and set it close. The bandages, such as they were, were only old rags, discolored and stiff with dried blood and God knew what else. He'd have to cut them off.

"Have we got a scissors? And a bowl. That's right."

Jinks filled a large bowl with steaming water from the kettle, added a heaping measure of coarse salt, and returned to the cabinets to find the scissors. He came back and handed them over, and Hugh began to cut away the bandages as best he could, but he could see they would have to be soaked before they'd come off. And God knew what he'd find underneath.

"God's balls." It was bad. He glanced at the girl's pale, still face, the high spots of fever the only color in her cheeks. Her heart-shaped face seemed delicate under the rime of grime. Fragile almost, despite what he knew of her hardened character.

She might be useless to him now, but he wasn't so callous as to leave her solely to fate. He would do his best for her, whatever he could. "Send for a surgeon. See if you can get Pervis, up at the hospital. And you'd better make sure we've got a clean knife."

CHAPTER 6

The first thing Meggs saw were the beams of a low ceiling above her head. She blinked to clear her eyes. The flickering light made her dizzy. She tried to raise a hand to block the light, but the movement brought a sickening blade of pain.

A deep, quiet voice sounded inside her ear. "Shh. Be still."

But she had never been very good at obeying commands. Especially when she was frightened. She tried to move, to sit up, but found herself pressed firmly down into what had to be the slightly uneven slats of a table. And the voice was holding her down.

"Let me go," she demanded, but her voice was weak and desperate.

"You're in no shape to go anywhere."

Meggs turned toward the voice and found it was the captain, holding her arm out in a grip like a vise. She could feel his hands hard on her forearm, but nothing more. His body was resolutely blocking her view. All she could see were white, white bandages, bloody-red water, and the cold glistening steel of a big knife laid on the table next to her head.

Panic rose, sharp and metallic, raking at her throat. "What have you done? Let me see. What have you done?"

A different voice answered, crisp and business-like. "Saved your hand, I hope. It was quite septic, but I think we've cleaned the putrefaction now. I think you'll keep it."

"No! Let me—" Meggs pulled her feet under her before the words registered. *Saved her hand.*

"Shh." That was the captain again. The words rumbled through his body and into hers where he held her arm against his chest. "Don't fight. Easy now. Thank you, Pervis. Much obliged."

"You know where to find me? Keep me apprised of any difficulties, will you? I can find my own way out." And then the snap of a bag and footsteps as Pervis, whoever he was, left.

The captain turned to view her with a faint crease in his brows, as if he hadn't expected her silly display of fear and squeamishness. "I'll let you sit up if you promise not to faint again."

Relief made her philosophical. Or careless. That was it. She felt strangely, as if at long last, she hadn't a care. Fear had a way of sorting out priorities. "Never fainted a day in my life."

"You did today. You've been out for a few hours now."

"Didn't faint. Smashed my head against the bloody floor, didn't I?"

She felt the chuckle rumble through him. "You did at that." He reached around to gently probe the back of her skull. "How's it feel?"

His hands on her head made her feel strange and light and exposed. "Like a hammer's been at it."

"Apologies. Sit up, handsomely now, and let me finish this bandage. You're as weak as a kitten."

"Still gave you that black eye."

He smiled over his shoulder at her. "And nearly cracked my jaw."

"We're even then, are we?"

"Not with this hand. Do you think you're ready to rise?"

But Meggs found she couldn't sit up, or didn't want to,

tucked tightly into the sheltering curve of his back as he held her arm clamped against his ribs. Instead she found herself turning, curling into him, into the heat that fairly rose off his linen shirt. Into the fresh clean smell of him. Like a new-mown field. Like heaven.

He still wore nothing but his rolled up shirtsleeves. She watched the light play off the golden hair on his forearm as his strong fingers wrapped her hand in a tight bandage. But his arm was bandaged as well.

"What happened?"

"You passed out."

"No. What did you do to my hand? And yours?"

"Soaked it in hot brine to loosen the crusted bandages and open it up to release the . . . Well, then we washed it. With strong soap. Something you could use more of, Miss Tanner. Something you should have done to this laceration at the start. I assume you cut yourself going over that wall, two days ago?"

Something inside, her pride she supposed, bridled at that— all that superior tone. But all she had left to answer was cheek. "Oh, yeah. Stupid me. How could I ferget? I got *loads* of soap and hot water in me lovely flat, up in Mayfair."

He stilled and turned back to look her in the eyes. "Like that, is it? Not even soap?" His face sobered until she could see that uncompromising granite. "Where do you live?"

When he looked at her like that, she felt more exposed than if she'd been naked. And he could go shove his bloody worthless pity. "Here and there. Never you mind." She tugged at her hand, still held so soundly in his.

"Well, as long as you take lodgement here, you'll wash. Regularly. You and the boy."

Boy? God and all the bloody weeping angels in heaven. "What boy?" she squeaked. Lord help her, she did. She squeaked like a rusty eel cart. Old Nan would be ashamed of her, giving herself away like that. But old Nan wasn't Timmy's sister.

"Your brother, young Mr. Tanner. He came sneaking around the back looking for you. He got to worrying about you, he said. With good reason."

"The boy don't have no part in this. Where is he? Let me see him."

"Easy there. Handsomely with that bloody hand—we've put a number of stitches into it. The boy's being bathed. And fed."

"Why? Whatchoo need to bathe him for?" She fought her way out of his grip to slip off the other side of the table. There were pots hanging from a rack above, close to hand. She could cosh him with one, if need be. "You keep your filthy hands off that boy. I won't let him be your plaything."

"My play . . ." he stuttered. His confusion quickly changed to a ferocious frown even as a high wash of color appeared across his cheekbones. "God's balls, girl. I am not a predator. I did not lure the child here for any such nefarious purpose."

"Right," she spat. "An' I'm the queen's sister. Everything about you is 'nee-farious.' Wouldn't want me, want us, otherwise, would you?"

"I don't want the boy. I only want *you*. I only spoke to *you*. But he seems to think he's necessary. He seems to think *you* can't get along without him."

"I told him to—" Meggs bit her tongue. Hard. She didn't need to be telling the captain every little bit of her business. "Where is he? Let me see him."

"Don't get your britches in a twist. He's eating us out of the larder." He shot a thumb over his shoulder. "You ought to feed yourselves more often—"

"Bloody shite for brains! You let him gorge himself? He'll be heaving it up in no time. Where is he?" She clutched her way doggedly around the table and across the spinning room. "Tell me!"

Himself hooked his thumb toward a set of rising stairs.

"Breakfast room. I didn't want him down here when we were working on you. And he needed feeding. You two have obviously been hauling sharp for far too long."

Meggs didn't want to hear anything more to add to the nasty feeling of guilt swirling around in her innards. "He needs Lenten fare, not a gorging."

She wove her wobbly way to the stairs he indicated, climbing up to the ground floor where smooth mahogany balusters swept upward in a dizzy, sinuous line all the way up three flights to the top floor. She could hear the captain following hard on her heels but paid him no mind.

"Tanner?" she called to the empty hallway.

"Meggs?"

She could hear him down the hall. She braced her way across the corridor, followed by the captain and then the fairy man, too late to do anyone any good, damn his pointy ears.

"Don't feel too good, Meggs." Timmy was lovely clean, but he had indeed eaten everything he could get his hands on. Several empty dishes stood on the tabletop.

She took him in her arms. "I know, you silly little piglet. Shh." She brushed his lovely clean hair away from his forehead.

"Meggs?" There was acute discomfort in his voice.

"I know, love. Come on. You'll have to shoot that cat." She fetched a stew bowl off the table by dumping its remaining contents onto an empty plate and began to rub his back as he started to heave.

"Aww. That's it for me," complained the fairy man. She sent his back a vicious look.

The captain stepped forward and took her shoulders. "You're not strong enough. Your hand needs—"

Another glare, one that ought to have made his damn cods shrink up inside his body for cover, kept the captain quiet as Timmy heaved up his supper. But he didn't leave, the captain, at least not for long. He came back with a cool, clean cloth for her to wipe Timmy's pale face, and he took away the damned bowl without a single comment.

When Timmy was done and exhausted from the efforts, he allowed the captain and her to lead him back downstairs, to a pallet the captain must have had made up on the kitchen floor. The poor boy was out like a rush light in less time than it took to pull the soft blankets over him. Meggs would have slept there, too, right beside him, but a strong hand came to her elbow.

"Come, you have to see to yourself."

"I'll stay with him." She was too weary, too bone tired to do anything else. She ached everywhere, now that she stopped to take inventory, not just in her hand and head. But the captain managed to haul her to her feet despite her protests. And he kept hold of her arm, propping her upright.

"You're in no shape to see to him. God knows how you're even standing after what we washed out of your hand," he growled, all angry complaint. "And you ought not to sleep after that bump on your head. What you need is a little nourishing food. Obviously, a very little. And a full bath," he muttered under his breath.

"A bath?" Jesus, what was she getting herself into, sounding all hopeful like that? But a bath? A real bath, with a tub full of warm water? God help her, it had been forever.

"A hot bath." He nodded at her, all grim determination. "You smell like a . . . stable. And God knows what other passengers you're harboring under that grime."

"I wash regular-like. I ain't got cooties."

"*Haven't* got. But that remains to be seen. Your clothes are filthy."

"Yeah, well, them's all I got."

"All I *have*," he corrected.

"Yeah, that, too."

"Nevertheless—a bath. You'll take it, or I'll *give* it. Your choice."

Something strange and liquid-feeling uncoiled and stretched deep in her belly. Probably just the thought of food. She hadn't eaten in a day, and she hadn't had anything that hadn't come off a cart in quite some time before that.

"I don't need no help. I know 'ow to take a bath."

"*Any* help." He looked her over again for such a long, still moment and with such focused intensity, she couldn't remember what she was supposed to think. Or what to hope. When he looked at her like that, as if he could see *inside* her, she wanted to hide. Inside him. Inside the strange generosity of his unwavering focus.

What in thunderation was she going on about? Clearly now, it was *she* who was well and proper dicked in the nob.

"In here," he directed.

The room at the end of the hall beyond the kitchen was nothing but a laundry. There were wooden drying racks suspended from the ceiling, and it smelled homey, of vinegar and starch and . . . verbena. How funny. Hadn't smelt that in years.

Oh, but a large copper tub stood in the middle of the slate floor, and beyond it, a fire glowed in the hearth. Meggs was drawn closer to the lodestone of the tub and let her fingers find the water. "Oh! It's hot!" Her hand was already at the buttons of the shabby, oversize shirt. It had been so long, so very, very long, since she had had the simple luxury of hot water. Her skin felt scaled and itchy in anticipation.

But he would never understand. He was nothing but gruff command. "It won't kill you. You're to wash all over," he instructed grimly. "From the top of your head, down to your toes. Under your arms and . . . all around." He turned his head away and pulled a thick, dry cloth off one of the racks. "Keep that bandage dry, or you'll answer to me. I'll find you some clean clothes to change into." He turned on his booted heel and slammed his way out of the room.

Once the door was closed behind him, Meggs skibbled over, quick-like, to check the lock and throw the bolt. Still, what was there to fear at this point? The captain seemed truly to be on the up and up. If he hadn't taken her when she was out cold and couldn't fight, chances were he wasn't going to try now.

And a bath. It was too much temptation to resist. She might risk nearly anything for a bath. And Himself, the captain, didn't seem at all interested in her person, so to speak. Seemed disgusted really. As if he feared he'd catch some dread disease.

That thought sent her good hand up to her hair. And back down to her buttons. It was something like hard labor to peel off her raggedy clothes, especially the tattered breeches, with only one hand, but slowly she got the job done until she was exhausted, bare to her skin, and teetering into the tub.

Lord, it was so hot her toes felt as if they might burn right off her feet, but it felt good, too, to lower herself slowly into the steam. Oh, Lord, she hadn't felt anything this warm in forever. She sat for a long, dreamy moment, luxuriating in the sublime feel of the water covering her skin. And the soap. It wasn't anything all perfumed and pretty, but it was clean smelling, like the wind after a snow. But warm. And clean and fresh.

She took up the heavy bar and began to slowly wash. In just a few minutes of one-handed application, she was exhausted but feeling cleaner than she had in years.

The pain in her head abated a bit, and the ache in her hand subsided to a dull echo of its former self. Meggs leaned her head back against the rim and closed her eyes, for just a moment, to savor the heat and warmth and freshness. She knew she ought to make sure about the money—make sure it had gotten to Mr. Levy's—and see to Timmy, but she would tend to that next.

Soon. Just as soon as she had a chance to rest.

* * *

Hugh tapped lightly at the door, listening for the tranquil, liquid sound of water from the tub, but the laundry was quiet. Too quiet. He keyed open the lock noisily, wanting to warn the girl and not take her off her guard. She didn't seem to treat very well with surprise.

"Miss Tanner?" It seemed a bit ridiculous to call a career criminal "Miss." The boy had called her "my Meggs." An outstanding piece of luck, that—the boy showing up. Hugh could use the boy instead, if the girl didn't heal, or couldn't use her hand even when she did. He didn't have the luxury of time to wait and find out. "Meg?"

Still, there was no answer. God's balls. He had left her alone too long. Dr. Pervis had warned it was a bad thing to leave a person to sleep for too long with a concussion of the magnitude she had obviously suffered. And Hugh's guilt at having helped cause said concussion, however inadvertently, was acute enough to make him vigilant.

He moved quickly to the side of the tub, already wondering if he ought to call the surgeon back, but his mind abruptly stopped functioning at what he saw.

A sleeping, naked girl. A wet, naked, pink-and-white-skinned girl, now all the accumulated grime had been scraped off. Except for her forearms, where the skin was not pale and white, but tanned. And from her neck up as well, her skin was slightly darker and wind-reddened.

Just like his.

But he was a man, a professional, an officer of his king and country. And she was only a scrap of a girl. She ought to take better care of herself. She ought not to have such stark evidence of having been out so long in all kinds of weather. She ought not to be sleeping, concussed and naked, pink and desirable, in his bath.

"You need to wear gloves," he whispered for no reason other than his need to say it.

"No gloves," she dictated from her stupor. "Interferes with the touch."

Well. She had a point. And domestic servants had rough, tanned hands. And he needed her to be a servant. Certainly she should look the part of a scullery maid. There was no need for gloves. There was no need for concern.

And she was at least semiconscious. Perhaps she was not so badly concussed as he had feared. Still, he was standing there ogling her like the callowest youth. "Wake up. I can't have you sleeping all night in a bath."

With that, she seemed to come to, her dark, sooty lashes battering against her lids, realizing exactly where she was. And exactly where he was. She squinted and focused on him, and sharpened up. Immediately, she curled herself into a little protective ball, her arms wrapped around her knees. "What do you want?" She tossed her little chin at him and his eyes were drawn to her full, almost pouty lower lip.

"To make sure you're clean and awake," he answered mildly. "Be careful of that hand."

She ignored his advice. "Why?" She wasn't in the least bit coy or pouting, only blunt and straightforward, belligerent and frightened.

He did her the courtesy of understanding her meaning. "To prove to you a point. That I do not have *nefarious*," he repeated her word, "intentions for either you or your brother. You are quite safe from me. You are here only to steal. This will be a purely professional relationship."

"That how you act professional, then? Barge into me bath? For your information, professional thieves do not share baths."

"They share everything. It makes no difference to me that you're naked. I couldn't care any less." It was, however, a trial to keep his gaze steady on her black eyes when he had much rather look elsewhere. "The point is, there will be no secrets between us. I have to be able to trust you. And you need to trust me and understand I have absolutely no interest in you other than your nimble hands." He didn't have to try to sound aggravated—he *was* aggravated. And tired. It had been a damn near thing with her hand. It might well prove to be a nearer thing yet. He scowled at the offending appendage.

"Yes, your hand, which I have gone to considerable trouble to save from having to amputate this evening. So keep that bloody bandage dry!"

The girl lifted her hand up immediately and set it well away from the water. She swallowed whatever saucy reply she had thought to make. "That who that man was, then?" she asked with difficulty. "He'd come to . . . ?"

"Yes," he answered with all the bite of his unreasonable anger. But at the blanching of her face, he strove to adopt a more reasonable tone. Hugh knew her fear. He'd had to face it a time or two himself, most recently when he had awoken near sick to his stomach with pain in the surgery bay of a ship outbound from Acre. "Mr. Pervis is a surgeon. A former acquaintance from the navy. He came over from the Royal Hospital, here in Chelsea."

She cloaked her fear in sullen stubbornness. "Never seen a surgeon in my life. Damn carrion crows."

"Well, you were damned *lucky* to have a man so skilled, so near, to be able to see to you. Perhaps you think I should have simply let you continue to rot yourself to death?"

He wouldn't let her break his gaze during the long silence, watching that uncomfortable truth sink into her face until she finally said, "I'm sorry. Thank you."

"You're welcome. Now, put your head forward. I'm going to wash your hair."

The sullenness came swiftly back. "I can wash myself."

"Not with one hand. Now put your head down or I'll dunk you."

She obeyed but watched him out of the corner of her eyes. He upended a ewer of warm water over her head in as impersonal a manner as possible. "Put your head back." It was easier this way, giving blunt commands. And when he growled, she stayed all curled up in the ball, not open and pink like she had been when he'd first come in. It was better this way. More impersonal, more professional.

He took up the bar of soap and worked the lather through her hair. He was as gentle as could be, mindful for snarls and the concussed spot, but also wanting to make sure she wasn't carrying any lice. But she looked clean enough. Under the foam of the soap, her hair appeared to be a dark sable brown, shot through with richer, brighter colors. It was long and slick straight, flowing at least halfway down her back in a dark fall of wet silk.

And truth was, he wanted to wash her hair because he simply, impossibly, wanted to touch her again. Back in the kitchen, he hadn't been ready to let her go.

He settled into an easy massaging rhythm, sliding his fingers through the silky mass, and soon enough she tipped her head back and closed her eyes, the very picture of simple bliss. Her plum-colored lips parted slightly as the water sluiced down the long slide of her back, down over the rounded curve of her flanks into the temping cleft of her sweet little arse.

God's balls. He'd remained celibate for far, far too long. Grime, dirt, potential lice. That was it. No thought of derrieres.

She held her bandaged right hand out, over the rim, but as he massaged her skull and worked his way around the tender lump on the back of her head, she relaxed, straightening her long, lean, muscled legs and letting her left arm slip down into the water as well, giving him an unimpeded view of her wet, glistening breasts.

And he felt his cock harden at the sight. He stepped away instantly, but he did not look away. He could not. She stretched her hand up to her head to continue the massaging motion.

With her eyes closed, not snapping at him with a gutter full of accusation, he could look his fill. He could feast his eyes on the pale, white shape of her breasts with their pink crests, the slide of her belly down to her long, coltish legs and the sweet triangle of dark hair at the apex of her thighs.

Hugh felt his mouth go dry and his own skin begin to prick with awareness. He'd known she was a woman. He'd seen her trim ankles and pushed-up bosom out on the street. But he hadn't expected this—this confounded, consuming attraction to her. She wasn't his type at all. She was nothing but grit and sinew, not a soft curve on her body. No place to find rest. Well, her breasts were curved, but her skin was not soft. It wasn't dewy and fresh. Even scrubbed until she was nearly red, he had felt years of St. Giles under his palms. A roughness caused by years of degradation, layers of endlessly worrisome work and toil. And somehow, it touched him in a way he couldn't explain. It touched him deep in a place he had hidden away within himself. So deep he had forgotten its existence.

God's balls. This was no time to go soft. He had a traitor to catch. He turned away. "Cover yourself."

She jolted back to awareness and curved her left arm across her breasts in a protective gesture. He all but threw the last pitcher of water on her hair to rinse it.

Then he pointed to the clothes Jinks had scoured up from God knew where, stacked neatly on a chair. There were all the necessary bits and parts, but he was in no state to point out small clothes and stays to her. "These should do for now. They're serviceable enough, but at least they're clean, unlike your present attire. Put them on when you're done washing. I'll leave you to dry yourself off." God help him if she would need help fastening them on.

He scooped up the dirty pile of clothing at his feet.

"Hey, where you going with those?" She reached out her uninjured hand, quick and acquisitive as a magpie. "Them's mine."

"*They* are filthy."

"Give *them* back." She made a grabby motion with her fingers. "I can get money for 'em."

Avaricious little sprite. To her everything had monetary value, even him. He would do well to remember that. "I'll pay you for them myself."

"Will you?" Her arm went still but didn't fall.

"I'll give you a shilling, if you promise never to wear them again."

"Done. But not all of 'em. A girl needs a thing or two, you understand." She still held out her hand, and when he offered them back to her, she rifled through the bundle and pulled some filthy linen strips aside. "Pockets," she explained. "Can't be a proper thief without good pockets under your outers."

He didn't want to think about unders or outers. That way lay terrifyingly certain madness. He balled the clothes into his fists. "May I take these now?"

"Take 'em away." She arched her brow as disdainfully as a queen and made a dismissive little flicking motion with her hand. "For all I care, you can even burn 'em."

"I'd like nothing more." Hugh pitched the bundle into the fire and stalked to the door. "Now get yourself bloody dressed."

CHAPTER 7

Meggs opened the door at his knock. Something like surprise registered on his face—the barest flicker of his brow and a quick downward movement at the corners of his mouth. Then those pale blue eyes were alight, skimming over her figure, making a catalog of her faults.

But all he said was, "You clean up surprisingly well. You were hiding quite a lot behind that grime."

Meggs tugged the drawstring on the simple neckline higher. "Never you mind what I was 'iding. I told you I knew how to wash."

"So you did. Do you also know how to eat?"

She made a rude sound.

"Yes. Well, let's hope you do better than your brother. Come back to the kitchen."

Timmy was still sound asleep on his pallet, and Meggs was relieved to see a second set of blankets lay on the floor next to him. The captain really did appear to be on the up and up.

Himself turned back from the hob and set a stout bowl of broth on the table next to a board full of thick-sliced bread and cheese. It smelled good, the broth, full of chicken and herbs she had forgotten the names of. And butter. There was a crock of butter. Her stomach made a sound of boisterous entreaty at the prospect of such plenty.

But she couldn't allow herself to fall to it like a stupid beast. She'd colic up as fast as Timmy if she did. And there was pride to be considered. Even old Nan had insisted on a sort of decorum at her plain table. But the captain was looking at her all queer.

"You gonna eat?" she asked to cover the strange heat in her face.

"No. I've already eaten. Go ahead, before it gets cold."

"How do I know it's not poisoned?"

"Because you're not stupid. Because I'd hardly spend hours getting the poison out of your hand just to put it into your belly." But in another moment he reached over, took the bowl in one hand, and drank down a gulp of the soup. Then he ripped off a piece of bread, picked up a chunk of cheese, and stowed it down as well. "There. Not poison. Now eat."

There was no room for disagreement in that voice. All commanding ship's captain. And she wasn't stupid. She sat and hooked the bowl up with her left hand and drank, and cautiously fed piece after piece of bread into her mouth. All the while, watching him watch her.

"When was the last time you ate?"

She shrugged. No sense inviting the lecture he seemed primed to give. "Now and again."

"Well, you'll eat here. Regularly. Consider it a perquisite. For you and the boy."

"Perquisite, is it?" Thought she was too stupid to even feed herself, let alone know what he was talking about, didn't he? Like some dumb beast, fit only for the dub. As if she didn't have ears or a brain in her head.

"It means an extra benefit arising from the situation we've agreed to."

"Do tell. I knew someone who would have liked that word, just the sort she would have used. Quite a collector of words, she was, old Nan." Do him good to hear he wasn't the only one knew how to talk. And she felt like talking. Must be the food in her stomach making her all garrulous. "Old Nan, my kidwoman. Loved words. Like 'garrulous' and 'exquisite.' 'That was an exquisite piece of work, my girl,' she'd say. Or, 'delicate.' 'You'll want a delicate hand with that lock, my girl.' Used to say good locks were like old maiden aunties—knew how to keep their secrets—so you had to cozen up to them sweetly. A great Kate was Nan. A picklock."

"Remarkable, a common picklock and kidwoman talking like that." He leaned back in his chair and regarded her steadily across the top of the glass lantern, his icy blue eyes probing and relentless.

"Nothing common about picklocks. Talent, that takes, skills and dedication. And she weren't always a Kate. Old Nan'd been a governess a long time before, afore she fell afoul of some toff's plans for her."

"Plans that turned her to a life of crime?"

She could hear that cold judgment in his voice, see it in the set of his jaw. Toffs like him never had it so hard as old Nan. Had no right to pass judgment on them that did for themselves what they could. But it would hardly be to her benefit to say so to him while he was feeding her up. And it would be foolish to tell him old Nan had taught herself to pick her employer's desk with a hairpin and take his ready lour, in desperation to escape being forced into his bed. Talk of beds wouldn't do. Despite the captain keeping his hands to himself in the bath, it wouldn't pay to wave a red flag under the nose of a bull.

She shrugged. "Plans that turned her to keeping food in her belly, regular-like."

"And how do you feel, now you've got food in your belly?"

She felt warm and, truth be told, a bit muzzy, but not quite all to rights. "Like a hammer's still at my head."

He gave a short, dissatisfied grunt. "How's the hand?"

"*I can number all my bones.* The breadbasket's aching, but not so bad as before."

He seemed to debate what to do next, but finally, he nodded and tossed his head in the general direction of Tanner and the blankets. "See if you can sleep." He got up and headed for the stairs. "I'll see you in the morning."

"All right, then, Captain," She returned his nod, all professional-like. "Good night."

She was asleep before Hugh had even returned from his study to douse the lantern and bank the kitchen fire. But he didn't leave her to her dreams and seek his own bed, as he ought to have done.

No. He pulled a chair up next to the fire and watched her sleep.

He told himself he stayed only because he ought not leave them. They were his responsibility now, the girl and her brother. Her brain might still be disordered from the blow to her head, and if he didn't watch her, she might, if she woke in the middle of the night, be foolish enough to run. She was, under all of her bravado, strangely, intensely shy of people. The years of hard living, of always looking over her shoulder, had broken her trust with the rest of humanity.

Not that he was any great example of trusting optimism. His experience had taught him most people were unworthy of trust in any form—even the illustrious, bloody Lords Commissioners of the Admiralty. But here he was, trusting a great deal of his future, not to mention a knighthood, to a pair of wary thieves who would take him for all they could and leave him flat at the first chance. So, he would watch them. Carefully.

But right now, they slept the sleep of the innocent, or at least the exhausted.

What was it she had said? *I can number all my bones.* Where had he heard that before?

He reached over very quietly and put the back of his fingers to her forehead—to check on her temperature. She was only mildly warm, not alarmingly so, and breathing evenly. He let his hands linger, sliding the backs of his knuckles across her high cheekbones and tracing the elegant arch of her eyebrow. Strange to think of her, this coarse creature of the streets, as elegant in any way, yet here, up close, there was an elegance, a delicacy to her features he would have denied a mere few hours ago.

She twitched and moved under his hand a little, uncomfortable—no, unaccustomed—to the simple touch of another human being.

And all he wanted to do, all he craved, was to be able to touch her, this strange, unfathomable girl. She had more faces than the surface of the sea, changeable and volatile. Pickpocket, housebreaker, and now, by her casual admission, a picklock to boot. His luck in finding her had been remarkable. She was very nearly perfect for his uses.

Too perfect. The vision of her bare skin and her white and pink breasts blew across his mind's eye. She was living, breathing temptation. And he would have to resist.

Hugh returned to the chair next to the stove and settled himself as comfortably as possible with a bum leg and a stiff cock. It was going to be a very long night.

Hugh came awake to the sound of the girl stirring from her pallet of blankets, the line between sleeping and waking abrupt and instantaneous. He still slept in naval watches, used to only four hours of sleep at a time, and so had checked on her often during the long night. He was relieved to see she sat up easily, sleepily pushing her hair out of her face and yawning wide.

She looked almost young, soft and innocent, reaching over to check on her brother first before she looked around the room, accustoming herself to her new surroundings until her eyes lit upon Hugh. She bolted up from the wool pallet of blankets, her face first scarlet and then an alarming, stark white.

"Handsomely, now." He surged to his feet. The last thing he needed was for her to keel over from dizziness.

But she was on her feet and steady, though wrapping herself protectively in one of the wool blankets. As if a piece of coarse wool would stop the direction of his thoughts. But he hauled his gaze from the sight of her tousled hair and flushed face. From her warm skin. From the idea of wrapping his hands around her messy braid and pulling her to him, up against his chest and . . .

"Morning, Captain." Her voice was quiet and froggy.

"Good morning. Let the boy sleep. How do you feel?"

"Like I been kicked by a horse." She rubbed her face with the back of her hand and pushed her hair off her forehead. "Where's the privy?"

Hugh's gaze automatically shifted to look through the high kitchen window, out to the dripping back garden gauging the height of the fence. Damaged hand and all, she could probably still make it over in a trice. "There's a chamber pot in the laundry."

"I'd rather go outside, if it's all the same to you." Then, as he stood there eyeing her dubiously, she read his thoughts perfectly and added with studied boldness, "You needn't take on. The boy's still here, right? I'd hardly pull a runner and leave him behind, now would I?"

"Wouldn't you? Isn't that what you did when you planned to come here without him? Or did you think you could just sneak out once you'd gotten your three hundred pounds?"

She didn't bat an eye. "What happened to 'we've got to trust one another'?"

The girl was clever. He'd give her that, damn her eyes. "Go on out to the privy then, though you may wish you hadn't. And mind that blanket on the wet grass. But come right back and come upstairs to my room. To my study," he amended, wanting no misinterpretation of his intentions. She would probably think the worst of him. "We have things to settle between us, you and I, and there's no time to waste before we need to get to work."

Hugh stayed in the kitchens, trying to keep himself from watching her walk to the back of the garden, until Jinks appeared to relieve his watch of the boy.

"See I wasted laying a fire in your room," the old tar groused.

"Aye. It'll still be there tonight." Hugh was in no humor for his former steward's pointed remarks. "I'll take my shaving water up myself, if you'll see to something mild for the boy when he wakes. But let him sleep if he can. And I've told the girl she's to come to my study directly she returns. I'll see her before breakfast."

Jinks tried to put a warning shot across his bow. "And how wise would that be now, sir?"

"Just the water, Jinks, without the dubious strategic advice."

But Jinks was too long familiar with his ways to be properly intimidated. "Don't know why you need a couple of scrappy bantlings, anyways. They'll only muck about my business."

"I need them because, much as I would prefer, I can't allow you to pulverize the Lords Commissioners into revealing their secrets without giving ourselves very much away. While a sound thrashing would be altogether more straightforward than mucking about with bantlings, Admiral Sir Charles Middleton has asked for discretion, and I aim to give it to him. We've set our course, now we'll sail by it. Thank you." Hugh took the ewer of hot water. "I'll breakfast in an hour."

"Aye, sir."

Hugh couldn't have taken any more than eight minutes to shave away his night's beard and change into a fresh set of clothes, but the girl was already waiting for him, standing in the middle of his study with her dress and hair set to rights, hands clasped demurely behind her back—the very picture of innocence. As though she hadn't a thought in the world of swiping whatever valuable she had probably already stowed down her bodice.

But he was keeping his thoughts, and his hands, well away from her bodice, wasn't he? She was here, at his insistent invitation, because she was good at swiping things. It only remained for him to learn how to manage her, this volatile little Kate.

The girl was perusing the bookshelves, and Hugh tried to imagine what the room, and indeed the whole house, might look like through her eyes. The book room was a study of light and shadow, with the gray morning light filtering in from the large front windows, leaving the dark mahogany paneling and bookshelves only dimly illuminated.

Without a fire and candles to warm the place, and bring the richness of the mahogany, and the brightness of the leather book spines to life, the room was hardly inviting. And yet, he was most comfortable here, in the only room besides his bedchamber that held his own personal possessions. His books, his telescopic glass, and sextant were out, on the desk and shelves—reminders of his other life, the naval career to which he was trying to return.

He'd been in London since early summer, recovering from his wounds, and he'd taken the lease on the house fully furnished so he might have the temporary comforts of land, without burdening himself with the more lasting attachment of permanent acquisition. He had planned to be there only long enough to recover his full strength, and now to complete the admiral's assignment and collect his knighthood.

But she would most likely be intimidated by this room. She was smart as a whip, but the room was everything she was not—refined and well educated. Comfortable. It's oak-paneled walls spoke of learning, tradition, and privilege.

"That's a powerful lot of books," she said by way of greeting.

"Aye." There was something about the way her eager eye swept covetously across the leather spines—no it wasn't simple avarice. It looked damn close to yearning. "Would you like to learn how to read?"

"Learn?"

"Yes. We will commence the actual work of emptying our suspects' pockets as soon as your hand has healed enough to allow it, but until that time, I have decided you will engage in a course of study designed to make you more useful to me." What was he saying? Teaching an illiterate girl to read might take months. He meant to be long gone once this assignment was complete. He meant to be aboard his own ship, not minding this lass's education. But his mouth seemed not to have consulted his head. "Being able to read will be an asset to you as well, afterward."

"Afterward," she echoed. And then a slightly crooked smile brewed itself on her mobile lips, as if she were amused. "Sorry to disappoint your low expectations, Cap'n, but I already know how to read."

"You do? Books?"

"Well enough. Told you old Nan were a governess once."

"*Was* a governess. Here,"—he reached for the volume closest to hand—"read this."

She flipped open to the frontispiece. " 'The New Practical Navigator, being a complete epitome'—that's another of Nan's favorites—'of navigation, to which are added all the tables requisite for determining the latitude and longitude at sea.' Nice, light readin', that?"

"No. It's full of errors." He took the book back and tossed it on the desk. "Can you write?"

"Not well enough to pass queer screens, but I'll do."

"You've tried to forge banknotes? My God, lass."

"Old Nan liked to see what her kiddies had an 'aptitude'

for. That was another of her words, aptitude. But screens wasn't my cup of gin. Had better *aptitude*," she pronounced the word with relish, "as a Kate. And a pick. And of course, also, a dab hand as a cracksman."

She was just full of unexpected talents and skills. Remarkable. "Can you do sums, as well?"

"Please, Captain," she said, as if he were embarrassing himself. "I'm a prime filching mort—a devilish good thief. I'd be an embarrassment if I couldn't add two and two and come up with five."

"Two and two are four."

"Aye." Her slightly crooked smile made dimples appear in her cheeks. "But I knows how to make 'em into five."

Every time he challenged her, she revealed another dimension, another facet of her talents and personality. And managed at the same time to knock his preconceived notions flat.

"Only if your hand heals. May I see it, please?" He held out his hand, already impatient to feel the touch of her skin.

She was reluctant, covering the bandaged hand with the other and holding it close to her body. "I kept it dry."

"Good. You will also endeavor to keep it clean. May I see it, please? How does your hand feel? Is it stiff? Or your arm? Pervis put in a number of stitches. Come over to the window, to the light." He walked over himself and pulled the curtains back farther, letting even more of the flat morning light flood the room. He needed to see her in the harsh light of day so he could banish his more ludicrous fantasies with practicalities. So he would think of ugly, black stitches instead of bare skin and soft pink breasts.

CHAPTER 8

"A little," Meggs answered as her feet were somehow moving all on their own, without a word of say-so from her brain, across the floor toward him. When she fetched up next to him, she felt again, as she had in the timber yard, the full size and strength of him. She was a tall, lathy girl, as girls went, but still, he towered over her like a treetop, with arms and shoulders all carved of oak.

He was back into his gentleman's rig this morning, coat, waistcoat, and cravat all in place, all clean and shipshape. Civilized. All that cagey power battened down under his hatches. He took her outstretched hand carefully, half turning away to hold it again tucked under his arm, steady against his side, as he plucked the tied linen strip free.

She pulled back awkwardly to keep from being hauled up against his backside with her chest plastered against his coat. He said he wanted them to be professional, so she kept her left hand fisted up in her skirts to keep from touching him.

But she couldn't do it, could she? Because she *was* a professional and he was making it so easy for her fingers to make business-like with his waistcoat pockets.

The captain was unwinding the bandage, and she found herself craning her neck around to see the surgeon's handiwork. There, across her palm, was a row of stitches, bristling black against her skin like an uneven quilt edge. Eight in all, she counted. Lucky eight. Jesus God.

"It looks good. Can you wiggle your fingers? Handsomely, now."

"What does that mean, 'handsomely'?" she asked his back. His broad, tall back that near blocked out the light. "It don't look handsome to me."

"*Doesn't.* Means carefully, with thought and deliberation. It's a naval expression."

"Do tell. I like it. The naval expression," she clarified, because he was touching each of her fingers in turn, running his own strong fingers across the tips and knuckles, sending soft waves of something nice lapping up inside her.

"Your hands are cold, but that's good, I think, or at least better than hot and septic." He sent a tight smile back toward her. "Flex your fingers again. Good. It looks good," he finished as he began to rewrap her dipper. "Pervis left a salve, to help in the healing and keep the scar soft once we take the stitches out."

"When's that?"

"Pervis said ten days." But there was tension and displeasure in his voice. And in his face. His jaw had got that hard look again.

"But you want me to get to your work sooner."

He shot a quick, perceptive glance at her over his shoulder. "Yes. I can only afford to give you a few days' grace."

"Right enough. We can get to planning your job straightaway." When he kept mum, and only kept on with the bandages, she prompted, "You gonna tell me what the job is, or is it some great ghastly secret?"

He turned, presented her with her hand, and took a long look at her with those probing, relentless, pale eyes. Didn't give much away. Played his cards close, the captain did. "The less you know the better."

If she was going to come through this job in one piece, she needed to assert herself with this formidable man. "Well, here's the thing. Seeing as you're new to larceny, you ought to take some advice to help you get rolling. It's best if you tell me everything about who we're going to dip, and why."

"If you should be taken up by the constables," he countered, "the less you know, the less you can give away. Safer for all of us."

What bloody effrontery. "I'd never peach. Never 'ave, never will. And I thought you said the traps couldn't bone me?"

His face colored strangely at her words, and his voice when he answered was strangely choked. "Should you be taken up by the constabulary, rest assured I will get you out. You'd be let off quietly, never fear."

"Ah. Tiptoeing through the hallowed halls of justice, are we? Right. But you leave me in the dark and I'll be like a grave digger—up to my arse in the business with nowhere to turn. That's no good for either one of us. So the more I know, the better. I plan as much as I can for every job—every last one."

"Even the MP on Cockspur Street? To my eye that looked entirely spontaneous."

"That one was," she admitted, "and look where it got me. Chased all over half of London, ruined me hand, and wound up here, contemplating unspecified felonious activities on behalf of His Fat Majesty, German Georgie. Something can always go bad. Planning is definitely better. So just what are we stealing?"

He took a long stroll behind his desk, where he sat in his chair and nailed that icy gaze to hers, sharp, like an axe. Weighing her out like an undertaker. Finally he said, "Information."

"Hmm. Tangible evidence, you mean, not just like hearing word of a deed? Hardest thing to get, that. Too many ways to keep it, too many ways to store it. That's why I like money.

Only a few places for a man to keep his lour and easy enough to find. But 'information' it is. Who're we going to start with?"

"A lord or two. Or seven."

"Seven," she repeated. "Lovely. Nothing like a challenge, is there? But I'm glad it's toffs—I likes stealing from the toffs. As a rule, they smell better and they have more lour. They are all toffs, aren't they?"

He was instantly all naval captain, all absolute command. "In all of these instances you are to take only the papers, if there are any. You are not to steal any watches or purses. Is that clear?" Oh, he was working himself into a fine glower.

"Depends."

"It does not *depend*."

She couldn't imagine how his jaw could set any harder. "It's like this—you're letting your honor get all in the way of the business. You just think on what happens if you relieve this lord of this information you want and nothing else. He'd know it were gone, and that someone was especially after *it*, and nothing else. He'd be wary and take a lam and blow the ken right away, see? But, if he thought he'd been cleaned of *all* his portable chattels, so to speak, like someone was only after his lour and took the papers by chance as well, he might be more inclined to wait and see. And when no one from the guvamint come after him, why he'd not be near as chary. D'you see? And then you can bone him for the drop, easy."

He looked away, all immovable, granite concentration. He didn't give away much, the captain. "I do see," he said finally. But he was unhappy about her logic, his lips ironed out to a hard line. "But you're not going to keep it. Neither the money nor the watches."

"What're *you* gonna do with 'em? Can't keep 'em around. Someone got wise to you, all that lour'd give you away, sure as a noose. You're gonna hafta fence it, and I'm yer mort there. I know my way around a few kens what won't cheat you blind."

"What *are* you going to do with *them?* There will be no illicit filching or fencing of *portable chattels*," he rumbled like thunder. "You will turn in each and every single piece of property you filch. Do I make myself perfectly clear?"

"Perfectly," she answered, arranging her face into compliant lines. And as sweetly as a vicar's daughter, laid his gold, pair case, openface, pocket chronometer on the wide expanse of desk between them.

Hugh had everything to do, to try to keep his mouth from gaping open and his hands from automatically patting down his waistcoat pocket. He knew very well what his watch looked like, though he stared at it laid out on the desk as though he'd never seen it before. As if he had not consulted it just before he came downstairs. Damn his eyes and her nimble fingers.

And he'd never felt a thing. He'd been too busy doing some feeling of his own, even if it had only been her hand. And yet he'd gotten lost there, amongst her nimble fingers. Fingers that would never be soft. But his mind had wandered happily off, imagining what other things such not-soft, agile hands might be capable of doing. To him.

Damn his eyes, he was a pig. She was trying to be useful and helpful and engage in the practicalities, and all he could think was how he'd like to "bone" her.

He cleared his throat. "Well done. Are there any other objects that do not belong to you, which you would like to return?"

She fished her left hand down her bodice and came up, one by one, with his letter opener, a small candle of sealing wax, and a Morocco leather bookmark. Her explanation was as casual as her shrug. "Just keeping my hand in."

He restrained himself from touching the four objects laid out on this desk just to feel the heat of her skin still radiating from them. "With just your left hand? Are you trying to tell me you think you're capable of going out in your current state, with your hand full of stitches, to take on this work?"

"You seemed like you was in a powerful hurry, yesterday. And you said you didn't like idlers. So I wasn't idle."

He leaned back in his chair to give himself a modicum of distance, both figurative and literal. To decide just why he was so loath to toss her out into the street to begin the work he so desperately needed completed. "As you so sagely pointed out, we'll only get one clear shot at this, then our suspects will become wary and make this task all the more difficult. I need you hale and hearty and able to function at one hundred percent of your ability. Or as near to it as possible. I can afford a day or two of grace, but no more. And you won't be idle. So, I don't mind you making an ass out of me, by keeping your *hand in,* in fact I'm all for it, but I will have you understand, this job is not a joke. This job cannot be attempted casually. A very great deal is riding on the success or failure of this mission, and on the job you're going to do. People's lives are riding on it. This war is riding on it."

"The war? On me?" Her voice rose precipitously.

"Yes, on you and on your skills. Do you understand me?"

She swallowed another saucy remark, as if she were well used to dining on nothing but her own wit. "Yes, sir."

"Good. I appreciate your skills. You're an admirable pickpocket, and we'll put that to good use, but what I will also require of you may be something more than the ordinary bit of thievery you're accustomed to. I may have to place you in certain houses, to recover documents and other objects His Majesty's government may deem necessary."

"Easy enough, Captain." She was unfazed by the prospect of housebreaking. "Now about these toffs—you know them all by sight?"

"Sit down." He gestured with impatience to a chair. She was going to tire herself out standing all day. He *was* in a hurry and he needed her to get some rest in the two days available, so she might heal as quickly as possible. "Some."

"You know where they live?"

"Some." She still wasn't sitting. In another moment he was going to pick her up and put her bodily into the chair.

"Wealth of information, you are." Her voice was dry with sarcasm. "Is there someone else from your navy portion of the govamint I can ask?"

Rawsthorne's contemptuous face leapt to mind. That was all he needed, for her to be exposed to the likes of Major Rawsthorne. For all her wit and sharpness, she would be no match for the casual cruelty he sensed in the man. He needed to find his traitor before the major had a chance to come poking around into his methods.

"I'll have all the necessary information by the time you're healed enough to start, if you'll sit your arse down long enough to begin that hand healing."

"Oh. Don't mind if I do." She perched said skinny arse on the edge of the chair and came right back at him, full of business-like insistence. "Look, I know you're a canny bloke, but you're an officer, all straightforward and honorable-like. But I'm a professional, a prime filching mort. You leave all the dishonesty and larceny to me. You just give us their particulars and Timmy 'n me'll take it from there. We can watch and follow 'em and see what they gets up to. See where they go and who they meet. See who's got expensive tastes or nasty habits, so we can best decide how to get the drop on 'em."

"I'll take care of that. You just heal."

"So you done this before then? You know how to tout the case?"

"As a matter of fact, I do. Rest assured, I know how to get the necessary information on my own."

"Waste o' time. Six eyes is better than one."

"Than two." But he could feel his face begin to smile at her obliviously mangled metaphors and mathematics.

"Six. You, Timmy, and me makes six eyes. I can watch toffs easy enough with a caw hand. And we'll let the Tanner tail 'em. He can patter after 'em all day's long, and those Lord Toffs won't be anything the wiser. An' another thing, you know where they're getting hold of this information you needs?"

"Perhaps." But her suggestion had merit. And he needed to remember what had made her so impressive, so perfect for his needs—her near invisibility in crowds. And the boy as well. Hugh hadn't seen him in Cockspur Street until he appeared out of nowhere to divert attention from the girl. They were seen only when they chose to be. It was a lesson he would do well to learn.

"Look, Cap'n. I thought you said we was gonna trust each other. I let you look at me in me bath, and you let me know everything you know and think, and already got planned up in that big, hard head of yours."

"I said we *were going* to trust each other." He answered by rote as the blood stood still in his veins. For a moment. Only a moment. Then it came roaring back with the force of a rogue wave, slamming through his body in a roiling rush. "You *let* me look at you in your bath?"

CHAPTER 9

He was answered by total, raucous silence. It was so quiet in the room, he could identify individual sounds outside the house: a carriage harness jangling and then rumbling by in the street, a wherryman calling up business from the water steps across Cheyne Walk, and the background bird calls from the trees.

But he kept his eyes on the girl and watched her try to master the curious rush of embarrassment flaming across her face. Meggs crushed her plush lip between her teeth as if she could call back the words, and her nostrils fluttered wide as she fought to control her breathing. Hugh hoped his face was not giving away as much as hers, but there was something distinctly erotic about the fact she had known he was looking at her. To know she had, in some small way, taken part in that lovely, long perusal. But he also knew he had to tread very, very carefully. If he pushed, she could easily revert to the almost feral, ferocious reaction he'd endured yesterday when she'd come into the house.

When the girl finally spoke, it was in a small voice, stripped of her usual St. Giles bravado. "You said I had to trust you." She gave a little half shrug, trying to be nonchalant, but her shoulders twitched unevenly as if the plain-spun work dress made her itchy. "And you didn't do anything when you was looking at me."

"So I did say," he agreed quietly. He understood, too, that she had bestowed upon him an enormous act of trust, which he needed to acknowledge with one of his own. "And no, I didn't do anything. I gave you my word."

But her coarse, street-tutored mind had traveled down an alley of its own. She sent him a narrow look across the side of her jaw. "Don't you like girls? Or are you a buggerer?"

God's balls. Hugh had to laugh or he would choke on his pride. And a rapidly rising need to demonstrate for her just exactly what he did like.

"I mean, stands to reason, don't it?" she went on. "Didn't touch me or nothing. And you're navy. Everyone says the navy's all rum and buggery."

"My God, lass. Your mind is an absolute sewer." He tipped his head up to study the ceiling, afraid to look at her. Afraid of what he might see in her eyes and of what he thought he might be hearing in her voice. "I'm not a sodomite. I *do* like girls. Women. Very much."

"Just not me."

Ah. Hugh forced a long, cool breath into his lungs. Just as he suspected—this was not about him at all, was it? "Just because I didn't force myself on you doesn't mean I didn't like what I saw. I did." He risked a glance at her. "Very much."

"Oh."

He saw confusion, but also, he thought, some disappointment chase across her face. No, he had to be imagining that. "But you don't like to be touched. And I'm a gentleman, despite all appearances to the contrary. I don't force unwilling girls."

"Oh." She was nodding slightly, trying to understand. For all her coarse worldliness, she was still strangely vulnerable.

"I understand your aversions. I can only imagine you have

been forced, in the past. Forced to do a great many things you didn't want to."

Color blazed up her cheeks, whereas her lips pinched down into a round little moue. It made him want to kiss the pain and regret away. To show her something of pleasure. To taste her sweetness.

But she would hardly welcome that. She had blackened his eye for so much as reaching out to take her cap off. His jaw was bruised from the force of her fear. "Is that true? You've been forced?"

"Aye," she finally mumbled into her shoes.

"Well, then." He had accomplished his aim, putting a safer, more professional distance between himself and this girl, and his infernal, unwarranted attraction to her. But her admission gave him no peace.

And she was regarding him now, staring really, as if he were some new species of animal. But he was only flattering himself to think it could be in fascination.

"You're a rum toff, you are."

"Am I?" He made his tone light to cover the idiotic spike of want lodged in his chest like a steel splinter. "Is that a compliment?"

She shook her head. "Never met a toff or a cove like you."

He decided to take it as a compliment anyway. "Thank you. Now then, as I have said, I am interested in your skills as a pickpocket and your remarkable adaptability and aptitude for role playing. And since you already know how to read and write, we can move on to preparing for your next role, that of housemaid."

"Oh, I done housemaid aplenty."

"Well, this will be different. You will actually have to become a maid and do housemaid's work here. Cleaning and scrubbing and such."

"Why? Waste of my skills, mop squeezing."

"Think of it as preparation. My plan will require you to become employed in our prime suspect's household, as a maidservant, so while you're there, you can intercept documents. You'll need to truly look and act the part, perhaps even for days, until you know your way around the house well enough to find and copy documents. So no one will be the wiser that they have been intercepted."

"Ah, so we're to run a rig, are we?" Those black eyes narrowed in appreciation.

"How did you think we should manage it?"

She pulled a face. "Thought we'd wait 'til the time was right and just heave the case. Play the darkmen's budge when the whole gill is safe at rug—asleep. I, myself, like to go in right after the toffs goes out of an evening and all the servants are shift of 'em, and happy to be on their own, and having as little to do as possible with their work. You'd only have to boost me through a window or some such and we'd fall to it."

"As much as the thought of *boosting* you through a window does for me, I'll take a pass." He could all but feel the lovely, rounded weight of her derriere in his hand. "You'll have a better opportunity to study and know where the right documents will be if you are employed for a time in the house. So a maidservant you will be. Here first, to learn, as well as wherever there happens to be."

"And are *you* gonna teach me? Or your fairy man there, Jinks?" She walked over to the bookshelf and swiped her finger through the rime of accumulated dust. "That'll be a treat. You got cobwebs here older'n Timmy."

She had a point. But— "Timmy? Timmy Tanner—what a name."

"Yeah, well, that's just what I calls him." Her smile was small, as if she was enjoying a private little joke.

"And he calls you Meg."

"Meggs," she corrected, her smile widening across her lips. "Tanners and meggs. Them's coins, 'int they? Money. Meggs means golden guineas, on account I'm so good at stealing 'em. And he's the same. Tanner's half a crown. What you call nicknames."

Hugh found himself smiling back. And here he had even called her *Miss* Tanner. "I see. Very good joke. *Noms du plume* as it were."

"*Noms de guerre* more like."

Hugh's ears pricked up instantly and sent a cold message to his gut, like a douse of icy seawater. Oh, that was something. The pronunciation. The inflection. The "R's" rolling from the back of her throat, like a native speaker. God's balls. Just who had he taken into his house and into his confidence? Admiral Middleton had warned him even the Admiralty was not safe from French spies, and there she had been, on Cockspur Street, exactly what he had decided he needed, so conveniently chancing by at the very moment he needed her. Damn his eyes. He had never believed in coincidence, and yet he had stupidly accepted her appearance as just that.

He made his voice calm and even. "Funny that, you speaking French."

She shrugged it off. "Like I said, I've got ears. Hear all sorts of things, I do. And old Nan were a font of gentry talk."

Perhaps. Perhaps not. This girl had untapped, uncharted depths. And he didn't have time to find the bottom.

He almost reached out to grab her, to haul her across his desk like a witless midshipman and shake the truth out of her. But she wasn't a witless midshipman. She was as sharp and lethal as a handspike, and he knew if he had her under his hands, hauled up close, he'd do other things than shake her. And his jaw still hurt like hell.

He fell back on his experience and put every ounce of menace into his voice and pinned her with his stare. "You listen to me, girl."

She went lividly, intensely still under his look, like a grenade before it goes off.

"Don't think to try and cozen me." He spoke in a precise, low growl. "Do not forget, I can *crush* you. If you even attempt to play me false, I will thrash you within an inch of your life. And *then* I'll start to work on you."

"I wouldn't advise a thrashing," she said matter of factly. "I don't react well to pain. I get angry."

He knew that well enough, given yesterday's bruising fight. But still it rankled, the necessity for her pugilistic skills. She was hardly more than a girl, not a prizefighter.

She was a *thief,* his logical mind insistently reminded him. A housebreaker, an accomplished and heartless pickpocket and robber. She was adept at all sorts of knavery, and he would be a fool to waste any compassion on her.

"Angry," she repeated. "It whets my appetite for violence. Nothing like a good fight."

Something inside him kicked over, like a fuse being lit. Fuck logic. Fuck compassion. This was different. Hugh looked at her fully, at this small bundle of sinew and bone, as the metallic tang of blood suffused his mouth like an opiate. God's balls. A girl with an *appetite,* a bloody *taste,* for violence.

He was appalled. And undeniably aroused. Because her words were like the echo to the savagery he kept latched down tight within, like black powder in his hold. Dangerous cargo.

This he understood, far too well. The taste for violence, for the heady rush of blood lust, was exactly what was suffusing his tongue at that moment. If he closed his eyes he could easily, effortlessly recall the addictive feeling of grim elation when his fist, or his sword, or his boot mashed into another. When he felt the ugly, satisfying lurch through his body as his blow slammed home. Oh, yes, he knew depravity.

Because it was all he could do to keep from kissing her, from shoving his tongue between her lips, to see if she could recognize the taste of it from his mouth.

God help him.

He fell back on duty to regulate his uneven breath. "Do not play me false," he repeated, for his own clarity. And sanity. "Do I make myself perfectly clear?"

"Aye, sir." She was still unfazed, as if she had no bloody idea the dangerous fuse she had nearly lit inside him. "You're a hard man, Captain."

"You have no fucking idea how hard." He let the silence stretch taut between them and never let his gaze waver. Never showed so much as an inch of softness. To show her the danger she courted when she played with him, however unknowingly.

Eventually she looked away. "Maybe I don't like the idea of working for a hard man."

He smiled at her, to show just how much of a bastard he was prepared to be. She wouldn't look at him in fascination now. "You have no choice."

Her gaze snapped back up to his, her eyes dark and feral, as wary as a trapped animal. God's balls, they were like to bite each other to death before this was over.

"You're a clever girl. It's strap or stretch on a gibbet. You must see, I can't let you go now, after everything I've told you. Not knowing where I live, what it is I'm planning to do, and for whom." He got up slowly and worked his deliberate way around the desk toward her. "You know everything about me—my name and rank, where I live, and that I'm working on an important secret assignment for His Majesty's government. And I really don't know the first thing about you. I don't even know your real name."

She let out an angry little huff. "Makes no matter. You can call me whatever you want. You will anyway."

"I would prefer to call you so you'll *answer*, and experience has proved your actual, Christian name will work best."

Another sarcastic breath. "Big of you, to assume I'm even a Christian." She was trying to goad him. And he knew it. Even as she spoke, she was up from the chair and moving behind it, keeping the small safety of the furniture between them. Clever girl.

But he wasn't going to rise to her bait and give her any justification for trying to bolt. He wouldn't chase her. Instead, he stopped and hitched his hip onto the front edge of the desk. "Yes, I am assuming."

She shrugged again, that uncomfortable twitch of her shoulders. "Well, Christian or Turk, Meggs is the only name I can remember."

It was a lie. But a relatively unimportant one. As she said, her name really made no matter. He only wanted to know, because he *wanted* to know. To know some part of the true *her*. "All right, Meggs it is. And Tanner?"

"Tanner, or Timmy will do well enough."

"All right, Meggs. I hope we understand each other quite plainly. This business is deadly serious, and there is no going back for us. No room for error. But I'm a man of my word, and you will be paid your seven hundred and fifty pounds for your services at the satisfactory conclusion of our tasks. So let us waste no more time on lies and gamesmanship, and get back to the task at hand. I am going to trust you. The toffs, as you call them, are actually the Lords Commissioners of the Admiralty. One—or at least one of them—is stealing secrets and passing the information to the French." He watched her closely for her reaction. "We need to find which one of the Lords Commissioners it is and put a stop to it, by gathering enough evidence to see him hung."

"Stealing secrets from the Admiralty? That's treason," she whispered. "I mean, I'm not one to quibble. Stealing is stealing, though everyone's got their reasons. Stealing a handkerchief'll get you hung. But treason. Treason will see you drawn and quartered before your heart stops spurting blood. Makes nipping a few gold thimbles here and there seem merely impolite. Cripes"—she blew out a big breath—"you do know how to pick 'em."

Her shock and pallor seemed genuine enough. "I didn't pick. This task was assigned to me. I don't have a choice, and now neither do you. Or the boy."

The mention of her brother sobered her out of whatever sharp shards of resentment still remained. Or perhaps she was simply too intrigued by the thought of the crimes and the money ahead. "Don't you get nothin' outta it?"

"Perhaps." He could give her that much. "I get to have my career back and my ship, *Dangerous*."

"Oh, aye, that'd be the one they give *you*, all right." She gave him the beginnings of a tight smile, her cheeky humor slowly reasserting itself. "Well, it's only ever two things—love or money."

"I don't take your meaning."

"Only two real reasons a toff, a lord, would commit treason—either he needs the money bad, or he believes in the cause. It'll be better if it's for money. Believers are the worst. Zealots they are—willing to do anything. The thought of being tried for treason don't faze 'em. Better hope yer man's in it for the lour, or this could get messy."

Oh, she was damn sharp, his larcenous little lass. "I'll keep that in mind."

"You do that. I know I will. Give me the jim-jams, zealots." There was that hard twitch of her shoulders, as if she could shake off the feeling like a wet dog. "Right, then. Lords Commissioners. These toffs all know each other, then?"

Sharp as a penny tack, this Meggs. He could at least let himself admire her professional acumen. She was a supremely able partner in crime. "Yes, they meet regularly at the Admiralty Building."

"And that's where your traitor's stealing secrets to sell?"

"He's definitely not *my* traitor, but yes."

She mulled over that information, scrunching up one eye in dissatisfaction at the direction of her thoughts. "That makes it tricky, you wanting to dip 'em all. A couple of men gets dipped on any given Sunday and that's bad luck. These toffs get to talking, and come to find they've all been bunged, and that'll put the wind up all of 'em. We gotta plan this out careful like. We gotta do it in a way they don't associate losing their purses with the Admiralty. Can't just wait for them to waltz out of the Admiralty and fall to our business in Charing Cross. We'll have to follow 'em, one, maybe two at a time, if we split up. No. Timmy's got the skills—he's a prime foyster and a good fagger—but we work best together."

At that moment her stomach growled with such resounding resentment even he could hear it. She needed to be fed.

"You leave that to me. Go down to the kitchen and get some breakfast, and then you can begin helping out in the household as best you can at the moment, with light chores and cooking."

She favored him with another long, scientific look. "Cookin'? Ain't you 'fraid I'll poison you?"

"And kill the goose that will lay your golden egg? No. And besides, you'll have to eat everything you make—and sit at table to eat it with me—and so will the boy."

"Across there?" She gestured over her shoulder to the large dining room sitting empty across the hall. "At that table, together? Under all those sparklies? You never!"

So she'd given herself a tour of the place. Of course she had. She was a professional.

"Yes, perhaps even at that table, under that chandelier."

"Well, I never."

"Oh, you will, Meggs. You will."

When Meggs made her way back to the blissful, reassuring warmth of the kitchen, she was astonished to find Timmy being fed up by a stout, no-nonsense woman with sky gray hair, and hands like a butcher.

"Where'd you come from?"

The woman straightened from the stove and favored Meggs

with a critical inspection. "You'll be the girl, then. Let me have a look at you." She put her hands on her hips and gave Meggs twice over before she nodded. "You'll do very well, I'm sure, but we'll get two things straight. Number one, don't be mouthy. Number two, do what you're asked, when you're asked, and we'll have no trouble at all. Now, I'm Mrs. Tupper. I'll be keeping the house for the captain and teaching you how to go on. You can start by eating your porridge, and when you're done you'll take the coffee tray up. Likes his coffee good and strong, the captain."

"You were here before—last night, then?"

"Of course. There you are, dear." She set another steaming bowl of porridge on the table. "Sit. Eat up while it's hot. Now where was I, Tims? Lord Bless me, Tupper and I—that's my mister, Tupper—have known the captain since he were a wee midshipman on *Resolute*. Years ago it was. How the time does fly. All right, Tims, you take that bowl to the scullery, and then your job is to take the hot water over. Be careful with that pail. That's it. They'll build up your strength, those pails will, till you're as strong as a gunner."

Mrs. Tupper turned back to the stove. "The captain'll want eggs and toast, I'll wager. Properly done." She heaved a cast iron fry pan about as if it were made of air. "Now, my girl, have you ever done kitchen or scullery work before?"

Meggs spooned down the creamy porridge. "No."

"Housemaid? Laundry?"

The porridge was sweet and warm and solid in her belly. Bliss. "Not a bit of it."

"Well, you'll learn, dear. You'll learn."

And learn she did, towed along like an anchor in Mrs. Tupper's smooth wake. In the course of one morning, Meggs learned where to find the silver and table linens, and how to set a proper table. How to lay out the coffee service. How to dust without mis-arranging things and how to make a bed. How to ladle out soup.

To be fair, she already had a good nose for where to find the silver in a house, but the rest was as new and unknown as a faraway West Indies island.

She learned how to scour a pot with only her left hand scrubbing, as Mrs. Tupper was constantly reminding her to keep her injured hand dry.

"You mind that fin, girl, or the captain will have both our heads."

But Meggs knew how to learn a thing or two for herself. Through the course of the day as she fetched and toted and hauled and emptied, Meggs was unsurprised to find that brisk, sturdy Mrs. Tupper had been, for the greater part of her life, a navy wife, living aboard ship with her husband, Tupper, until he was badly wounded in action at Toulon. She also learned that Captain McAlden, who had been a mere lieutenant then, had, along with his friends, been quite the heroes and had saved Mr. Tupper's life. Nothing was too good for the captain in Mrs. Tupper's opinion. She had come all the way up from Dartmouth, down the coast in faraway Devon, to keep house at his request.

And she wasn't going to put up with any nonsense, questions about palm trees or straggling. Meggs hopped to it all day long, until the afternoon waned and she was as worn out as an old dishrag.

Each meal seemed to start almost as soon as the last plate from the previous meal had been scrubbed and stored away. Mrs. Tupper was as demanding and uncompromising as old Nan had ever been, but Meggs liked her. As with Nan, a body knew where they stood with Mrs. Tupper. She was firm and tough, but she wasn't mean or hard. She never so much as cuffed her, despite numerous mistakes. And when she got it right, the lady took a delighted pride in her accomplishments. Put her in mind of Nan, more and more.

Except Mrs. Tupper fed her more. Loads more. Every time

she turned around, there was a bit of bread and butter or cheese. Or coffee and milk.

Oh, Lord, she hadn't had milk like that, fresh and thick with cream, in so long. Since before. Before she'd become what she was. Before she'd ever learned to have a care in the world. And she was going back to that, by all the saints, her and Timmy both. That was why she was here, working like a red-faced skivvy. So she could get her money and leave London for good, and put it all, everything she'd become and done, behind her.

And when she did, they'd have a home of their own, like this one.

It was a fine house, though not much lived in. Now that she was assigned to clean the rooms, she took a sort of proprietary interest in them. In the great, big pond of mahogany she polished in the dining room and the lovely parkland of walnut parquet she mopped and polished on the floor of the drawing room. At least the dining room had table and chairs. The drawing room was strangely empty, the few bits of furniture and rugs piled up in the corner, waiting for Himself to unpack and set them to rights.

The only room, besides the bustling kitchen, that gave hint to the life of the house was his study. This was where he must spend most of his time. The room certainly seemed to reflect his personality, or at least as much as she knew about him. A large desk dominated the room, with two straight-backed chairs marched in front of it, as if he liked the people he dealt with to be uncomfortable, or at least not at ease. She certainly hadn't been.

There was no great, important portrait painting of either Himself, or an ancestor, on the wall. There were some smaller ones of ships propped on the bookshelves, a single pair of prints of bee anatomy behind the desk, and a mirror set so high above the fireplace mantel she couldn't even see herself, but other than that it was plain and spare.

But there were loads of books. If he had really read them all, she was surprised he didn't have a squint. And not just on the shelves, but piled on the corner of the desk and open on every surface, scattered here and there, as if he were looking at them all at once. As if they were all vying for his attention. The books were the only thing not neat and tidy and squared away.

And there were more rooms, above. Meggs looked up the curve of the baluster to the bedchambers. Where Himself would sleep.

Mrs. Tupper told her she wasn't needed to go in there to clean—Mr. Jinks would see to the captain's things. But she had a brain, hadn't she? And all her stupid brain seemed to want to do was imagine what might lay behind the closed door.

Would it be helter-skelter with books, like the study, or would it be like the man himself, straightforward and contained? Have to be a powerful big bed to house a man like him. And there it was again, a picture of him, etched across her brain, colors and all, lying on that bed, tawny and naked as the day was long, looking up at her with those pale, hawk bright eyes.

Lord almighty, what was wrong with her? Her brain must be disordered from all the rich food, the work, and the skull bashing. A girl could get herself into deep, deep trouble thinking about a man like that.

Thinking of a man like the captain at all was asking for nothing but trouble.

CHAPTER 10

A bell rang from deep in the kitchen, and Meggs went rattling down the stairs, trying to shake the graven image out of her head and get back to work.

She set the big-deal table for supper, as directed by Mrs. Tupper, with the most beautiful things—silver and linen and cut glass and porcelain so fine the light passed through it. She set out the big tureen of soup while Mrs. Tupper brought over a platter of roasted chicken, served with potatoes and peas. Spare fare, Mrs. Tupper had called it. Looked like a bloody feast to her. She had to swallow to keep herself from slavering down her face like a mongrel dog.

And then Himself gimped in. He looked tired again—in his body anyways—the limp made his footfalls slow and deliberate. But his eyes were bright and sharp, searching each one of them out in the room. She ducked her head and stepped back, determined to play her part of housemaid to perfection. Anything to get her out of the kitchen and back to what she did best. Bunging pockets wasn't easy, but it surely beat this working for a living. Mop squeezing had gotten old mighty fast.

At Himself's nod, Mr. Jinks and Mrs. Tupper sat down on

one side of the table, and she and Timmy were directed to the other.

Lord, but he'd really meant it. They really were going to sit down together at the table. She had set the lovely places herself, and still she had not let herself believe the captain would really take his meal with them, as if it were the most normal thing in the universe. What a rum cove, to take dinner with his servants as though they were guests and gentry. Good Lord and all the glowering saints. Her face felt as hot as a biscuit. She couldn't remember the last time she had sat down at a dinner table, and it wasn't even the gleaming acre of polished mahogany that filled the dining room upstairs from one side to the other. But she had, once. Before.

For the past few years, meals, such as they were, had been taken on the street, standing up or hunched on a convenient stoop or bench, eating hot pies from a vendor's barrow. Another memory intruded, of a crude wooden table at old Nan's, the kiddies all packed in elbow to elbow shoveling what little food there was into their mouths before it could disappear.

"Tanner," she whispered out the side of her mouth, "watch the captain, when he eats, and do whatever he does. No, you turnip, not the wine. You're too young. Mind your manners."

Only they hadn't got any manners, anymore, had they? Timmy had been a baby, before. He couldn't remember. He ate like he was in a prison, all hunched over his soup bowl, as if he needed to defend it.

But she had another, dimmer memory in her head. Of linens the color of daffodils and fresh milk in creamy stoneware jugs. And pies. Filling the air with the smell of apples and cinnamon. Meggs reached her left hand up to the edge of the table to finger the intricate curl of the sterling silver fork.

"Don't even think of pawning it." The captain's voice intruded upon her reverie. "Anything missing will be deducted from your pay. At replacement value, not at whatever you get if you fence it."

He was a sharp cove, no doubt about it. But he didn't know everything. She slid her hand back into her lap and kept her memories to herself. Daffodils. Creamy milk. And flowers. Flowers fresh from a garden, in pots—no vases—around the house.

And plates. Like this one, porcelain with pale flowers and lines of gold painted round the scalloped edge. Her mother's hand, so soft and white on the stem of a wineglass. Had they sat at tables like this one? She searched her memory, but the only other thing she could recall was the mellow glow from the candles and the feeling of warmth.

Oh, the soup was good. Potatoes and leeks and cream. Warm and smooth as butter. Heaven.

When the soup was finished, Mrs. Tupper motioned for Meggs to clear the bowls away to the sideboard while she uncovered the serving platters of chicken, potatoes, and peas. When Meggs sat back down again, the captain turned those probing eyes of his to her to make conversation. Or at least his style of conversation, which was more like an interrogation.

"Do you like to steal?"

Nothing like reminding a girl of exactly where she sat in the world, though tonight she might be allowed to be fed her dinner like a nob. She glanced at the cold judgment of his eyes, but didn't pause. "I like to eat."

"So I see."

That was bloody rich—big man like him, who looked as if he'd never missed a meal in his life. She put up her chin and faced him. "It's like this—if I could eat without stealing, I wouldn't steal. But I never did figure out how to have the one without doing the other."

"I see." He took a long sip of wine, still wanting to find his answer. "So you don't get even a bit of a thrill when you are successful?"

"Well now, that's just human nature, innit? But usually I'm too busy worrying about my neck, or Timmy's, to feel any thrill." She made herself take a breath and relax, civil like. He was only curious, was all, however lowly it made her feel. "I do like how I feel when it's done. When a job is over and everything's done and secured. That's nice for a bit. But I only ever feel successful after my pockets are empty. And then I have to start all over again, don't I?"

"I imagine what you must have felt was relief. And perhaps, pride."

"I like to steal *and* eat." Timmy laughed from her other side.

The captain smiled at him in encouragement. Meggs frowned. He shouldn't do that. The captain should be encouraging the boy to be more like him, a gentleman, instead of gallows bait.

"And you're good at it." The captain was smiling at Timmy, completely unconcerned with her, though she sent him a ferocious scowl. As if he thought it perfectly all right to let a twelve-year-old boy, with more enthusiasm than sense, loose on the streets of London on his own. Hadn't she just told him today they worked best together? She'd give him a bloody big piece of her mind. She'd—

Meggs snapped her neck to swivel her look from one to the other. How would the captain know how good the Tanner was, unless . . . ?

She rounded on her Tanner. "What did you do?"

Timmy wasn't holding his cards close. He was bursting to tell her. "Went out just this afternoon, the cap'n and me, on our own." He was full of manly triumph at having finally gotten around his overprotective sister. "I showed him round, tipped him the dub, so he'd know what it were like. Tailed a nob in his carriage, all the way straight into Mayfair. Took a hackney, we did. I sat up with the driver so's I could keep a close trail of the nob n'all. You should get your own carriage, Cap'n." He talked right across her as if she wasn't there. "A bang-up rig, like a curricle or a phaeton. That ways, I could sit up right behind, like the prime bucks in the park, and tell you where to go."

She'd like to tell them both where to go. This was her job, her rig, and they had gone off without her. Left her behind like cold bathwater, to mop and clean up after them, while they were out roystering the afternoon away.

"Tanner don't—"

Himself cut her off, his voice calm but carrying. That voice that could get heard over cannon fire. "You did very well, today. Both of you." He smiled at her, but it was meant just to make her shut up—it didn't even warm the corners of his eyes.

She had nothing to give him but surly resentment. "Told you I knew how to eat."

He ignored her. "Thank you for a delicious dinner, Mrs. Tupper." Then he cut his sharp eyes across to Meggs.

She knew that look well enough already, though it was softened with the barest bit of a smile, telling her to mind her manners. She bobbed a respectful nod to the housekeeper. "Thank you, Mrs. Tupper."

"Thank you," echoed Timmy without any prodding.

Well, there were manners there enough to fill a boat. And dishes enough to fill the wash bucket to overflowing. Lord, but that was going to take an age. And them all filing out, leaving it for her. Mrs. Tupper was handing her plates and platters to carry off to the scullery, so she couldn't get a moment private enough with Tanner to give him a piece of her mind.

Thankfully, it turned out she didn't have to do all the washing up alone, though Tanner was playing least in sight. Mr. Jinks and Mrs. Tupper worked right alongside her, Jinks handling all the wet, sloshing bits while she was to dry the plates and take them back up to store in the butler's pantry between the dining and breakfast rooms.

The rest of the house was quiet, but there was light and a murmuring of voices coming from Himself's study. She tiptoed her way across the hall parquet, silent as a knife, to listen at the door.

The captain. And Tanner.

She would have burst in. She should have. She was supposed to be protecting Tanner, wasn't she? She was supposed to take care of him and make sure nothing awful or *nefarious* happened to him.

But her throat felt hot and tight, and she couldn't keep her mouth from twitching around. He had left her out. *They* had left her out, both this afternoon and now. While she was cleaning and working, they were sitting up here, pretty as you please, talking and laughing.

Her eyes began to burn with heat. Oh, fie and damn. She wasn't going to cry. She wasn't. Old Nan had taught her better. But—

"Go on," the captain's voice was saying, "you're falling asleep in your chair. Take yourself off to bed." And then a scrape of chairs.

Meggs ghosted her way across the hall and down the stairs before they had so much as cracked the door. She smothered her rage and fear and frustration by savagely sweeping out the kitchen, until captain sought her out.

"Normally, I would tell you listening at doors was a bad habit, but under the circumstances, I suppose it's appropriate."

There was nothing she could say that wouldn't make her look six ways a fool. So she kept her breath to cool her porridge.

"Come back up to the study. You've made a decent start, but there's more work to be done before we turn in."

Something in his voice—something remote and hard—made alarm scurry through her like a hungry rat. And that "we turn in"—there weren't any pallets laid on the floor tonight.

She touched the sharp knife she'd nipped into her pocket earlier. It calmed her to feel it tucked close and ready. But the captain was already clomping unevenly up the backstairs, paying her and her knife no never mind.

Did no one in this bleeding house use the main stairway? Waste of all that damn mopping and polishing, if you asked her. But no one was asking.

The study smelled of fire, of something burned that was different from the heat of the coal in the grate. There was a wisp of paper, curled and blackened on the hearthstone. The captain had been burning papers. Probably something he didn't want her getting ahold of.

But now, he was passing her another piece of paper. "Tell me what you make of this."

"Dunno. It's writing, innit? But it's not right. It's all my eye and Betty Martin." She held the paper out, to hand it back. He shook his head and didn't take it.

"Jibberish, do you mean?"

"Yeah."

"What language is it?"

She looked again, more closely. "These supposed to be words? So it's a code then? Like flash patter and the like?"

"Good. Yes, a little." He was nodding at her, all encouraging.

"And it's not gonna be the King's English is it? Didn't think we had this many two-letter words in English, do we? Then again, I suppose we do, but it still don't look right."

"Very good." The light in his eyes was all for her being clever. Made her feel warm and happy inside when he looked at her like that. Made her forget about needing to keep knives in her pocket. Guess that was the pride he was talking about.

"Can you cipher what it says?" she asked him.

"Yes. I wrote it, as an exercise for you."

"Well, I dunno what it says." She shrugged, all nonchalant, but she didn't like to admit it. That pride again.

"You will, lass. I'll teach you how. Come here." He pulled a chair up next to the desk and sat, motioning her into the other. "This is what's known as a simple Roman code. It's a basic shift of the alphabet. The secret is to find the most common letter."

It was like a puzzle, a game. "There—the 'M's.' "

"Good, that was quick. Now, to decipher it, you have to know the most common letter in English is 'E' and in French also. And the most common set of double letters are 'LL.' "

"So some of these is really going to be 'L's' instead of 'T's.' "

"You've already cracked it."

"Oh, I get it. So I put 'E's' in for all the 'M's'?"

"Try it. You write out the alphabet, like this. That's the code alphabet. Now under the 'M' you try an 'E', and then fill in the rest of the alphabet in order. Now—"

"Now, I look at the code paper and I put in the underneath alphabet letters."

"And see if you can make it intelligible. Go ahead." He smiled and sat back, all gratified satisfaction. Seemed she wasn't the only one with pride. But it made her smile, too, this pleasing him. Made her insides all warm like pudding.

She had the message decoded, but not understood, in no time at all. "Well, that's French, innit?"

"Very good. It is. What's it say?"

"Well, I can read it like. I can make the sounds of these words. *'Ah,'* well I get that anyways, *'que ta bouche me couvre de baisers, car ton amour est plus exaltant que le vin.'* But I don't know what it means."

His face was all careful, watching stillness, his gaze zigzagging across her face. He was testing her. "I thought you said you'd been taught French?"

Oh, he was scary clever. "No, I didn't. Said Nan knew French, on account of her being a governess, and used fancy words. *'On dit'* and *'comme il faut.'* Used to make her laugh, talking to us kiddies like that. But I don't know what all them words mean." She waved her finger at the paper.

He looked at her for a long hard spell, his steel blue eyes probing for the truth. But then he just got up and said, "You've done enough for one night. But this will be a nightly exercise, whether I'm here or not."

"Where're you gonna be?"

"Out. Following our suspects into places where you, my lass, would be most conspicuous."

She gave him her patient look. "Never been *con-spicuous* a day in me life. Made my reputation on it."

"So you'll fit in at a brothel? Or a gaming hell? Or a fashionable gentleman's club?"

"Oh." Well. That'd teach her to brag like a jackass. "Leave that to you, I will, thank you very much."

"Thank *you*. Now up to bed with you." He rose and seesawed his way toward the door.

"Up? I'll sleep down in the kitchen. Night, Cap'n."

"I've had Mrs. Tupper make up a room for you. And one for Timmy as well."

A room? To herself? What was that stupid flutter of hope in her chest? She batted it down like a moth. "I don't mind the kitchen. I like to be close to the fire."

"You'll be warm enough. There are plenty of blankets." He looked back at her over his shoulder, frowning at her idiocy. "Wouldn't you rather have a proper bed instead of a pallet on the floor?"

She made like it was no import. "I'm used to choosing the softest plank."

That stopped him. He smiled at her strangely—his mouth tried to turn up at the ends, but it didn't reach up to his eyes, and his voice got quiet and grave. "I imagine you are. Let me show you, and then you can choose."

Talk of beds, however soft, still made her nervous as a lamb at a butcher's. "What about my brother?"

"I imagine Mrs. Tupper already showed him up. He was exhausted."

Timmy didn't have a right to be tired, the little traitor. He'd been the one larking about on carriages all day while she'd been made to scrub and mop.

But Meggs hugged her hurtful resentment close and kept her knife closer, and followed cautiously after him, up the narrow servants' stair, into the attics on the top floor of the house, where there were small, but private rooms with low, slanted ceilings. The captain had to bend his back to fit under the roof. He filled the narrow doorway, frowning at the lack of space as he gestured her into one of the rooms.

He took the single candle and set it on a chest of drawers, illuminating the narrow room with its dormer windows with curtains—*curtains*—closed across the glass, shutting out the blank darkness of the night. Gingham curtains. It was small, but light and airy and clean. So clean, it smelled of lavender. And the bed, even the spindly, narrow, iron-framed cot, so lowly it was fit only for his servants, was a bed the likes of which she had not seen for longer than she could remember.

"It's not much, I grant you." The captain stayed in the doorway, slouching against the frame and looking grimly about the room. Looking for things she could steal, no doubt. He needn't bother. He could lock her in for all she cared. She'd even prefer it.

He didn't understand, did he? He had no idea the temptation he offered. The money was nothing in comparison, really. Money, she could eventually get. She would have grubbed and stolen and saved and eventually, with luck and perseverance, she would have had the money.

But a room of her own. With a bed?

It was a real bed. With a real mattress and real sheets and blankets. It smelled like starch and lavender. It smelled like paradise. She let her fingers glide momentarily across the counterpane. "Where's Timmy?"

"Right next door." He hooked his thumb past his shoulder. "Would you like to check on him?"

"No, thank you." She wasn't quite ready to talk to Timmy yet. She'd rather wait till he was asleep before she checked on him. Though it would be the first time in forever they had ever slept apart. Or in beds, for that matter. Meggs wondered if she should mention that to the captain. What would he think, to know she and Timmy had most often slept like sheep in a barn, one practically atop the other for warmth and comfort? But if Timmy found he could sleep without her, she could certainly find her way to sleeping without him. Probably.

She turned round and bobbed a curtsey to the captain. "Thank you, Cap'n."

"You're welcome." Himself shifted his hands to hang on to the top of the door frame, but he didn't leave. It left them, the captain and her, in the small, yellow circle of light cast from the remaining candle and awkward, penetrating silence.

She stood there facing him, her heart galloping away in her chest, feeling the heat of her blood leach out into her skin. What was she supposed to say? What was he going to say? What was he going to do? Surely with Timmy, however he had been won over to the captain's side, right next door, surely the captain wasn't planning to try anything?

But Himself stayed still, looking at her with those cunning, icy hawk eyes for a long moment, giving nothing away. Finally his mouth moved slightly, as though he might try to say something and was still testing the taste of the words before he spoke them. Or as though he might try to . . .

There was that damned flutter again—hope. Or indigestion. But she didn't want to find out. Not tonight. So she nodded to him once, all professional-like, and then, without a word or any further to do, she shut the door firmly closed in his face.

Meggs turned the lock and waited. Waited for him to say something. Do something. Anything.

Nothing came. And then, after a long minute, there was the heavy sound of his uneven tread down the stairs and away, below.

Meggs let out her breath on a long sigh and moved slowly into the room, touching everything, letting her hands and her eyes work together to confirm the reality, the solidity of each and every object. It was all real. She sat down on the side of the bed to test the mattress, springing against it a little, and put her hand out to touch the plump pillow and the soft linen night shift Mrs. Tupper had left folded on the bed. She'd thought of everything, hadn't she? Such thoughtfulness brought a hot, itchy fist of gratitude welling up in Megg's throat.

It had been such a long time since anyone had thought of her, or thought of her needs. But here she was, wasting time and a very good bed on mawkishness. But first, no matter how sore at him she was, she had to check on Timmy.

He was curled up in the nest of quilts like an exhausted puppy. "Meggs," he smiled up at her when she touched his face. "Isn't this the best?"

"Try not to get too used to it."

"What's the matter with it? Prime setup it is. All the grub we can eat. I grown an inch since we come, in just one day, Mrs. Tupper says."

"She's only being nice to you, on account the captain needs our work."

"You don't like him, do you? Why can't you be nice to the captain? Why can't you make him like you, so's we can stay and work for him?"

"It's not like that, Timmy. It makes no matter if the captain likes me. He hired me—us—to do this job, and after that, he's going to go back to sea. Mrs. Tupper says he used to have a ship of his own before he got his leg near blown off, and that he'll be going back to it, once we do his dirty work."

"Cor. Ship of his own." Timmy yawned out the last of it. "Wouldn't that be nice."

"Hmm. Good night, my Tanner."

"Meggs." His voice brought her back. "Stay with me?"

"Sure, love. Just let me get out of my apron and I'll come back in."

The plain work dress and apron Himself had given her had a drawstring up the front, and the stays laced up frontways, too, as servants' clothes did, so she was out of it in a trice. She peeled down to her shift, laying the sturdy gown and petticoat over the iron railing at the foot of the bed. Then she checked the lock one more time, just to be sure, before she peeled off the shift as well, to wash herself with the warm water and soap.

It had been so long since she had had either privacy or clean clothes, really clean—the nightgown was new, never been worn before—she was loath to dirty it even by sleeping in it, even though she'd had her first real bath in years and she was clean. Really clean. She took another deep breath of herself. And smiled.

But it was chilly. She waited no longer to throw the nightgown over her head, pad across the hall, and slide in next to Timmy. It was so lovely to slide her legs along the clean, soft linen. The quilts, for there were two of them, pressed down comfortably, the weight making her feel secure and safe.

Oh, he had no idea, the captain. Lord, to think of all those years with nothing but maybe a pallet on the floor and some scratchy, wool blankets to share between them. And they had been lucky to have that. Old Nan had been a generous kidwoman, as kidwomen go. But Nan had never had sheets like these. Sheets that were enough to make her forget her resentment of Timmy, and all her troubles, and the mess she was in.

Oh, Lord, she'd have sold her soul a time or two just for the chance to be as clean and well fed and encased in downy warmth as she was now. And would be again.

She would take the money and be finished with it. And he had said amnesty yesterday, hadn't he? If he truly meant what he said, she could leave London and know she wouldn't have to spend the rest of her days looking over her shoulder, waiting for the sword of Damocles to drop down on her neck.

She'd ask tomorrow. No she'd insist, but right now, she'd let herself sink into the heavenly abyss of the feather pillow. Tomorrow was soon enough.

But it wasn't. It never was. Something could always go bad.

CHAPTER 11

His second day of the tutelage of his thieves had been hell—tedious and then exhausting. The boy had gotten hurt while they were on Lord Harold Cummings's trail. Stupid mistake. At a chance word from Hugh, the Tanner had darted too close to a brewers dray and ended up slightly the worse for wear. He escaped with only a profusely bloody nose where his face had collided with the corner of the wagon, and a goose egg–size bruise on his temple.

Timmy had taken it all in stride, only whimpering a little when Hugh had mopped up the copious blood with his handkerchief. And thankfully, the boy hadn't been concussed. Hugh had more than enough of that to worry about with Meggs as it was.

Hugh's leg ached like a hot ball of tar was lodged in it by the time they made it home to face Meggs. As they came into the kitchen, a movement in the garden above caught his eye.

She, Meggs, was taking in the washing before the afternoon waned into early winter twilight. It was a Monday, and under Mrs. Tupper's regime, like nearly every other house on the block, linens of all descriptions had been hung out in the fitful sunshine to bleach and dry.

Hugh moved to a better vantage point to watch her. He felt

more than a little ridiculous—an officer of His Majesty's Navy, spying on a maidservant, even if she was an accomplished, professional thief—but he didn't want to be seen. It seemed important to be able to watch her without her knowing it, without her putting up that hardened veneer of cheek she tossed over herself like a heavy sea cloak whenever he came into a room.

She was out in the cold afternoon without so much as a shawl, and she hugged her basket close to her side as she scurried under the lines of clothing. Her skin looked pale and white in the chill air, and he noticed something he hadn't before, a mole, dark and intriguing, against the side of her neck at her collarbone. Beckoning him to let his gaze linger on the long slide of her alabaster neck, running down to her shoulders and on her fine hair, one long tendril dancing loose across her nape.

She wasn't precisely beautiful. She was too spare and prickly for English beauty. No, she was more like an exotic plant from a desert. They, too, had blooms. And she all but hummed with a potent, alluring life force that blossomed out of her face. When she wasn't masking it.

Meggs moved directly to the makeshift line strung across the garden and began to unpeg the wash. He watched her swift, economical movements with a sailor's appreciation of her agility and physical dexterity. There was grace in each one of her movements. She shook out the clothes, tucked them under her chin, and folded them against her body, smoothing her hands down the fabric to flatten them out. He watched as she quickly unpegged and folded one of her own chemises without even thinking about it, then she hesitated in front of his small clothes.

Was she embarrassed? He was almost embarrassed for her. No, not embarrassed. The heat under his skin was something entirely different.

After her initial hesitation, she moved quickly, taking down the drawers and folding them in a rush before she moved to the next piece of clothing. It was a shirt—one of his linen shirts. There were several of them on the line—he went through at least one a day. She shook it out once, an elegant, forceful snap of her wrists, and then slowly, as if she couldn't decide if she really wanted to, she crushed the shirt between her hands and brought it up to her face to visibly inhale its scent.

He nearly staggered. His fingers dug into the wooden windowsill to keep himself steady, gutted by the intimacy of the gesture. He understood her impulse far too well. He wanted nothing more than to bury his face in her neck and inhale her scent, her very essence.

And with that simple action, she also told him the compulsion was not by any means one-sided. She felt an attraction, too—perhaps not as strongly as he—but she felt it nonetheless. Their curiosity, at least, was mutual.

By the time she brought her basket in and saw Timmy, Hugh was across the room, accepting a hot mug of cider from Mrs. Tupper.

Meggs reached her brother as fast as a rifle shot. "What happened?"

Timmy smiled sheepishly and shrugged her off. "I'm all right."

She ignored him, combing and cataloging his body with her hands, feeling across the architecture of his bones and searching with her hands for something broken or out of place.

"I'm all right, Meggs," Timmy insisted. "Leave off. It's just a bloody nose."

"It is not. It looks like you got clouted. What happened?" she asked again.

Tanner's eyes slid toward him. "We had a bit of a dust up," Hugh answered.

She visibly battened down her temper and raised her eyebrow in silent question, simmering hot, like the pot of cider on the stove.

"Don't take on, Meggs," Timmy begged quietly. "Not in front of the captain."

Hugh couldn't name the look that washed over her face, but somehow, she got paler, her eyes dark as coals. "Meggs." Hugh touched her elbow lightly. "Let Mrs. Tupper mother him up for a moment. She has a vast amount of experience with battered-up lads."

Mrs. Tupper chuckled as she tilted up Timmy's head. "Don't I just? Helped patch the captain up a time or two, when he was only a wee bit older than yourself." She gave the boy a critical inspection. "You'll do, lad, you'll do. Now, let's get you a pot of warm milk and chocolate. And perhaps some clotted cream. The cream here's not so good as in Dartmouth—the cows here in London being . . ." And she was off, rattling copper saucepans.

But Meggs was spitting mad. She'd rounded her elbow out of his grip. "No."

"Come up to my study." It was an order, however quietly given. "I'll buy you a drink. I know I could use one." He moved off, up the stairs without waiting for her to follow, and she stomped up behind him, each stair step a noisy complaint against his lack of vigilance.

He threw his battered sea coat on the chair in the front hallway and headed for the tray of decanters behind his desk.

"I don't like spirits," she groused from the doorway.

"Then read a book while I get one." He wasn't normally the sort of man who felt a driving need for spirits, but after only a few days in *her* presence, he began to understand its appeal.

"And I'm not going to read a book, I want—"

"You want to rail at me, like a fishwife, for an *accident*. An ac-

cident, which could have happened anytime, and did, according to Timmy, happen all the time before you two came here.
An accident, like the one which befell *you* and brought you to
my door, in a state of putrefaction the likes of which I haven't
seen outside of the navy. Here." He shoved a small glass of
sherry into her hands. "Drink up. It'll make you feel better."

"I don't want to feel better," she insisted stubbornly, afraid
to let go of her armor of indignation. She was fair quivering
from it. "And you are changing the subject."

"Which is your brother, and what you plan to do with him
once he grows up. Or what *he* plans to do with himself, once he
grows up. Or sooner."

She stood stock still, pale and flat, like the water before a
gale. He braced himself, anticipation of the potential violence
of the coming storm thrumming through him.

And then, she simply burst into tears.

Oh, fuck all. He had absolutely no idea what to do with a
weeping female—especially Meggs, the girl who didn't so
much as shed a tear when she tore open her hand or when
they stitched it back together. And now, in the turn of a moment, she had become a watering pot.

"Come now." His voice sounded stupidly, unnecessarily
gruff. "It's not as bad as all that. He was only roughed up,
though I'm sure I aged a couple of years in the process."

She folded herself abruptly into the chair, staring at the
bandage over her hand, as she wiped at her eyes and tried to
pull herself back into order. Likely brooding over all the dicey
chances life still held in store for her and her brother. For all of
them. "What happened?"

"We were over near the docks along Cheapside. Timmy
said you used to live near there."

She tossed up that tough little shrug. "Lived here and
there, over half of London."

"Is that how the two of you have the map of London in your

heads? I must have chased you through every back alley from Charing Cross to Covent Garden, and the Tanner showed me hidden paths along the docks not even the rats use regularly."

"It's how you stay alive, knowing your way around, and two ways in and three ways out of any street. But what happened? Just give me the bad facts."

It was no wonder she was a successful thief—she didn't give up easily. "We had trailed my Lord Cummings down along All Hallows Lane. Some rather unsavory friends, our Lord Cummings has. When I stated my wish that if you had been with us, you could have picked his pockets to find out what he had collected from the gentlemen of the wharves, Timmy said he could do it and darted off unmindful of a brewers dray swinging up from the warehouse."

"Something can always go wrong." She shook her head like a dog, insistent in the need to fight. "You shoulda taken me. He's not careful like he needs to be."

"And I daresay he learned that. He made a mistake—and I'm more than sure he'll remember it. Nothing like a little pain to drive a lesson home. I've seen it time and time again with boys under my command. He'll not make a mistake like that again. And I need you here."

"But he needs me to set him off on a job right. He's only little."

"He's not that young. I went into the navy when I was only a little older than him."

"It's just—he's at this dangerous age. He thinks he knows everything and there's no possibility of failure—because it hasn't happened yet. Only it hasn't happened, because I *do* think about all those possibilities of failure. And I plan for them. Contingencies and backups. He's too impatient and headstrong to do that."

"Impatient and headstrong. Difficult traits." He smiled. Such obvious irony.

"All he wants to do is get the job done so he can eat. All of a sudden, he can't remember old Nan making him go hungry for not getting it right."

"While you make yourself go hungry, even if you do get it right?"

"That's not the point."

"Isn't it? What did you say—impatient, headstrong, and stubborn?"

She had the grace to flush, her face heating like a sunrise, pink and blue at the same time.

"Speaking of impatient, let me have a look at that hand." *Speaking of impatient.* There were layers and layers of irony, need, and self-denial in this conversation. "You're keeping it dry?"

"Yes. And clean. Mrs. Tupper helps me change the bandage if it gets too soiled."

"Good." Hugh picked up a candle branch and brought it to the other side of the desk, then pulled his chair up close to hers and began to unwind the linen strips. "I saw you taking in the laundry."

He felt almost . . . exposed. Rather like at sea, when he might order the gun ports opened to see if the enemy were prepared to engage. But also, exposing the limits of his own firepower.

But she floated just out of range. "Waste of my time, my skills."

"No," he clarified quietly. "I watched you."

"Oh? Oh." She tried to pull her hand away on that quick intake of breath, but he held it firm in his own. He could feel the rush of her pulse through her wrist, and her breath grew shallow even as she worked to keep her feelings hidden, crushing her plush, plum lips under her teeth.

"It's healing nicely." He stroked lightly along her palm. "Are you afraid? Of me?"

Her response was an honest whisper. "I'd be a fool not to be."

"And you're not a fool. And neither am I. I'm a gentleman. If we ever decide to do . . . anything about this curiosity, this"—he hesitated and then decided to name it—"attraction between us, it will be by mutual desire. Do you understand?"

She didn't answer, just watched him with those huge, dark eyes.

"And until that time of mutual desire, nothing is going to happen. You have nothing to be afraid of." He leaned forward slowly and very gently placed a kiss on her forehead.

And left her in peace.

Instead of shorter, the days seemed to get longer, no matter the number of hours between the late dawn and the early twilight. More scrubbing, more sweeping. Despite her appeal to Himself to let her go out to do real work, the captain still wouldn't take her out. Timmy, goose egg and all, got to be out of the house all hours it seemed, whereas she was made to keep cleaning.

It was enough to make a mort go mad. And despite all his quiet talk about mutual curiosity, the captain acted as if she didn't even exist. She'd hardly seen him from one end of the day to the other. Made her surly as a drunk pimp, it did—grouchy with no good reason for it.

And what in the blazes was that awful noise? Meggs paused as she hauled on the pulley rope for the laundry drying racks suspended from the ceiling. It sounded somehow like the clanking of swords crossing. In *Chelsea?*

She poked her head out into the kitchen only to hear heavy footfalls shivering the ceiling far above her head. "What on earth is that?"

Mrs. Tupper didn't even look up from kneading her bread. "Never you mind. You just get on with that ironing."

"Not bloody likely," she muttered to herself. The heavy muffled footfalls resounded again, vibrating down so that the copper pots in the rack overhead jangled. And then Meggs heard Timmy's voice, raised in a shout.

She abandoned the irons and followed the sounds up two flights to the drawing room, where she discovered the reason why all the furnishings were massed in a heap against the side wall and the curtains left fully open to flood the room with light.

The captain and his man Fairy Ears were fighting each other with long, skinny, shining blades. Jinks was stripped to his shirtsleeves, but the captain—the captain was bare from the waist up. He was . . . well, *bare*. All tawny skin. And muscles that moved, glowed, and bunched. They had dimension and form, like you could go and put your arms around and hang on to them. Or feel around your shoulders.

Lord help her.

Of course, that was *if* a girl wanted to feel a thing like that, which she didn't. Got in the way of business, muddied it all up.

They were completely immersed in their deadly business, paying her no never mind, but it seemed to be only an exercise and not an actual fight. Himself directed his man, instructing, "I want to try that riposte again."

"Right, sir."

Timmy was here, too, the little shirker. He stood near the corner with a turkish towel but also with a tipped blade of his own. Jesus bloody God and all the bleeding saints. They had been teaching him swordplay.

In another moment, the captain felt the hole she was boring into his back with her stare and stopped. He motioned Timmy to go work with Jinks, who set the boy into a series of prancing footwork. Then the captain walked over to her, still wearing nothing but his skin. It was near impossible to focus on her anger with all that glowing nakedness. She didn't know where to look.

But the captain didn't think a thing of it. Sauntered over as if he were in the queen's drawing room taking tea with the court. "Your brother has caught on quickly."

Meggs could peacefully shift her gaze across the room to the Tanner, swiping away with his blade like a bloody cavalier. "Yeah, well, he's a clever lad, in't he?"

"He's more than clever. He shows a considerable amount of potential."

"Do tell." Meggs wasn't in the mood for all this chatty, informative taradiddle. She was surly and mean feeling. Hurt really, if she were to be honest. This was her bloody rig, wasn't it? He'd wanted her expertise. "You lads going to prance around all day, or are we never going to get to the business at hand, of letting me do what you're paying me for and steal?"

If he was taken aback by her sharp tone, he never let on. He was all stoic, immovable captain, full of what old Nan would have named *sang-froid*. "You'll begin when your hand's well enough."

"It's well enough to push a bloody mop all day. Don't know why it shouldn't be well enough to do fencing or fleecing, whatever you need. So let's get on with it."

He chewed on that for all of two seconds. "Let me see." He reached out for her hand.

She snatched it behind her back. If he saw the blister burns from the irons, he'd find another reason to keep her cooped up all day. "It's fine."

He tried that icy-eyed gaze of his. "Aren't you in a fine pet this morning?"

"So maybe I am. Maybe I get annoyed when I'm doing all the work around here, and you three are prancing about like . . ." She ran out of nasty things to say. Where was old Nan now when she needed a cutting word? "Letting Timmy mess about in there, instead of doing his share."

"It's good for him. I told you, he's got an aptitude." He tossed aside the sword. "You might think of him for a minute, instead of yourself. You might think of what will happen to him if you stay on your present course through life. I know you're devilishly proud of your prowess as a 'prime filching mort,' but you know as well as I, you'll most likely end your days on a gibbet, and the boy with you. You ought to think of what he might become instead."

"You bloody . . . How *dare* you?" she hissed at him. "You have no bloody, fucking idea what I think about, or what I plan, or what I've spent *years* planning to do. I *sold* myself to you like a slave, you blind bastard, for that boy! I've done all this, everything, to get him out of the game. I've taught him to read and write against his will. I've nearly starved myself, saving up every cursed penny I could steal, so that boy, my brother, can have a future."

Lord help her, she was shouting so loud every ear in the house was sure to be ringing with it, but once she had begun, she couldn't seem to stop.

"I cut my hand wide, fucking open on the goddamned glass of that wall, so he could have a meat pie! So don't you *dare*"— she needled a finger into his chest—"tell me what to do. I don't need advice from a bloody cripple who doesn't know anything about us, and who's going to throw us out of here like yesterday's dishwater once you've got what you need from us."

And with that last blast of meanness, she flung herself down the stairs and ran all the way back to the laundry, where she slammed the door shut in Mrs. Tupper's astonished face.

Behind her, the house was echoing with empty, waiting silence. She couldn't stand it.

She yanked a thick shawl off the peg, threw open the door she had just slammed shut, and stomped her way out the garden door.

"And where do you think you're off to?" Mrs. Tupper stood with hands on her hips.

"Out. I'm sorry—I'm going out." She had to be out in the

air, moving and doing and thinking. She needed . . . Oh, she didn't have the faintest idea what she needed anymore. She had to get away before she said something else ludicrous and mortifying.

For all her stern, no-nonsense, Mrs. Tupper had a soft heart. "Then you go on up to the herb garden there and get those things I told you. You remember?"

"I remember." Her voice sounded hot and stupid, like there was a fist inside her throat making her windpipe feel raw from not crying. From feeling so useless. She wasn't useless. She *was* a bloody prime filching mort, not a damned mop squeezer. She was old Nan's girl—finest there was. If he wanted proof she could filch, she'd give him bloody proof.

CHAPTER 12

She ducked around Mrs. Tupper, ran up and out through the side gate, gave some stupid cove who was hanging about the lane, the stink eye as she fled by—what the hell did he think he was looking at—and headed north along Paradise Row to the Physic Gardens.

The gardens themselves were mostly brown and bare, and covered with a silver white rime of frost, but there were still rose hips and witch hazels to be cultivated. And toward the back of the garden were glasshouses where Mrs. Tupper's precious herbs could be bought.

But Meggs would get to the bloody herbs just as soon as she did a bit of business with . . . who? There—a doddering old Quakerish fellow in a long, old-fashioned coat and cape was meandering his way out of the garden.

Cawed hand and all, it would be simple enough to bung him. He was an easy target, slow and unsteady on his pins. And rich. She didn't normally like to steal from old people, but he was well enough set up, and she was madder than a toad full of pins.

And her nasty, analytical brain had already made its catalog: old-fashioned black frock coat of beautiful, tight merino wool over a long waistcoat, all fastened with a long row of polished, silver buttons. Purse in the outside pocket of the coat, right side.

All she had to do was brush by a fraction too close and give his spindly frame a bit of a bump. And then, as she played the Good Deed Doer and reached out to catch him, she plucked up his purse like an egg from its nest.

"Goodness, sir! Take care, before you do yourself an injury." And as they both brushed and straightened their disarranged clothes, she emptied the lour silently into her special pockets and let the purse drop to the ground underfoot.

The old man smiled and waved her off, oblivious to all the business under his nose. "Thank you, dear girl."

Almost enough to make her ashamed. Almost, but not quite. And off she went toward the herb sheds, where Himself caught up to her before she'd even reached the thyme. She'd seen him coming, of course. Hard to miss a man like the captain. Especially when he looked mad as a bear with a sore head. Well, that would make an even pair of 'em, then.

He was dressed rough, with only his sea cloak pulled on over his shirtsleeves. Come after her in a rush, he had. Knew she would be up to no good. His face was taut and set, but he only took her arm to lead her out of the way and said tightly, "Don't you think that's enough?"

The Bible said to turn the other cheek. All she seemed to be able to go was give it. But giving cheek was her stock in trade. "Enough for what?"

"Enough for one bloody morning. You make one stupid mistake and you'll blow my whole operation. Not to mention get yourself hung by midday. That was William Forsyth, one of the founders of this garden, as well as being the bloody Royal Gardener, whom you just robbed."

"Well then, here. You take it." She passed over the lour, which he took, and the next moment shoved back at her as if it were a snake.

"Don't give it to *me*."

"Why not? You said I couldn't keep it. And you said I couldn't get nicked."

"God almighty. I don't have time to sort out your tantrums."

"I'm not a child."

"Then stop acting like one."

"Stop treating me like one. And stop stealing my brother from me."

Oh, Lord, now she'd gone and done it. She closed her eyes and started to walk away. To get away from him and the mortification that threatened to swallow her whole.

He stopped her with a hand at her elbow, gentle but solid-like. He meant to have this out now. He spoke in that instructing voice of his, firm but patient. "I am not trying to take your brother from you. I have been doing exactly what you so cogently advised me to do, make use of his abilities to tail and follow people. We've learned a great deal about three of our most highly placed subjects in the past two days."

"You could have learned twice as much if you'd a let me help."

"I shouldn't have to explain this again. You're a clever girl, so put that devious brain of yours to work. I need you to be a housemaid. It's important. It will become more important in a few days' time when you're employed in one of these men's house."

"So why you gotta teach Timmy to fence?"

He took a minute to answer, as if he hadn't thought of the reason himself yet. "I thought it might be good for him to have the company of men. Look, Meggs, I can see you're protective of him, but a young boy needs more than just a sister. He needs a man to show him . . . well, how to be a man."

"But he's not a man, is he? He's naught but a boy."

"I was twelve when I went away to sea. And he's years ahead of where I was in terms of maturity and sharpness, or toughness. He's had a much harder life."

"Mayhap, but in education, where does he measure up?"

She flung her arm out in frustration. "He can barely read or write. He's as sharp as they come with money and shop signs and the like, but nothing more. Nothing that will make him a gentleman."

Sweet Jesus and all the saints. Why couldn't she just keep her mouth shut? Oh, he was surprised at that. He couldn't keep his eyebrows from flying upward in astonishment.

"I didn't think you were ambitious for him to become a gentleman."

She had already said too much. "Yeah, well, that'd be a lark, wouldn't it?"

"It would be a bit of a stretch, but not unheard of. It could be accomplished." He was weighing it out seriously. "I could see it done. And with the money I'm paying you, you could certainly afford to buy him a naval preferment."

"In the navy? In the middle of a war? You're out of your skull."

"Best time for advancement." He looked away, and she could see that toughness flowing across his face, the way water carved lines in boulders.

"Doesn't he have to be a gentleman to start?"

"Do you think *I'm* a gentleman?"

"You? Don't make me laugh. If there was only one thing I knew in the whole world anymore, I know that."

He gave her a big piece of that chewed-up smile, the one that made him look a little silly and completely harmless. "Thank you. If I am a gentleman, it's because I became one. I wasn't born a gentleman. My father was a hardworking, industrious Scots farmer, but barely a gentleman. I became a gentleman because I went into the navy. And the navy was the making of me."

"And you think it could be the making of the Tanner?"

He looked her in the eye. Honest man was the captain. "I do."

And she was getting tired of fighting. "Maybe you're right. I know he won't listen to me anymore."

"I've a friend who's presently the captain of a sloop on Channel duty. Working with the Revenue and staying on patrol. Fairly easy, if tedious duty. But he owes me a favor and might take your brother on as a midshipman."

"And that would make him a gentleman?"

"It would make him an officer, eventually, and gentleman will follow."

"But what if he got blown up, like you, or drowned. He doesn't even know how to swim."

He had no reassurance to give her. He knew her better than to try. Something bad could always happen. "It'd be a damn sight better than being hung for a handkerchief. You can't treat him like a child. And *you*"—he turned those icy, furnace eyes on her—"can't afford to act like one."

He was right. This was business. He was counting on her to be a professional. She took a deep breath and tried again. "I'm sorry. But my hand is fine. I can dip for you. So please, leave off the mopping about."

The tension eased out of him on a deep breath. But he still said, "I can't."

He turned to walk her back toward the glasshouse, and she saw the cove from the lane—the one who had eyed her. He was picking his way across the garden plots without once looking down at the rows of plants. But he did keep darting glances at the captain. That was six ways from wrong.

"Right then, sir." She raised her voice and held up her hand, ticking off Mrs. Tupper's list as if he had just given her instruction. "Thyme for the fish sauce, marjoram, dill weed, and vanilla bean, but only if it can be got cheap enough."

"Meggs? What are you on about now?"

She smiled meaningfully the conspicuous cove and lowered her voice. "Fella there's got an unseemly interest in our busi-

ness. No, don't look. You just take your time going home, nice
and slow—an easy promenade along the river here so you
don't hurt that leg, and leave him to me."

"I'm not so crippled as all that." His voice was both question and warning. "What are you planning?"

"As you like to say, Captain, the less you know the better.
And I've got Mrs. T.'s herbs to buy, haven't I?"

Less than an hour later, Meggs gave him the information
like a present.

"He's army or I'm Betty Martin. Handkerchief in his pockets, embroidered, with the initials R.E.—careless that, to have
his initials—and plenty of lour. Made it ever so difficult when
you went out by the water stairs for him to get a wherry down
river, when he hadn't the fare to follow. He went off up the
Row, but see now"—she pointed out from behind his study
curtains—"there's his replacement. Come up river in a wherry
from the Whitehall steps. I recognized the waterman—you
know the fella—nasty, greasy, yellow beard, squint eye? But
look at the way yer one's walking there, back and forth—all
military. Stiff rump and spine. Don't have a decent slouch to
rub a-tween 'em, those two boys. And that bag he's got slung
across his coat there? That's got the Broad Arrow on it. That's
British Military issue then, right? And don't get me started on
the boots—him and the other one. This one's let 'em go all
scruffed up, but every popinjay and macaroni on Bond Street
could tell by the cut and the leather, they's every inch Horse
Guards."

He smiled at her, and it was like a warm fire had been lit, all
pleasure and comfort. Oh, Lord, when did she come to this, to
feeling like he was the sun and she was a little weed in the
ditch, desperate for his rays.

"Lass, you are a credit to your profession. Your Nan would
be proud of you. I know I am. Well done." He sat down in the
desk chair and leaned back, pleased and relaxed. "I think it

safe to assume our watchers are what are commonly called Intelligence Men."

"Never say. Fancy that—hiring men like that to do the thinking for the rest of them. Shame really. No wonder the war's not going so particular their way. Someone really ought to train those boys up."

He laughed outright. "I'll take great pleasure in telling them you said so. Thank you."

"You're welcome, Captain."

"I wonder if I might be permitted to give you something in exchange? By way of a reward?" He passed over a small parcel, all wrapped up in paper.

She untied the twine and found a thick cloak, plain and serviceable to be sure, but on the bottom, all wrapped in beautiful, foiled paper was a bar of scented, milled soap. She breathed in the scent. She could not allow herself to use it when she was stealing, but until then, perhaps she could wash her hands with it before she went to bed so she could have the scent to breathe off her fingers all night long. That would be heavenly. She got a warm, quivery spot deep within her at the thought.

"Thank you for the clothes. And the soap. I can't use it, of course, when I'm working."

He looked a little put out. Offended even. "Why not?"

"Mark of a good thief—never leave any trace, even a scent. Have to be invisible, Nan used to say that. Taught me to use my nose, just like my eyes, or my ears. But it was lovely, the soap. Thoughtful-like."

"You're very welcome." He looked pleased, even if he wasn't quite smiling.

Like he might have had a quivery spot all his own, the captain.

Hugh stepped out of his front door feeling almost lighthearted. Must have been because he had actually slept last night. Or perhaps he was just getting used to the dreams. Or perhaps he was very much looking forward to this morning's work—bearding the putative lion in his den. With luck, he might even provoke a fistfight. Anything to appease the rolling hunger surging through his blood. The thought of putting his fist into someone's jaw pleased him to no end.

Bloody minded, that's what he was this morning. And happily so.

Thanks to a message from Admiral Middleton's inestimable clerk, and through his own contacts, Hugh had all the information he needed. He knew exactly where to find Major Rawsthorne within the warren of rooms between the Privy Garden and Little Scotland Yard.

The man Meggs had spotted in the Physic Garden, Robert Ellis, as they had identified him, followed him downriver like a netted sardine. Hugh disembarked his wherry at the Whitehall stairs and made a meal of climbing up to street level and making his slow, ponderous way across the greensward and into Little Scotland Yard. Once through the gateway, Hugh changed his pace, just for the fun of it, to pass quickly through the stone corridors. Ellis had to jog to keep him in sight, until he fetched up at the unmarked and unnumbered offices of Major Rawsthorne. If the major was surprised at being run to ground in his own warren, he hid it well, only displaying his annoyance and displeasure by snapping his fingers at a subordinate to close the door Hugh left purposely open.

"McAlden, isn't it? I hope you've come to make your report."

Hugh returned the major's lack of courtesy. "Rawsthorne. Good." He opened the door again and called down the hallway, "Robert Ellis? Come now, Lieutenant Ellis, don't malinger out there in the corridor. Major Rawsthorne would like reports to be made." He turned back into the room and without further preamble, instructed, "Call your dogs off, Rawsthorne."

"I beg your pardon?" Rawsthorne rose instantly behind his desk.

Hugh gave him the look that had made hardened seamen whimper in their sleep. "Your men. Ellis, Mickeford, and Greens. The men you've had watching my house and following me about the city. Stand them down. They are interfering with my ability to do the job Admiral Middleton entrusted to me. They are about as obvious as a fireship, hanging about Chelsea. Teach them to do their job properly, but don't use me to do it. Good day."

Chapter 13

Hugh spent the rest of the morning making arrangements for the afternoon. It would have been much simpler and less time consuming to have taken Meggs with him to Whitehall, but he didn't want her to be in any way mixed up with Rawsthorne or his men. It was one thing for him to play with Rawsthorne's fire, but if he involved Meggs, or let Rawsthorne get even a hint of her, he might not be able to protect her or guarantee her amnesty.

And here she was, the object of his obsession, putting fresh tapers into the candlesticks in the entry corridor. "Are you ready to get to work?"

"Me? Right now? Just like that?" She dumped the rest of the candles into a convenient drawer. "But I have to know what we're doing. Need to plan. You can't just go off like a cannon shot and hope you hit something. You've gotta aim."

God, he loved how this girl's mind worked. "Duly noted. We'll be heading up to Town in a private coach, to St. James's, where we will 'dip some toffs.' "

Her smile of appreciation was so dazzling, his heart hammered off beat and his sense of anticipation sailed a notch higher. "We should be able to find at least one of the gentlemen on our list at his club on St. James's Street."

"Oh, I do love a bit of work down St. James's. Right then. I'll need to look respectable—especially as you'll look like you fit in. You wait here." She evaporated up the stairs.

When she came back down four minutes later she looked— respectable, nothing more. Nothing to remark upon. Which was in and of itself remarkable, since he found her so remarkable, so intriguing. But somehow she masked it—her own character, her charisma—and became another character all together. She should have been on the boards at Drury Lane— she'd have made a fortune collecting the baubles of the rich playboys, instead of having to steal them.

But Hugh found he didn't like the image of her as available to other men. Even imaginary men. He could only console himself with the knowledge that if she had wanted to become an actress, she most certainly would have done so. But she had not. She had chosen to become a thief, much to his current benefit.

"Will you be warm enough in that? Why aren't you wearing the heavier cloak? That's why I bought it for you."

She had two wool shawls wrapped around her. "Wouldn't look me part in such a nice, new cloak. Draw attention that would."

"A cloak? What possible difference could a warm cloak make? Other than keeping you from contracting a pneumonia."

"It's not just the cloak. A girl like me, a servant, could never be seen with the likes of you, her master, in new clothings 'less it was a business proposition of an entirely different sort, see?"

Hugh stifled—yes completely stifled—the smile twisting at his lips. He would not remark upon the "proposition of an entirely different sort." He would *not*. "You're sure?"

"Oh, yeah. Dressed like this, no one sees me. Too old and you're interesting, like a cart wreck—they gotta look. But women in the middle of life—middle class, middling looks—

people barely ever sees them. It's like they're invisible. Gang o' kids, a loose boy or two, or a sharp-eyed bloke they don't know, and everyone's got their hand over their purse. But some plain-dressed, plain-lookin,' plain-spoken woman? Nobody pays a lick of attention, so they'll never be able to recognize her again. Made my fortune on it."

"Your fortune? Some fortune, if you lived in a tenement near Bull Wharf," he teased, but there was nothing casual about his avid curiosity about her life before he came to know her.

"Ain't in the Thames wharves now, am I?"

"*I'm not* in the Thames Street wharves," he corrected automatically.

"Oh, we're well educated today, are we?" She switched effortlessly to the better-spoken, well-modulated tones of the lesser gentry. "My fortune is not hidden in some rookery but is under the direction of a very reputable firm of brokers in the city, allocated equally between the safe and sound five percents and other, more productive investments."

Hugh wasn't sure which surprised him more, the easy accent or the mention of the reputable firm of brokers. "You've a broker in Cornhill Street?"

"Threadneedle. Standing appointment every other Friday." At his look, she put up her chin. "Not every thief is an idiot who trades his fence for blue ruin. I am very good at what I do, Captain, and I'm no fool. I thought that's why you collared me?"

"Yes." But he had never in a million years thought uneducated street thieves were salting it away in Threadneedle Street. But he should have. She'd had him send the money there. "Ah. Levy and Levy."

"Bright one, you are."

"And does Mr. Levy know your money comes from ill-gotten gains?"

"Matter of fact, he does. Asked me that very question once. And I told him."

"Not very scrupulous, your Mr. Levy."

She rounded on him, full of aggravated righteousness. "He's got every scruple he needs, and so do I. I can't change what I am, what I've become in my life. If I hadn't started thieving, I would have become a beggar on the streets. Or worse. How honest is that, just setting there, all pitiful, begging for a handout? At least I work for my money. I worked hard for Nan, I worked hard for Timmy and myself, and I'm damn sure working hard for you. And you needed my work and my skills, don't you forget, Mr. High and Mighty Captain, while you're polishing your scruples to a glossy shine."

That speech was both elegant and extremely heartfelt. "I stand corrected."

That set her resentment back down on her heels. "Well, all right, then. You ready to go?"

The private carriage was on loan from his mother, Viscountess Balfour, from her extensive stables behind Berkley Square. It wasn't often he asked for a favor, and his request of her had been answered by the arrival of her second best, and he noted with thanks, unmarked town coach. His leg was improving, but it was too stiff for a second cold wherry ride upriver.

He put Meggs inside, and Timmy was to play Tiger and sit up with the driver. Hugh planned to have the coach leave them at the Inn of the Crown and Scepter, halfway up St. James's Street, where they might pose as passengers in transit while they watched the clubs, White's and Brook's, on opposite sides of the street. Today, they were looking for Thomas Williams, an MP who usually came to his club in the late afternoon, on his way from Westminster to Mayfair, and left after a drink or two.

Meggs was smiling as the carriage edged down the congested street. "What is it?"

"Oh, I've worked this little stretch of the city a time or two. Took a couple of purses right over there, near Little Ryder Street, that first morning, before we saw you."

It seemed half a lifetime ago already.

They had pulled up in front of the Crown and Scepter, when he saw another of their suspects. "There's Lord Stoval, coming out of White's. I hadn't planned for you to follow him, but he's one of the Lords Commissioners as well. He lives over near Grosvenor Square."

"Forrest green coat there?" She blew out a huff of breath. "It's all over, Captain. There's your sharper. Got something down his tail pocket, he has. From the inside, looks like. That's hard to bung. We might get at it, if we do a bulk and file with the Tanner, but it's devilish tricky, and anyway, a man that jumpy'd be fly to us."

"For God's sake, Meggs, speak English."

"Bulk and file? The Tanner could jostle him while I do the business with his pockets, but your man there would be fly to us. He'd know—he's all but waiting for it. Look at him with his eyes about the place like a sharper. On the take, that one is, and edgy. Written all over him."

He could see some of what she meant as he watched Stoval stride through the archway. To his eyes, the man did appear tense, but no more than that. "Tell me why you think so."

"One side of his coattail is heavier than the other—falls lower and pulls the fit of the coat off. Look at his hands on his stick. Tight grip, tense. And it's too heavy for fashion, that stick. And he's no need for it—he's not a gimp, like you. Now, see that—he's touched his coattail twice now as he's walking to his carriage. Just the barest pat, but like he's checking his goods, see? And—I don't know—something about his eyes. Too sharp. No doubt, Captain, he's your man." She crossed her arms across her chest, completely satisfied with her almost instantaneous assessment.

"All that in fifteen seconds?"

She shot him an eyebrow and cocked her head to the side, a look of both superiority and pity. "Let me ask you something. How long does it take *you* to look up at the sails of your big ship, with all them masts and spars and ropes, and decide which one is set wrong?"

He couldn't help but smile. With one analogy she had convinced him.

"Seconds, am I right? That's because you're a professional navvy, all trained up for it. It's your job, innit? Well, this is my job, taking the lay of a man. Spent hours and hours, and days and days, I did, walking up and down streets with old Nan, her in her governess rig and me as her charge. Asking questions and questions. What did I see? Where was his hands? What hadn't I noticed? Teaching me to look harder, making me figure it all out, until I could tell who had meggs and who had pennies, just from the way their pockets creased. You take my word for it, Cap'n. He's your man. That's money in your bank."

"As much as I wish you may be right, we must still be thorough. And methodical. There are three other men left to investigate, and we can't discount a one of them until we know the contents of all their pockets."

"It's your money to waste as you see fit. Who's next?"

"Thomas Williams, Member of Parliament for Grampound. And there he is. Bath superfine, buff breeches, boots."

"You're getting better at this, Cap. Waistcoat carmel brocade, fine gold watch, good chain, jeweled pin in his cravat. Tempting that. Slight tremor in his left hand. That'll be his weak side. Right." She clambered out the carriage door and would have disappeared in the blink of an eye, but he let loose a volley of Anglo-Saxon oaths that effectively stopped her.

Even Timmy let out an appreciative whistle. "That's prime oath making, that is, Cap'n."

Meggs smiled at him from the curb, not daunted in the least. "Nice that. Not a single repeat."

No trepidation, nothing, from the pair of them. He must be losing his touch. "Oh, go on then, goddamn it. Go on after him."

Hugh climbed out more slowly, stiff from sitting, and almost lost track of them, so fast did they move. He followed Meggs's progress from the opposite sidewalk, and his palms all but itched with the desire to take action. He hated being so bloody useless to her and having to keep out of the way. And he felt strangely nervous for her, this first time watching her pick a pocket for him.

He recognized the barely noticeable tension in her face, the quiet flare of her nose before she began to work herself into character. She pulled a small piece of paper out of her pocket, like a note or a direction, and then glanced up at the buildings as if looking for a direction. Then she was behind Williams and stepping on his heel as she brushed past, between the shoulders of two men as they passed each other. Williams seemed to catch her, then back away, tipping his hat to her before he turned across the sidewalk traffic to the doorway of his club without ever pausing. And Meggs was still walking up the sidewalk, dithering with her message for another moment before she ducked into a shop.

Timmy appeared out of nowhere, passing her, and then reappeared on Hugh's side of the street. "Hold your horse, mister?"

"Did she get it? Do you—"

The lad gave him a stupefied look. "Of course. Passed me a dummee."

"What's that?"

"Pocketbook."

Hugh nodded in comprehension and glanced over his shoulder at the shop.

"She'll meet us back across the park," Timmy advised. "Best not to look back."

She was there already, sitting demurely on a park bench, the picture of respectable nothingness, by the time they arrived, made slower, no doubt, by his uneven gait over the even, browned grass.

She smiled as they approached, her face pinked and shining with pleased delight. He saw a gleam in her eye—a breathless exuberance and excitement. Was that professional pride? Was that what he himself looked like when they had cut out those boats at Toulon, or when *Dangerous* had cut the line at Aboukir Bay?

And something else. Ah. As she looked up at him, and smiled, and raised her brows, he realized it was expectation. No matter she knew she had done well, she was waiting for him to tell her so. Waiting for his approval. The heat in his gut he had endeavored to keep on a slow match burst into flame. God's balls but she was going to kill him, making him wait. Making her decide to want him.

"Well done, all. Very well done. Now let's get back to Chelsea before the light's gone." Even he could hear the grimness in his voice.

They examined Mr. Williams's personal chattals, as Meggs was fond of calling them, in great detail. Along with the pocketbook was Williams's purse, his watch, the stickpin from his cravat, and a small tin of snuff. Meggs was nothing if not thorough.

The pocketbook was a revelation of orderly and exemplary note keeping. It held a detailed list of each and every appointment for the day, day after day. Committees, votes, and positions on various bills were given the same amount of space and attention as social engagements. Beside each appointment entry was a column, listing each and every expenditure paid out, from Hackney carriages to his tailor. From its pages they could recreate Williams's exact day, each and every day.

"He'll be a breeze to finish investigating with all the names—his bankers and other appointments in the city. I don't see any names here that give me pause."

Meggs looked over his shoulder. "We should ask Mr. Levy. Save you time. He knows everyone there is to know in the city. You should ask him about all your list of toffs. Or I could ask him for you, seeing as you don't know him. Likes me, he does. Says I'm enterprising."

There it was again, that angry pang at the thought that other men might admire Meggs—for any reason. Why should Mr. Levy not admire her? She brought him business and she was very clearly enterprising. It was an admirable trait by any standards other than that of aristocratic society. He pushed the ridiculous pang of jealousy aside.

"Thank you, but I already have my own firm of brokers and men of business who have already conducted such inquiries on my behalf." But conscious of her need for praise, he added, "But I thank you. It was a very good suggestion."

Meggs nodded, but she still looked unhappy, frowning at the pocketbook.

"Meggs? Did you have another suggestion?"

"No. Not really. Poor man. All neat and tidy. Won't be able to function without his little book, I shouldn't wonder. Makes me feel bad for taking it."

"Morality from a thief?" He was only teasing, but his words set her off like a spark put to priming powder.

"Don't you condescend to me. Yes, I'm a thief, because I'd neither face nor fortune, and I needed—we needed—to live," she said with cutting precision. "And being a thief is a damn sight harder than just lying on your back and spreading your legs like a whore, so don't you think if I *could* have, I'd have done that sooner rather than waste years learning how to steal proper and fast? I've got all the morals I need. And I know once you copy all those names down, you can take that book back down to White's Club, so he can have it back and get on with his life. It's only right."

He'd not thought of it at all. For all his jealousy about her past, he'd never thought about what might have brought her to thievery at all. That to become a thief had been a difficult choice. He had supposed, now that it was put in front of him so baldly, that she had been raised to it from infancy, as were all of London's thriving pickpockets, with no thought as to other or less criminal careers. But it did take skill and a nimbleness that took years of training.

She was different from all the rest, however. Hugh had a hard time believing all of London's pickpockets could be as accomplished as she. She could be almost anything she chose. Certainly, when she was working, she *was* any number of characters, hardworking and honest. He couldn't forget how she had almost made him believe she *was* a seamstress. He was counting on the idea that she could *be* a housemaid.

So why did he get the feeling she *chose* to play Meggs the thief, just like she chose her other roles? Why did she choose to remain a vile-mouthed, hard-talking guttersnipe, when she didn't have to? "Let's talk about your accent."

There was that stillness, that pause, that told him she'd gone instantly wary. "Why?"

"Because you dropped it this afternoon."

"Captain. I'm a prime filching mort. I never drop nothing."

Exactly, he wanted to shout. There it was—she rolled out "Meggs" the way he would cast loose the guns to keep his enemies at bay. "You put on a respectable accent as easily as you put on your respectable clothes today. Can you do it all the time?"

"Different accents?"

"Yes."

"That is easily enough accomplished." The well-modulated tones rolled off her tongue as if she were a Mayfair governess giving a lesson in elocution. "Will that be all, Captain McAlden?"

"Can you do others?"

Oh, God. There was that smile, pert and saucy and delicious.

"Perha'ps yew'd prefer a bit of a burr, or then again"—she switching to an Irish lilt—"something with a bit of a brougue? I used to be able to do a bit of a Frenchwoman, but that was Nan's specialty—the émigrée she used to call it. I'd have to practice for that."

"Your Nan taught you all that?"

"Some. Got a ear for it." There was the shrug. "It's fun."

"So why do you still talk like you're from St. Giles when you don't have to?"

"Dunno," she lied. "Wouldn't get no respect on the streets talking like a nob."

"But you're not on the streets now, are you?"

"Perhaps. But I will be again, won't I—when we've served our purpose here and you're done with us. Isn't that so, Captain?" She waited a long, long moment, waiting for his confirmation, daring him to lie to her face.

When he didn't do it, she simply nodded and rose. "Good night, Captain."

"Good night, Meggs."

But he still didn't know the answer to her question.

CHAPTER 14

The first week of Advent brought not comfort and joy, but a cold, raw wind, ripping sideways through clothing. Meggs hugged her hands round her middle and thanked God the captain wasn't a stingy man with his lour. The new cloak was warm as toast. With her shawls wrapped round her tight, she could keep out the worst of the biting cold.

The captain wasn't happy to be sniffing after this toff today. It went against his grain to suspect a navy man.

"Nathaniel Phillips is a political appointee to the Admiralty Board, but he's a naval man through and through. Started as a clerk in the Victualling Office before he moved to the Admiralty as assistant secretary to the First Lord. He's lost a brother and two nephews, killed at sea in this war. He's been with the Admiralty upwards of thirty years, though he sat for Parliament as well. Doesn't stand to reason he'd sell the Admiralty's secrets," he'd groused.

She didn't have the heart to tell him a man, or a woman or child for that matter, would sell just about anything if they felt they had to. And only a friend would know enough to betray a body. The captain already knew all that well enough. And he was a thorough, fair man. If he had to investigate a man he considered a friend, then so be it. He was going to do whatever the job took, no matter if it was personally distasteful to him.

Had to admire a man like that, a man with principles.

So when the older gentleman in question made his unhurried way out of the Admiralty onto Whitehall, they fell in behind with nary a wrinkle. She sidled herself closer to the sheltering bulk of the captain, delighting that for the first time she was not ashamed of the way she looked next to him. Today the captain was wearing what he called his "undergardener's rig." He was dressed in old nankeen breeches and a leather journeyman's jerkin, covered by a long, disreputable coat and topped by a wide-brimmed, dark felt hat.

At first glance, he looked like the kind of man a prudent person would leave alone, but to her, he looked most like his real self. A natural leader among men. Capable and commanding, without the need for any sort of rank. All the layers of civilization peeled back, leaving nothing but the man himself.

But she couldn't moon about thinking how fine the captain looked, she needed to keep her peepers open and fixed on their toff. She had reckoned he'd be making for his town house in Mayfair. Perhaps she'd do a bit of pocket work as they made their way among the travelers from the inns along Haymarket, just to shock and amuse the captain when she passed him a thimble or two. But the old nob stymied her by heading in a different direction, up Whitcomb Street.

She glanced at the captain to see what he made of that, but he just soldiered on, marching with his stiff gait and keeping his hat low and his eyes on the geezer. They worked their steady way from Whitcomb across the warren of small, angular blocks to Leicester Square, where the toff nipped into a florist shop. In order to watch him through the windows from a safe distance, Meggs found a quiet passageway between two buildings across the square and pulled the captain into it, so he might lean against the wall and rest his leg. Must be a pow-

erful hurt to make a man that big and that strong take to limping.

But the passageway was narrow and they had to squeeze up
together a fair bit to stay out of sight. The captain leaned one
shoulder into the wall and turned his back a bit to the street,
to block the worst of the wind. His body made a momentary
cove of warmth and calm around her, a respite from the hurly-
burly of the sidewalks.

He was so near, so big and masculine. She swallowed her
jim-jams. "I suppose we ought to make it look like you're
chatting me up. Like we had private things to say to one another."

"Oh, aye, that should work." He smiled down briefly. "It
would be the most expected thing in the world, to see a man
and his lass looking for a quiet corner."

His lass. Along with the rough clothing, he let the rough
Scots burr come out in his voice. Oh, Lord, the way he said it
made her wish with all her heart she could be that lass. When
he was so himself like this, it made her want *not* to be herself,
not to be Meggs the prime filching mort. It made her want
something else, something clean and free from all the burdens
of the past. It made her want to be better.

It made her want to do *something*. "Yes, well, but you can't
keep track of your toff, turned as you are, and I can't see over
you, so it might be best if I stand in front of you like so." She
eased herself around the front of his chest, so her back was to
the street. "So's people think you're looking at me, instead of
eyeing his Lordship, there."

Oh, that was harder still. Her eyes were level with his chest,
and as he shifted to stand straight, so she could move by, his
chest seemed to expand and radiate heat like a warm stove.
How nice would it be to lay her head there? How sweet would
it be to be the lass who got to do that? She edged closer as if
she were in his embrace, and his hands did come up to her

arms. He rubbed absently along her upper arms, as natural as could be, chafing his hands along the wool, against the cold.

"You shouldn't be looking at me, of course. You should keep your eyes on the shopfront. This is just a cover."

"Just a cover," he repeated, but his eyes flicked down to hers, icy hot and penetrating. And there went her insides, all to quivering like a Christmas pudding. When he looked down at her, his mouth and his lips were just there, right there, in front of her, so that all she had to do, all she needed to do, was rise up on her tiptoes and she would meet his mouth, and solve this strange dilemma that had brewed inside her.

"He's bought a posy. And he's moving again. Come on." He turned her by the shoulders and they were off, across the square and headed north again through oddly angled streets, dog-legging it around to Hays Court and cutting through the mean little wedges of pavement over to Crown Street.

Here on the edges of St. Giles, the neighborhood deterio-rated into dingy tenements, and as the streets became meaner, she felt herself become so, too. Here, in such a place, she didn't bother to hide the quickness of her eyes or temper her walk to portray a timid housemaid. Timidity and temper-ance had no place in St. Giles. Here, she put up her chin and dared people to look her in the eye.

The captain felt it, too, the difference. He kept pace with her, even with the limp, although he couldn't mask it com-pletely; it seemed to her his stride took on a rangy, hungry quality that earned them some extra walking room on the pavement. Most people saw a cove like him bearing down on them and just faded out of the way. Even the drunks had the little sense God could still give them to keep well clear. Ex-cept of course the ones who were too far gone to notice where they were.

They passed one such place, where a gin shop's patrons had spilled out from under a meagre awning, into the street. Some patrons were so drunk, they sat out on the curbing heedless of the cold ground, stupefied against the raw weather from the blue ruin.

He caught her arm to pull her out of the way of one man who reeked of vomit and gin. She could see disgust, the abhorrence of this class of people, in the lines etched around the captain's mouth.

"They'll kill themselves, drinking that." Hugh hated to think that could have been her. If she'd lost the use of her hand and couldn't steal, if she hadn't possessed the force of character to keep herself away from blue ruin, or any other kind of deadly spirits. If life had dealt her just one more misfortunate twist, she might be the one strung out and insensate in the doorway. "They're nearly dead from it."

"Well that's the point, innit?" She was impervious to his pity, wearing her armor of cheek and guile. "And who can blame 'em? A day out in this misery makes them want to die, so they can go straight to hell and finally get warm." She was grinning up at him to show that was her idea of a joke. Gallows humor. *"Both the innocent and the wicked he destroys.* Might as well get what you want, if that's to be the way of it."

"Isn't that from the Bible? Did you ever drink at a place like this?"

"Not my style. A lot of kidmen do give their kiddies beer or gin of an evening to keep them quiet, but Nan didn't stand for that sort of thing. Dulls the senses. You have to be sharp to stay alive as a pick or a Kate. Just like this rig."

She was smiling at him in a way that felt very much like camaraderie, something he had only ever felt with his brother officers. But she was no brother. He could never forget she was a woman. Every part of her, each and every part that made up her whole, called out to him. The urge to touch her was so strong it lodged firmly in his chest, heated and burning away at his breath, until he had to shove his hands deep into his pocket to stifle it sufficiently.

But she didn't notice. Just forged on, keeping Phillips well within her sight, staying professional. "Real question is," she mused, "what's a toff like him doing in this part of town? And walking? This far? Nob geezer like him takes his carriage—unless he's doing something or going somewhere he don't want anybody to see. Maybe he's got nasty habits?"

The area held an opium den or two, and there were brothels and prostitutes littering the byway. Even a man like Phillips might be tempted. "Perhaps."

Ahead, Phillips came to the crossing at Greek Street and paused. Meggs took the opportunity to slip a shawl out from under the cloak and lay it over her shoulders, on top. She answered his unspoken question with one of her shrugs. "Any bit of a disguise helps. Just a bit of something different. Makes it hard to keep trace."

He took her advice and pulled his hat off and stowed it in his pocket. "Different it is." And he saw to his chagrin his hand had thoughts of its own, had reached out to pull off the mob cap she was wearing and touch the pretty, dark brown silk of her hair. He curbed the impulse ruthlessly, lest she react badly and violently to his touch, and it came off as a light, friendly cuff across the head. And that way he did get to touch her hair, after all. Soft and smooth as running water.

He turned away and ran his hand carelessly over his own head, just to feel the contrast. Just to exhaust the impulse to touch her and peel away the layers of hardened street to find the girl beneath.

She didn't shy away. She was nodding. "Suppose we might could try and look like . . . well, sorta like sweethearts. You know—people who look like they only got eyes for each other, don't make nobody suspicious. And a person could still see a lot with someone's arm around their neck, looking all innocent."

"*Anybody* suspicious," he corrected automatically. But his mind was sailing ahead, unresponsive to his helm. She was giving him the perfect excuse to touch her. His body immediately heated a degree or two hotter. He was both thrilled and then jealous—with whom had she run this rig, as she called it, before? In how many of these doorways had she been kissed? "And you never looked innocent a day in your life."

"Ha. Try me."

Oh, he wanted to do more than try. "All right." He slung his arm casually around her shoulder and felt her shiver beneath him, as if she were uncomfortable at his touch, despite her bravado in suggesting it. No. That wasn't it, for she had reached up with a cold hand to hang on to his wrist where it fell across her shoulder, the very image of a pleased sweetheart. The shivering was because she was cold, even with the new cloak. She still didn't have enough meat on her bones. "God's balls. Here."

He swung his rough, old sea coat off his shoulders and around hers, completely enveloping her. He put his arm back around her shoulders and moored her up tight alongside. "A fellow out with his lass would keep her close then, would he?"

"Aye, I suppose." There wasn't a lot of encouragement in her voice, but neither was it discouraging.

"And touch her a little?" He casually smoothed the loose hair away from from her face. "As if he'd earned the right to?"

"Oh. Aye, I suppose that, too."

"And he'd probably smile at her, too, now and again."

"He might," she agreed quietly, ducking her head down to hide a small smile.

When she didn't object, he became emboldened with his success. "Might he also want to take her hand in his?" He did so, catching her hand up and towing her across Oxford Street at an ungainly run, heading for where he'd let Phillips disappear up Rathbone Place.

She was laughing and breathless, but she shook her head in disagreement. "Not a man looks like you. Holding hands is for kiddies. Man like you'd never."

But, he was pleased to notice, her fingers remained interlaced with his. "A man like me?"

"Too sharp by half for that kind of love play. Look like you know your business, you do."

God help him. Her frankly assessing look had him instantly as hard as a loaded cannonade. "But if you were my lass, it would be my business to keep you happy."

She laughed outright. God help him, the sound of her unbridled delight hit him like a broadside. He tensed his gut to withstand the blow her simple happiness inflicted upon him.

She let go of his hand, though he tried not to let her. "We're in St. Pancreas—that's three parishes he's crossed now." She hitched the lapels of his coat closer.

"You warm enough?"

She nodded. "You?" Her eyes shifted to his leg, where his limp was growing more pronounced. "Why don't we bung him now and have done? Save ourselves the trouble of this parade."

He didn't want her to think he was weak. "I want to find out where he's going first. He may stop if we dip him now."

Her smile widened. "Starting to think like me now, you are."

He felt like kissing her. Right there on that cheeky, plush mouth. "Don't worry—he won't walk all the way to Hampstead." And indeed, Phillips turned off at Percy Street to clew up at a neat little doorway of Number Four Little Charlotte Street, where he was greeted at the door with an enthusiastic kiss from a woman half his age. Hugh slouched into the side of the building on the corner and pulled Meggs up next to him.

"Well." She cast her gaze at the surrounding neighborhood. "Didn't think a toff like him would live here."

Could she really be that naive? Her? "He doesn't live here.

Not for long anyway. That is undoubtedly the home of his mistress."

"His mistress? Geezer like him? Right out in the open in the doorway like that? In the middle of the day?" Her face had gone three colors of red. "And him walking here like he was all proper and buying a posy and holding his head up, easy as you please."

He was surprised to find her so judgmental. "If it makes you feel better, his wife has been dead for years. It's rather an accepted thing for a man in his position to keep a mistress."

"Maybe toffs and aristos," she conjectured. "But if Mr. Tupper ever tried to do a thing like that"—she pointed at the doorway—"I think Mrs. Tupper would put him to bed with a fry pan."

It was such a vivid image, he laughed and caught her back against his chest. "That she would, but I can assure you Mr. Tupper would never do such a thing."

She tensed against him, but when he made no other move, she slowly accepted the casual intimacy. "Well, I suppose it's not so bad if his wife's dead. But I don't see why a toff would want to have a mistress when they could have a beautiful wife, all clean, and pretty and lovely. With beautiful, clean clothes."

He could hear the wistfulness in her voice. Somewhere under all that brass and cheek, and larceny, was a girl who wanted to believe in fairy tales, and happily ever after, even if she knew better. "Men want different things from a mistress than they could ask of a wife."

"Like what?"

God's balls. The possibilities boggled his mind. But how could they be having this conversation? Was this some sort of ham-fisted attempt at flirting? If so, she was even worse at it than he was. "Wives are ladies."

"So?"

"Ladies don't do . . . certain things."

"Oh." She stewed that around in the pot that was her brain.

"Oh. Gotcha. That the way it's gonna be for you then, when you get a wife?"

This was an easy answer. "I'm not going to get a wife—naval men shouldn't have wives. It would condemn her to a life of either hardship or loneliness."

"Oh. Then you'll get a mistress? You got one now?"

Hugh wasn't sure what he heard in her voice. "Why do you want to know?"

"Dunno. Just asking. None of my business, I suppose." She looked away at the house and didn't ask again.

He leaned down close and tightened his arms around her ever so slightly. "Meggs," he said, just so she knew he was talking to *her* and not playing pretend. Not simply flirting. "I don't have a mistress. And you should know, it's not all force and coercion. It can be very nice. It's *supposed* to be very nice."

She went instantly still, in that aware, wary way of hers. "Is it?"

"Yes. It's a lot like this, being up close with no bad feelings, no one doing anything the other doesn't like. Do you like it with my arms around you, like this? Do you like it when I touch you like that?" He gently brushed that wayward skein of hair away from her nape.

She nodded infinitesimally.

"Remember that, Meggs. And know, if you want it to happen, when it happens, between us, it will be very, very nice."

She must not have believed him. After his comment, she kept unnaturally quiet for the remainder of the afternoon as they followed their quarry back south toward the park, silently emptying both Phillips's pockets and his mistress's reticule with ruthless efficiency and a noticeable lack of cheek.

Once home in Chelsea and ensconced in his study, his examination of the evidence turned up nothing of interest. Hugh was glad. It had gone sorely against his grain to have to suspect Phillips. But now that left only two men, Lord Stoval and the Earl Spencer himself. Neither prospect pleased him very much, but with Admiral Middleton's clock ticking away the days, while the Admiralty leaked secrets like a rotten bilge, he was going to have to choose. The best he could do was trust Spencer couldn't have ordered an investigation into himself and concentrate on Stoval in the hopes Meggs was right and he was the traitor.

And preliminary reports from his various contacts were not in Stoval's favor. Despite a sterling reputation within the *ton*, whispers from the City and among the men on Change was that Stoval's pockets were to let. He had dealings with a surprising high number of different banks and at least one disreputable moneylender. There was the large house in Mayfair, at the corner of Grosvenor and Park Lane, and a wife who entertained lavishly.

And Hugh had to send Meggs there. The prospect gave him no ease. Neither did his leg, stiff and aching from the long walk. He reached out and absently massaged his thigh muscle, pressing out the knots of pain.

"Does it hurt often?"

Hugh looked up to find Meggs studying him, instead of her codes. Not surprising, because she almost always solved the exercises quickly. She had a knack for patterns and picked them out easily enough. When he didn't answer her, she abandoned the desk and came around behind his chair, slowly, tentatively, as if for once she wasn't sure of what she was doing.

"If you like . . ." she began, "I can rub some of the stiffness out." She set her hands to his shoulders and began to massage the tense muscles in his neck. "Used to do this for Nan all the time. And her hands, when she got the rheumatism in her finger joints."

Her agile fingers were digging deep, searching out the tension along his shoulders. Hugh searched for something normal, something innocuous to say to cover the astonishing sensation of her hands on his body. "Your hands are strong."

"Have to be, don't they? Old Nan used to insist I give her shoulders a rub every night so my hands would get stronger."

He could hear the smile in her voice and thought he could see it in the reflection of the dark window. "How old were you when you first began to steal?"

Her hands stilled for a moment. "Twelve. Nearly thirteen."

"As old as that?" "Prime filching morts" of her caliber were usually trained to their art from the cradle.

She gave no reply, only kept up the steady, rhythmic massage. God help him, it felt beyond good. "And your Nan taught you? Why did she wait so long?"

"Only met her after I'd already begun."

"What do you mean? Did you work for a different kidman?" He didn't like this jealous hunger he had for information about her past, and the people who had influenced her, but he couldn't seem to stop it.

"Nope. Only ever had Nan. Began on my own, I did."

"How?"

A long silence was interrupted only by the popping and hissing of the fire while she decided what she wanted to tell him. And then she let out a sigh. "I didn't mean to be a thief, actually, but we were hungry and cold, and we were nearly out of money."

She must have had parents. And yet they were curiously absent from her tales. "Your parents?"

"Dead."

Of course. What else made a child of the streets? "So you just started stealing?"

"No, I started whoring."

It was if she had kicked him in the jaw. Again. Every time he thought he knew or understood her, she overthrew all his ideas. It was such a complete reversal of everything she had said, he didn't know what to believe. He felt the faint stirring of anger in his gut, but whether it was aimed at her or at whomever had turned her to prostitution, he couldn't tell. He turned and tried to focus on her reflection in the window. She stood behind him, partially obscured by the back of the chair.

"But I never could. I was twelve. Couldn't attract anyone. Not even in Covent Garden." She gave a little self-deprecating laugh. "And Annie—she was a blowen used to work the Garden—felt sorry for me, so she gave me a particularly nice flat of hers. Young. And clean. He was roaring drunk, but obviously wealthy. So I went with him, but he was just so drunk, he couldn't even manage his clothes. His purse fell right out of his pocket and he didn't even notice. So I took the purse and left him propped in the doorway." She pushed up her shoulder and shrugged, the way she did when she was trying to prove it didn't matter. But it did.

A doorway. She hadn't even had enough money for a room, a bed to . . . God's balls. At twelve years old. Hardly old enough to be left on her own, let alone left to whore for food. The tight feeling deep in his gut was anger. Black anger, eating away at him. Because he'd seen a hundred such girls before and walked past, dismissing them from his mind as soon as he was across the street, or in his house, or back on board his ship. He had done so that very morning.

Her hands kept up their steady, relentless assault and she spoke matter of factly, with her head tilted to the side, as if she hadn't thought of it in a long time.

"It was a really fat purse, enough to keep Timmy and me for a fortnight, but it made me bold. So I went begging. Actually, I was only pretending to be begging. I was looking for more drunk young peers. I went down to St. James's, where we were just yesterday, and watched them slip and slide out of their clubs late at night, and I just followed one or two, and gave them a bit of a bump in the dark and said, "Sorry gov-'ner," and made off with their purses. And that's how it started. I only did drunks for about a year, until I got more proficient. And then Nan found me. But I still like drunks best."

Hugh visualized it all in his mind, easily seeing the desperation that would have driven her. He had to admire her spirit, her adaptability. Some people, the people in what passed for "Society," would have starved. Any of the young women his mother pushed his way would have simply withered away before they took any real steps to provide for themselves. It had taken courage, nerve, and backbone. Yes, he did admire her. She rather reminded him of himself.

But twelve. It nagged at his mind. What had gone on before that?

"And you, Captain?" She cut into his thoughts. "How did you come to take in "bantling thieves" for the benefit of His Majesty's government?"

"You shouldn't listen at doors."

"There's a lot of things I shouldn't." Her thumbs found a tense spot. "Mrs. Tupper says you were Post Captain and a hero at Aboukir Bay, and that was where you were injured."

"No. It was afterwards. At Acre. A different battle, on land. I was—as one might say—out of my element."

She was quiet for a long moment, her hands slowing. "How did it happen, then, your leg?"

"Simply blown to pieces. Our own damned artillery piece, brought up from one of our ships, exploded. I was hit." He could hear the bitterness in his voice and taste the sour tang in his mouth. He wasn't normally given to such obvious self-pity. Self-loathing, perhaps. It must be the brandy. It could have nothing to do with the way her hands felt upon his shoulders, how he could smell the slight fragrance of rose soap on her hands. The soap he had spent nearly an hour purchasing for her. "God, that feels good." He closed his eyes for a moment only, determined to right himself, to still her hands and stop the deep feelings springing from the surprising intimate moment.

Hugh opened his eyes and saw her reflection bending down toward him for a moment before she raised her head back up. She had been about to kiss him. He was sure of it.

But she had already started to pull away. "Your fire needs to be built up."

Hugh clasped his hand over hers on his shoulder. "Thank you. For your kindness," he said quietly. "That felt very nice."

She was pulling away. And he didn't know how to stop her.

"Don't worry about the fire. Take yourself off to bed. Tell Mrs. Tupper the same. Good night."

"Good night, Captain."

The ache in his leg was gone, but it had been replaced by one in his heart. He really was going to have to cultivate a taste for something stronger than brandy.

CHAPTER 15

"Come along sifting that flour! Dinner's serving in two minutes. No, keep sifting. Else we'll have lumps in the gravy. Or worse." Mrs. Tupper sniffed suspiciously at the flour sack.

"Awful lot of bother for nothing," Meggs opined. "Don't know why you want to sift out the bugs. Might as well eat them. They'll give you more nourishment."

Mrs. Tupper's mouth gaped open like a hooked mackerel. She put one hand on her hip and pointed emphatically toward the kitchen stair. "That's enough of that. Go on with you. And take that roast up with you. No sense in going empty-handed."

They were to eat in the dining room, proper, all of them. Meggs was seated, awaiting the rest of the household, when she heard the captain come up behind her, his gait making the floorboards creak unevenly. He came and put his hands over her shoulders and rubbed them a little, just like she'd done last night, thumbing into the tight, tense muscles along her spine. Giving her a bit of the jim-jams. But in a nice way. He seemed to do that every chance he got today—give her a touch, quick and sure. But nice. As if he liked making sure she was near. Or as if he wanted her to know he was near and she could rely upon him. Either way, her insides were fluttering like a jar full of fireflies.

He leaned down to speak quietly into her ear, and she felt the stir of his breath along her skin. "I would appreciate it if you would keep all species of insects out of my food, no matter their dubious nutritional value. I've had more than enough of that in the navy, and I don't wish to experience it again in my own home."

"Sorry. I didn't realize. I was just giving Mrs. Tupper a bit of—"

"Cheek. Yes. And she's proper flustered."

The captain backed away as Timmy came in, but when he went to his own seat, she could see he was smiling—the chewed-up smile where he was trying not to, but had to anyway. She smiled back.

Near the end of the meal, the captain held up his glass of claret and said, "Well, Meggs, it's time to send you off. Tomorrow's the day."

The flutter of nervousness turned into pinwheels. But she was looking forward to it, in a way, to prove herself to the captain. Perhaps even impress him. "Who's it to be?"

"Lord Peter Stoval. The house is Number Twenty-Four Upper Grosvenor Street, corner of Park Lane. So we'll be able to keep a watch on you, or at least the house, from the park."

"How am I to get in?"

"We have reason to believe the household will shortly be in need of a maid, and you will present yourself at the kitchen stairs, bright and early tomorrow morning, excellent references in hand and hopeful smile on your face. And you will either be hired or you will make a reconnaissance of the premises and find a way of reentering the house."

"And how do you know they're wanting a maid?"

The captain chewed on another piece of his smile. "They've lost a girl from their kitchen just this morning. Seems she decided to take an impromptu visit to her sister in

Yorkshire, and while she is there, she will surely decide to take a wonderful position as housekeeper to a lovely old gentleman who lives a simple retired life in the same village as her sister."

"Jesus God. You're gonna nab 'er, ain't you?"

"*Aren't* you?" he corrected. "No, we're not *gonna*"—he took another sip of wine—"we already have. And before you get your petticoats in a twist, the girl has not been harmed in the least and will even see just the improvement in her situation I have described."

"You mean, you already got her that position all lined up? Before you sent her off to her sister in Yorkshire?"

"Yes."

She let out an appreciative whistle. "How'd you manage that?"

"I have friends."

"I could use some better friends, it seems. Then I could see an improvement in *my* situation. But seems I'm to remain a mop squeezer. Right then, how 'igh and mighty does a maid at Number Twenty-Four Upper Grosvenor Street need to be?" She made her accent all toff-like.

"Not at all high or mighty. Scullery maid's the job. Very pleasing and quiet, but they seem to like handsome girls in his house, so I've no doubt you'll be chosen."

"Handsome. Does that mean you think I'm handsome?"

"You'll do."

"Handsome. Even in the scullery." She looked down at her hand. "Have to have these stitches out."

"Hmm. Yes." He reached out his hand, flat on the table, as if he meant for her to place her own hand in it. And she would have, except Mrs. Tupper interjected.

"Right," the housekeeper said. "You just bring these down to the kitchen, and I'll have those stitches out in a jiffy." She stood up and started clearing away the plates.

Meggs could only follow. Coffee and stitches. Not exactly what the captain had in mind, judging from the disapproving looks he was giving from under his brows. He was all battened-down sternness with this hands folded across his chest and tucked under his arms, like he had to hold them there to keep from taking the scissors out of Mrs. Tupper's hands.

The mental image of the captain's hands trying to hold those tiny, bird-shaped embroidery scissors was beyond ridiculous. His big fingers couldn't even fit through the loops.

"What's so funny?" He smiled and frowned all at the same time. It made him look silly and young. And made her insides melt into a puddle.

"You. She's not hurting me."

"Then stop biting your lip."

"I'm not biting— Oww!"

"There, there," Mrs. Tupper cooed. "Just a bit sticky. Almost done. There, that's the last of them."

And then the captain had swooped in and was pressing a hot, moist towel to her paw, sopping up the last little bits of pus and blood from the threads, then holding her hand pressed between his. "How's it feel?"

He was talking about her hand, but she couldn't even feel it, the way he was standing so near, all warm and solid. Her stomach was trying to make those funny little flips again. "Umm. Good." She flexed her fingers a little, feeling the tug of the scar. "I'm that glad to have 'em out. They were getting itchy. Itchy palm means you're coming into money, old Nan used to say. Let's hope she was right."

"Yes, let's. Come upstairs to the study so we can go over the last of your instructions, as well."

He went ahead, and she followed after helping Mrs. Tupper and Timmy tidy up, so that he had already poured himself a drink from his liquor tray by the time she came through the door. "Care for a drink?"

"No." She threw herself into one of the chairs in front of the fire and contemplated the scar. It didn't look half bad. And more important, her hand worked just as well as ever.

"How about a sherry?" he asked over his shoulder.

"Don't really think I'm ladylike enough for sherry."

He chewed his smile into submission and got right back to the business of frowning. "You'll do." He walked over to his desk and tossed her a small bundle he pulled out of the top drawer.

She caught it reflexively and weighed it out with her hands for a moment. "What's this then?"

He merely nodded at the sailcloth-wrapped package in her hand, so she carefully untied the string and unwrapped a heavy roll of flannel. "Set of picklocks? You never!"

They were beautiful—finely made and well balanced. Steel and brass. Very fine. And a gift. From him. "What'd these set you back?"

He waved aside all questions of cost. "I want you to have them in case you need them at Stoval's."

"A set like this will have me finding excuses to use them. It was right kind of you."

"Kindness had nothing to do with it." His voice grew rusty and gruff. "You need the right tools to do this job. You can't expect Lord Stoval to leave miscellaneous, secret communications from the Admiralty lying out on his breakfast table for you to find."

He was trying to put her on her guard. As if she hadn't practically been born on her guard. Still, she wasn't about to argue with him. He had given her another gift. "Oh, no, right you are, not him. Sneaky, chary bastard, he is."

"Agreed, so I want you to be careful."

Was that real concern in his voice? She tried hard to ignore the feeling of happiness brewing inside her like hot tea. No. He was only being professional, that was all. But still, it was a gift. Just like the soap. Finer than was called for, if they were being strictly professional about it. "Right you are."

And he was being very professional, staying all the way across the room and looking all stern and captainlike. "If you need anything, you've only to send word."

She made her voice cheerful and professional, as if she wasn't all over jim-jams at the thought of leaving his house. "Let's hope I can make friends with the bootboy. Oh, do you think Mrs. Tupper might give me a jar of those toffee sweets of hers? That'd go miles for bribery and favors."

"I'll have her do that." He came close enough to hand her a small glass of sherry before he retreated behind his desk, still frowning as if he were displeased and looking all gruff ship's captain.

And so she babbled on to cover the uncomfortable silence. "Funny, how I like this, the sherry. All smooth and rich, like a grand lady."

"So if you need help, you'll send word?"

"Can't think that I'd need any helping."

He made a rude sound of disagreement. "I'll look for you on market days. Stoval's household often sends one of the scullery maids out with the kitchen maids and the cook when they go to market. The footmen are too grand to carry market baskets."

"Which market?"

"Shepherd's, south down Park Lane, is their usual, but I'll look for you at Covent Garden and Hungerford Market if you don't appear at Shepherd's."

"Right you are." It was nice, knowing she could count on him. It made her feel sure, solid, and safe inside. Knowing he would be looking out for her. Made her feel . . . not important, but well, necessary. As if she were, perhaps, as necessary to him as he was to her.

But he didn't say anything like that. He only said, "Take care of yourself, Meggs," in a voice gruff with command.

"Don't you worry, Cap'n. I can take care of myself." She would make him proud. She would make him glad he had taken all the trouble with her hand.

"I don't doubt that, Meggs."

"Thank you." But if he had that much confidence in her, why wasn't he smiling? Why was he as stern and grave as if she were going off to war? "I'll bung the case and be back before you know it, but you'll be careful with the Tanner while I'm gone, won't you?"

"I will." He turned his face away to look into the fire. "Now off to bed. I'll see you in the morning."

When he checked on her that night, making his silent way up to the attics as he had done almost every night in the quiet wee hours of the morning, she stirred. For the first time, she woke while he stood there, shielding the candle with his hand to mute the light, braced for her reaction.

Which was nothing but a small, almost imperceptible movement of her head before she asked, "Is it time, then?" in a voice cottony with sleep.

"No," he assured her. "Go back to sleep."

She half rolled to peer at him. "What's wrong?"

"Nothing. Just checking on you."

"Oh." She blinked her dark, shining eyes at him slowly, sleepily. Beautifully. "Are you worried? That I'll get it wrong, or bolt on you?"

"No," he lied. He was worried. But not that she'd bungle the job. She was too professional for that. "Go back to sleep."

She turned over with the slightest flounce and settled herself back into the mattress. Like a long, lithe cat, though there was nothing kittenish about her. Meggs seemed to take up the whole mattress. One arm was thrown over her head and the other fisted up a hank of the coverlet. Her legs were splayed out in opposite directions. Even as he watched, she kicked a foot out from under the sheets, disrupting the bedclothes, as she twisted her bare foot around to rest uncovered atop the coverlet.

It was just a foot. Just a combination of flesh and bone to be walked upon and to propel her across floors, through doors, and down alleys, but it was small and strong and arched just so, and it was hers.

My God, he wanted her. He wanted nothing more than the mindless oblivion that would finally come when he could look at her with nothing, no jobs, no distractions, no worries, between them. When he could sink himself into her narrow warmth and release himself into her.

But it was late, and she was asleep, and she was his charge. She had a long, important job ahead of her on the morrow. And she hadn't asked him yet.

Still, he couldn't bring himself to leave.

She sighed and rolled over, and in the warm, mellow spill of light from the candle, the gaping neckline of her night rail revealed one perfectly round, small breast, with a nipple the soft pink color of the inside of a seashell.

His mouth was suddenly very, very dry. He stared, finding the peak of her other breast through the sheer, batiste fabric of her nightdress and back to her bared flesh. Round as the palm of his hand. So pink. So improbably, incongruously soft. The air in the tiny room felt so hot it was a wonder he didn't burst into flame.

But he did not move. He was calm. He was not going out of his mind with undisciplined need.

How in the hell had this waif gotten under his very skin, into every fiber of his being? How in the hell was he to keep his hands off her?

By being a professional. By remembering his duty and what he owed to his country and Admiral Middleton. By remembering Major Rawsthorne would be happy to see him strung up by his testicles if he failed. He had a job to do. And to do it, he needed to send her into danger. He needed to let her go.

But there was something about the cadence of her breathing.

"Meggs?" he asked quietly. "Are you awake?"

"Mmm."

"Meggs, are you *letting* me look at you?"

She took two more deep breaths. "Are you looking?"

"Yes. I am."

Her mouth curved into the slightest, almost secret smile.

He felt delight. She made him feel ridiculous, unreasonable delight. He settled his back against the wall and stood there, watching her breathing settle back into sleep, trying not to think about what it was going to feel like when she was gone.

"Cap'n?" she murmured. "You still here?"

"I am."

"You gonna stay all night?"

Hugh's breath bottled up in his chest. "If you don't mind."

"I don't." She patted the top of the quilt before she rolled her back to him. "You can sit on top."

It wasn't what he had hoped for, but Hugh didn't dare say a word as he eased his bulk down to sit on the bed next to her. His long legs reached all the way to the wrought-iron railing of the footboard.

"Good night, Meggs."

"Night, Captain."

Hugh crossed his feet at the ankles and shut his eyes. The scent of her soap, of roses and jasmine and something else, something uniquely Meggs, rose up around him. He put his head back to rest against the wrought iron of the headboard.

It was deucedly uncomfortable. And heavenly.

Himself wasn't there when she finally woke up early in the winter dark. She had lain there beside him for hours, feeling the weight and press of his comforting bulk, afraid to move, not knowing what she should do to make him want her. Waiting for him to do something. But he hadn't, and somewhere in the long, dark night she must have fallen back asleep.

And he seemed to have used up all his conversation in her room. He didn't say anything through breakfast and kept silent all the way through the hackney carriage ride up toward Mayfair, until she got out along a deserted stretch of Hyde Park.

"The house is over there." His voice was like the groan of an oak tree pushed too far by the wind—stretched hard. He stayed in the carriage, but he pointed the way, looking across the street at the house and scowling ferociously. And then he took her hand and squeezed it. Hard.

But that was all. Not that she was expecting anything else, but when he let her go, she felt the loss of him all the same. She was filled with the same inept indecision as last night, unsure of how to make him happy with her.

There was nothing to do but get on with it.

"Well, then. Best be off. Cheerio, Captain." And with that, she dove into the traffic and into her new world.

The interview with the hatchet-faced housekeeper behind the big desk took only moments and went just as the captain had told her it would.

Mrs. Trim, the housekeeper, wore a plain black merino gown, a lace cap over her steel gray hair, and a look of unamused dissatisfaction. The clasp of keys pinned to her waist was, in Meggs opinion, conspicuously small. A housekeeper without keys was like a constable without a badge—responsibility without authority. Interesting. So who did have the keys?

"Your name, girl? And your references?"

"Meg, ma'am." Meggs bobbed her head and passed over the letter the captain and Mrs. Tupper had contrived. "Only the one, ma'am, from London. Housekeeper I work for now, ma'am."

"And why have you been let go?"

"Oh, no, ma'am. Closing up the house they are, on account of the master's health and Mrs. Tupper going with the family back to Dartmouth. I didn't like to leave London. Mrs. Tupper said she'd put it all in her letter, ma'am."

Hatchet Face perused the letter for a few moments. "Seems in good order. She says you're strong and obedient." Hatchet gave her a look like a blade, trying to cut away the lies they'd concocted. Meggs attempted to look strong and obedient and have no opinion about anything whatsoever. "When can you start?"

"Straightaway, ma'am."

"Good." She rang a bell on her desk sharply. "This is Mrs. Cook. She will be in charge of you."

"Thank you, ma'am." Meggs followed the silent cook back through the kitchens to a steam-filled corner, where two beefy-armed girls were toiling over basins filled with roiling water. "Here, ma'am? Right. I'm Meg." She nodded to her girls. "What's first?"

"You can scour that pan. Settle her in, Dorcas."

Two full days of scrubbing and scraping, and nothing else. She could have been at the captain's toiling away for all the difference it made, except for the feeding—and the kind words. Hatchet Face Trim was no Mrs. Tupper. No wonder the servants were all Friday-faced with no camaraderie. During those two days, Meggs wasn't even let out of the kitchen unless it was to go to the servants' privy or to climb the servants' stairs to the attic room she shared with the two other scullery maids, Dorcas and Maude.

But it wasn't all wasted time. Meggs found out a thing or two about the house without ever leaving the steamy environs of the scullery. The elaborate panel of bells calling for servants to attend to the rooms above was located to the side and above her station at the sinks. Two days gave her a fine idea of who was where, and when.

Lady Stoval didn't breakfast till noon, and then she spent the hours before dinner taking the carriage out to make calls or receiving visitors in her private suite of rooms on the second floor.

Lord Stoval spent his days split between his office on the ground floor and Westminster and the House of Lords. But the study was still in use by his private secretary, Mr. Falconer, who had his own room below stairs—as did Mrs. Trim, the housekeeper, Mr. Lawson, the butler, and Cook. Mr. Falconer was said to be either very diligent or worked to death by Lord Stoval, for he was often heard working in the study well into the evenings while the other staff were preparing the dining room for dinner to be served just across the hall from the study.

In Meggs's opinion, that study was the clear place to look for Stoval's illicit secrets, for the simple reason that no one else in the house, not Lady Stoval, or the housekeeper, or even the housemaids, was allowed within its sacred walls. Word in the servants' hall was no one but Lord Stoval, Mr. Falconer, and occasionally the butler were allowed inside.

People weren't secretive unless they had secrets to keep, and it was a very secretive house, top to bottom. When Meggs was let up to her room the first night, they were even locked in by the housekeeper. She heard the bolt fall and immediately went to try the door.

"Don't bother," Dorcas offered as she slouched herself across her cot. "That's Trim's prevention against—what'd she call it, Maudie?"

"Amorous congress," the other girl supplied.

"Yeah, that's it. My old ma called it tupping, plain and simple. But there's none of that under old Trim. So don't even start thinking about the footmen. Not that they'd ever look at us lowly sculls."

On the second night, after the family came in from their evening just as the clocks of St. Alban's Chapel struck two o'clock, Meggs decided to give her lovely picklocks an airing.

In the quiet concentration of the dark, Meggs was able to pin the single bolt after a quick, silent conversation with the lock, who was a bit of a biddy, old and tired, and of the same low opinion about locking girls in. She was happy to give over her secrets on a quiet sigh and let Meggs slip out onto the narrow upper corridor with no one else the wiser.

There was a lantern on a small table at the top of the stairs. Meggs didn't bother to light it—she'd learned well enough how to see in the dark—but she did take the new candle from the lantern, as well as the extra candle stubs stored in the drawer below. Something could always go wrong, and if anyone came looking for her, she wanted to make sure they'd have a hard time lighting their way.

She barefooted her silent way down the servants' staircase to the ground floor, listening for a long moment for any sound of activity. But the household seemed to have settled down safe at rug, asleep, so she moved out through the swinging door and made a cursory inspection of the front corridor.

Damned if every door didn't have a lock. Dining room, breakfast room overlooking the rear gardens, billiards room across the hall, and last but not least, His Lordship's private study. Every single door held at least one lock, but the private office had two. Lord Stoval, it seemed, didn't trust a single soul. And that made him untrustworthy.

These locks, she found, were not in the least way related to the old biddies upstairs. They were of the newest design with shiny brass plates advertising their presence, and they were rather beefy, designed to impress as well as prevent. They were big bruisers that relied almost entirely on brute strength. No delicacy of touch was needed here.

She forced as much tension as she could muster on the gate and loosened the first big fellow up with a heavy raking before she set each of the tumble pins with a sharp jab. The bolt fell with a hearty click, and Meggs held her breath, stretching her ears out into the darkness to see if anyone would take notice. Evidently, no one but his Lordship cared enough about the household chattals to bother.

The second lock, on the door handle itself, was big but typical for a Mayfair household and was just a matter of form—a few moments of careful raking and she was in. She closed the door behind her and flipped over the deadbolt. And inhaled the redolence of pipe and cigar tobacco, wool and leather, while she waited for her eyes to adjust to the darkness. And cloves—the air was heavy with the bitter tang of cloves. Someone had a sore tooth.

There was only a sliver of a moon hanging over the city, but it threw a weak silver light through the windows on the Park Lane side of the room. Meggs carefully eased the curtains closed so no one could see the light from her small lantern.

When she lit the little shuttered glim, the narrow beam of light illuminated a dark, wood-paneled room with a huge desk taking up most of one side. Rich, red and green Turkish carpets covered the floor, and two leather wing-backed chairs sat in front of the cold fireplace grate. Over the mantelpiece was a huge portrait of a be-wigged Restoration dandy in bright military regalia, all be-laced and be-jeweled. On either side were smaller oil paintings, one of a family group, all wide, bug eyes, and long, insect necks.

The things some toffs would rather have than money. Never ceased to amaze her.

It was a fine room, but dirty as a sty. The dust had to be inches deep. The housemaids had clearly never been allowed in to clean the place. Word was it was Mr. Falconer's business to see this room was kept tidy, and it was Meggs's professional opinion that Mr. Falconer was nothing but piss poor at the job. But that was all of a piece, because Mr. Falconer, she had found, was not at all well liked. In fact, he was just short of reviled. He did not associate with any of the other servants—he did not take meals with them. He did not use the servants' stairs. He had his own key to the house, which he entered from the secondary entrance on Park Lane. Where, visitors with business with Lord Stoval could enter the study through a small vestibule attended by Mr. Falconer, rather than use the front door of the house. Mr. Falconer had his own small room below stairs, accessible by a separate, private exterior areaway stair below the Park Lane vestibule. He did not fraternize with any of the other servants.

As Falconer had gone out for the evening soon after Lord and Lady Stoval, and was not expected back, Meggs hoped to search the study without his interference.

It was easy to see what they did in here—there were almost tracks through the fine sheen of dust on the desk, chairs, and shelves. There was all but a rut in front of one book, Burke's *Reflections on the Revolution in France*. It seemed to be the only book anyone bothered to read. What did it say that was so intriguing to Lord Stoval?

Right, then. To the business. Big desk—four top drawers and four more beneath on each side, all with small ward locks. The only good news was that the lower locks looked to take the same key—that made them immediately less important. But the top four looked, with the glim held up tight to the keyholes, as if they took different keys. Damn, but someone had secrets he wanted to keep. But simple little ward locks weren't going to keep anyone who knew their business out. So, what else?

Ah. There it was, a stout, iron-banded and studded coffer chest, to the left of the desk, next to an extra side chair. That would be where Falconer sat when he was taking instruction from Lord Stoval. The big strongbox would be closer to Falconer than Lord Stoval. Stoval was a strange paranoid to delegate such responsibility to another man. Hadn't Nan always said, only a man's closest friends knew him well enough to be able to betray him?

Meggs knelt down in front of the strongbox to have a look. Lord, but it was a beauty, and no dust here. This box they used. Often. Iron it was, forged sheets, with iron bands riveted over the whole in a christ-cross pattern. This grande dame had multiple lock mechanisms—a top keylock, which probably threw at least six bar bolts across the inside of the lid for starters; two dogs at the back; another keylock on the front, along with two bars and staples for padlocks outside.

Knocked Meggs back on her heels, all that. And the old dame was beautiful as well. The key locks were beautiful work, pierced and chased, but the one on the lid had a clever escutcheon covering—probably had a spring mechanism that had to be turned in conjunction with the key to spring the bolts. Devilishly clever. Had to admire work like that. And re-spect it. It would take her hours and hours to tickle the secrets out of this lady, one by one, and then figure how the sequence of locks worked. Nan would've loved a challenge like this box. Test of professional acumen, she would have called it.

Meggs held the glim up close to the escutcheon on the lid. It read 1794, Hermier, Paris. But England had been at war with the damn Frenchies since the Revolution began before that. What was Lord Stoval doing with a coffered chest in his house in London, made by a Froggie after the war started? That was what was called corroborating evidence. The captain couldn't convict a man of treason just for having a French cof-fer chest, but she'd eat a golden guinea for dinner if he couldn't scragg Stoval based on what she was sure to find inside.

But she wasn't going to crack that beldam this night. The chapel clock chimed the half hour in warning. And there was still Falconer out. No one was up to any good at this time of the morning, and didn't she know it? But still . . .

Meggs got the glim up and took another look at the desk.

Most people put their valuables to their right side. But some-thing—hell, she didn't know what—but something about the way the extra chair and the strongbox were placed to the left made her go to the other side. She worked her tension spring and single hook pick and waited patiently to make friends with the lady, who graciously yielded her virtue without a fight. Low and behold, the drawer held another damned lock-box. Money? She couldn't take the chance of rattling it, but it was a simple little mechanism, young and barely tried. Silly little bit of fluff gave up her secret easily and to only the hook.

It was full, not of money but keys. Here they all sat, like ladies at a tea party, smiling up at her. Brass, steel, and iron. She'd—

There was a jingle of keys on a chain and then the sound of the locked gate to Falconer's areaway stairs being engaged. No time.

She doused the glim, silently flipped the lockbox shut, stashed it back in the drawer, and thumbed the lock cocked on the drawer in less than four seconds. She was at the dead-bolt on the door at six, waiting. When she heard the outside gate swing open, she opened her door, and then as the gate clanged shut behind Falconer, she shut hers. And she was off, behind the silently swinging baize door as Falconer unlocked the areaway door.

Well. Meggs let her thumping heart settle back down to normal. She was going to need a powerful lot of locksmith's putty to copy all those keys.

CHAPTER 16

"I'll need that pot for the fish stew, quick-like," Cook bawled through the steam.

"Fish stew," Dorcas grumbled. "The whole place'll stink of it. I hate fish."

"Why's that?" Meggs asked as she threw a handful of sand into the pot for grit.

"All them dead eyes, lookin' at me."

"Gives you the jim-jams, does it?" Meggs raised up her voice a notch or two. "Not me. I know how to pick a fish."

"Think so, do ya?" Dorcas was caught between not wanting to have anyone able to do anything better than she and her native revulsion to the fish. Or to doing any actual work. Hard to tell.

"My old dad were a fishmonger, down Billingsgate way." Meggs lied away, happy in the knowledge she at least knew her way around the Billingsgate market on the east end of the city and could picture the very fellow she would have liked for an imaginary, fishmonger father. "Gone now he is, or I'd be working the market still, not scrubbing pots, but I can tell you how to get a nice piece o' fish, firm and fresh-like."

"That so?" Cook had her red, strangling hands on her hips and gave Meggs a new look.

"Yes, ma'am. Gotta have a nose for the fish. You pick by the smell and the color of the flesh, depending on the type. But no matter the type o' fish, firm it ought to be, but not stiff. If it is, it's too old. Unless you want smoked. But my da was only fresh." Meggs rinsed out the copper pot and set to shining the exterior with her apron. "Nice piece of haddock, you'll want this time o' year, for a stew, won't you, missus? And you'll want to get there good and early. That's the real secret. They load in at dawn."

And that was how a girl ensured she was to accompany Cook to market of a morning.

Hugh had been lounging around the fringes of Shepherd's Market since dawn, watching the wagons of produce come in from the farms to the south and west, and barrows full of fish wheel up from the stairs at the Thames.

He was dressed in his old worn-down togs, a souvenir of his former days on assignment with his friend James Marlowe clearing out a nest of smugglers on the Devon Coast, the first of Admiral Middleton's "special" assignments.

Hugh liked the kit because he didn't have to pretend he was a gentleman when he was rigged up in the old fisherman's wool pants and sea boots, thick-knitted jersey and cap. He didn't have to mind his manners or listen for the remnants of the Scots burr he had been taught to scrub out of his accent.

Finally, by the time it was light enough to see the frosted breath in the air above every head, he saw Meggs, scooting along like a duckling in the wake of the big, red-faced, waddling Cook. He hefted a crate and meandered his way through the produce until he reefed up next to her at a fishmonger's stall.

"Hello, Meggs. You're a sight for sore eyes." It was only relief, that bonfire in his gut. He was only relieved to know she was safe and that things were going according to plan. He had felt as if he had ordered a man inshore to cut out a ship from an enemy harbor, not knowing if he were sending him to his death or to triumph. But sending people out was his job.

She blushed, even though her nose was already red from the raw cold. "Hello yourself."

"D'you know this fella, girl?" demanded the Cook.

Meggs shot him a nervous, fidgety glance. "I do, ma'am."

Hugh tugged the brim of his cap. "I'm an old 'quaintance of Miss Meggs, here."

"Miss Meg is it?" she demanded. And Meggs had the good sense to scoot under the protective wing of the woman's arms, as if she were deferring to the woman's judgment. "How is it I've never seen you round this market before?"

Hugh was about to give the very obvious answer, that he'd come looking for Meggs, but she spoke before he could. "Know him from my Billingsgate Market days, ma'am. He's one of the lads worked my father's stall afore he died. God rest him."

Just like that, a story as smooth and plausible as if they had rehearsed it for days. "God rest his soul," Hugh echoed. "Take your basket for you?"

"Thanks all the same." She laced her arm through Cook's. "I'm with a Mayfair household now."

"Come up in the world." He gave his hat another tug. "Good girl."

"Thanks." She smiled up at him and then looked to Cook for approval. "How's the fish this morning."

"Not so good as Billingsgate." Oh, her eyes brightened at that piece of flummery. It was nice, playing this way, impressing her.

"Of course, you wouldn't think so." Meggs tossed him a wink and moved toward the nearest stall, taking a deep inhale of the assorted fish as if she could divine just the right one by smell alone. For himself, after years at sea, Hugh was fairly impervious to the briny stench. It wasn't so bad now, in winter, but God help the stink come the summer. A couple of hundred years' worth of fish scales shimmered in tiny rainbows underfoot. But Meggs poked and sniffed her way across the stall as if she were a French perfumer until she came up with a couple of healthy-looking specimens. "What do you think, ma'am?" she asked Cook.

While the Cook was dickering with the fishmonger over the price, Meggs wandered away from the stall, giving them a small measure of privacy to talk. And talk she did, quick and competent, one hundred percent professional, all traces of the flirt gone.

"Place is locked up tighter than the Crown Jewels in the Tower. Thinks he's got things worth stealing, Stoval does. It's going to take a long while to get through all his locks. Only a few have the freedom of the house, and not even the butler has all the keys. Even the larder is cocked up tight every night. And so are the servants. I hate that, being locked and shut in. I need locksmith's putty and plenty of it. Can you get me some?"

"Shh. Slow down. Putty. I'll get it. When will you next be out?"

"Dunno. Lied my way into this. Hope to God that damned fish ain't off."

"*Isn't* off. It's fresh. I saw them load it off the boats myself. We don't have much time. Be careful," he ordered, the same way he would if she were one of his men. But she damn well wasn't one of his men. Hugh took a quick look around, casing the market over her head, and then in a flash of impulse pulled her tight to his chest and kissed her soundly on the mouth.

He shouldn't have done it. He had no business doing it. He could say, if she asked, if she protested as she ought, it was all part of their disguise—he was supposed to appear as if he were courting here. So he kissed her. He lowered his lips to hers and took what he wanted. What he had been wanting since the first time he saw her.

Damn her eyes, she had no business being that soft, or that sweet. Her lips were too plush, too full, begging him to take them between his own, and tongue and nip and worry at them. She had no business opening her mouth ever so slightly on an exhalation of pleasure, so he could slip by and press himself to the petal soft interior of her—

They were in the market. He pulled back. His blood was pounding away at his veins like a sledgehammer. But then, because he couldn't help himself, he kissed her once in the middle of her forehead before he pushed her away. "Off you go."

She nodded automatically, but her gaze was soft and unfocused as she turned to rejoin the goose of a Cook. Meggs turned back once to look at him and give him a smile of such simple, pure happiness, he felt a pang as real as a saber thrust through his chest.

Meggs had to wait another two days for Falconer to be out at the same time as Lord Stoval in order to find a convenient time to do a little cracks work. It went faster this time. Now that they'd met her, the bully boy locks on the door merely shrugged their beefy shoulders and let her in. She went immediately to the left-hand drawer of the desk, and having previously made the wards' acquaintance and pried out all their secrets, she was past the gates and into the drawer in a jiff. The lockbox inside was even less trouble.

She had the flattened roll of putty Timmy had passed to her in the areaway stairs while pretending to sell roasted Spanish chestnuts, all prepared and wrapped in linen. She rolled it out on the desk and set to work, ward keys first, pressing first the sides and then the key end into the soft putty. She worked quickly, methodically pressing one after another, sorting them aside and keeping track of how many she had done. It was all going swimmingly.

And then, suddenly, she heard the rattle of keys, not at the areaway steps where Falconer usually went but at the Park Lane vestibule door.

Bloody blue fuck. Five keys left.

She scooped them up and slid them straight down her bodice. She couldn't douse the glim until she had the rest of them back into the box and latch down, box locked, and into the drawer and closed. She snibbed the candle of her lantern out, blistering her fingers to kill the telltale smoke.

There wasn't time—the corridor door was too far away. Already the second lock on the door from the vestibule into the study was being keyed and was turning.

Meggs scuttled under the huge desk and slid up tight to the front piece, thankful for the heavy oak construction. She stuffed the glim under her skirts, both so the metal couldn't reflect against any light and to cloak the smell.

After the creak of the door, there was silence. Then the hollow sound of footsteps retreating onto the stone floor of the vestibule, followed by fumbling to strike flint for a light. Meggs ripped the white mobcap off her head and stuffed it deep into her pocket with the roll of putty and turned her face away from the opening to present a completely dark aspect. Cobwebs tickled at her face, and she closed her mind to the thought of spiders. The room hadn't been cleaned in so long, the carpet was bound to be teeming with wildlife.

She waited until the footfalls returned, hushed by the thick, dusty rug. The single candle dimly illuminated the room, casting the edges in deep shadow. There it was, the strong, almost overpoweringly cloying scent of cloves. The next sound was from above, where he must have placed the candle on the desk. Then the jingle of keys again and the complicated mechanical sound of bolt locks disengaging. He was at the strongbox. She heard the catch release and then nothing as the well-oiled hinges slid silently open and the back of the lid came to rest against the desk with a soft thunk.

There was a rifling of paper, or perhaps books, and then he

came round the back of the desk, pulled out the chair, and sat. Meggs crushed herself even smaller, folding into herself and forcing all but the barest minimum of necessary air from her lungs. Falconer's feet, and she knew now it was he from the dark stockings and breeches, came within mere inches of connecting with her shin.

Meggs fought to control her breathing and stay calm, lest Falconer feel her nervous heat. But he was busy jangling more keys into a lock, and then the right-hand drawer clicked open. Interesting that the secretary should have access to all the locked areas. Perhaps Lord Stoval had reason to be paranoid if Falconer had copied all the keys and made free with the contents of the desk. But Falconer only withdrew several sheets of paper and set himself to work.

For the next several minutes the only sound was the quiet, wet splash of the pen dipping into the inkwell and the slow scratch of the nib across the paper. No wonder Falconer had to work all hours of the day and night if this was what he did. He was incredibly slow at the business, laboriously drawing out each and every letter. If this was competence for the secretary of a peer of the realm, then perhaps even Timmy had a shot at respectable employment.

Time dragged on. There were more sounds of paper or pages being turned—she couldn't tell which—and then a few more excruciatingly drawn out bits of writing. The pen dipped and tapped against the inkwell once more, and then he was away and flying, writing much faster.

What on earth? And then the loose parts of her brain snapped into place like so many tumblers in a lock. She had made much the same sounds not five nights ago, copying out and deciphering the codes the captain had set before her. Could Stoval have delegated his dirty work to his secretary? Good Lord and all the lady saints, she was fairly itching to see just what he was writing above her head.

But it was a no-go, with his leather shoe dangling precipitously at the end of her face. Finally, he set the pen down, pushed back his chair, and . . . stopped. He inched forward on the seat and then bent down to pick something up to the left of the desk.

And picked up a ward key.

Stupid, careless bloody . . . Meggs shut her thoughts down hard. She couldn't get upset, not even with herself—she'd only make some sound and give herself away. She had to think. Falconer was holding the key, turning it over in his hand. Then he reached for his key ring and rifled through them, looking for the right key for the left-hand drawer's lock. He was going to search the key box. Damn, damn, damn.

Just as he was turning the key, a carriage rumbled up out-side the Upper Grosvenor Street entrance, and Falconer paused. Another moment or so, and the hall outside was filled with the sounds of footmen running and opening the doors, and then the voices of the butler, Mr. Lawson, and Lord Sto-val himself, walking and talking in the entrance hall.

Falconer abandoned the drawer, and Meggs listened to the sounds of him opening the locked study door leading into the front corridor. He must have spoken from the door of the study—his heels didn't click upon the black and white marble floor of the hall.

"My Lord Stoval," he interrupted the butler in the middle of some discussion.

"Yes, Falconer," Stoval answered. "What is it?"

"If I might have a word, my lord?"

"Yes?" Stoval sounded irritated. "Make it quick. I have to change for dinner."

The door closed the two men into the study, the soft Turk-ish carpet crushing under their feet and sending up little puffs of dust.

"You have been careless with the keys, my lord."

"Of course I haven't. You know I don't bloody well have the

keys." There was more than simple irritation between these two men. Stoval was . . . resentful.

"I would like to remind you," Falconer continued, with a slight lisp that told her his mouth still held a clove, "that the security of this room, and our *business* here, is of great importance to the success of our endeavors. Leaving keys on the floor, where anyone might find them, is careless."

"Anyone? You and I are the only ones in here to find them."

"Which is my point entirely."

"Look, you're the one with all the keys and the locks and the . . . methods. I do my part and the rest of this"—Meggs could only imagine Stoval made a gesture.—"is up to you."

"A great part of my doing, as you say, my part, is making sure you are able to do yours." Falconer was as smooth and lethal as he could be, around a mouthful of cloves. Lord, but that must be some toothache.

"Fine. Mind the keys. May I go?" Definitely resentment. Stoval could give lessons to schoolboys. But why should Stoval be asking *permission*—albeit sarcastically—from his secretary? There was no doubt at all in Meggs's mind there was dicey business in this ken, but just who was the masher and who the spud she hadn't quite figured out. And if she didn't get her arse back into the kitchen before dinner, she'd be out on her bum before she could find out.

Thankfully, with Stoval gone back the way he'd come, Falconer seemed to be done as well. He put the loose key back into the lockbox in the drawer without counting the remaining keys, and he took himself out the door and down his stairs to dinner. Her mistake cost her naught.

Meggs forced herself to count to one hundred before she bolted. But upon rising, she saw Falconer had made one tiny mistake of his own. He had left a blank sheet of paper, on top of which he had presumably written his letter. The faint tracings from the pressure Falconer had used to write his letter were still visible. She could make use of that. She snatched it up and was gone.

Meggs made it back down to the servants' hall only a moment or two before Falconer swept in. The normally bustling hall went quiet. Servants seemed to collect at the kitchen door, curious at the sight of the secretary who never deigned to be seen among them.

The butler, Mr. Lawson, looking as though he'd like to be anywhere else and doing anything else, came in behind Falconer and cleared his throat. But everyone was already listening.

Almost everyone. Out in the kitchen Cook said, "What's going on here?" at the inactivity and was instantly hushed.

Falconer stepped forward. "I should like to make it clear that the working areas of the house, Lord Stoval's private study as well as my own rooms, are strictly off limits to all of you."

Meggs watched him from under her cap, back demurely atop her head, as he attempted to intimidate the rest of the servants, from the footmen to the boot boy, with his stares.

"And if I find any person who is out of their place, or has overstepped their bounds and trespassed upon those rooms, I will take their punishment into my own hands. Do I make that clear?"

Posturing fool, he barely looked at the women, who rather naturally moved closer together near the doorway like ewes confronted by a wolf come into their meadow. Meggs huddled up with the rest of the sheep and let the quivering kitchen maids hear her whisper, "Gives me the jim-jams, that fellow does, with his yellow eyes and soft hands." Murmurs of assent rose around her.

Except for Dorcas, who looked at her sharp.

Meggs thought she might be ready to peach her out, so she

linked her arm with Dorcas's and steered her back to their station at the sinks.

"You been out of your place, haven't you?" Dorcas asked
out the side of her mouth.

"Just wanted to see my fella," Meggs groused. "Don't see
how that's any of old Fancy Pants Falconer's business. Coming in here, telling us to mind ourselves."

Dorcas made a sound of emphatic disgust. "He thinks he's
better'n the rest of us, with his keys."

"Exactly. But thanks, Dorcas, for keeping that to yourself.
Much obliged. I'll make sure you get my helping of pudding
tonight."

"You don't want it?" Dorcas was suspicious of any altruism.

"Got all the sweetness I can handle from my man." And
they laughed together as Meggs blew out a long breath of
worry and plunged her hands back into the scald bath. She
hardly felt it, she was that relieved at the outcome of the day.

Make no mistake, Falconer was up to something more than
a load of mischief, and he was a nasty, mean, toad of a man.
She'd be damned happy to get this job done and see the last
of him.

Hugh paced back and forth along the strip of Hyde Park,
the way he used to pace the quarterdeck of his ship awaiting
the outcome of a shore sortie. What did Meggs always say?
Something can always go wrong. His experience told him she was
right. But all he could do was wait.

In another few minutes, the cold and the ache in his leg
would drive him into the carriage he had hired to cruise the
edge of the park, as a station for him, or Timmy, or Jinks to
maintain a constant watch on the house. He wanted to be
nearby in case Meggs should need any help. Though much
good it did him. Or her. She was bloody well on her own.

But there on the areaway steps was a familiar head, the

loose strands of her fine hair gusting up around her face in the wintry chill as she worked her broom. He was across the roadway and to the railing as fast as his leg could carry him.

"Meggs." He made to walk past inconspicuously, but she snagged his hand and pulled him toward her.

"It's all right. They think you're courting me. Come up close."

He didn't need encouragement, crowding her into the fence and taking her into his arms. Assuring himself she was all right. "How are you? Have you got it?"

"Fine. Some. Here's the putty." She slipped a bundle inconspicuously into his coat. "I'll need 'em back quick as you can manage. I had to nick the five keys there and they'll be missed. It's Falconer, the secretary, who's in on it with Stoval. They're both in it up to their necks and no doubt. But the evidence is locked up tighter than the bloody Tower of bleeding London."

"Meggs, I don't know if we'll have time to get keys made. We're running out of time. The meeting of the board has been pushed back to accommodate us, but we can't wait much longer. We have to have evidence now."

"Try this." She passed him a sheet of blank writing paper. "It's an impression of a letter Falconer wrote. I think it may be code, but I haven't had time—" She shook her head. "They keep us working something chronic. He's *always* in there. And it takes so long to pick every lock every time. That chest is going to take hours and hours to crack, unless I can sort out the keys."

Hugh could see the purple circles under her eyes and feel how small and fragile she was under his hands. They weren't feeding her enough. She shivered in the cold biting wind, and he wanted to bundle her up and take her home. Keep her safe and warm. But that wasn't what he was going to do. He was going to order her back into the house. "Lass, listen. We're running out of time."

She looked deflated, as though the breeze had run out of her sails. Almost defeated. He hated that he would have to ignore it. "Take the keys back. You'll need them. Go in at your first opportunity." He made his voice quiet and commanding. This was a mission. She was his subordinate, his agent, trained to do this job nearly from childhood. And he used his personal knowledge of her ruthlessly. "I need you to do it, Meggs. I'm counting on you. I know you won't let me down."

She nodded, weary and tired to her soul but determined. "I'll do it, Captain. You can count on me."

CHAPTER 17

It was a good afternoon for a ransacking. The rain poured down like vengeance, muffling sound, and twilight came early, casting the kitchens into semidark. All the dishes were done from the day, and dinner was just going on the boil. The family was to dine from home, so it would only be the staff. Much less work.

The call bell above her head rang for the Park Lane vestibule door—Falconer was going out. She had to take this chance. Meggs tried to think of an excuse, a reason for her to do what she was doing, but she couldn't even come up with a pretext fast enough for being outside in the areaway to make sure he had gone clear of the house.

Dorcas did it for her, snickering, "Looking for that big man o' yourn, are you?"

"Oh, aye. Well, a girl can hope."

Falconer was coming around the corner and passing by the front of the house. Meggs ducked back down the steps, out of the rain, before she caught his eye. She didn't think he noticed her as he went by, walking straight down Upper Grosvenor Street and out of sight.

Meggs came back in and took off her apron. This was it. It

was now or never. As the captain said, they were too bloody out of time for the niceties of subterfuge.

"Where are you off to?"

Meggs turned back to see Dorcas and Maude eyeing her. "Going to see my man."

"He out there?" Dorcas asked.

"Can you cover for me? Please?"

"Trim finds out, you know she'll give you the boot without a character."

Maude shook her head and advised, "Oughta make him marry you, Meg. It's not right he don't, and you going to him all hours of the night."

So they had heard her. But still they hadn't peached her out, bless their pot-scrubbing hearts. "That's exactly what I aim to tell him, Maudie. Wish me luck."

"Luck, Meg," they chorused, and let her go.

She ran upstairs only long enough to get her picklocks, and set the jar of Mrs. Tupper's candies out on Maude's cot for them both to find, before she went down to the study, through the locked doors, and straight to the strongbox. Meggs set to it, but the clock had soon ticked away an hour, and still she hadn't made it through the first sequence. The falling darkness made her close her eyes and concentrate on the feel of the way the tumblers were spaced, but it also made it hard to find her picks. And she couldn't get the sequence right. Meggs lit a single candle, and she stood up for a moment to say a quick prayer to the soul of old Nan for guidance and to walk around the box to see if there was something—some other catch like the escutcheon—she might have missed.

As she walked by the bookshelf behind the desk, her eye was caught again by the little trail through the dust where someone had repeatedly reached for Burke's tome. For a moment all she felt was the puzzlement. And then it came, that strange tingling feeling, the quiet stillness when everything else fades away except the pocket or the lock—or—the certainty. She sat herself in the chair at the center of the desk and turned toward the book, reaching out with her left hand. Because Stoval was the left-hander. And Stoval didn't have the keys. Stoval reached from this spot to that book. Often.

She hooked her fingers around the back of the spine and pulled the book out. It was surprisingly light for such a thick book. Because it wasn't a book. It was a clever little box—and it was full of what she could only suppose were cheat sheets for the code books locked up tight in Falconer's strongbox. And they were all in a cramped left-slanted writing. Stoval.

Meggs took only two seconds to think about what she should do. She pulled the entire contents of the book-box out and shoved them straight down the front of her bodice, so the sheets were riding flat along the busk. This had to be enough evidence to at least arrest Stoval and Falconer. Once they had them secured, the captain could come in and go at the strongbox at his leisure. All she had to do was get the sheets to the captain quick-like, before Stoval figured they were gone.

So she replaced the book-box on the shelf and was about to walk straight out. The urge to run was so strong. No. She turned around. Much as she would have liked to leave the strong chest half unlocked, if she left *any* evidence, it would put the wind up both Falconer and Stoval. The captain needed enough lead time to do things legal-like. She quickly stowed her pick set down her pockets, doused the candle, and made sure everything was put to rights.

It was then she heard the unmistakable sound of a key being inserted into the lock of the hall corridor door.

Bloody blue fuck. How had she missed hearing anyone on that clacking marble? There was no time. She had to get out the only other door—the private vestibule. She mussed her hair out of its pins and pulled her neckline loose as she ran. By the time she made it through the study door and was safely in the vestibule, the full scenario had worked its way through her brain. *Brazen it out, dearie, but make it real.* Meggs took one last moment to shove her breasts as high as she could get them, wet her lips, and subside back against the door with a sigh of lazy satisfaction.

It was only another second or two before Falconer burst through the door and wrenched her by the arm, twisting the skin over her wrist. Pain burst up her arm and settled in for the duration. Falconer had a grip like a debt collector with a mean streak. Here was a man who did not mind causing pain. Jim-jams didn't begin to cover the fright crawling along Meggs's skin.

"Oowww!" she bawled. "Lemme go!"

"What are you doing here?" Falconer demanded.

"Oh, Mr. Falconer. Lord Stoval." She bobbed an awkward and painful curtsy within the secretary's viselike grip as Lord Stoval appeared in the doorway. Falconer was a blade of cutting suspicion, sharp and probing, his eyes darting all over the vestibule and back into the study. But Stoval's gaze was much more obedient. Meggs took a series of rapid little breaths designed to make her titties rise and fall quickly, keeping his attention focused. While Falconer cased the ken for anything missing, Meggs used her free hand to slip a tiny pinch of putty into the bolt of the door behind her back, pinning the lock open.

"I asked you a question. This room is forbidden to servants."

"Yes, sir. I knows." She made her eyes wide and let all her very real fright come into her voice and her face. "I weren't in that room, I promise," she pleaded. "I just slipped in here for a moment or so . . . so's I could stay warm, outta the cold."

"You came *in?*" Lord Stoval asked.

Meggs bit her lip and did her best to look all soft and rumpled and appealing, even as her courage was wobbling like a loose cart wheel. "I know I weren't supposed to, my lord." She let her eyes swim just a little with the shine of tears. "But they was always watching in the kitchen stairs. And a girl can't get a man to make an offer with everyone staring. I just needed a bit of privacy to get him in the mood, see?"

Lord Stoval began to chuckle.

"This is not amusing," Falconer sniped. "How did you get in here?"

"We was in the doorway, talking like, but the door was open, so's we just slipped in, outta the rain."

"We? Who did you let in here?"

"For God's sake, Falconer," Stoval objected. "Look at the girl. I'm sure her skirts are still damp. It was merely a lover's tryst. Go back to the kitchens, girl."

"No." Falconer was insistent and he had not released her wrist. "How did she get in here? The door is locked."

"No, it ain't." Meggs stepped aside to let the winter wind blow it open. Falconer let go of her arm to ratchet at the lock.

"Really, Falconer." Lord Stoval's voice was replete with smug disdain. "You need to take better care with your precious keys."

The palpable antagonism flaring between the men gave Meggs the perfect opportunity to back quietly out of range. But she couldn't just run—and certainly not toward the dark carriage trolling slowly past at the edge of the park. If either Falconer or Stoval had even an inkling of what she'd stolen, or for whom she had stolen it, they would take a lam faster than the captain could have them arrested. They had to believe they were still safe.

"Come back here," Falconer snarled at her as he chased her out on the wet pavement.

Meggs darted into the middle of Upper Grosvenor Street, where she was sure to catch a crowd. "You keep away from me, you leacher!" she bawled.

"I'll have you dismissed."

"No you won't, cuz I quit!" Meggs was yelling at the top of her lungs so the whole street would hear. "I won't work in that bloody house another minute. And if you ever try to hurt me again, I'll have my man come find you and fillet you into pieces with a fish knife, you sorry excuse for a—" She picked up a small chunk of broken cobble and whipped it at him. She missed, but the piece landed exactly where she hoped it would, crashing through the window pane next to Stoval's head with a spectacular shower of splintering glass.

And then she turned and ran like hell. Away from the captain and into the alleys of London.

Twenty minutes of running hard, of backtracking and skirting through passageways the size of a penny, made sure Falconer lost track of her. Damn, but why was it always as wet and cold as a dead whore when she was caught out of doors? If she stayed out in the rain, trying to find her way back to the captain any longer, the cargo down her front would get wet and the ink would run. And all her bloody evidence would be ruined. She couldn't wait. Chill rain was sluicing through her hair—she'd lost her mobcap somewhere in her run—and the clothes upon her back were already soaked through.

There was really only one alternative. She had to get the sheets of codes dry. Old habits died hard. If anyone from Stoval House was looking for a larcenous, missing scullery maid, they'd have a devilish hard time finding one.

CHAPTER 18

It was agony to wait. It did no good to tell himself she was a professional, or that she had been living off her wits and agile fingers for years. Or that she knew her way through every alley and byway in London. Or that she was as lethal as a handspike.

Hugh had seen her back out of Stoval House, bawling like the proverbial fishwife, pelt Falconer with her rock, and take off like a wild hare. He tried to keep after her, but she was too fast and had too much of a lead for him to follow on foot. And then the traffic snarled and slowed to a crawl, making the carriage all but useless. She had disappeared into the cold, wet streets like the rain—invisible.

For a long while he cruised the park, waiting in hopeful anticipation for her return. But when night set in, and still there was no sign, he began to grow uneasy. The doubts he had pushed aside in the pursuit of duty came back to assail him tenfold.

Why hadn't she run to him? Had he asked too much? Had he left her alone, unsupported, in Stoval House, too long? Had he given her an impossible task? Or worse. Had she just simply run?

He had warned himself, hadn't he? He had known he was

asking for trouble by trusting a cynical thief who would leave him flat at the first chance she got. He had trusted an untrustworthy criminal, and as a result he was going to fail Admiral Middleton, the Admiralty, and his country. And now he would have to go tell them.

Hugh reluctantly had Jinks turn the carriage toward home, and in too short a time, he was drawing up in front of the house in Chelsea, where Admiral Middleton was wearing down the carpet in his study.

Unfortunately, Rawsthorne was there as well, making himself at home behind his desk, looking into every shelf and corner and cataloging whatever it was he was seeing into the back of that manipulative mind of his. Hugh was of half a mind to be rude, just to pick a fight. But putting off the inevitable would serve no one. Bad news had to be delivered as quickly as possible.

"Well, Captain?" Admiral Middleton asked directly.

"It's Lord Stoval, sir. I am quite confident of that, despite the fact that I have a very small amount of evidence to date, but unfortunately—"

There was a sudden clatter at the door as Timmy pelted into the room, and for a long, strange moment Hugh couldn't conceive of how Timmy had grown so much taller or what he was doing interrupting their conference. But when the sopping-wet urchin all but threw himself into his arms, he knew that the wet body he was holding was Meggs, shaking from cold and exhaustion.

"I ran," she panted. "Near all the way. Devil of a time shaking him, he was that mean, but I tipped him the double in the Dials, and I ditched the maid rig cuz'—"

"Shh. Get your breath. Sit down." Though he was loath to let go of her for even a moment, he set her back in a chair so she could rest and catch her breath. She swiped off a disreputable hat and pushed back the loose ends of her hair, dripping and shaking off water like a stray cat. But all her lovely,

dark, long hair was gone, chopped off somewhere in the latitude of her chin. It looked as though it had been lopped off
with hedge shears. "Christ. What happened?" And then, because he had already said too much in front of Rawsthorne, he
added, "Do you have the evidence?"

"I've got it. Codes." She was taking in air in great gulps.
"Couldn't make the big box—eight bolts—too strong. But I
got these." And then she was fishing a packet out of her shirt-
front and pushing it into his hands. "I tried to keep them dry."

She had wrapped the papers in a small length of oil cloth.
Smart, smart, clever girl. And he was an ass, an unmitigated,
undeserving jackass, for ever doubting her.

"Is it enough? Can you get him with those? That's Stoval's
writing, I'm sure. He's left-handed. See how it slants? The
other piece—the blank I gave you—was Falconer's. Right-
handed. And these codes should decipher it. I couldn't get
into the strongbox," she repeated, anxious for it not to be a
failure. "I swiped those papers—didn't have time to copy 'em.
So you've got to act fast, because if either Stoval or Falconer
goes looking, they'll know they're gone and something's afoot.
Is that all right? Will it be enough?"

"It should be more than enough." Hugh passed the packet
to Admiral Middleton and then swept his own sea cloak
around her shoulders. "Try to get warm." He would have
kissed her, right there in front of God and the admiral, but
Rawsthorne was prowling behind him, so he had to be content
with chafing her arms. "Go down to the kitchens. Mrs. Tupper
will have something hot for you."

She shook her head, like a stubborn little terrier, not willing
to leave until she knew. "But is it enough? Did I get the right
stuff? We could get back in on a dark job to heave the case, I
suppose, but—"

Hugh laid a finger across her lips to stop the flow of nervous
babble.

"Have a look at those codes, Major," he suggested. "Can you make anything out?"

Rawsthorne's attention was diverted to the evidence Admiral Middleton was laying out on the table, so he left off peering at Meggs to sit down and examine the evidence. They worked in silence for a very long while, and Hugh was obliged to go over and give his opinion on the work. He tried to keep an eye on Meggs, who was shivering in her chair as wet and cold as a bilge rat.

"Do you have everything you need? I need to get the boy seen to before he takes ill."

"We do. We'll take it from here." Rawsthorne finally nodded his head and then moved toward the door.

"Quietly, Major Rawsthorne, please. Arrest him as discretely as possible. Do we understand each other?" Admiral Middleton asked.

"Lord Stoval shall be swept under your rug as quietly as you should wish. You may leave it to me."

"Thank you, Major. I'll await your progress. Good luck." When Rawsthorne had left, Admiral Middleton came to shake Hugh's hand. "I thank you as well, Hugh. You've done very well with an enormously difficult task, and it is much appreciated. Go ahead and see to the boy."

Hugh drew what felt like his first full breath in hours, or even days. They were done and the traitor was as good as hung. So why didn't the fist holding tight to his gut ease?

Meggs was home. She was safe. But he wasn't. He was coming apart at his seams. Because now, in the moment after her triumph, he had no reasonable reason to keep her.

Mrs. Tupper insisted Meggs soak in a steaming hot bath to steep the raw cold out of her bones. That suited her well enough, though she was anxious to hear from the captain if Stoval and Falconer had been successfully taken up.

But she was tired to the bone. And cold. So she gave in to Mrs. Tupper's fussing and was glad. The bath was thawing her out nicely. A bowl of soup and a nip of that sherry of the captain's, and she could fall into her lovely bed, warm and happy. She had done it. She had done it for him. She hadn't let him down. So why hadn't he said a word of congratulations? Or even thanks?

It was all of a piece—the captain prowling into her bath without so much as knocking. Had a penchant for interrupting a good soak, the captain did. Meggs curved into herself to hide her body, but he wasn't even looking at her. He was ranging around the room like an angry animal pacing the edges of its cage. Raw discontent sloughed off his shoulders. The only civilizing touch was the drink in his left hand. Every few moments he would swirl it around in the cut crystal glass and take a gulping drink.

"Well, am I meant to guess? Is it finished? Did you get them?"

"We got Stoval. Took him coming out of White's."

"Serves him right. Taken like a thief in the middle of St. James's. Stupid bastard. Hope you checked those pockets of his."

"Claimed it was all Falconer's doing—that he had no idea Falconer was a French agent, only that he owed him money. So you were right, weren't you, about it being either for the money or for the cause? Only you seemed to have found one of each."

Meggs chose the better part of valor and refrained from crowing, "I told you so." The captain's mood didn't appear to be receptive to such insight. "But what about Falconer? Did you get Falconer? He's the dangerous one."

"He has thus far eluded our net, damn his eyes. He's likely halfway to France by now."

"What?" No wonder his discontent was like sulphur in the air. And she wasn't far behind him. "I can't like that one bit.

You've got to take him. He's a nasty piece of work, that Falconer. He can't be let off." She shivered the creeping unease off her shoulders. "At least you can string up your toff for treason. They'll give you back your ship for that, won't they?"

"Perhaps. But it's all to be dealt with quietly, so don't start looking forward to any public hangings at Newgate. Bloodthirsty little wretch. I thought you might have some compassion for your fellow thief."

That tore it, the captain calling her names. "If they'd a caught me, do you think they would have showed me any compassion? Falconer would have cut me into a thousand pieces and taken pleasure in doing it. And Stoval would have just watched. They deserve everything they should get, the pair of them. They ought to be strung up in the middle of Hyde Park so everyone could see. Dealt with quietly. They hang children for stealing little better than a handkerchief, and you'll let these treasonous bastards, whose *nefarious* deeds may have cost hundreds of soldiers—and sailors, don't forget the sailors—their lives, let off quietly. If that doesn't just fuck all."

"I didn't say *I* wanted to let them off. I happen to agree with you. But I take orders same as you. And I do what I'm told."

"Well, I done my part, what I was told, and if you didn't get your man, then it's no skin off my back. I ran the rig neat and square. No one could say I didn't."

But the captain wasn't saying anything else, good, bad, or indifferent. He just wolfed around, watching her bathe without the slightest awareness of her body. Of her nakedness. Of *her*. Of the massive impropriety of his presence in the room. Jesus God, he wasn't her bloody brother.

When he ranged closer to the tub, she looked up to see his face, ruddy and dark in the heat of the room. "You look like God's revenge against murder."

He took another ruminative sip of his drink and then

reached out to finger the blunt, uneven edges of her wet hair, his voice rough with some dangerous anger. "You're no good to me as a boy."

That was bloody rich. She wouldn't be treated like a blasted piece of equipment that needed to function to suit his needs and his moods. Well, he could have his bloody mood. She'd been chased across half of London, scared and wet, and she had been cold and tired for hours doing his work for him, and she was fed up with belligerent men thinking they could stalk into her bath and intimidate her.

She stood straight up in the tub, water sluicing down her body and splashing on the floor, naked as the day God made her. "Don't bloody well look like a boy now, do I?"

He was on her, over her, picking her slick, wet body up and carrying her the two steps backward, up against the wall before he could even think about what he was doing. But he was so tired, so bloody, fucking tired of thinking. So he wasn't going to think at all.

At that moment, after such a night, the only sane thing to do was feel. Feel the warmth of her body, heated and slick from the bathwater, and let his hands roam where they would—everywhere he longed to touch but had for so long denied himself. Up her sides, past her heaving ribcage, over the seemingly fragile strength of her collarbone and shoulder, along the line of her jaw, up into the blunt ends of her chopped-off hair, down the slide of her sleek flanks. Each a marvel of warm, wet silk.

But it was her mouth. Her filthy, heathenish, taunting, tormenting mouth. He fell on her like a starving man, made ravenous and crude by unreasonable hunger, eaten up with lust and longing. He was empty of finesse. He could take no time to savor the solace of her chapped, gasping lips. He pushed aside his promise that it would be nice, and tender, and sweet.

She was no tender, delicate flower, and he had nothing of sweetness left in him. He was beyond, already delving deep into the honeyed warmth of her mouth, fastened to her like a succubus, taking every ounce of heat and pleasure he could from her.

It was inevitable. He had known it from the start. He had wanted her like this, flushed with passion and writhing against him, from the very first moment he had seen her long, trim calves and delicate ankles.

She was kissing him back, her hands raking through his hair, clutching him to her sleek, animalistic body, her improbably soft, full lips greedy and wanton opening to his. He slanted his mouth across hers to deepen the kiss. She tasted of rain and clean cold, and her essence mingled with the Scotch whiskey in his mouth to create a potent, heady brew. He was drinking her in like a man dying of thirst, parched to his core and gasping for the solace only she could give.

She made a hungry sound, and he swallowed it into his mouth as she arched against him, begging with her body for his touch.

And he could not wait. He could not breathe. He had to be in her.

There was no time for preliminaries. His fingers were at the buttons of his breeches and freeing his rod. His hands were too impatient to ascertain anything more than the glorious heat and slick entry to her body, before the blunt head of his cock found her unerringly. All he could do was appease the black vortex of his want and drive home into her with all the force of his raging need.

Yes. Oh, God, finally yes.

"No!" The shocking, inarticulate but unmistakable noise of agony and betrayal bounced off the walls of the small room, piercing the haze of his lust.

Hugh opened his eyes and pulled back enough to look at

her, to see her, pinned against the wall by the force of his body. She was strung as taught as a bow, not daring to move, her eyes shocked wide open. Not even daring to breathe.

And he knew. He felt. He understood.

She was, improbably, insistently, unmistakably a virgin. And he had fucked her against a wall.

"Christ," was all he could manage. He was appalled. He had acted appallingly.

And like that, he eased his brutal grip of her hips and let go. He stepped back. "I'm sorry."

"No, please," she gasped.

He could only see the misery he had brought as she hid her face and slid down the wall, her arms wrapped protectively around her middle to shield herself from any more of his brutality.

It was all his fault. She was his charge. His responsibility. He should have had greater restraint. He should have understood her protests. He should have been a gentleman.

"I'm sorry. Please. I'm leaving," he reassured her. "I won't bother you— I'm sorry."

He turned away and shoved himself back inside his breeches and buttoned up the fall as quickly as possible. Two more steps and he was at the door and through it. Leaning back against the stout wooden panel to catch his breath, to pull himself together.

The kitchen was mercifully and suspiciously empty. There wasn't a sound in the house, as if the boards and plaster were holding their breath to see what further havoc he was going to wreak.

What had she done? One moment he was kissing her and she was kissing him, every touch of his lips against hers felt like sparks exploding under her skin, and then he was gone. He had lit a bonfire in her body and then just walked away, leaving her charred to a cinder. He said something and turned on his booted heels and simply left. He didn't even have the good graces to limp, as if he'd been thoroughly worked over. As thoroughly worked over as she. He simply left her like she was garbage he no longer wanted to deal with. Worthless. Not worthy of his consideration. Once more, abandoned.

The pain reached all the way through her, from the sharp shock inside her belly all the way out to her fingertips. She felt as if he had left her in a hundred broken pieces, scattered over the floor like shattered glass. She would never fit back together again.

But she *had* to scrape herself together. She had to move and get away before he came back. She'd be damned if she ran out of another house into the rain with nothing but the clothes on her back. She'd be damned. She had warm, substantial clothing upstairs in her lovely attic room. And money. Enough for a hackney. Enough to get her a night at an inn. And she could go to see Mr. Levy in the morning to get her the rest of her money. There was no stopping her from having that.

Once in her room, she piled on everything woolen she owned. She didn't care that he had bought and paid for them. She had bloody well earned them, and she had every right— *every right*—to take them with her. The job was done, and it was time for her to move on.

Timmy wandered up with a slice of orange in his hand. "Whatcha doing?"

"Get your things," she ordered. "We're leaving."

"Don't be daft, Meggs." He laughed.

She snapped back, "Don't be bold. I told you to get your things."

"Jesus, Meggs. Why do you want to leave? It's warm and dry here. He feeds us up, every day, and the jobs are dead easy."

"Just get your clothes. Put them in here." Between them they probably didn't even have enough to fill the portmanteau.

"But Meggs, we ain't even ate. I don't wanna—"

"Shut up. Stop arguing. Just shut up and come."

"Jesus, Meggs." Timmy backed away, hurt and bewildered. She had never spoken to him like that before. She had never acted like that before. She had never felt like this before. As if she were simply broken. "I don't wanna go. I'm not going," he argued. "I'm gonna stay with him."

Meggs could no longer hide the feelings blistering to the surface. Everything, absolutely everything, was falling apart. Everything she had hoped and dreamed and planned was ruined. They were never going back to Tissington. She was never going to get married and have a quiet, happy life. Her life was ruined, and it was all *his* fault. God, she hated him. She hate, hate, hated him, and she couldn't spend another moment under his roof.

"Fine." She turned her back on Timmy, so he couldn't see the rush of useless tears filling her eyes, and finished her packing. The money took longer. She had salted it about the room, a few pounds here and there, under the lantern, stuffed in the mattress, under a drawer. The bulk was beneath a floorboard that didn't want to be pried up. It didn't help her eyes were so full of hot, angry tears she couldn't see.

She headed down the stairs, quiet as a dead mouse, but there he was, the captain, coming up the way she was going down. Timmy was with him, looking up at her. Traitor. He pointed, and the captain looked up to see her.

Damn him. He'd taken the only person she had to love.

"Meggs?" As the captain called up the staircase, she bolted for the backstairs.

"Meggs. Don't." His voice chased her up the stair. Tears were blurring her eyes, and she grabbed up her skirts and ran the whole way down, out into the kitchen past Mrs. Tupper and out the passageway toward the garden door. If she could make it to the gate—

"What on earth?" she heard Mrs. Tupper exclaim.

She had almost reached the door. The latch was under her hand. The door was open an inch, and the cold, damp, coal-fired smell of the night was filling her nose. And then his hand was over hers, pushing the door shut.

"Meggs. I'm sorry." His voice was at her ear. He was directly behind her, his hands wrapping around her upper arms, trying to hold her back. "I'm sorry."

"Let me go. Let me go. Why can't you just let me go?" She was crying now, damn her eyes. Sobbing like a ninny. She ought to be ashamed of herself, but it hurt so bad, all that raw feeling piled up high in her throat as if she had swallowed glass. Cut into a thousand pieces and leaking salty, stinging tears.

"I can't let you go," he whispered. "You know I can't."

He turned her by the shoulders and hauled her against his chest, and she was pressing herself into the wall of warmth, trying to hide. Sniffing and snuffling, and gasping for air like a bleeding mackerel.

"I'm sorry," he said over and over. "It was all my fault. I shouldn't have. I shouldn't—I'll make it up to you. Only don't go. Please. Stay."

"Please stay, Meggs." That was Timmy behind him, somewhere down the passage.

"Come now, lad," Mrs. Tupper chided. "You leave them be. Our Meggs isn't going anywhere this night. Catch her death out in this cold and damp, why I shouldn't be surprised . . ."

Her head was still bowed against his chest, the ends of her hair hanging down lankly around her ears. Hugh held on to her, crushing her against him, physically preventing her from leaving. He didn't have the words to convince her—all thought was drowned out by the furious panic clawing at his chest when he realized he had driven her away. He had done this.

But he could undo it.

"Please, for your own sake, at least stay the night. You can't go out into this filthy weather. If you still want to leave in the morning, I'll make arrangements. But please, don't just leave."

She took a deep, shuddering breath and turned her head to lay wearily against his chest, not fighting anymore. He lowered his lips to her forehead to try to show her with his mouth what he could not put into words—despite what he had done, she was precious to him.

His lips met her skin and came away singed. Hugh replaced his mouth with the back of his hand. She felt scorched. "Ah, Meggs, you're burning up. We've got to get you to bed."

"No!" She shot her hand out against the doorjamb.

"For God's sake, Meggs, I'm not going to bed you. I'm going to put you into a bed." Hugh scooped her up and carried her all the way up to the bedchamber adjoining his, the one that should have belonged to the lady of the house.

When he placed her on the bed, she immediately sat up and swung her legs off the side.

"No." He crowded her back. "You need to be in bed."

"I'll go to my room." Her tone was plaintive.

"No." He couldn't explain it. He needed her near. He needed to take care of her, but he wasn't prepared to sit up all night on top of a narrow spindly cot again when there were better arrangements at hand. "There's no fire there. This one's already laid." He suited action to words and stepped away from her to light the fire, keeping one eye on her huddled figure. She stayed put on the edge of the bed and finally moved to unwrap one of the shawls swaddling her body, but the effort seemed to exhaust her.

"Let me help." He began to undress her gently, but quickly. He thought to strive for the same sort of impersonal treatment he had given her when she had first arrived—that first prophetic bath—but somehow, after what he had just done, it seemed wrong. So he unravelled the shawls and pulled out her hairpins slowly, carefully, giving her time to accept his help, building her trust. But when he moved to take the pins out of her bodice, she jammed her elbows down tight and crossed her arms over her chest. "Lass," he coaxed, "I've seen you naked before. You're ill. You couldn't even sit up if you weren't so bloody stubborn. There's nothing holding you up but willpower. Mrs. Tupper will be up in a moment, but we've got to get you out of these clothes and into bed."

She allowed him to get her down to her chemise, and he left it at that. There was no sense in aggravating both of them. But when he knelt down to pull off her sturdy shoes and peel away her dark, woolen stockings, he couldn't miss the faint smear of blood on her inner thighs. He was stabbed by a jolt of remorse so fierce it damn near made him queasy. Damn him for a bloody savage.

Hugh retreated across the adjoining doors to his own dressing room to find and wet a flannel cloth in the basin. He returned to her and stood for a few moments in idiotic indecision before he simply handed it to her.

"You need to wipe . . . yourself off."

"I suppose so," she said in a small voice, as if she really didn't know, as if she had yet to understand what had happened, what was happening to her body. She wiped off her tear-stained face.

"No, lass, there's blood. On your . . . legs."

Two spots of hectic color burned their way high on her chalky cheeks. "Oh."

Damn him for a lunatic. She was a street urchin from the Cheapside docks, for God's sake. Surely she knew the basic facts of life? Surely a girl who was on a first-name basis with various Covent Garden whores knew? But then again, he had never, in a hundred years, expected her to be a virgin. He had not thought such a thing could be even remotely possible. But it had been. And he, of all people, should have seen it. He turned away. "I'll see to the fire."

When she was done, she dropped the cloth by the side of

the bed and crawled stiffly under the covers, curling into herself. Shutting him out.

Hugh pulled the bell pull, and in another minute, Mrs. Tupper trundled in.

"She's got a fever," he informed her as he opened the door.

"Oh, I knew it," she said as she came around the bed and laid a hand on Meggs's forehead. "I didn't like the look of her this evening. I just knew she'd taken a chill. Out in all that rain and cold. Open your mouth, lamb." Mrs. Tupper held up a candle and peered into her mouth. "Putrid throat," she pronounced.

"It's just dry." Meggs finally spoke. "If I might just have some tea, I'll be fine."

"Certainly tea. With lemon, if one can be found, and honey. And whiskey. And a hot mustard plaster."

Meggs made a sound of protest but only managed to let out a croak.

"Should I send for the doctor, Captain?" the housekeeper asked.

Meggs swallowed hard and insisted, "I'm not going to die of a stupid cold." He could hear the stubborn aggravation in her voice. "Just leave me alone. Please." She turned her back to him.

"Just the tea for now, thank you, Mrs. Tupper, and liberally laced."

When the housekeeper had departed, he moved closer to the bed. "Meggs."

"Please, go." Her voice was the merest whisper.

"In a moment." He had a few more things he wanted to say. "We have to talk, Meggs. Your virginity—"

She made a brusk sound of dismissal. "Hardly matters now," she muttered as she picked at the coverlet without looking at him.

"Stop it. Of course it does. Why didn't you tell me?"

"I did. I told you I wasn't a . . ."

"Whore. Yes, but there's a fair amount of middle ground be-tween virgin and whore, wouldn't you agree?" He shoved his hand through his hair, tugging at his scalp, trying quite liter-ally to get a grip on himself. "You might have told me."

She turned to look at him then—her gaze as level as a blade, no hiding. "You wouldn't have believed me."

She was right. He wouldn't. He hadn't. He'd seen and thought only what he'd wanted to think about her, only what his body had demanded he see. To take what was offered. "You told me you had been forced."

"Well, yes . . ." she scrunched up her face, remembering. "But not *that*."

"If not *that*, then what the hell were you talking about?"

"Forced to steal. Forced to live like rats, shivering together for warmth. Forced to eat garbage lying in the streets to stay bloody alive. Forced—" Her voice was giving out.

Damn him for an ass. "Shh. I'm sorry. I understand."

"No, you don't. You couldn't possibly."

"Forced to do things you're not proud of, to stay alive. I *do* understand."

She rolled up to sitting, and when she spoke, her voice was scratchy and raw but full of conviction. "I *am* proud, I don't care what you or anybody else says. I am proud of what I learned to do and how I kept us alive. I'm proud I made the best of it. I *refuse* to be ashamed, do you hear me?"

Hugh closed his eyes against the wash of recognition flood-ing through him. Oh, yes, he heard her. *Things only turned out best for those who were prepared to make the best of the way things turned out.* This was why he could not keep his distance from this girl. Because she was the echo of himself, stripped of the civilizing veneer. They were savages together, the two of them.

At least, that's what he had thought and why he had done what he'd done in her bath. It was what he *wanted* to believe.

But he had been wrong. He had lived in the world long

enough to know and understand the cost, what it must have been like, with the life she had been forced to live, to keep her body unto herself. It would have taken restraint, and self-discipline, and careful, careful vigilance. And he had ruined it. He had ruined her.

"Meggs. Lass, I know what I did with you—to you—hurt you badly. In more ways than one. I have no excuse, except to say I made a grave mistake, thinking that was what you wanted, too. And I'm sorry you didn't. I understand that now. But I've never wanted another woman the way I wanted—the way I still want—you."

He had wanted her from the very first moment she'd walked into his library and pitted will and her body against him. He'd wanted her when she had thrown her clothes at him and told him to burn them. He'd wanted her so badly, his balls had ached for days.

He still did. So when Mrs. Tupper brought the hot, sweet tea liberally lashed with laudanum, he stomped downstairs and locked himself in his study, where he got himself a drink. And then he got himself another. And another.

CHAPTER 19

Hugh was about to let the first Scotch whiskey of the morning smolder its way down his gullet when he saw the elegant, emblazoned carriage roll to a well-mannered stop at his front door. For a long moment, he thought seriously of going to ground and barring the door. It was why he had chosen to live in remote Chelsea in the first place, so he might avoid unnecessary visitations of this kind.

But hiding would be cowardly, and he was not a coward.

He was standing in the front hall behind Jinks, having discarded the drink, and straightened his coat and cravat when she was announced.

"The Viscountess Balfour, Captain."

"Hello, Mother." He kissed the soft satin of her cheek.

"Hello, darling. Thank you."

"May I show you in?" He held his arm out toward the door of the study.

"Not up?" She glanced up the staircase in the general direction of the drawing room. "Still no chairs?"

"Nary a one."

"Well," she sighed, "I live in hope."

He settled her into one of the leather chairs before the fire.

She looked light and bright, and entirely out of place, an exotic, tropical bird with her beautiful white hair and her cheerful lavender gown and lace. Even nearing fifty she was still as elegant, graceful, and stylish as she had been in his youth, though the fine merino wool of her high-waisted gown couldn't be much of a match for the chill she claimed made her feel arthritic. But she probably kept fires lit in every hearth at her elegant town house in Mayfair, unlike his inhospitable self. "May I offer you some refreshment?"

"Ah. Yes, please, tea would be lovely. Thank you." She drew off her bonnet and shook the droplets of rain onto the hearth. "Such dreadful weather."

"Now, to what do I owe the pleasure of this visit? Especially in such dreadful weather?"

"You needn't take that tone. You sound like your father. I came to visit."

"You came to meddle in my business and to tell me I ought to marry."

"Gracious, no!" She frowned at him. "You're hardly fit for civil drawing room conversation, let alone charming some poor girl into marriage. You'd make an absolute mess of it. Whatever put such a thought in your head?"

He couldn't possibly answer her. He strove *not* to look at the ceiling. *Not* to think about who was up there, in a bed, just beyond the ceiling plaster.

When he didn't answer she continued. "I've only come to see you. To see how you get on."

"I get on just fine."

"Yes, I can see that you do. You look stronger. More vital. Your limp has become hardly noticeable. It can only mean this hermetic life you've chosen does suit you."

"Mother, I'm hardly a hermit."

"All right," she conceded with a smile, "this *private* life you've chosen. It seems to suit you. I'm glad. Though we hardly ever see you."

He snorted.

"You know I only want to see you well and happy."

"I know nothing of the kind."

"Don't be so contrary. It's an unattractive habit. Terrible. Your father never could break himself of it. But you"—she bestowed upon him a warm, beatific smile—"are a better man. Self-disciplined and intelligent. You get that from me."

"So I do." Actually, he had gotten self-discipline, as well as most other forms of discipline, from the Royal Navy, but he didn't argue with her. It would only prolong her visit. Not that he didn't love her, or wasn't secretly pleased by her call, but she was as curious and sly as a fox. Another ten minutes and she'd sniff out the girl asleep upstairs like a scent hound. "And *you* are too self-disciplined to have come here without a purpose."

She bestowed a smile upon him as if he were still ten, and her pleasure was his reward for being so clever. "Just so. I am hosting a dinner party, and I find my numbers have come to an inconvenient and unlucky thirteen. I need you to put on your uniform and fill a chair."

"Merely fill it? I won't have to talk to unmarried, eligible girls?"

"A few, perhaps, but there will be only one you'll have to speak to at any length, at dinner. But you needn't worry—she won't do for you at all. She's a hearty country girl—your aunt Lucille's niece on her husband's side—and from what I understand, very managing. We'll find a nice, befuddled vicar for her to marry and manage, but dear Balfour doesn't want one at his dinner. A vicar, that is. Political people mostly, but Balfour asked for you especially. You know he admires you."

He did know, but he hadn't given any thought to turning his place as favorite stepson to his advantage. " 'Know how to keep your mouth shut at the right time,' was, I believe, his opinion."

"High praise, in his view. And he's right. You do understand all these political subtleties, though I know you don't care for them yourself. Nor do I. Intrigues." She shook her head as if the machinations of the House of Lords were beyond her feeble, feminine abilities, when she was as shrewd as a vixen. That was probably why Viscount Balfour had married her. If there was another reason, he chose not to think about it. She was, after all, his mother.

"So you'll come? It would be a very great favor to me, darling. And you aren't doing anything but getting better, clearly. Look at all these books. You ought to get some help in. But what you really need is a quiet evening out, every now and again."

What he needed was a not so quiet evening *in*. In bed, with the young lady upstairs, convincing her, he did understand more things than she . . .

"Hugh? Are you quite all right?" His mother was peering at him in concern.

"Hardly a quiet evening, when I'll have to pretend to listen attentively to some girl's enthusiasm for the Briarly-St. Badgley church fete."

His mother's smile was somehow all the more charming when she tilted her head that way. It was like a secret weapon, that tilt. It made him ridiculously willing to please her.

"But there. No other young man would even *understand* the need to listen attentively to the planning of a village fete. You must come. I won't take no for an answer. It's this evening, of course, so set that disreputable valet of yours to brushing your blues and shining up all that gold braid."

"If I wear my uniform, I'll outshine your country girls in all their pale muslins."

"But you're not for the country girls, so it doesn't signify. Wear the dress uniform."

It was against naval custom for an officer who was not on duty to wear his uniform. His mother knew that. And yet she had insisted. It must mean her husband had heard of his success with Admiral Middleton. Clearly his family was burgeoning with spies of every sort. All the more reason for his mother to depart. "I'll come."

"Eight o'clock." She rose and let him kiss her again. "I knew I could count on you. Balfour will be so pleased."

But what she meant was that *she* was already pleased. And really, whatever machinations she was up to, that was all that ought to matter. "I hope he will."

He saw her down the steps and to the carriage himself.

Hugh tried to keep himself busy writing all the necessary reports for Admiral Middleton, but after his mother left, the house was too quiet. Jinks had taken Timmy out with him on one of his errands or another. Hugh found himself wandering from room to empty room. Trying to keep himself occupied, trying to keep from admitting all he wanted to do was watch *her* sleep. Feast his eyes on the sight of Meggs unmasked, unprotected by that formidable veneer of distrust and cleverness.

But when he entered the room, her dark eyes were open and, he wanted to think, a little less wary. "How are you feeling?"

She slowly pushed herself up to sitting and crisscrossed her legs beneath the covers, like a lazy cat arranging itself. She was, perhaps, still at bit muzzy from the laudanum. "Who was your lady friend?"

The lawn nightdress was draping itself interestingly across her shoulders and breasts. Hugh was sure he could see the sweet, pink crests beneath the sheer fabric. He moved away to busy himself at the fire.

"I don't have a *lady friend*."

She let out the smallest huff of scorn. "Then who was she? She smelled beautiful. The whole house is perfumed with her—gardenia and something else. Is she your mistress?"

"Good God, lass. If you didn't notice, she's old enough to be my—"

"Didn't look that old. Didn't move like she was old, though I didn't get a good look at her face from the window. All bedaubed in lace she was. Even her hat. She was a prime article."

"She will be eminently flattered to hear you think so. She is my mother."

There was a long pause as she tried in vain to control some emotion. It proved itself, as it so often did, to be cheek. Sweet, opiate-influenced cheek. "Fancy *you* having a mother. And here I thought you'd sprung straight from the loins of the devil himself." But she smiled a little in that saucy way of hers, amused by her own joke.

God help him. He was going to choke on wanting her when she was soft and sweet, and half undressed.

"I have to go out this evening, to a dinner. It will involve tidying up business with the admiral, I expect." He let himself walk closer so he could see the luminous light in her dark, glossy eyes. "Meggs, I want to talk to you when I return. We haven't spoken since yesterday, and I want to make sure you aren't still thinking of leaving."

It was a long, excruciatingly uncomfortable minute, while his blood pounded in his ears, before she replied. She spoke quietly, but she tossed up that shoulder to try to shrug off the truth. "Don't have anywhere else to go."

He picked up her hand and kissed it. "You don't need anywhere else to go. You belong here."

Hugh presented himself at the Balfour town house on Berkley Square at precisely one minute after eight o'clock in the evening, even though he knew his mother could not intend to serve dinner until at least nine and he would have to endure a full hour of the Briarly-St. Badgley miss.

So he was surprised when Balfour immediately strong-armed him into the midst of a group of influential lords. Hugh wasn't sure if the attention was a reprieve, or a sentence, but he couldn't help but be pleased to be singled out by Balfour's praise.

"Can't tell you how pleased we are to hear of your success. My stepson has been approved for the King's honors, in consequence of his numerous exemplary offices for the Crown. You're to be congratulated, Captain."

Hugh would have been more pleased simply to be given back command of a ship to secure his future success, but beggars—especially beggars to the Board of Admiralty—couldn't be choosers. "I thank you, sir."

And he certainly wouldn't have chosen Major Rawsthorne for a dinner companion. Hugh was exceptionally surprised to find him part of the group. But his mother had said it would be "political." So he had been warned.

"Major Rawsthorne." Hugh acknowledged the introduction with a small bow. "Didn't know you were acquainted with Viscount Balfour."

"I make it my business to know everything about men of influence. And about the people I become acquainted with in the course of my duties."

Such posturing, such playing of roles and donning of metaphorical masks. Hugh wished Meggs were with him to see it all and to amuse him with one of her characteristically blunt, colorful observations. She would know exactly how to take these people.

What a load of prittle-prattle, she would probably say of the evening. On the other hand, he was sure she would have enjoyed watching and cataloging all the characters: the hearty country girl, the sophisticated London miss, the elegant and gracious matron. The generous patron and the bluff young Lord. Even the insidious, professional bastard.

"You've come up roses for old Middleton, at the Admiralty.

Young Captain McAlden here has managed quite a nice little piece of intelligence work," Rawsthorne announced to the group. "We might want to recruit him."

So much for Admiral Middleton's request for discretion. Clearly Rawsthorne had none. But that was, of course, Rawsthorne's modus operandi, to puff up himself, and his service, at the expense of others. But it gave Hugh leave to dislike Rawsthorne more than ever. "I thank you for the offer, but no. The navy suits me perfectly."

"No? Just as well. Although you might want to take some advice—the benefit of greater experience. I'll warn you against 'going native,' as we used to say in India. Don't want to get too comfortable with the lower classes, even in London. I shouldn't like to warn you here, in your mother's home, but it won't do to, how should I say, dabble with the servants. Not good breeding."

Hugh forced himself not to react. Not to reach out and choke the life from the bastard. Just because Rawsthorne was an unmitigated ass and no gentleman was no reason to ruin his mother's dinner party with a satisfying bloodletting. And he wouldn't be effective helping Admiral Middleton if he made a public spectacle.

But Rawsthorne misunderstood Hugh's silence and laughed in derision. "You see, you're not the only one who knows how to find out things people want to keep hidden."

"Hidden? You are mistaken. My life is an open book. Anyone may see I serve the navy at all times."

"Yes, even when you're on half pay as an invalid. It does help to have additional help in such times." He looked meaningfully at Viscount Balfour.

Stupid, blind, pompous bastard. It was one thing for Rawsthorne to take his verbal potshots at Hugh—he was fair game. But Rawsthorne stepped over the line when he included Meggs, and now his stepfather in his careless talk. Discretion be damned. Two could play this game. "I imagine it does. It is a comfort to know I reached my rank before my mother had even met Viscount Balfour. But is there someone here of particular influence you'd like me to introduce *you* to?"

If he was going to burn his bridges, he might as well strike the match. And he was in the mood for a bloody bonfire.

CHAPTER 20

Hugh was not used to hangovers. They were as new as the guilt that dragged at his conscience like a sea anchor over his behavior to Meggs—he had never before earned either condition. And so, head in hands to halt the vicious, queasy pounding behind his eyeballs, and slowly nursing down a mug of bitter, black coffee, he was singularly unprepared when Meggs waltzed into his study first thing the next morning with her armor of worldly derision firmly in place.

"So what's it to be, now, if I'm not to be a mop squeezer? Learning to become a courtesan or mistress, I suppose? Learning how to fuck men's secrets out of them?"

She might as well have slapped him.

"Is that what you think?" he growled over the bitterness lodged in his throat. Did she know him so little to think he'd do such a thing? How could she think that, after the careful, respectful way he had been treating her? Damn her eyes for still not trusting him when he had done everything in his power to prove himself trustworthy. If that's the way she was going to act, he was through with masquerading as a gentleman. "Well then, if you insist, we ought to get started right away. Take your clothes off so I can have a good look at you."

"What?" She was stunned, as shocked as he'd been by her

accusation. Good. Two could play this game. He let the unworthy surge of satisfaction goad him on.

"Isn't that what a pimp, a flash man, would do? Get a good
look at his merchandise? I didn't take a good long look at you
the other night. But from what I remember, I'd say we'll need
to fatten you up a bit. You're a trifle on the sleek side. A man
doesn't want a lathy wench. A man likes a woman pillowy."

She was staring at him as if she'd never seen him before.
Good. She'd been warned. He'd told her he was a hard, hard
man.

"That's what you assumed, wasn't it? That I would want to
turn you into a courtesan? Courtesans need to be soft and
voluptuous. A courtesan's body is her weapon. I have absolutely no doubt that in time, you could learn to become
quite lethal."

"I don't think—" she broke off, enraged and hurt. Her
voice, and indeed her whole body, was trembling.

"You do *think*. You think so fast, you could give yourself
whiplash. You were thinking I'm such a prick, I would *fuck*
you, take your maidenhead, simply for the expediency of getting you to spread your legs for other men."

She blanched, the only traces of color in her face two spots
high on her cheeks. She turned away, toward the door. "You
flash bastards are all alike. You spout all noble—"

He was around the desk and had his hand hard on her wrist
before she could move a foot. "Alike, are we? Is that why you
offered your body to me in that bathtub, because I'm like
every other man? Is that why I kept my hands off you for
weeks and weeks until I was fit to be strangled with wanting
you? Is that why I left you, rather than take advantage of what
you had so stupidly and blatantly offered? Rather than start
your 'training' by giving you a thorough fucking right then and
there, against the wall, like a three-penny uprighter in a doorway?"

She struggled, pulling her arm away, so he hauled her back

against his chest. He loomed over her from behind, his lips at her ear.

"How foolish of me, to think I wanted you for *myself*. For *your* own self. How foolish of me to want *your* body. Your scent. Your skin." He let his hand snake around her tiny waist and move lower, pressing his palm flat against the hollow of her belly, holding her against him and letting her feel his body surrounding hers. "Do you really think I would treat your body as if it were merchandise—mine to do with as I wanted?"

She wouldn't answer. Her silence battered at him, driving him on. He could feel the tattered remnants of his careful self-control tearing away. He reached up and speared his fingers through her ruined hair, fingering the blunt, uneven strands. "If I ran you like a pimp, I would never have allowed you to cut your hair. A courtesan has lovely, flowing hair. Hair that a man could run his hands through and tangle his fingers in, to pull her head back, so he could tongue and kiss her."

He suited action to words, dragging apart the careful attempt she had made to put up her hair, pulling out the pins and tugging her head back and exposing the long, vulnerable slide of her throat. He set his teeth to graze against her sensitive skin, and she shivered, her shallow breath echoing softly into his ears. Ruthlessly, he drove her on.

"A man likes long hair." He let his hand slide deliberately lower over her skirts, down her belly to her mound. He lowered his voice to a rough whisper. "Except here."

She swallowed hard, and the pulse along her throat leapt. "No."

"Yes. Especially here. Courtesans are well groomed all over. The object is to display their sex. I would have done some . . . judicious trimming so your cunny would have been displayed to advantage."

He felt the tight tension coil through her body, and the movement resounded through him, roaring through his blood.

"Oh, yes. Foolish of me, not to have done. I would have enjoyed barbering you."

Her eyes slid closed, and her lips fell open in shock. And
arousal. He felt her body's surrender, and a carnal mixture of
lust and triumph poured into his veins, allaying the savagery
of his need.

"And I would have made sure you enjoyed it, too. Very
much. I would have made you feel the same want and hunger
I feel. And I think all this belligerent talk is just an excuse. An
excuse to make me see you as a woman. Let there be no doubt
in your mind—I do. I see you. I want you." He cupped his
hand firmly around her sex; he could feel her heated pulse.
"You're throbbing. And warm. I wonder if you're getting wet.
Shall we see? Shall we see if you actually want me as much as
I have wanted you?" He lowered his voice to an intimate
whisper. "Shall you open your legs for me and let me see?"

Slowly, inexorably, so she would feel every last inch of material as it dragged over her legs, he began to gather up her
skirts. Her hands opened wide in the air, not daring to touch
him, but needing some anchor, fingers searching vainly until
she grasped them tight into fists.

Looking down over her shoulder, he pressed flat into her
belly with one hand, and with the other he pulled her skirts
away so that she was naked from the waist down except for
her stockings. The coarse black wool was a shocking, deca-
dent contrast to her smooth white thighs. The erotic image
burned itself into his brain. His mouth went dry, and the air in
his chest grew heated and tight. His erection pulsed against
the thick wool twill of his breeches.

She tried to cross her legs, to hide herself. He stilled her
with a firm hand on her thigh.

"God. Look at you. Look at yourself." He drew her legs
apart so he could see that dark triangle of soft curls covering
the entrance to her sex. "How could you think I would want to

share you with any other man? How could you think I would let anyone else inside you? How could you not know, I wanted only you, and you alone?"

"I didn't—"

"You do now. I can see you. I can see what my touch—*my touch*—does to you and your body."

"Please." She was shaking her head, her whole body trembling under his hands.

He would ease her fear. He would replace it with longing. A longing as fierce and powerful as his own. "Oh, I will please you, Meggs. I will." He rubbed his jaw along the slide of her cheek. "You're already pleasing me. Open your legs wider for me so I can touch you. So I can begin to please you."

Her chest was rising and falling erratically, but she opened, slowly inching her thighs apart. The moment she did so, he speared one long finger into her silken warmth. Her knees buckled as she made an inarticulate but unmistakable sound of surrender.

Her passage clenched around him, and his own blood thundered in his ears, the force of his arousal leaving him nearly shaking. He moved to stand in front of her, to tip her face up with one hand while he stroked her passage with the other.

Nothing was going to stop him from having her. But not like this. Not on any old piece of furniture that came to hand. Not in the middle of the room, where Mrs. Tupper or Jinks could come upon them. Not carelessly. Not this time.

He had waited years to have the right woman. This woman. No other. He wanted to take her fiercely, but with deliberation. "I want you upstairs. Privately. Behind a locked door. Face to face, so you know the man who's making love to you. So you know it's me inside you and no other."

Hugh lofted her up against his chest and carried her up the stairs, taking the steps two at a time in his rush to get her up to his room. She hid her face against his neck and said nothing. But she did not protest.

He set her down and turned away to thumb the lock, surprised to find his hands shaking and fumbling at the task. But he had waited so very long, his body could no longer hold his desire in check.

When he turned back, she was standing halfway to the bed, her face turned to the window, pale and still. Unreadable. He tried to make his voice soft to hide the sharp, jagged edge of his need. "Meggs."

She looked up at him, her eyes wide and dark in her pale face. So dark, trying to hide an ocean of fear. Making choices was always frightening.

"Are we going to do this? Together, of our own free will?"

"I . . . Please do—" She stopped, struggling as if she couldn't breathe.

"Please what? You have to tell me, Meggs."

She stood before him, trembling, her breath rising and falling in audible agitation. But she looked him in the eye. "Promise you won't leave me again. I couldn't bear it if you leave."

"Shh. Easy now." He took her hands with his own and kissed each palm, then took her face in his hands and kissed away the salt tears until he found her exquisitely full lips. He opened his mouth to kiss her slowly. Gently, softly. "Sweet Meggie. Easy, love, easy."

He pulled her tight into his embrace and held her there as if it were the most right thing that had ever happened to him, as if she belonged there, as if he never had to let her go. "I promise."

Slowly, as if they had all the time in the world, so slowly he could savor each and every moment, each and every sensation and press it upon his memory, he kissed her. Slowly, so she could cry off and stop at any moment. Slowly, so she could choose to go each and every step of the way, he peeled off her clothes, one by one. He took his time, watching and feeling, seeking out each bit of newly bared skin with his eyes and his fingers.

Her body was finely made. Her skin under her clothes was white and pale, a contrast to the brown of her neck and her arms—testimony to a life lived out of doors, working, making a living. Just like him.

He had told her a man liked a pillowy body, but all he wanted was her, this sleek woman-girl. This lass, as slender as a lath, aroused him as nothing and no one ever had. He had said he would have changed her, made her different, but there was nothing he would change about her now.

He wanted to discover everything, to explore every part of her. Her hands—her fingers long and tapered, so quick and agile. So skilled, so erotic. Her scent—he slid his nose along her neck and into the blunt, fine silk of her hair, to inhale the intoxicating scent of her, of subtle roses—the soap he had purchased for her.

She was still afraid, her body quaking like a loose sail, even as she pressed herself to him, burrowing against him, and clasping her hands tight around his waist. So when he had her down to her shift, he picked her up and put her in the bed, under the covers, and set himself away from her to undress himself.

And he did this slowly as well to savor the way it felt to bare his body for her eyes, to know the next thing he would feel, after the air on his skin, was her body, soft and warm next to him. And when he was stripped, and his rampant erection jutted from his loins, he stood and let her look at him. Let her choose again.

She reached out one hand to the flesh covering his ribs, her touch light and tentative as if she could not quite believe he was real.

"I don't know what to do," she admitted. "I don't—"

"Shh." Hugh climbed onto the bed and kissed her quiet, caressing her with his mouth and his hands, running his fingers down the bare skin of her arm and then back up to trace the delicate line of her collarbone. The taste of her was like a drug he had not known he craved, exotic and intoxicating.

"We'll go slow, and wait for you to catch up." He kissed the hollow at the base of her throat. "And I'll tell you how beautiful you are. And how long I've wanted to kiss you."

Meggs had no defense to such piercing sweetness. Something inside her eased, even as other parts shifted restlessly. "I don't want to go slowly," she whispered. "I just want you to want me."

His mouth at first whispered across hers, his lips somehow both firm and soft against her skin, lulling her with their gentleness and, luring her into a new world of tender sensation.

"No. Please," she heard herself beg. "I've been so lonely. I don't want to be alone anymore." She closed her eyes against the hot sting of tears and opened her mouth against the pulse of his neck. The beat was strong and hectic, and she nuzzled against his rough skin with her nose and mouth, smelling and tasting him, breathing in his warmth and strength. "Please."

He cradled her jaw and kissed her more deeply, hungrily even, pulling her into him with strong, purposeful hands. "Show me," he breathed. "Make me understand."

How could she make him understand, when she didn't understand herself? She felt as if she might shake apart with all the worry and need trapped inside, scratching and clawing its way out. But along with the fear was this overwhelming compulsion to bind him to her. Her hand was already fisting hard in his short hair, pulling it taut between her fingers, holding him tight so he had no choice but to stay.

His answer was a welcome growl. "God, yes, that's it."

She closed her eyes and concentrated on the welcome force of his kisses, on his firm mouth, moving insistently on hers.

"Open your mouth to me." The dark promise of his low voice vibrated through her. Desire blossomed along her skin and began to melt into her bones. When he ran his fingers over her chemise, down the swell of her breast to pluck at the peaks hidden beneath the fabric, she made a fierce, needy sound. Her body arced into the rough friction of his hand, pressing her breasts against him to feel more of the drugging sensation. He tugged the shift down impatiently, molding his palms around her aching breasts. She gasped as his calloused fingers rasped against her sensitized flesh and sent hard darts of delight shooting through her. Then he gathered her nipples like ripe berries between his fingers, rolling them firmly until the pleasure went careening every which way inside her. When his mouth followed his hands, Meggs thought she would break into a hundred pieces at the exquisite contrast of his warm mouth and cool teeth.

She clutched at the strong, curving muscles of his upper arms, anchoring herself to him. His body was fiercely beautiful with its heavy covering of muscle over bone. His skin was warm and golden with a light sprinkling of golden hair across his chest. He was a marvel of heat and light, strength and power. She dragged her palms up over his shoulders and hard across the flat nipples.

He groaned at her touch, a deep sound of satisfaction, so she did it again, pressing her hands more deeply into his muscles, taking longer to trace the curve of his chest and the interesting ridges of his stomach.

When he rose over her like this and stroked her body, so fiercely, so intent in his need to give her pleasure, how could she not give herself to him? How could she not open her body and soul up to him? She wanted, she needed, to feel him next to her, skin to skin. She grasped the hem of her shift, and he sat up to help her peel the last barrier away from her body.

"Tell me you're sure," he ground out. "Tell me you want this. You want me." His eyes, pale and molten, burned into her.

"Please."

"Say it," he insisted.

"I want this. I want you."

His mouth crashed down hard, pressing her lips open and heating her from the inside, the blistering sensation of his tongue rough against hers. Pouring himself into her, filling her with his need. "Say my name."

"Hugh," she breathed into his mouth. "I want you, Hugh."

She repeated his name over and over, like an incantation, as he came down hard on top of her, licking and sucking at her breasts. His body felt strange and immediate against her skin, sleek and sliding, and then rough and prickling as his legs intertwined and tangled with hers. His hands dove into her hair, turning and angling her head to his advantage. He kissed every part of her face—her eyebrows and her nose, her cheeks and the corner of her mouth—with a thorough desperation, as if he could not get enough of her taste.

Meggs kissed him back, loving the whiskey tang of his mouth, savoring the texture of his raspy skin abrading hers, and glorying in the weight of his body pressing her firmly into the mattress. She wanted to discover everything about him, experience every texture and taste. She loosened her grip on his hair, brushing it against her palms like newly mown wheat.

She wanted . . . something to ease the fist of tension that was a pain deep inside her, between her legs. Every sensation that began somewhere else—her skin, her hands, her breasts—plummeted deep within and ricocheted back, spreading and radiating through her body. She was breathless with it, breathing in pants and gasps as if she had run a long way. But she was running toward something, not away. Toward Hugh. And with him, toward pleasure. Toward desire.

Her hips had begun to rock against him, sending sparks of urgency sizzling across her skin.

He watched her move with hunger stark in his eyes. "Look at you. You're perfect." He traced his hands down her flanks to her hips, skimming across her belly and spanning her pelvis with his large hand. He pulled the linen completely away. "I want to look at you. I want to see you. All of you."

Heat like a wave roared across her skin and burned deep as his hand slipped lower, tangling his fingers in her curls and stroking her thighs, then pushing them apart. The unholy tightness within her reached such a pitch, she felt as if she were going to break apart, shattering into splinters of feelings.

"I've wanted for so long to touch you," he whispered as he slid a single, long finger inside her.

This time, the sweet pain came from within her, from wanting more of this, more of the sweet, slippery friction. He moved his hand subtly, and the tension inside her grew tighter still. His hands drew across her like a bow upon a fiddle, and she felt undone. Her legs were open, she had opened them, and his knees were pushing them farther apart. And another finger joined the first inside her, pushing, stretching harder now. He turned his hand within her, and his thumb brushed lightly across her flesh.

She made a sound, part anguish and part demand, as her body bucked up of its own accord, seeking, demanding what it wanted. What he could give her.

He kissed her more roughly now, and she kissed him back, wanting the fierceness, wanting the strength and push and surfeit of feeling. His breath came harsh and ragged in her ear. "I can't. My God, Meggs, I need you. I want—"

"Yes."

"Tell me you—"

She didn't even wait for him to say the words. "Yes. Please. I want you—"

And he was pressing against the tight heat, pushing into her and filling her from the inside with sensation and weight, pinning her to the earth, and to her own body, so she wouldn't fly away from herself. "God, Meggs."

He looked hurt, almost anguished, as he rose above her, his hands sliding up to rest beside her head, tangling in her hair.

She reached to him, to stroke his face, to ease his pain. He kissed her hand and began to move within her, tentatively at first, watching her face with those pale, hot eyes. She closed her eyes to the first hot rush of pleasure and smiled, letting the heat and the light that came from him wash over her. She was drowning in the pleasure he gave her.

"Yes." When she whispered that word, just one simple word of encouragement, everything changed.

His body shuddered above her with some inexpressible emotion. The sound that tore out of him was one of barely contained savagery, a growl of hunger and unappeased need. And his body moved to follow, pushing and rocking into hers with a building force, making heat and need pound through her in a headlong rush.

She needed—she wanted. Her hands were clutching at him, her palms tingling with feeling that ran rampant through her body. Her legs were moving, pushing, helping her to rise to meet his thrusting hips. She planted her feet flat against the sheets and pushed up, and white heat blazed from the harsh, cataclysmic joining of their bodies.

He came up on his knees between her legs and reared back, clasping her roughly by the hips and pulling her straight into him. She must have cried out. She heard the keening sound echo around his chamber, but she was too lost to the fire of his body and the strength of the pleasure rocketing through her. Over and over, wave after wave of deepening bliss rolled through her, pushing her closer and closer, urging her higher.

And his hand grappled its rough way across the scoop of her belly, and his fingers grazed across her, there, and drenching heat and blissful icy water exploded in her belly, and she was gone.

CHAPTER 21

She came back to herself slowly, floating down as if her body were a river, free and flowing within its own banks. And Hugh was right there next to her, holding her, touching her, stroking his hand lightly along the length of her skin. It was strange and wonderful, this physical closeness, this intimacy. He seemed not to have exhausted his curiosity about her body. He was looking at her hair, running the choppy strands through his hands carefully.

"I am sorry I upset you by cutting it." Her voice was small, as if it traveled a long distance to arrive at her lips.

"Shh. No matter," he murmured, and kept touching her, making her feel new inside herself, as though she had never fully used her senses before. Then, he rolled up on one elbow to look at her, with one of his legs angled across hers, and contradicted himself by asking, "Why did you?"

She automatically tried to shrug away the question, but he was too close.

"Tell me."

"I was scared. I suppose, I wasn't really thinking. I wanted to make sure the papers were dry, and I was getting soaked. And cold. So I went to the rag traders, and then, I thought it would be best, if they were looking for a girl, that I be a boy.

It's always easier to go about unmolested at night if you're a boy. And I didn't think it mattered."

"It doesn't. All that matters is you got back safely." He gathered her to him, her back tucked snug against his chest.

"And that you got the evidence you needed? Then you're not angry?"

"No." His words vibrated through her body as he shifted subtly behind her. "Does this feel like I'm angry?"

His mouth came down to gently kiss and worry at that spot, that sensitive place where her collarbone met the side of her neck. Sensation flared anew under her skin.

"No." She wondered if he could hear the capitulation and encouragement in her voice. "But you said you didn't like it."

"I've changed my mind." He ran his hands through her hair, over and over, tugging and drawing it out, fanning it through his fingers. Stroking her like a cat. "I've decided to be enthralled. Because now I can see the back of your neck all the time without moving your hair. I can use my hands to do other, more interesting things." His palm slid around her hip to span her belly and then stroke lower.

She closed her eyes and felt the glorious heat of him all around her, surrounding and pressing into her, fanning her arousal to life. She wanted more. More of his heat and his comfort. More of the intensity of his unwavering focus. More. "Yes. Please."

He took her permission to steal both hands around her hips and arrange her legs so she was open to his touch. She let him, surrendering her will gladly to the coming pleasure.

"Is this what you want?" he asked as he slid one long finger into her flesh, his palm warm and rough against her mound.

"Yes." She could feel the hot strength of his erect rod against her bottom, and she arched back against him, seeking the exquisite friction of his body and his hands.

"You're wet," he rasped into her ear. "Your body is ready for me."

"*I'm* ready for you," she answered.

And then, in one strong movement, he rolled her forward onto her belly and came over her, pressing her down into the mattress. The air whooshed out of her lungs on a gasp as the weight and strength of his body settled over her.

"Hugh?" His name felt strange upon her lips. Everything felt strange. He was kissing the skin along her shoulders, loving her with little biting nips that sent shocking rays of sensation shooting down deep into her belly. She shouldn't like it so. "Hugh!"

"Hush." He laced his fingers through hers on the sheets. "Does it feel good?" He let his glorious body slide along hers, rubbing against her. The shocking little sensations intensified and ignited a low fire of tension that built between her legs. She clenched down the feeling, but it only brought tight waves of yearning pulsing up from her belly, pushing higher through her whole body. Crushed against the mattress, her breasts began to swell and ache for his touch. She tried to push back against him, to appease the chaos of sensation rioting through her, but he held her down with the weight and power of his body above hers. His large palm settled into the small of her back, holding her still before him. "Do you trust me?"

She didn't know what to answer. She didn't trust anything, not even the waves of pleasure lapping at her belly.

"I'm going to teach you to trust me," he whispered into her ear. "I'm going to teach you to trust this." He reached between them and stroked his hand up the cleft of her bottom.

Her body knew the answer, rising up into his hand, his touch. But she did trust him, far more than she trusted herself. Because she knew already what she had given up to have this—this man's possession of her body—and feared what more she would be willing to give.

"Open to me," he pleaded in a gritty voice. Her body reacted to his words with a spike of lust that made her clench and spasm in opposition. The feeling intensified as he impatiently urged her to comply, kneeing her legs farther apart. "Yes."

She could hear the urgency in his voice and breathing, and she could feel it in his heavy, possessive touch. And it felt good to know she pleased and aroused him in return. She had gained power as well by putting herself into his control.

The thought sent another wave, shocking in its intensity, careening under her skin, urging her on, urging her to abandon herself to the power of his body. Of his need for her.

Her own need, to possess and be possessed, to love and be loved, rose in response.

He sat back on his heels and ran his hands slowly around the curve of her bottom, dragging his palms and fingers down the long muscles of her legs to her ankles. She felt the heat of his gaze and the touch of his hand opening her flesh, readying her for his entrance, arranging her for his pleasure. The liquid heat of her body rose like a tide inside of her, carrying her along on the ocean of her surging need. Carrying her toward him, toward the pleasure that awaited just out of reach.

And then he put his hands upon her hips and surged into her with a strength that shocked a cry from her mouth. Her body bucked up into his, defiant and eager in its need.

"Hush." He came over her, to push her deep into the mattress, to still her with his weight and his body. He covered her hands with this own and laced his fingers through hers. "Hold on," he instructed.

And she did. She gripped his hands as if she could hold herself to the earth while his body created heat, and need, and bliss within her. He took her with fierce sweetness, strong and unyielding, while murmuring encouragement into her ear. She could not keep from crying out in wonder every time he rocked into her body, sending what little thought remained spinning into endless sensation. Meggs closed her eyes and held tight to herself, resisting the urge to let go, to hurl herself off this cliff of jagged passions.

Her cries only served to inflame him, her capitulation to encourage him. He let go of her hands to hold her hips and thrust harder, deeper. Held captive, surrounded by his body, his heat and scent, she could only feel him and his possession. She could only welcome his dominion over her body. His hands ranged over her back, around her shoulder, and down to steal under her chest. She pushed herself up on her arms so he could reach her aching breasts and roll the tight peaks between his thumb and forefingers, the rough abrasion sending fierce stabs of arousal twining with the pleasure coiling deep in the pit of her belly.

He lifted her up and onto her knees before him, then pulled her back against his chest. Every feeling, every sensation intensified. The cool of the air against her heated skin, the aching bliss of his hands, rough on her body, rasping at her nipples and then lower. The pleasure and the heat of his skin behind hers. The sweet friction of his body plunging into hers, sending liquid fire billowing under her skin.

"Meggs. Meggs," he called, and there was desperation and triumph in his voice, and he pitched her forward and plunged into her with ferocious, searing abandon. And then with a suddenness that shocked her, she came apart, flying away, soaring upward into the sky.

She woke up warm, as warm as she'd ever been, but devilishly hungry and uncomfortable. Her hand hurt from being slept on. By him. The source of all the delicious warmth. And noise. He made a deep breathing noise as he lay on his back with one arm thrown over his head. All male strength and abandon.

She inched her arm free and debated going in search of food. Instead, she spent the moment looking at him, strange and curiously blank in repose. Meggs didn't think she liked the way he looked asleep—inanimate, all his cares and concerns erased and pushed far away. She liked him awake, with those intensely searching eyes alert and sharply focused. Full of cagey, raw energy. Strong and reliable.

Oh, Lord help her, but she wanted to rely on him. Just this once, she wanted to let go of all the plans and strategies and just be here, in his bed, in his arms. For a little while at least. He hadn't spoken at all of what was to come next, if he expected her to stay or go, or keep thieving for him. He had said an unspecified amount of time—but how long was that? And what was to come after? She knew the answer—knew what it had to be. He knew what she was, what she had chosen to become. If she was ever going to put this life behind her and go respectable, she was going to have to leave all traces of Meggs the thief behind. She needed to start fresh and put all the mistakes of her past behind her.

And lying with Captain McAlden was a mistake—a glorious mistake—but a mistake nonetheless.

She followed the contour of his well-muscled arm as it lay over his head, almost reaching out to touch the skin on the inside of his elbow, when he suddenly rolled over her, all awake and alert.

"And do you like what you see?" he asked in his sleepy growl.

"You snore."

Improbably, he smiled. "Do I?"

"Yes. Hasn't anyone ever told you?"

"Mmm." He kissed the side of her neck. "No. Never woke up with anyone else before."

Something about the unguarded, spontaneous way he spoke made her pause and look at him sharply. "What do you mean?"

Hugh could hear the pointed curiosity as well as the dawning incredulity in her voice. He slowed his hand, and instead of pulling her close as he wanted, he settled for brushing a stray lock of hair off the frown she was pleating into her forehead. This was not a conversation he was particularly enthralled to have. He would much rather talk about breakfast. Better yet, he would much rather have *her* for breakfast. So he concentrated on distracting her by exploring the texture of her lips. Her soft, plush, mobile lips. But she was drawing back to stare at him.

He rolled off her and subsided onto his back. She was too clever by half.

"But . . . Oh, right. A man wouldn't want to spend a whole night with a . . . I mean that would cost a lot . . ."

"No. That's not it at all. You are simply the first."

He stated the fact without any elaboration.

But she sailed right on by, holding to the same tack. "To spend the night here, with you? Am I meant to be flattered?"

"Very much so." He turned to smile at her. She really had no idea. And that was fine.

But she was a clever girl, and she continued to look at him, concentration and puzzlement darkening her eyes. "Very much so?" she echoed his words before she asked quietly, "How many women have you had?" Her question was so characteristic—direct and straightforward. No dancing about the bad facts.

"Had?" He drew out a moment, teasing her with it. Teasing himself.

"Had. In the biblical. Tupped. Fucked."

He fought down both his laughter and his urge to lecture. He had to remember she knew no better. He had to remember her education, such as it was, came from London's grimier streets. "What we did was not *tupping*. What we did, what we *do*, is make love."

She retreated a little in the face of his tone, but then repeated quietly, "How many?"

He thought of another evasion, but decided she deserved to know the unvarnished truth. "One."

"One?" Her brow screwed down in confusion as she rolled up onto her elbow to examine his face for evidence. "Only one other?"

"No. No other." Hugh felt neither embarrassment nor pride. He had his reasons for his choices, but they amounted to only one thing—she was his choice. "*Only* one."

"But that would be . . ."

"You."

"No." She rolled onto his chest, gripping his arms, peering at him, as though she could find the reason written across his skin. "But you're . . ."

"Eight and twenty. Is that so hard to fathom?" He reached for her. He had to touch, to strengthen his connection to her. To make her understand. "How many men have you been with?"

Her eyes sharpened to black bullets. "You know—"

"Just so," he finished quietly. "And are you dissatisfied? Or craving the company of others?"

"No," she answered slowly, as if she were reckoning as she spoke.

"So there you have it." He brushed the sheet and blankets down, uncovering her like a gift to himself so he could stroke along her sleek flank. "It's not that complicated."

She closed her eyes a little at his touch, but then shook her head. She couldn't let it be. She continued to search his face for something she could understand, something she could believe. "Every toff I've ever met, or ever known, or ever heard of, sticks his cock into *anything* willing. And even unwilling, if you listen to some of the housemaids. But handsome as you are, I can't believe you've ever had a shortage of willing girls."

He shrugged away the suggestion. "Like you, I'm simply not promiscuous. And I don't believe in a double standard. But I thank you for the compliment. It does me no end of good to know you find me handsome." His hand slid around to trace the sensitive underside of her breast. "This is all I want. This is all I need. You."

She made a pleased, agreeing sound, and Hugh wanted to kiss it out of her mouth. But she whispered against his lips. "Then how? How did you learn to do that, to make me feel all golden and happy inside?"

He did kiss her then, taking her sweet mouth and kissing the small puckers of worry smooth. "Meggs. Lass."

"I mean, I knew about it," she explained between kisses. "Heard all about tupping, even seen it a time or two—people going at it in a doorway. But I never imagined how it could make me feel. You've never done this before, either, and yet, you can make me feel like my body was raining sunlight."

It was a wonder he didn't float away on the lazy rush of pleasure. It was beautiful. She was beautiful. He kissed his way across her eyes. "But there you have it. Imagination. Inspiration. For instance, this, right here—" He traced his fingers lightly over the delicate scoop of her hip bone. "I find this fascinating. I find it *erotic*. There's a word for your collection. Do you know what that means, erotic? Inflaming the passions. It means, it makes me feel the need to touch you. To be touched by you."

"So if I feel the need to do . . . this"—she rolled her sweet, sleek, softly naked body atop his—"I could?"

"You can do whatever you want," he assured her.

"Can I do whatever I want to you?" Her eyes were avid, roving over his body in fascination.

Hugh wondered vaguely if he could expire from pure, undiluted lust. He threw his hands out wide. "Have at it, lass."

And she did. She stretched full out on top of him, the soft friction of her skin whispering hot, erotic promises along his flesh. He touched her in encouragement, his hands cradling her face, his thumbs tracing tender, sweet circles across her cheek and lips. The first touch of her plush lips to his was soft and tentative, a mere taste until she grew more sure. She opened her mouth to kiss him, taking his lower lip between hers to nip and suck, to draw him deeper into the velvet softness of her sweet mouth. He let go of all thought when she sent her tongue out to tangle with his, exploring him with eager, unbridled curiosity.

And then she drew back abruptly, her mouth open and panting from her exertions, her eyes wide and avid, scanning his body for more ways, and more places, to explore. She was sitting across his belly, her sweet rounded arse pressing into his very attentive cock. She was a sight to behold—her pale, white skin flushed and rosy, her dark hair and eyes an exotic contrast. He showed her how to explore by example, reaching his hands up to cup the perfect roundness of her breasts and brush the pink crests of her nipples.

She groaned in response and leaned into him, filling his hands. And then she did the same to him, running her palms over the muscles of his chest, exploring, her nimble fingertips tracing the flat shape of his nipples before her mouth descended to kiss and tongue him the way he had done to her. "Do you like that?"

"God, yes. I like anything you do. Everything you do." She was his fantasy come to life, her body sleek and moving under his hands, her ruined hair brushing along his skin, her hips pressing against his.

"Anything?" She ran her hands up his arms to push his hands over his head and lay against him again, moving and stretching, trying to appease her need for greater contact. She kissed him again and again, and then, when her lips weren't enough, she used her teeth on him, nipping along his neck and jaw, pain and pleasure melding together in bursts of fire along his skin.

"Yes," he groaned in her thrall.

She pushed away again, dragging her nails across his chest as she sat up. She rocked back against him once before she slid back even farther to sit across his thighs and take his erection into her hands. "Anything?" And she stroked him with her clever, strong hands.

Her hands fisting along his length felt beyond good—the bliss was exquisite. The sight of her seated atop him like an earthy sprite, working her magic on his body with her nimble hands and her plush open mouth, was like spark to powder. And when she wiggled even farther back so she could lean down and stroke him with her lips, he thought he might explode.

"My God, lass. Yes," he encouraged, his voice thick with lust.

"I don't know," she asked, out of breath as she came up for air and slid her hand back down his flesh, "how your skin can be so soft, and yet so hard." She licked him like a candy, once, twice, before she covered him with her lips and took him again into the velvet warmth of her mouth. She closed around him, stroking him with her tongue and abrading him with her teeth, urging him closer and closer to the keen edge of his need. When her hand slid lower to take the weight of his balls, caressing him in her palm, he thought he might expire from the jolting rush of dark pleasure.

But then the heated bliss of her mouth was gone, only to be replaced by her hands, as she slipped forward and rubbed his cock against her mound. "I want you inside of me."

"Yes." He was eager to oblige her, so as her nimble hands continued to stroke his engorged flesh, he reached between her legs to find the heated entrance to her body.

"What are you doing?"

"Making sure your body is wet and ready for me."

But Meggs didn't want to be led. She laced her own fingers with his, stealing her way into her own body. Hugh thought he might come right then and there, so powerful was the rush of carnal heat at the sight of her with one of her hands wrapped around his cock and the other one stroking the slick entrance to her body.

"Do you like that?" she asked, but she already knew the answer, her eyes dark and glowing with the newly discovered knowledge.

"Yes," he gritted, rapidly moving beyond finesse, beyond anything but sharp-honed need. He speared his fingers through hers and took the dew from her cunny to slick over his cock. And then he was gripping her hips and guiding her—but it was she who had his cock in hand and was easing him into her lush, warm flesh, sliding down onto him, the slick circumference of her passage tight and clinging. And when she moved atop him, slowly rising and falling upon the length of his cock, he had to close his eyes against the crazy rush of blood through his veins. Over and over, the sweet heated friction of her body drove him inexorably higher.

He tried to lie back. He tried to let her set her own pace, but she was whimpering with need and rocking harder and harder, flinging herself down upon him. And then her hand was grappling around his neck, pulling him up so she could slide her legs forward, around his hips, and wrap her arms around him for purchase, to shudder hard against his loins. Her head was thrown back, her face nearly contorted with concentration, as she strove to feed her body's hunger .

He leaned back on his arms for leverage to angle his hips to give her more pleasure, more of the exquisite, torturous, heady friction as she pushed her body against his. He found more of his own pleasure in watching her abandon, in hearing her cries.

But when she began to call his name, begging and pleading for her release, all thought began to close down until there was nothing but dark ravening need. He gripped her hips and pumped himself into her ruthlessly, again and then again, building his need like a wave until finally it crashed down upon him. He heard her orgasmic scream, and all hell broke loose inside him as he exploded into her.

CHAPTER 22

By midafternoon a wet snow had begun to fall, blanketing the world outside in gray and white. Inside, they had not yet left his bed, though they were both awake. Hugh was content to bask in the glow of her contentment. But, while they didn't have to get up and go out into the cold snow, they would have to get some food, sooner or later. Later was an easier thought.

"Are you comfortable?"

Meggs sighed like a cat. "Warm as toast. Sleeping with you is like sleeping next to a cast-iron stove."

"That does not sound comfortable."

"Hmm, no, it's lovely. I meant it as a compliment. I've never been so warm."

"Well." He was inordinately pleased to be able to give her so simple a pleasure. But he made a joke of it. "Let me set this phenomenon down in my log book. Tuesday, the tenth of December, in the year of our Lord seventeen hundred and ninety-nine: Meggs gave me a compliment."

They laughed and Hugh's heart and body felt . . . aligned, for the first time in his life. No not for the first time. But in a very long time.

The thought was there in his mind in an instant. He could

marry her and live quietly. He could make her a captain's wife. She seemed particularly adaptable—she might even like the rather rough and tumble of life at sea. He'd never seen the advantage before. Indeed, he served with only one captain who had his wife aboard, on a first rate that hadn't seen much action, back when he'd first been a midshipman. But to have Meggs to hand, to talk to, to have the benefit of that agile, quick mind. Not to mention having her in his bed.

"I've been thinking."

She laughed. "Have you? Don't know how you can possibly tup and think at the same time. I can't."

"Don't say tup." He wasn't sure why it bothered him, only that it did.

"Why not?"

"It's vulgar."

She sobered, in that quiet way of hers, going intensely still beneath his hands. "But I am rather vulgar, aren't I? That's what thieves from the Cheapside docks are. I can't change who I am."

"You're only vulgar when you choose to be. I think you can choose not to be."

"And you want me to choose not to be." Her voice was guarded and careful.

He made his voice deceptively casual, though his response was every bit as careful as hers. "Probably. But it's what you want to choose that matters. Now, do you want to know what I've been thinking or not?"

"Yes, of course."

"I was thinking about what comes next. I did tell you about my friend, Captain Marlowe?"

The carefulness made her voice even more quiet. "In the navy, yes."

"Well, I wrote him, just to see if what I proposed for your brother might actually be possible."

"Oh. For the Tanner. And?"

"And, I've received his reply. He will take your brother on as a servant—which is a sort of way of saying he'll be an apprentice at first, to see how he goes on. Marlowe is adamant about making sure it's what the boy wants. Marlowe was forced into the navy, and even though he loves the life, he won't stand for any boy under his command being made to join against his wishes. But if it is what Timmy wants, and Marlowe thinks he's capable—which I have no doubt he will—he'll make him a midshipman and teach him lessons in seamanship and navigation, and all the skills it takes to be an officer, a gentleman sailor."

"A gentleman." She rolled away and looked at the ceiling for a very long time.

Hugh didn't rush her. He knew what Timmy meant to her—she had devoted her entire life to his care and upbringing. And change, especially a change that would take her brother away from her, was always going to be difficult and frightening.

Finally, she just nodded. "Then it's settled then, is it?"

"Only thing is for you to say yes. And the Tanner to be asked, of course."

"Yes." She nodded again, though her lip was buttoned down trying to keep it from quivering. She didn't like this whole idea, but she knew it was for the best. "Best if you tell him. Or ask him."

"Are you sure?"

"Yes." She pulled on bravery with the bed sheet as she moved away. "I'm sure."

Timmy was ecstatic. They settled the business between them and made the arrangements in less time than it took for Meggs to case a mark. Mrs. Tupper agreed to accompany the boy down to Dartmouth by post chaise and deliver him to Marlowe, whose housekeeper she really was. Now that Meggs's training as a housemaid was done, Mrs. Tupper felt she had paid her debt of gratitude, and she wanted to return to Mr. Tupper in Dartmouth for the coming holidays.

It was also, Hugh knew, Mrs. Tupper's emphatic way of letting it be known she did not approve of his new relationship with Meggs.

"I'm too old not to speak my mind, sir," she had told him when he had finally left Meggs, and the closed confines of his bedchamber, in search of food. "That girl deserves better." Her sharp criticism was all for him, but he would be relieved to spare Meggs the mortification of hearing any of it.

They were to leave in two days' time. And that left Hugh exactly one day to figure out what he was to do with Meggs. He could think of only one way to go about the business. He took a hackney coach to the door of Number Forty-Five Berkley Square.

His mother saw him immediately.

"Hugh, darling, what could be wrong? What brings you here?"

"Why must something be wrong for me to visit my mother?"

She fanned her hands through the air impatiently. "Because. Tell me at once." She waved him into the chair beside her.

"All right." He eased his bulk cautiously into the delicate-looking silk-upholstered armchair. "I would like your advice and assistance in helping someone to . . . learn how to go on in Society, a little. A very little."

The pleased surprise he had expected did make a brief appearance in her face—her eyes lit and the tiniest of smiles curved her lips—before it was replaced with a certain wary caution. "A little? I will, of course, help you do so. But I'm enough of a mother to want to know why."

"A simple favor."

"Simple? I see. And what is the name of this simple woman?"

"Why must it be a woman?"

"Because I didn't think, even after all these years in the navy, it would be a *man*. And because you're cagey about nothing else in your life but women."

It was not quite shocking, but definitely disquieting, to be so easily read by a woman he hadn't spent more than two days with in the past ten years. "You would make a formidably spy, Mother."

"So would any woman worth the name mother. It's our job to figure out our men's thoughts regarding such things, for you don't seem to want to do it for yourselves."

She had him there. He most definitely did not want to examine his thoughts regarding Meggs too closely. They were foolish in the extreme.

"But you have not answered, Hugh. Who is she?"

Hugh took a deep breath. "Someone entirely unsuitable." He could think of no other way of putting it. Meggs was— hell, he didn't even know if Meggs was her real name. She didn't trust him enough to tell him. And he couldn't bring himself to trust the rest of his life to someone he truly knew so little.

"For *you?*" His mother's eyebrows were flying away with astonishment.

"Yes, for me," he scowled back. "Who did you think?"

"I don't know," she cast about. "A fellow officer's sister from the country or someone like that sweet Miss Burke, now Viscountess Darling, whom you seemed to like so well, and who didn't know anyone of consequence in London. You've never spoken . . . Is it quite serious, then?"

"Yes. But it's more complicated than that."

"How so?"

As Meggs would say, it was best to lay out the bad facts. "She's a thief. An accomplished pickpocket and picklock from the Cheapside docks."

His mother's hand went to cover her mouth. He had certainly surprised her. "You can't be serious. You can't. To want me to turn this pickpocket into a lady?"

"Not a lady, like yourself in the ton, but just generally, to help her, so she knows how . . . to go on." At his mother's continued stare, he felt forced to explain. "She's important to me. She's remarkable. And I'm sure you'll be pleased to know, she thinks you're a 'prime article.' "

"Does she? Well, I am flattered. Important and remarkable?" She looked away into the fire for a moment. "I see. Tell me, then, how long has she been . . . with you?"

There would be no fooling this woman, no side-stepping of the truth. "A few weeks."

"My dear child." She tilted her head to the side as she regarded him. "Surely you must understand, you're merely infatuated with her."

"Please, Mother, I think I know the difference."

"Do you? You who have steadfastly avoided the company of females of good family?"

"That's not true. You spoke of Miss Burke, and yes, I will admit, I *was* a little infatuated with her. And this is different. Very different. This girl, well, she means a great deal to me."

She asked very quietly, but deadly serious for all that, "Do you do this, this wanting to help her on in Society, for her, or for yourself?"

Oh, she was canny, his Scots mother. He was doing this for himself, in the name of helping Meggs. But truly it was for himself. It was selfish, and foolish, and nearly impossible, but he had to try. He had to see if it was possible. "She has no one else in the world to help her."

"And it is like you to want to play her Galahad. However foolish, or misguided, it speaks well for your unselfish character."

"Hardly unselfish. I *do* want it for myself, as well. I love her."

"And does she love you?"

Hugh felt all the import of her question. She was not just asking about Meggs. She was asking if he knew the difference. He did. "I believe so. Not that she'd admit it."

Her face registered another surprise. She was too much of a mother not to understand how anyone could find her son less than lovable. But she rallied. "Well," she said with a brave smile, "if she loves you, that's all the suitability she needs."

"I've come to tell you, I'd like to make a . . . an adjustment to our arrangement."

Meggs was instantly on her guard, dropping back from the connecting door to her room and pulling on the tough veneer of the street as if it were a handy cloak. Up came the shrug, as if whatever he would say made no matter to her. "What's it going to be then?"

"A removal to Mayfair. To Berkley Square. To my mother's house."

That stopped her cold. "Your mother? Whatever for?"

"She's agreed to teach you to be a lady."

"You want me to become a lady? Why? Ladies don't steal things."

He laughed. "You'd be surprised."

She thought for a long moment before she asked, "Does your mother know what I do. Or what you do for the navy part of the government?"

"Not exactly," he hedged. "But you and my mother are completely agreed on many subjects, one of which is that no one *sees* women, especially women of either a certain class and age. And in society, few young men see young women of good family as anything more than breasts and foolishness. That'll be the hardest part." He couldn't stop himself from touching her plush, full bottom lip with the backs of his fingers. "Hardest thing I'll ever have to do—teach you to act *foolish*."

Meggs returned his teasing with a strangely bittersweet smile. "I just may surprise you. I fear I can be as foolish as you might need me to be."

"I hope you will. So, you've done maids, and you've done boys, and now we need to turn you into a pretty girl. A young woman of good family."

She made an unmistakably rude sound and crossed her hands over her bodice. "How on earth d'you plan to do *that*? And you still haven't told me why?"

He let the second question slide and crossed to her, taking her hands in his. "With you, as in all things, it will be easy. You'll need nothing more than a lovely dress and attractive hairdressing to change from a cygnet into a swan."

She was not mollified by the implied compliment. "A pretty girl is a pretty girl, whether she's covered in silk or clad only in rags. Any man with half an eye for beauty can see that."

"Are you fishing for compliments? But it's no great lie to tell you, you are a very pretty girl." She was not actually conventionally pretty. She did not have the milk and roses complexion, or apple-cheeked, blond warmth of the stereotypical English beauty. Her eyes were too dark, her features were too delicate and fey to ever play the milkmaid.

"Is this another of your impossible assignments? Hedging your bets on that knighthood?"

God's balls. "How do you know about that? It was meant to be secret."

"Please, Captain. I'm a prime filching mort. It's my job to find out things."

"Hugh." He leaned down to nuzzle meaningfully at that place at the edge of her neck. That place that made her smile, that hopefully started the sunshine raining down inside her.

"Hugh," she agreed, becoming softer and more pliable under his attentions.

"I'm good at finding things, too. Like these lovely things." He made a reverent obeisance to her breasts over the fabric of her bodice.

"Ah, well." She let out a long tremulous breath. "But they're easy enough to find."

"True," he kissed one peak into tight agreement through the fabric. "But you will also, no doubt, come to appreciate I am a man who understands subtleties." He traced the rim of one finger along the sensitive underside of her breast, drew a line along the turning of her arm and up, over the white, sensitive skin at the inside of her upper arm.

She shivered under his touch and he stepped away. "I'm going to lock the door. Don't go anywhere."

"And where would I go?"

"Nowhere." He smiled and kissed her. "I told you, you belong here."

Lord, she was as nervous as a pigeon among the company of cats. The hackney was winding its way into the heart of Mayfair. Huge, terrifyingly elegant town houses rose up on either side of the street.

"Meggs, don't fash yourself. It will be fine." He was trying to be all relaxed and civilized today, all smooth gentleman. But his jaw was set like stone—like flint, just as the Bible said. It did not exactly bode well.

"But why—"

"Meggs. She knows all about you. And she knows all about us. And she still invited us here."

He wasn't going to tell her why, so she should give up trying. "I've never met a viscountess."

"Then I can tell you, she is exactly the same person she was before she became a viscountess—thoughtful and charming. She was a gentleman farmer's wife for far longer than she's been a viscountess. She's lovely, don't worry."

The thought gave little enough comfort—every man thought his mother at least part a saint, whether she was a gin whore or a viscountess. But true to his word, Viscountess Balfour was lovely. And thoughtful. And nice. The white town house on Berkley Square was large and very beautiful, but she greeted them at the door, herself, as if she had been awaiting their arrival.

"May I introduce you to my mother, the Viscountess Balfour. Mother this is my . . . this is Meggs."

"Meg, my dear, welcome." She held out her hand, and then leaned in to kiss Meggs on the cheek. "I'm so happy to have you here. Hugh has told me all about you."

"Oh, dear." She gave the lady a nervous curtsy. "I had hoped to pass myself off with a greater degree of credit."

"Nonsense! You are most welcome." Her eyes were every bit her son's, a blue so pale and beautiful it was shocking, but they were softer somehow than her son's, perhaps because they were almost always creased up with a smile.

"Thank you, my lady. I'm very obliged."

"Not at all. With Hugh's sisters all grown up, I'd like nothing better than to have a young lady about the house and help bring her out into Society." Hugh's mother led them up and into a gorgeous yellow drawing room the size of a guild hall. "I've called for refreshment, as I'm sure you'd like something warm after your journey up from Chelsea."

"It is not the other end of the earth, Mother."

"No, but it is the other end of London, and the day is bitterly cold. We don't all have your hearty constitution, Hugh. Now, Meg. What a lovely name. But we'll have to introduce you in the world, or at least in the drawing room, as something other than just Meg, my dear. Miss . . . ?"

There really wasn't a hint of meanness in the inquiry, and Meggs thought if there had been she would have found it, so carefully was she weighing every word. But Hugh had been right—so sweet, so kind, right through to the bone kind, and lovely. Meggs didn't want to lie. She wanted to begin as she meant to go on, with both the captain, Hugh, and his mother.

"Evans." Yet, she couldn't bring herself to give all the truth out at once, carte blanche, as they said, so she gave it to the smallest falsehood she could manage. "Miss Margaret Evans."

She was inordinately conscious of the weight of his eyes on her. Would he know? Would he guess it was real, her name? He didn't seem surprised. He merely smiled, a small, infinitesimal crinkling of his eyes only. But she had forgotten, they had already decided, her and Timmy, that using Evans was what was best for him as well, going into the navy.

"I didn't know Captain McAlden had sisters."

"And an older brother, too, Francis, but he is still ensconced in faraway Scotland, as are my daughters, his sisters Catriona and Elspeth, so I have no company except his poor self." But the viscountess smiled at Hugh and held out her hand to him, so Meggs knew they shared a real affection. But of course they must. Why else would the viscountess take her on, except to please her son?

"I'm glad we'll be able to spend some time together here before we leave for the country."

"The country!" There she went, sounding hopeful. More than hopeful—enthusiastic.

But Hugh had spoken at the same time, and his response had been far less than enthusiastic. "The country?"

"Yes," the viscountess confirmed, "I'd like you to come to Balfour with us for the holidays."

"Holidays? Can't remember when I last celebrated the Christmas holidays." But they were both, she and the viscountess, looking at Hugh.

"Oh, I'm glad—it will be such a treat," his mother began before he could say anything. "I will confess to a little machination, as I would very much like Hugh to come with us, but I think he would be more inclined to do so if you were to agree to come."

Meggs felt herself poised on some kind of precarious point between mother and son, and not understanding which way the wind ought to blow. "He has been very kind to introduce you to me."

"Yes, he has been kind to both of us because he knows how lonely I've been here in London without company. My husband's family is all grown, too, and living in the country. You will meet them soon enough. But now you are come to me, we shall be wonderfully busy. We will have time to get to know one another, and then, when we go to Balfour, it will only be family and country friends. You'll have plenty of time to find your feet, so to speak."

"You are very kind." Meggs couldn't think of what else to say. "And where is Balfour?"

"Somerset," Hugh answered. "At least two days' drive." His voice was dry and tight. He was not pleased at the idea.

"Have you traveled much, my dear?"

Meggs brought her attention back to the viscountess, who seemed to think her son could be managed by ignoring him. Perhaps Lady Balfour was right. Meggs had not learnt any way of managing him—even the obvious. "No. Only a little, and a very long time ago at that."

"Then I hope this will be a treat."

"Thank you, ma'am. I mean, Your Ladyship."

"Ma'am is perfect—it's what Hugh calls me, so it is of course what you shall call me, as well. Now, I do not wish to embarrass you, but I must ask you a great indulgence. I have not had the opportunity to buy clothes for a young lady in quite some time. I hope you will allow me to make you a present of a dress or two before we leave for Balfour? You must do me the great favor of making you quite the thing. I've been longing to steal a march on the local matrons, and we must also think of poor Hugh."

Viscountess Balfour was every bit as smart and single minded as her son. How clever to couch her thinly veiled attempt to bring Meggs's clothes up to snuff as a gift to her, just to save Meggs the embarrassment of worry over the funds. "Poor Hugh?"

"Why yes. Since Hugh will do nothing to give the local matrons hope for their daughters, we must take the pressure away from him by offering you as an amiable dinner companion to their sons. Do indulge me. And of course we must have a ball. A Christmas Ball."

"A Christmas Ball?" That voice was all captain, getting sorer than a caged bear.

But the viscountess just sailed on, immune to his growling. "Really, we must call it an Advent Ball, since it will be before Christmas. Margaret must have an opportunity to dance."

"But, ma'am," she stammered, "I don't know how."

"Then of course, you must learn. You will stay, and we will spend our days shopping and dancing. Oh, my dear girl, you must let me buy you a ball gown. But we must let Hugh go. I fear his eyes are starting to glaze over at the thought of dress shopping. You may go, darling. You are no longer needed. I have dear Miss Evans under starter's orders. But of course you will return this, and every, afternoon, so you might be useful. You will be available this afternoon, won't you, darling?"

"Available?" For the first time in her experience, the captain looked almost afraid.

"To dance. Surely you understand Margaret must have someone with whom to dance? How else is she to learn?"

"You know I don't dance."

"Nonsense." His mother waved away what looked like ten years of personal preference. "Your leg is clearly better, and dear Margaret will feel so much more comfortable dancing for the first time with someone she knows. And with your . . . difficulties of grace, you can't help but be understanding if she has trouble remembering steps."

The captain knew Meggs could remember the tumbler set of a lock she'd picked six months ago. She was highly unlikely to forget a dance step. But she was attempting to look as innocent as a milkmaid behind his mother's back.

"Perhaps, ma'am, it would be too difficult for an arthritic old sailor, like Captain McAlden?"

The corners of his incandescent blue eyes crinkled up almost imperceptibly. But she knew. His look told her he would step all over her toes, just to teach her a lesson. But perhaps she could teach him a thing or two as well. Dancing might have its advantages, after all.

CHAPTER 23

His mother did not have a sense of humor. Or perhaps she did. However it was, she was determined to keep them well apart. Viscountess Balfour arranged for them to travel to Somerset separately, be separated at dinners, and room in separate wings of the house. She was taking no chances with Meggs's reputation. Even if it damn well inconvenienced her own son. This was *not* what he had asked for. And his mother damn well knew it, damn her canny blue eyes.

His only opportunity to speak to Meggs after his arrival was in the drawing room, with the room already packed with dinner guests. Meggs was seated with the ladies at a settee, but she wasn't attending to their talk. In fact, she rather burst his bubble of anticipation when she noticed him not at all when he joined the assembled party. She was staring into the wood fire roaring away in the huge hearth.

"Miss Evans?" And when she did not respond, "Meggs?"

"Oh, Hu— Captain McAlden. What a pleasure it is to see you again." She made to rise, but he waved her back into her seat.

"What were you looking for there?" He gestured to the flames.

"Nothing." She turned back to the hearth. "I'd just forgotten."

"Forgotten what?"

"The fire—what it was like. The wood smells so good, so warm and inviting. I'd just forgotten is all."

How strange. If she knew wood fires, chances were that at some point she had lived in the country. Funny, he'd never suspected that. To him, she was so wholly a creature of London, with her encyclopaedic knowledge of its streets and alleys, its ways and people, from Billingsgate Market to Chelsea. And yet, here she was, dressed in a demure, light-colored dress of the finest make, looking every inch the quiet, contemplative country daughter.

"You look very nice," he told her. "Very demure."

She gave him a flash of her cheeky smile. "Oh, yes," she whispered, "I'm as demure as an old whore at a christening."

He was laughing even though he knew he shouldn't. He looked back to see if anyone was attending their conversation and spoke quietly. "God's balls, Meggs. Don't talk like that. You need to keep out of mischief and learn how to be a young lady."

"Out of mischief?" She began to smile. "Imagine that. Whatever shall I do with myself?"

"Learn needlework, I suppose."

"Hmm, boring. But I suppose I could learn easily enough. I *am* good with my hands."

"God help me, don't talk like that, either. I'm meant to be a gentleman and keep my hands off of you. So please don't tempt me. Help keep me to the straight and narrow."

"Yes, I've been instructed to cleave to the path of righteousness myself. I'm to make myself agreeable to the young gentlemen and ladies through dinner and cards. Your mother makes all the young men sound like choir boys, but I know better. I'm only hoping I haven't bunged one or another of them when they were down to London sowing their wild oats."

Hugh hadn't thought of *that*. No wonder she was uneasy. "You're safe here. No one will recognize you. Remember, you made your fortune on it."

"I could make another fortune sharping them all at cards— go back to making an honest living."

"Not card sharping, too?" Where did her list of felonious skills end? The skirl of misgiving in his chest widened into caution.

"Oh, aye. Old Nan taught us all to cheat. Famous games we'd have, with the whole lot of us all trying to cheat each other. Half the deck would be up the kiddies' sleeves, until there was nothing left to play with." She smiled at the fond memories.

That was what he had been thinking—he so *liked* this girl. One wouldn't think she could have any fond memories of growing up in the hell that was the slums of London, but she knew life was what you made of it. And she was clearly determined to make the most of this opportunity, as well. If he thought, in the ensuing days, he occasionally saw a glimmer of sadness, or apprehension in her dark eyes, she hid it well from the others.

His mother had made arrangements for a dizzying array of winter outings—shopping trips to the local village, daily visits to the neighbors, walks and sled rides in the parkland, the gathering of winter greens to decorate the house for the coming Advent Ball, and nightly dinner parties.

Throughout it all, Meggs smiled sweetly and made herself agreeable to everyone. She held the other girls' packages and purchases when there were no gentlemen handy, she complimented the young ladies on their clothing and good looks, and she laughed delightedly whenever one of the choir boys made a joke. She was doing exactly as he had asked and was going on splendidly. Everyone declared Miss Evans completely charming.

So naturally, he was in hell. Because not once through the first two days of activities had he been allowed to so much as sit next to Meggs in a carriage, walk with her in a lane, or converse with her at dinner. They were always surrounded and accompanied by others.

Meggs and he were also housed at what could only be termed a deliberately inconvenient distance. Meggs remarked upon the distance on the third day, when they chanced to find themselves alone—for the first time—whilst looking for the orangery, where there was to be a game of charades.

"It's such a very large house. My room must be in the next parish over, it's so big. The footmen ought to run a toll gate in the upstairs hallway."

"They're too busy running a dice game in the carriage house." But he really wasn't attending to what he was saying. Despite his mother's injunctions, he was not about to let the opportunity to be alone with Meggs pass. He took her by the elbow and guided her left, instead of right, and found a suitably empty corridor.

"And me without me fulhams," she was saying.

That brought his attention back. "No loaded dice, Meggs. No gambling. No card games of any kind. You are not to fleece the choir boys out of their allowances. However much they might deserve it."

"Allowances." She scoffed. "Someone needs to tell me how *that's* not stealing. And they call me a thief."

"They should only ever call you Miss Evans." He checked the corridor behind them.

"So proper. I'll try to remember that. And what will you be calling me?" She attempted to devastate him by tilting her head to the side and looking up at him through the dark fan of her lashes. God's balls. When had she learned that particular trick?

"Are you flirting with me, Miss Evans?"

"And what if I were, Captain McAlden?"

"Well, in accordance with custom and honor, I believe I am obliged to flirt back."

"Really? And are you dreadfully accomplished in the art of flirting?"

"Unfortunately"—he shook his head in solemn disappointment—"I find I'm woefully out of practice. But I wonder . . ."

"Yes, Captain?"

"I wonder, if *you* might be so kind as to lend me your assistance in this endeavor?"

"Well, I will have to check my schedule. But I do feel certain I can find the time for an endeavor of such great import."

"I thank you." He bowed over her hand. "You are too kind to this arthritic, old sailor."

"Yes. I do hate to tell you, the young ladies do worry about the extent of your . . . infirmities," she advised solemnly. "Sadly, for their sakes, I find I am loath to set them straight. But how much time, do you suppose, will we need to devote to your study of flirting?"

"Oh, a goodly amount of time, I should think." He tightened his hand around her wrist and swung her around as he opened the door to a small closet and backed her in, shutting them in the close velvet darkness.

"Why, Captain McAlden, how clever you are to—"

He kissed her taunting mouth with all the hunger eating him alive from the inside. It was all he could do to keep himself from plundering her mouth and every other part of her body. He wanted to stamp himself into her, to mark her irrevocably, to tell every other man his mother had introduced her to, to stay the hell away. She was *his*.

"Oh," she breathed as they broke apart. "No wonder they call that tipping the velvet."

"My God. I need to— I want to—" He couldn't think. He could only feel the surging need swamping his body.

"To fuck me?"

The raw carnality of the whispered words washed him in a wave of unadulterated lust, drenching him with unspeakable craving. "My God, lass."

"I want it, too," she confessed into the hushed dark, "the fucking. I want you to fuck me."

Hugh found his head tipping back, his eyes closed in something approaching prayer, to ward off the power of her words. "You shouldn't say that."

"What? Fuck? Don't young ladies of good family fuck? Is it too vulgar for them?"

"Yes. Of course. But it's not just—" He had to remember her upbringing, her life on the London streets, the people she had been exposed to. She couldn't be held responsible for the heat firing deep in his belly, for his coarse, earthy response to her choice of words. "It's . . . dirty."

"Is it? But underneath this pristine dress, I am rather dirty. A dirty little thief. And I think you must like dirty, Captain." She reached out across the few inches of utter darkness and found him unerringly. "Or at least your yard does. It's growing."

He swore, violently and profusely, and felt nearly insane from the effort to keep from putting his hands upon her in the urgency and violence of his need. In savage lust.

"Is that dirty, too, 'yard'?" She stroked the length of his shaft through the rough wool of his breeches. "Though it seems to like me saying its name."

He grabbed her hands up and pinioned her wrists over her head as he bore her back into the wall. "Stop."

She wasn't at all intimidated. She arched her body against him. "But you don't really want me to stop. You like it. And so do I. I've missed you." Her mouth brushed along the side of his cheek, close to his ear. "I've missed it when you press your yard against my belly. It makes me want to do dirty, vulgar things to you. It makes me want *you* to do dirty things to me."

God help him, he wanted it, too. He wanted it with an inarticulate violence that left him astonished and shaking. And so he indulged himself, enthralled by the carnal lust between them, by dragging his hands down the vulnerable length of her inner arms to the underside of her breasts. "What sort of things do you want?"

He heard her intake of breath and felt her warm exhalation brush over his skin.

"I want you to touch me."

"Here?" He traced below her breasts, along the raised waistline of her dress and up the curved sides to the pins securing her scooped neckline.

"Yes," she breathed.

He pulled out the pins and let her bodice fall before he set his hands back upon her, tracing her curves above her low stays, palming the sweet roundness of each breast through the light fabric of her chemise. "Do you want me to take this down?"

"Yes."

He let his hands find their unseeing way to the ribbon drawstring of the chemise, pulling apart the tie and loosening the fabric enough to tug it down so her breasts were exposed above her stays to the heated air. "And now what?"

She was breathing faster now, and it gave him great pleasure to imagine the way her bare breasts would look rising and falling, their pink crests tight and waiting for his touch. But she surprised him.

"Now, it's my turn. To do dirty things. To touch you." And she set her clever, agile fingers to the buttons of his breeches. The fall came quickly undone, and she was loosening the drawstring of his small clothes and pushing the linen apart before he could stammer his assent.

"God. Yes." His hands found the delicate peaks of her breasts just as hers closed around the length of his shaft.

And just as he would have moved forward to kiss her—to take her mouth with his own, and fill his senses with her taste and texture—her clever hands were sliding down the length of his thighs. And she was kneeling in front of him.

"God. Meggs, not here. I don't—"

Oh, but he did. He did. He did like the feel of her warm, strong hands closing around his cock. He did like the feel of her agile fingers drawing up and down the length of him, sending pleasure shafting through him. His head tipped back against the wall, and he shuttered his eyes against the heated bliss of her mouth closing around him. He did love the feel of her hands digging into the flesh of his thighs as she steadied herself and began to suck and lick him.

It was pure, dark, unadulterated bliss, deeply carnal and undeniably pleasurable. He found himself holding her head in his hands, pulling the pins from her carefully arranged hair and trailing his fingers through the soft, fine, short strands, then letting the silk glide through his fingers as she pleasured him. Her soft, sweet mouth was hot and tight; her tongue and teeth pushed his bliss higher and higher until he was forgetting himself, losing grasp of reality. Losing touch with everything but Meggs and the roiling, churning chaos of pleasure ripping through his body.

The first wave of his orgasm was just beginning to roar through his body, when there was a succinct rap at the wooden door to his right.

"Hugh?"

Holy fucking— He swiveled instantly so that his back was to the door and Meggs was hidden from potential sight. His hand tightened against her head, not allowing her to withdraw or move so much as an inch.

"Do not open that door." He spoke quietly, but there was no question but that it was a command.

"Hugh, I must say this—"

"Go away, Mother."

"Hugh, this will not do. There are rules, and I know you were raised to obey them. I am counting on you to be a gentleman and behave yourself. Now, get yourself out of that closet immediately, before I have— Just put yourself to rights and get back to the party. Do you understand me?"

"Yes, ma'am. Now go *away*."

He waited until he could hear her footsteps retreating down the hallway. Despite his restraint, Meggs had pulled herself away.

"Sweet Jesus God, I'll never be able to look at that woman in the face again." Her voice was shaky and she was clambering to her feet, inadvertently brushing up against him. "I should not have done that."

"No," he lied, pitching his voice low. "You shouldn't." His hands stopped her from rearranging her bodice. "It was very wrong of you. And I daresay it was very wrong of me, as well."

"Yes." But her voice was breathy and perhaps a little unsure. "I should go."

"You should," he agreed again, but his fingers were tracing the tight peaks of her exposed nipples, and her breathing fractured into shards. And he was no better, his unfulfilled release still humming through the bones under his muscles. "But you're not going anywhere," he growled. "Not with your talk of dirty things and liking to fuck. Not with your breasts so exposed and responsive to my touch."

Her breathing broke apart, gasping and labored as he continued to caress her. Hugh ran his rough palms up the long slide of her neck, framing her jaw in his hands before he speared his hands through her unruly, disheveled hair. He loved the way it felt sliding through his fingers.

"You got to do what you wanted to do, before we were so

rudely interrupted, and now I'm going to do what I want. And what I want is to turn you around so I can bite your neck." He turned her hips, nudged her a little roughly against the wall, and set his teeth lightly to her nape. It was only a little nip. "To mark you," he whispered in her ear. "As mine."

Meggs made a needy, greedy little sound of surrender, and Hugh felt such a welling of almost savage lust, he feared he could not hold it back. But he had gone too far for restraint now. He took up her hands and raised them over her head against the wall.

"Put your hands here and don't move," he ordered.

But Meggs wasn't the sort of girl who took orders easily. "And what if I don't?"

He pushed his hand into the small of her back, pinning her against the wall. "Clever girl to ask," he whispered, crowding against her. "What happens if you take down your hands, or move so much as an inch, is that I won't fuck you."

"But we can't—"

"I think we can. I know I can. I think I will." And he began to gather up the yards of materials that made up her skirts and petticoats, rucking them up, until he could feel her sweetly round bottom filling his hands.

He ground himself into her, bending her like a sail as he reached lower to touch her. His fingers found the slick opening of her body and stroked her until she was wet to his touch and ready for him.

"Yes," she begged on a ragged whisper. "Touch me. Please."

He heard the whispered plea, and dark heat consumed him. He did as she bid, sliding himself into the tight, exquisite constriction of her body. She was lush and small and perfect, urging him toward the heathen darkness of his soul with her carnal words.

He should teach her not to talk like that. He should teach her to say other things, softer, gentler words for the beauty of her body.

But not now. Now, he would glory in the dark, forbidden pleasure her whispers brought. He would let go of all the constraints of civilized behavior. He would fuck her as she had asked, as he wanted to, rocking into her, pressing her hard against the wall and stamping her with his possession.

His hands were grasping her hips, holding her still before him, and still she arched back and pushed her sweet arse against his loins, asking with her body for more, for everything he could give her.

She bucked and undulated and whimpered so sweetly, he ground his teeth against the idiotic, paradoxical rush of tenderness. He let go of her hips and rounded his arms around under her upper arms and shoulders, and into her hair. He fisted his hands in the silken strands, tugging her head back so he could tongue and kiss her. To cover her soft mobile lips and fall into the infinite sweetness of her mouth and the clinging velvet of her tongue.

He felt as though he were on fire, flames seeping out of his skin. His clothes were too tight, and yet he would not let go of her to take them off. He could not, for even an instant, forgo a fraction of the bliss pouring through his veins, pumping physical rapture through his body.

Her hands were still over her head, but she pressed them into the wall, pushing herself off as she thrashed back against him. He brought his palms to her breasts, roughly pinching her nipples between his finger and thumb, and she made a soft exultation of unbearable ecstasy as she came. Her womb convulsed around him, and a tumult built within until it became a raging riot of deafening sound and overwhelming feeling. He joined her climax, flinging himself into her with annihilating abandon.

It was many, many minutes before the crescendo of their labored breathing began to abate. Hugh turned Meggs around and gathered her to him. He would help her put her clothes back to rights in another moment or two. But not yet. Not until the last flare of rapture had faded like twilight out of his bones.

"Lass," he managed as their gasps subsided. "Did I hurt you? Are you all right?"

"No. Yes," she answered, and her head fell against his heaving chest. "I've never been so right in all my life."

Chapter 24

M eggs wasn't exactly sure what to do with all the country outside the windows. The other young people seemed to think almost nothing of bundling up and tromping off across a pasture to go to the village, but Meggs was vaguely overwhelmed by all the snow and trees. She had longed for this, to be in the country, for so long, but she had forgotten how . . . *real* it was, how quickly one might lose one's way when one didn't know the landmarks, or how cold it was when the wind blew hard across the fields unbuffered by building or walls.

And only people who owned more than one set of boots could contemplate such a frigid walk. Despite the fact that she was currently clothed as finely as any of the angelic young ladies and their choir boys, she was not one of them. She could not be. She did not own any of it. She was a thief. And she had chosen to become what she was, and no matter what Hugh so obviously wanted her to become, there could be no turning back. She knew now that she had been foolish to dream of it, foolish to try. She would never be able to wash away the years of crime and misery with a few foolish weeks at a house party.

She wandered back through the house, glad of the solitude. Glad for the time to sift through all the conflicting feelings being there, in a house in the country, brought out. To sort through the memories rising around her like ghosts. Meggs wandered into the music room, drawn by its soothing green color and plush velvet chairs. It was airy and lovely, with a large, floor-to-ceiling bay window overlooking the snowy lawn. Meggs let her fingers glide over the keys of the beautiful pianoforte, lightly so no sound would come out of the keys.

It had been so long since she'd even seen, much less sat down at, such an instrument. She slid onto the bench and quietly, very tentatively, played a single note. The tone bounded out of the pianoforte, resounding and dancing about the room playfully.

How often had she pictured her mother seated thus? She could see her in her mind's eye, so slight, almost fragile, so beautiful and happy sitting at the pianoforte in the back parlor of the rectory. The light used to come in over her head, from behind, lighting up her hair, all golden in the afternoon light.

Meggs moved her fingers onto the keys and hesitated. She wasn't sure if she could remember. But she could remember the scales. She picked her way up one, awkward and off time, but she kept at it, warming her fingers up, and then up and down the keyboard she went three times, with increasing speed and agility. How did it go, the song her mother used to play—that beautiful *impromptu* she would play for Father? It had been so long. Meggs hummed along, trying to pick out the notes, letting the tune flow up through her mind, letting the beauty of the music wrap around her and pull her in. Indulging in memories best left forgotten.

Hugh returned to the house through a side door after two hours of tromping through the snow, strengthening his leg and working off his lust. After yesterday's encounter, it was a wonder he didn't simply burst into flame any time he saw or even thought about Meggs. His mother could find him by the trail of smoke and dust he left in his wake.

As he closed the door behind him, he heard music, tentative but wending its way slowly through the corridors. But all the bright young things were out—he had seen them across the fields. Curiosity, or instinct, had him following the sound until he pushed open the door to find Meggs seated at a pianoforte. Her head was bent down, gazing in concentration at the keys as she picked her way slowly, but surely, through a passage, and then, with more assurance, began the melody over again.

His heart kicked over at the implication. Meggs was playing. She played the pianoforte. She had had training. She had at one time in her life lived with an instrument. She was playing a piece of baroque music with a delicacy and refinement completely at odds with the position in which he found her. Everything—her rough accent, the speed and efficiency of her larcenous skills. Her unabashed embrace of her criminality. The lack of any sort of moral compass—everything he knew of her was completely at odds with what he was hearing.

And then his eyes moved from her hands, her lovely, agile, quick hands, to her face. As she settled into the piece, she closed her eyes and a smile blossomed across her lips, and transformed her countenance into a beacon of transcendent joy. It was so intimate, so personal a joy, he felt he ought to look away, but knew he could not. Beauty unfolded over him as if she plucked and strummed something, some chord deep within him.

And as he watched, a tear formed in the corner of her eye, a momentary glitter of water that fell in a single drop down her cheek. Hugh was stunned. What ghost of memory had the music called up from her past? If he hadn't seen it himself—that moment of wistful longing—he would have thought he imagined it. He hadn't thought she had a wistful bone in her body.

He had pushed off the wall and was striding toward her. "Meggs."

"Oh! Hugh!" She abandoned the pianoforte and came toward him in a careless rush that made his heart too glad.

"Where did you learn to play?"

Everything open and glad in her face shuttered down in an instant. She turned away and indicated the instrument with a careless shrug. "Here and there. Old Nan's trick. Good for the fingers, she used to say. Helps to keep them strong and quick. Got an old banger from some gin house, I reckon. Nypers all over Seven Dials tickling the ivories."

She was lying. However much it might actually be true that old Nan might have gotten ahold of an instrument to strengthen her kiddies' hands, Meggs was hiding something.

"Meggs. Where did you learn to play?" he repeated.

She darted a glance at him under her brows, at once mutinous and wary. "If you must know, s'pose it was me mum. I remember she were a fair hand." Her accent slipped back into the cadence of cant.

"Don't." He moved closer to look into her eyes. "You don't need to talk like that."

A door opened down the corridor. Meggs's eyes went to the door and stayed there even as she answered him. "I can't be what I'm not. Not with you. I can't."

She was backing away from him. He stayed her with a hand. "Meggs. Please. I beg you."

She was there in a soft rush, in his arms, pressing her plush lips to his in a bittersweet kiss. But still, he wanted to devour her. He wanted to take her mouth in a way that told her there could be no more half truths and evasions between them. "Meggs, you trust me with your body, why won't you trust me with what's in your past?"

"Please," she begged in a soft whisper, "don't ask me. Because if I let you, you will break my heart." And as the footsteps drew nearer, she turned and fled the room.

Dinner was not comfortable. Meggs had been seated next to the earnest local clergyman, the Reverend Mr. Phelps, who seemed to regard her with trepidation. She had hoped to be seated nearer to Hugh so she might try to talk to him. To make him understand the way it stood with her. She had taken great pains with her dress for the evening, hoping her outward appearance would bolster her confidence, but he was staring reproachful daggers at her across the table. She took a quick swallow of claret and vainly searched her mind for suitably innocuous topics of conversation.

"Do you have a particular favorite among the gospels, Mr. Phelps?"

The curate looked at her with new eyes and settled into a lively lecture about his preference for the Gospel of St. Mark, and she relaxed a measure. The viscountess smiled her approval, but Meggs disciplined herself not to look to Hugh and his steely, probing eyes for his approval. What did old Nan used to say? *"Know your own measure, dearie, because you're only as good as you think you are."*

When the snow began to fall, brightening the courtyard, and the guests began to depart to spare their horses, lest their carriages slip and get mired in the snow, the viscountess linked her arms with Meggs's and waved good night to the last of their evening's guests.

"Thank you, Standard." The viscountess took a candle branch from the butler. "I'm going straight up. My dear, I hope you had a lovely evening." She kissed Meggs on the cheek.

"Thank you, ma'am. You were very kind."

"Nonsense. No more than you deserve. You did very well indeed. I shouldn't be surprised to find Mr. Phelps leaving flowers, or at the very least a card, tomorrow morning. Oh, Hugh, dear, are you still up?"

Captain McAlden—and he was captain now with the way he was looking at her, as though there was a reckoning about to come—prowled into the hallway like a cagey bear. "I am."

"We're going straight up. Good night, dear."

"I'd like a word, if I may, with Miss Evans."

The viscountess pursed her lips and gave him back the mirror of his own blue glower. "Now, Hugh, you brought her to me, and I would be remiss if I let any girl under my chaperonage meet alone with a man, even if he is my son. It has been a long evening, and I think it would be best—"

Hugh cut his sharp eyes to Meggs. Best to get it over with. "It's quite all right, ma'am. I'm happy to speak to Captain McAlden for a moment before I go up to bed. I'm sure it will only take a moment."

Viscountess looked back and forth between them, then settled her eyes on her son. "Behave yourself."

"I take your point, Mother. I will not keep Miss Evans long."

Viscountess went off to bed, leaving Meggs alone with the bear, who looked very, very hungry. "You should be nicer to your mother. You are the one who asked her to take me in."

"This is not what I asked her to do. But speaking of mothers and lies, that was quite a bouncer you told me earlier, about that *etude*."

Meggs said nothing but kept her face turned to a study of her toes as she made a circuit of the large entry hall, keeping distance between them. It hadn't been an *etude*, it was an incidental piece of music. Her mother had told her, and she had remembered because she had liked the sound of that word—incidental.

But Hugh did not appear to be in the mood for quiet. "I asked you a question, Meggs."

The bully boy crept back into his voice, though he would probably think it was mere ship's captain, expecting his answer by rights. Why did he have to be like this, so relentlessly probing? Why couldn't he leave well enough alone? And why, damn it all to hell, *why* did she still want him like air, and breathing, and water? "No, you didn't ask me a question, you accused me of lying."

"Where did you learn that music?" His tone was hard and

uncompromising. "No one in a kiddie ken teaches English Baroque composers."

The anger and frustration and wanting all piled up inside her, pushing and shoving to get out. "How would you know? How would you know anything about it? You, who grew up among all this. You, who haven't known a day of want in your life."

"For your information, I did not grow up 'among all this.' My father was not a viscount. I grew up in Scotland, a gentleman farmer's second son, who had to make his way in the world and earn every advancement in my profession."

"Well, good for you."

"And no matter the temptations, or the need, I've never stolen or lied—" He stopped himself abruptly.

But she still felt the blow. After everything, this was what he truly thought of her. Hurt and anger, and pride, made her voice as quiet and stunning as a blade. "No, you hire out for that, don't you?"

His face turned to flint, registering the bitter truth of her accusation.

"Yes," she answered for him. "That's what you need me for, to do your lying and stealing for you."

"Is that all it is to you, Meggs? All *I* am to you? A job?" His own accusation was low and quiet, but just as lethal.

"You don't need me for anything else. Once I've done whatever the next job is, stealing like a 'lady,' you'll have no more use for me. You'll go back to your ship and I'll go back—" Oh, sweet Lord, there was the despicable heat welling in her yes. Nan would have clouted her. She ought to clout herself, but she was too tired. Too scared and tired of fighting. Always fighting, for every penny, for every advantage, for every scrap of his attention.

Because no matter how warm, or well fed, or well paid she was, without him, she would be alone. "I don't have anything, anywhere, or anybody to go back to."

Damn his eyes. How could he just stand there, looking at her as if *she* were the one breaking *his* heart. This time, when she left him, she kept her head high and made herself walk.

She couldn't sleep. Too many things were crowding into her mind, too many useless, tormenting feelings and memories, crowding and careening around in her gut.

She hated feeling so alone. Every time she thought of her brother—so far away out on the cold, wet sea—she couldn't imagine he could be happy. Or warm. While here she was, tucked up beside a blazing fire with warm shawls and eiderdown to insulate her from the winter cold and damp. She sat cross-legged on the bed and watched the snow trace out the shapes of the trees outside the window, and she listened to the miraculous hush of the falling flakes. This was what the Christmas season was supposed to be like, but instead of happy, she felt hollow. Even when she and Timmy had had next to nothing, she'd never felt this alone. This empty. Warmth and cheer and security were nothing without someone to share it with.

What was to become of her now? What was she going to make of herself? She had felt herself to be hanging at the edge of something irrevocable before tonight, but her argument with Hugh had brought it back to the front of her mind. She was poised precariously between her past and her future, with no bridge, no way of getting from one to the other.

A muted knock at her door, and at her answer, Hugh's dark silhouette entered into the firelight.

Meggs felt awkward, uncomfortable, and wary. He didn't look like a man intent on a reconciliation. He looked as sober as a hanging judge, ready to pronounce sentence. "What is it?"

He said nothing as he came in but sat next to her on the bed. "I'm sorry. I'm . . . I'm such an ass in a drawing room. I had meant to give you this tonight. But we ended up arguing. Well, here." And held out a small, wrapped present.

She looked at it without moving to take it, stupefied by surprise. Of all things, she could not have predicted he would want to give her a present. It was a small box, with an uneven, blue velvet bow. He had wrapped this himself.

"It's for you. I know it's not Christmas yet, but I thought . . . I wanted to be the first to wish you Happy Christmas."

"You came here to give me a present?" Was this a new tack, to call himself an ass and then cozen his answers out of her with gifts? Lord, but it would probably work. "But I don't have anything for you."

"You're not meant to." He put it in her lap because she still hadn't ordered her wits enough to take the silly, thoughtful, darling thing.

"Thank you." She picked it up and ran her fingers across the plush velvet.

"It is traditional, upon receiving a Christmas present, to actually *open* it."

She smiled then, mostly because his tone was just aggravated enough to be silly.

"Is it?" She pulled the scrap of velvet fabric loose slowly until she uncovered a lovely gold filagreed cross; it was decorated in an intricate interlacing pattern with a single pearl at the center, hanging on a delicate chain. Oh, Lord. It was so very, very lovely. So very, very innocent and perfect. It was everything she wanted to be. It was nothing she was.

"It's so beautiful. I've never—" She had no voice. Heat was gathering deep in her throat and behind her eyes. Dash it all. She clutched the cross in her hand because she couldn't put it on. "Thank you."

"You're welcome. Let me put it on for you."

"No. I couldn't, really—"

But he was already taking it from her hand and looping it over her head from behind. The light chain settled around her neck, just as his hands settled on her shoulders, and his fingers traced the contours of her collarbones.

"Hugh, I know you mean to be kind, but it's not that simple. I can't—"

"Hush. Yes, you can."

His mouth joined his hands, and he kissed the nape of her neck. And then, that spot on the side. That place where sensations skittered and shivered under her skin to make every muscle in her body tense and quiver in expectation. He did not disappoint.

This is what she needed, what she wanted—this contact, this warmth. His warmth. When he was with her like this, she could push aside all her doubts about tomorrow and be happy in these fleeting moments of his tender attention.

He kissed his way up the sensitive tendon to her ear, arousing her desire by slow degrees, turning her breath light and golden. His teeth closed down on the lobe of her ear, tugging her head around until she turned, and his lips were there, upon hers. His mouth was warm and drugging, and she was where she wanted to be, wrapped in his arms, held by his strong hands, kissed by his astonishingly clever mouth. She loved how muzzy and warm he could make her feel, how sensation burrowed down deep into her very bones, until she wanted to burrow into *him*, to taste and touch and give pleasure to him, just as he was giving to her.

And even as his mouth played upon hers, his hands were stripping the batiste sleeping gown over her head, as if it were nothing more than lace and cobwebs, until she was naked before him. He pushed her back onto the bed, and shivers ran riot across her skin, not from the chill of the air but from the heat in his icy eyes.

"I love it when you let me look at you." His strong hands dragged across her flesh. "At this." He traced the curve of her breast. "And this." His eyes swerved over the course of her belly as his finger traced the architecture of her hip bone. "And this."

His hands skated farther along the inner sides of her thighs to ease her legs apart. And stopped cold.

"Meggs," he breathed very carefully, "what have you done?"

He was poised above her, his eyes raking her body. But his chest rose and fell rapidly behind the confines of his shirt and waistcoat.

She took a deep, emboldening breath, uncertain and a little overwhelmed now that the moment had come. She had to show him. She had to convince him that she wasn't a simpering, innocent miss, and never would be. Not even for him.

She let her hands flow down across her body, outlining her curves and plains, until her hands reached her mound. She undulated a little, conscious of the picture she must present to him, all tousled curls and ripe, pink flesh. Like the courtesan she had once accused him of wanting her to be. Only now she was the one who wanted. She wanted him to see who she really was. "You said," her voice the barest whisper, "you would have done some judicious trimming and so I—"

His mouth dove down upon hers, ravenous and demanding, the probe of his lips and tongue like a drug for her needy body. He broke the kiss to rasp into her ear, "I also said, I would enjoy barbering you, so next time, let me do it for you."

The heat and desire in his eyes washed across her body like an intimate touch, tumbling and cascading deep into her being. Her eyelids closed as her body arced like a wave beneath his hands. A cry of anguish and need and pleasure flew out of her throat.

He rose up on his knees and moved between her legs so he could stroke down her belly with both hands. "Do you remember that word, 'erotic'? Inflaming the passions? And how it makes me feel the need to touch you? It makes me want to do *this*."

He pushed her knees wider, baring her fully to his gaze. "It makes me want to look at all the pink, erotic parts of you." He gazed at her body, slowly and deliberately, letting her watch him look at her. Then he bent to kiss the tiny, dark birthmark on the inside of her thigh before he put his mouth to the delicate folds of her flesh.

Meggs forgot how to breathe. She forgot everything but the feel of his mouth upon her. There was nothing but the subtle probe of his tongue into her body, and the tight bud of pleasure, where his mouth closed softly over her.

She threw her head back and closed her eyes as he stroked her lightly with his tongue. Her body was warm and spilling heat, quivering under his caress. Needy, inarticulate sounds flew past her lips, urging him on.

"Shh, love," he admonished.

But she couldn't help herself, couldn't stop. The needy, mindless cries came with every delicate touch of his tongue to her flesh. And then it was too much. He moved to replace his tongue with his hand and whispered his thumb across her. She bucked up into his hand and rained heat and sunlight across his palm.

She was panting audibly, feeling every inch of skin, every pore on her body, and still he did not relent. He slid one long finger inside her, and at the same time he smothered her gasp with his other hand across her mouth. He rose above her, a dark, looming silhouette, touching her deeply and intimately with his hands.

"Shh. You have to be quiet. Or I'll be forced to stop doing this." He speared another finger inside her, and her body arced up to greet him. "Or this." And he turned his fingers to press upon her *there*. And it was too much. Again and again. It was bliss and heat and need and—

She needed him. Needed to feel him. She wanted him everywhere, wanted to touch and taste him as he had touched and tasted her. She licked the salt of his body along his open shirt, and when she came to the meat of his sculpted shoulder muscle—she bit him. She didn't know what came over her, but when a sound of deep animal appreciation howled out of him, she did it again.

She bit his hand as he muffled her cries, and he was there, covering her, meeting her body with his own, feeding her need for heat and friction. He had only loosed the flap on his breeches, and it was somehow erotic that she was beneath him, open and naked and pale in the reflected firelight. All this while he was above, dark and clothed, with only the pale, incandescent light from his eyes shining down at her. Looking at her body, watching every little thing she did, each arch and sigh.

She reached up to fist her hands in the linen of his shirt, to feel the starch and smell his clean scent, and to tether herself to him, before she flew away again. Before she abandoned herself to the carnal heat, pushed higher and higher by the buttery texture of his suede breeches rubbing against her inner thighs as he rocked into her.

Her breath was coming in unmannerly, groaning pants. Surely the rest of the house could hear her and would know what she was doing. She covered her mouth with her own hand, desperate to hold back, to quiet the gasps and moans of pleasure stealing out of her mouth with every powerful surge of his body into hers.

"That's it." His voice was rough and urgent. "You have to keep yourself quiet or I'll have to stop fucking you."

"No!" she breathed and flung her hands out wide, digging her fingers into the coverlet, holding on for all she had. "You can't."

"I can." He surged into her, deep within to touch her womb, and then he withdrew nearly to the end. "And I will. If you can't keep quiet."

"I will."

"You can't moan."

She bit down on her lip and shook her head side to side, thrashing the feelings out of her.

"You can't scream when I fuck you like this." He hooked his hands under her knees and pulled them upward, bearing into her roughly, deeper into her core, the pain and pleasure of his body rubbing against hers, meshing and melting into heated bliss.

And her heart exploded and flung her into the black velvet darkness.

CHAPTER 25

Meggs put off all thinking, all worrying, and all planning for the future until after the Balfour Advent Ball. She was going to allow herself to float along, buoyed above the ocean of care for just a little while longer. Or at least as long as she possibly could.

Her time within the approval of Society, of his family, wouldn't last much longer, but she held on tight to her little dreamtime. All her other dreams had fallen away—of returning to her own home in the country, of taking up her life anonymously, of finding the peaceful love she had once known. They were nothing but a foolish, childish fantasy. But this, this joy she got from the joining of their bodies, was real. It would make no difference if she lived out the rest of her days as his mistress. She could not reclaim what she had lost. She had ruined herself irrevocably the first moment she had decided to turn thief, the first moment she had compromised the principles she had been raised with. But there was nothing to regret in the fierce bliss he gave her. If that was all the passion and joy she was to know for the rest of her life, then so be it.

The evening of the ball came bright and clear, the moon lighting the dry roads so every family of the neighborhood of

Balfour arrived in good time. The viscountess did all the work of introducing her.

"The connection is really quite slight. Do you remember Eugenia, Countess of Whelmshire? My second cousin. No? Lovely girl, went to school with her, married superbly. Well, this is her youngest sister Effie's daughter's girl. But no matter, it's such a treat to have a girl in the house, someone to fuss over and dress. Makes me feel young again, all the tinkering and plotting after the young gentlemen."

Meggs had nothing to do but smile and look sweet and happy in her beautiful iced pink silk ball gown and beautiful cross necklace. And she *was* happy. Though Hugh had been far away, at the other end of the table at dinner, he had spoken to her.

"You're to dance the opening set with me—that is if you'll have me."

"Of course." She smiled up at him. The expectation of being able to hold his hand and look up at him for twenty minutes all together, without once having to hide her feelings, was its own kind of bliss.

And so when the musicians began to play, and her captain stepped up to claim her, she smiled at him as if he were the only person in the room.

"Miss Evans."

"Captain McAlden."

"Come, let us dance, and you can pretend to be charmed by my clumsiness."

"I don't have to pretend." She laughed and was rewarded with one of his rare, almost silly smiles. But then as they danced, he grew more serious, more focused, until it was *she* who felt as if she were the only person in the room. When he looked at her like that, that way he had of making her feel as if she was not dressed at all but standing before him clad only in her skin, she blushed a startling crimson.

"Stop looking at me like that," she admonished when they came together.

"Like what? How am I looking at you?"

"As if . . ." Heat rose across her face, but it did not stop her from smiling. "You know very well what you're doing."

"No, I'm not *doing* anything. I'm merely thinking about *doing*. And planning to do later. Very much later. Don't forget that as the choir boys try to charm you into kissing them."

Heat set in under her skin and hummed along there in happy anticipation. The evening became a whirl. After the first set, the viscountess returned to lead Meggs around for more introductions. With each turn about the room, young men seemed to materialize out of nowhere, asking for the privilege of one of Miss Evans's dances, if she had them to spare. She played her part, accepting demurely and dancing with each gentleman who asked without talking too much, or revealing anything about herself. But it was all lovely, lovely, lovely.

And so she was completely unprepared when the viscountess steered her toward a tiny, elderly woman seated at the center side of the room on a chaise.

"My dear Anne." The viscountess greeted her friend. "May I have the pleasure of presenting my protégé, Miss Evans? Margaret, I would like to introduce you to my great friend, Her Grace the Dowager Duchess of Fenmore."

Meggs stumbled to a standstill. And felt her heart give out, crumbling into hot icy pieces within her chest. But it only felt as though it had given out, for she was still standing, still breathing, still expected to speak and say something into the strange, echoing silence between them.

"Your Grace." She looked the old woman in the eye, determined not to blink, not to so much as stammer. She couldn't help it—there was ice and something more—blame and hatred coming from her voice.

The old lady was noticeably ruffled, taken aback at her

nearly insolent tone, though she appeared to have a better grasp of the civilities. "I'm sorry, Miss . . . ?"

"Miss Evans," the viscountess supplied. She frowned at Meggs, her eyes full of concern. "She's my cousin's . . . Are you quite all right, my dear?"

Meggs looked back at the duchess, who was staring at her, baffled and unsettled. Meggs knew she was supposed to say something, to make some sort of apology, but she could only stare back. Then Hugh appeared out of nowhere at her side, murmuring something about the heat and needing air, leading her away with an uncompromising grip at her elbow.

"What has gotten into you?" Hugh was looking at her sharply, those eyes steely and unblinking. "You're antagonizing the Duchess of Fenmore. You're supposed to take the role of a simpering, witless, young thing, not sparring verbally with Her Grace."

"I'm sorry." But she wasn't, and he knew it from her voice, which was still shaking.

"Meggs? What is going on?"

How could she explain? There was nothing she could say that he would believe. "Nothing. You're right, it is hot and close in here."

"Try to remember your behavior will reflect directly upon my mother."

The mention of the viscountess had a strong effect. "Yes," she agreed. "I understand. I am sorry. I need to go to the withdrawing room."

And she was sorry now. She felt awful, the disconcerting jumble of feelings over the past weeks nothing in comparison to the seething roil of poison in her gut. Meggs had imagined this moment a thousand and six times over the past years, had pictured the meeting, but in her dreamlike scenarios, she was joyful and triumphant, while the old lady was to have been weeping and contrite. But this had been horrible—awkward and unfulfilling. The moment had come and gone before she could compose herself enough to get past the dry burning in her throat and say anything to the point.

The withdrawing room was helpfully equipped with a tray of champagne glasses, and Meggs took one and gulped it down. Bubbles immediately came up into her nose, and she thought she might sneeze, but she didn't, so she took another, more cautious sip to erase the raw dryness in her throat. No wonder people thought it was wonderful. The wine tasted light and bright, and wonderful—it tasted like hope.

So she took another swallow. And another.

Who cared about one old lady? Not her. There were choir boys to fleece.

Lady Balfour took her son by the arm. "Hugh, darling, just some motherly advice. You're sadly dimming my triumph with your lovely Miss Evans by this atrocious dog in the manger show."

"She's not my Miss Evans."

"Really? Then to what purpose is all this? Don't be silly. You're as transparent as a window glass. Now come along. You're scowling ferociously at Mr. Blythwyn while he dances with Miss Evans, and it won't do. You look as if you'd like to throttle him."

Hugh was reminded of a similar comment he had once made to a friend, Colonel Rupert Delacorte, in exactly this same situation. And look what had happened to him—tied up in knots by the ravishing Miss Burke, instead of throttling her. But the Ravishing Miss Burke was not a liar, a sneak thief, pickpocket, and robber. She was not a "prime filching mort."

Hugh didn't know exactly what it was about Meggs tonight, but he couldn't take his eyes off her. Nor could he relax his guard. Something was wrong, and he damned himself for a fool in instigating this whole experiment. He should have known she would not be able to resist the compulsion to steal. She was working the dance floor as if it were Covent Garden.

As for Blythwyn—he was taking every opportunity to leer down the front of Meggs's gown. "Damned Welshman."

"None of that," his mother admonished. "He's merely talking to her, and she is talking back, learning to use that lovely smile of hers just as you wanted. You wanted the girl to move in society, and she's doing it. Pray don't dim her triumph with your misplaced disapproval."

It would hardly be a triumph if someone caught her with her hand in their pocket. Her lovely smile would do her no good then.

His mother took his silence as assent. "Thank you. I would suggest you go and flirt with some other young lady, but I know that's far beyond your powers of civility."

"Is that what you call what she's doing—flirting?"

"Hugh. Only in the best way, the correct way. A girl has to flirt and talk, otherwise young men just stare at their bosoms and plot how soon they can drag them off to the nearest dark spot." She turned those canny, vixen eyes on him. "There, the dance is finished. There are some people I'd like her to meet."

Meggs came off the dance floor glowing. She gave him what he could only call a mischievous smile as she brushed by. And then he felt the slight tug on his waistcoat. He reached immediately into his pocket—only to find two watches.

"God's balls, Meggs, what in blazes do you think you're doing?"

"Have to keep my hand in, don't I? I get tired of stealing yours all the time, though it is the nicest."

And away she went, with his mother murmuring vague things about "—my poor cousin's girl. So happy to have her with me. Gives me a chance to bring a girl out at last. Such a pleasure. How do you like her frock? Don't you think she looks well in that silk. Madame Egremont, of course." All as light and sparkling as champagne.

Just when Hugh felt his mood could not be made worse, he

spied Major Rawsthorne strolling toward him, looking like a
rat amongst the chicken eggs. There was only one reason he
would be approaching Hugh after their last set-to—he was
looking to make trouble.

"Surprised?"

"Not particularly," Hugh lied. He should have spoken to
Balfour about expurgating his guest list after his last en-
counter with this bastard. "To what do we owe the . . . honor,
Major?"

"Oh, country air, festivities, charming company. Although I
must say, I am surprised to see you here. Thought you'd still
have yourself chained to old Middleton's side. You have a reputation as a man who cares little for finer society."

"I consider it a privilege to serve the admiral and His
Majesty's Navy, in any way I might be asked to do so." God's
balls he was beginning to sound as pompous as Rawsthorne
himself.

"Clearly. I was just telling Lord Cummings"—who had
strolled over to join Rawsthorne—"you quite stole a march on
me, young man. Captain McAlden, here, handed us a traitor,
all but convicted of his crimes, along with all the evidence—
and still I know nothing of how this miraculous feat was accomplished. Still waiting for your report."

Lord Cummings of the unsavory friends down on the
Cheapside docks. To what purpose was this bloody game?
"I'm sure the Admiralty will forward you a copy in due time. It
is nearly Christmas, Major. I hope the admiral's staff has better
things to do than copy out reports."

"The war doesn't stop for Christmas, Captain," Rawsthorne
hectored, pious as a parson. "But you are here to celebrate, no
doubt. You should be well assured of your preferment. Although the second man, your traitor's accomplice, slipped
through your hands."

"My hands?" The anger Hugh had tried to stifle, out of re-
spect for his mother and Viscount Balfour, not to mention to

keep Meggs safe, seethed to the surface. "I gave your department everything you needed to arrest the man. You jeopardized my . . . men, gathering that evidence on Falconer for nothing. You let him go with your blatant arrest of Stoval in St. James's."

Rawsthorne smiled, taking obvious pleasure in toying with him. "We won't quibble on a night like this. The intelligence leak from the Admiralty has at last been stemmed, and that was all you were required to do."

Hugh shut his mouth over his anger, though he felt hard and edgy with the need to smash his fist into Rawsthorne's fucking face.

"Yes, we're all here to enjoy ourselves." Rawsthorne made a show of looking about him, though Hugh knew the moment he spoke what the major was about to do. "There are some lovely girls about. That young lady is your cousin, I understand."

Raw hatred and fear—oh, yes, he'd be a fool not to fear Rawsthorne, the same way he would be a fool to underestimate an opponent at sea—surged and heated his blood. The violence rising from deep within him felt more and more inevitable. But he had to be careful now. Rawsthorne was purposefully baiting him, and the bastard must have firepower— he never would have engaged with Hugh unless he felt he had the advantage—but he was, as yet, keeping whatever he knew to himself. But Rawsthorne could bloody well stay away from Meggs. "My cousin is not available to dance with you. Do I make myself clear?"

Rawsthorne smiled. "Explicitly, old man. It is all quite clear to me."

Meggs watched the exchange between Hugh and the army major with interest from her vantage point at the top of the set she was currently dancing with the curate. Mr. Phelps proved to be an obliging and surprisingly energetic dancer, thankfully leaving off all mention of the gospels during the set. And he did not tax her with inattention when she became involved in watching Hugh's exchange with the major.

Hugh did not like that man. Not one bit. If she were the major, she would have been scurrying far away. The captain was looking more and more like God's revenge against murder, but the major—why the major was egging him on.

And now the major was sauntering away and taking out a gold and enamel snuff box to serve himself up a pinch. Filthy habit that, old Nan used to say, and Meggs could only concur. What a toad. It would give her great pleasure to serve him up to the captain like a trophy.

When the dance ended, she snagged another glass of champagne from a passing footman and headed in the major's direction.

Hugh saw it all at a distance, as if the events unfolding before his eyes were happening at the end of his spyglass, miles away across the sea of bodies in the ballroom. Somehow, someway, despite his injunction, wrongly, stupidly, Meggs was being led out onto the dance floor by Rawsthorne.

Hugh was going to kill the bastard—his mother's ball and the scandal be damned. He was going to pummel Rawsthorne until he was nothing but a bloody piece of pulp.

Every nerve in his body was on alert. His right hand was searching his belt for the sword he was not wearing, because he could not wear his uniform or weapon while he was not on active duty. *She* was his duty.

She tossed a smile to him across the floor as she turned in a figure, away from Rawsthorne—that cheeky, mischievous smile that brought dimples out in her cheeks. But she had turned back before Hugh could make a gesture—his hand cutting back and forth across his throat—to stop whatever lunacy she thought she was about.

On she danced, laughing and smiling at all the other dancers. And then everything slowed, and the edges of Hugh's vision seemed to close in until there was nothing but Meggs. She began a figure and then went the wrong way. And crashed into the wall of Rawsthorne's chest. Hugh wanted to shout, to jump between them, but it was already over, and other hands had intervened to help Meggs up and steady her, and put her on the right way. She was laughing gaily, smiling, and apologizing as if she hadn't a care in the world.

As if she hadn't just robbed Rawsthorne blind.

Hugh had to get to her. He had to stop her before anything else happened. He fought his way across the dance floor as though he were trying to make way against a running tide. He bumped into the dancers right and left. He didn't care. He had to reach her.

Finally, finally, he caught Meggs by the wrist. "Excuse me. Cousin Margaret, my mother requires you."

Meggs gave him a huge smile and allowed herself to be led away. As soon as they cleared the lines of dancers, Hugh felt another unfamiliar weight settle into his pocket. He fished it out without looking and let it drop to the crowded floor as he towed her on. "Are you out of your bloody mind?"

"Yes!" She was all sauce and dimples.

"God's balls. You're drunk."

"Am I? I don't feel drunk. I feel wonderful!"

Even as she leaned in closer to the warmth of Hugh's chest, Meggs felt another hand close around her wrist like a manacle.

"A word, *Miss* Evans," Major Rawsthorne hissed through clenched teeth.

"I beg your pardon, Major." As if there weren't already players enough, Mr. Blythwyn stepped innocently into the fray, back to claim his second dance. "But Miss Evans is my partner for the next dance."

"No." The major didn't so much as look at him. His eyes remained fixed on her. "I have unfinished business with Miss Evans."

"Your *business*"—Hugh gave the word a dubious inflection as he loomed over Rawsthorne—"will have to wait. Miss Evans is not at your disposal. Let her go."

Meggs very much hoped that she would not be disposed of at all in the course of the evening, but she was glad of even the temporary reprieve.

Rawsthorne snarled, "Where is it?" And right there, in front of God and everyone, he yanked her toward him and started to frisk her, his hands roving up and down her body in search of the stolen snuff box.

Meggs repressed her instincts to mash the bastard's cods in right then and there and instead did what any proper, gently bred young lady being escorted by Lady Balfour would do. She screamed loudly and with great vigor, and wilted into a faint.

"Unhand her this instant." That was her captain, all snarling bear, even as he caught her.

"She stole my snuff box," the major fumed.

Well, points to him for awareness. But points off for sheer stupidity. No matter that the captain was all angry command, the stupid, handsy bastard continued to try to frisk her quite thoroughly, even as Hugh tried to pull her away.

"I don't know what he's talking about." She opened her eyes wide and went all wounded doe. But the major, clever bastard, wasn't buying one Drury Lane farthing of it.

"Of course she does." Rawsthorne's voice rose with his mounting frustration. "I doubt this little baggage with the light fingers is even your cousin at all."

There was a general chorus of "oohs" from the crowd of guests as people drew back and simultaneously pressed forward, anxious to hear every word.

The captain was as smooth and cool as an iceboat. "Is that

what you're looking for, major?" He pointed to the snuff box, halfway across the floor. Oh, he was a clever one, her captain. She hadn't even seen him ditch it. "You dropped it on the dance floor."

Rawsthorne stalked away from them and snatched it up. But his anger and his potential humiliation had made him find a new target. "Is that how you did it, McAlden? Gained your knighthood by employing this little whore to steal your secrets and save the Admiralty from dishonor and humiliation?"

Hugh helped her to her feet and spoke into the screaming silence quietly, but there was no doubt that the entire assembly heard every word. "You do both Miss Evans and my family, not to mention His Majesty's Royal Navy, a grave insult by such careless words."

"Spare me your Scottish family honor," Rawsthorne sneered. "You may have fooled the rest of the world with your fancy piece, but I know a two-penny St. Giles whore when I see one."

"I have no doubt *you* do know a great many things about St. Giles whores," her captain enunciated coolly. "And I'm sure you will do me the honor, Major, of seeing you into hell at your earliest convenience."

"A duel?" scathed Rawsthorne. "I'm not going to fight a duel over a thieving whore. Find your consolation between her legs if you need to."

There was an audible intake of breath as the ballgoers registered their shock at such language.

"Since you refuse to act the gentleman—" Hugh stepped closer and backhanded Rawsthorne across the face with a slap so hard, the man stumbled sideways from the force.

There were shouts and screams, and ladies actually fainted as Rawsthorne leapt at the captain but was restrained by the hands of others. The mark of the blow was livid against his sallow skin, and blood was oozing from the corner of his mouth.

But Meggs could barely register the crowd pressing forward. Or even the two men at the center of the turmoil. Everything faded until she could only see the old woman advancing inexorably across the widening expanse of floor toward *her*.

Hugh's rage was such that he was entirely, effortlessly calm. Everything faded but the deep, abiding sense of certainty and the snarling face of the man he would shortly kill. He did not see the small but formidable old woman until she was upon them.

"That will be quite enough of that." The Dowager Duchess of Fenmore stepped in the fray, followed directly by his mother and Viscount Balfour.

"There will be no duel." The old lady commanded them with the casual haughtiness only a dowager duchess with decades of having her way could produce. And although her remarks would seem to have been directed at the men, she was bearing down upon Meggs like a warship under full sail, parting the waves of gawking bystanders with the menace of her cane.

"Throw that blaggart out with the dogs." The duchess flung her hand at Rawsthorne as she came near. "I will not hear another word of his outrageous raving. This girl cannot possibly be any of the vile and despicable things he has said. This girl is *my granddaughter*."

And then, for a change, all hell broke loose.

Everybody spoke at once, and the crowd surged forward. Hugh was trying to go forward as well, trying to reach Meggs, to stop this strange travesty before it was too late. But there were too many people.

He heard Viscount Balfour take charge. "Maitland," he addressed his eldest son, "please see to the musicians while I escort Major Rawsthorne from the premises. Eleanor, perhaps the duchess would prefer to retire to your sitting room, and we can end this spectacle."

"Now, I'll never stand a chance," the young man at Hugh's elbow complained. "It was bad enough when she was only your cousin, but now she's the granddaughter of a duchess, she's far beyond my touch."

Hugh looked back to see Meggs throw him a desperate glance over her shoulder as she was all but frog-marched out of the ballroom like a prisoner with the dowager on one arm and the viscountess on the other. He followed quickly on their heels, taking the stairs two at a time to reach her before this stupid travesty went any further. But even once in his mother's private apartments, he could see there would be no chance to steal her away. The old lady had Meggs in a death grip—her knuckles were stark white on Meggs's pale upper arm.

And they were not alone. His stepfather had returned, taking command of the room even as others came in. Hugh was nearly swallowed up by the cacophony of voices, each one more strident that its neighbor, each voice insisting on having its opinion in the matter heard.

The current Duke of Fenmore, the cousin of the dowager duchess's husband, the late duke, was speaking. "My dear Anne, are you quite sure?"

The dowager was strident. "I am sure. Margaret Evans. I could scarce believe it. You took your mother's name. I knew it the moment I saw you. Oh, my dear girl." The woman was grasping Meggs's hand tightly. "I would have known you anywhere. You're the very image of her."

Meggs looked absolutely stricken, as though she were about to toss up her accounts. Hugh had only once seen her so devoid of color or animation.

His mother was trying to inject some measure of sanity. "Your Grace, I don't think that Miss Evans could possibly be who—"

"Please, Eleanor. I know my own grandchild. I have all the proof I shall need."

"But the law is another matter entirely," the duke cautioned quietly. "I understand your—"

"You know the proofs as well as I, Charles. The child had two identical birthmarks on the inside of her arms, just above the elbow." Duchess took Meggs's hands and held her arms up, turning them inward. A collective gasp rose from the group. "And another mark."

Hugh's blood went cold as the old lady sailed on, heedless of the destruction in her wake.

"On the inside of her left leg, in the shape of a house wren. At least that's what they thought when she was born, and why her mother called her Birdy."

A chill settled into Hugh's bones. The dusky tan birthmark was still quite recognizable. He had lingered there, on the inside of her white thigh, to kiss it, just last night.

Tears were streaming down Meggs's face, marbling her cheeks with red and white splotches. The duchess was still holding Meggs's hands, but her own had begun to tremble.

"It only remains for you to tell us, dear child."

Meggs nodded and spoke through her gasping sobs. "It's true. My name is Trinity Margurite Evans. I was born on October the thirteenth, in the year of our Lord 1779 to Margaret Augusta and Lord Arthur John Evans in the village of Tissington, where my father was Rector of St. Mary's Church on the estate of the Fitzherberts."

Hugh was beyond stunned—he felt gutted. As though she had fired a cannon point blank into his chest. The dowager closed her eyes and reeled a little. The duke was there instantly, steadying her before she could fall.

"And the boy?" the old woman managed when she had collected herself. "Your brother."

"Timmy is . . ." Meggs met Hugh's eyes for the first time but didn't speak. She looked hunted, a wild animal finally run to ground.

Hugh found his voice. "He is currently on duty as a midshipman in His Majesty's Royal Navy, under Captain Jameson Marlowe of the sloop *Defiant*, on Channel defense."

The dowager turned her horrified face to him. "What is my son's heir, the Duke of Fenmore, doing on Channel duty, as a midshipman of all things?"

"I was not aware of the boy's identity." His gaze was back at Meggs, staring hard, trying to urge her to stop this utter madness. "I was trying to do what I could to assist the boy in a profession, as he seemed to have no other . . . benefactors."

"Yes, yes, of course." The dowager took a fortifying breath, and then as someone pressed a glass of sherry into her hand, a fortifying drink. "But you will send word to have him returned directly."

"Your Grace." Hugh could do nothing but bow.

At the same time the current duke spoke, very kindly. "Anne, perhaps it would be best to verify the identity of the children before—"

"Verify away, Charles. Yes, let us please make sure it is all right and tight and all the lawyers happy, though I hate to think it will rob you of the dukedom. But in the meantime, I want that boy home." She turned to Hugh. "And you will assist me. You, who appear to have been seeing to my grandchildren's benefit."

It was hours before Meggs could finally get free of all the tears, and questions, and hand holding. The dowager duchess had not wanted to let her out of her sight, but she had finally been persuaded by Viscountess Balfour to retire and let Meggs do the same.

But instead of going to her own rooms as she ought, Meggs ran to Hugh's, and went in without even knocking.

He was prowling in front of the fire like a caged animal, staring into its depths with an empty glass in his hand. But he did not in any way look pleased to see her. She thought again of the Bible verse—*I have set my face like flint.*

He wasted no time. "What in God's name do you think you're doing? This is beyond all—" He bit off the rest of his words, as if they left a bad taste in his mouth.

"I know I shouldn't be here, but I had to talk to you. I had to explain—"

"How can you possibly explain? I'm not going to assist you in this swindle, Meggs. It was one thing to rob every gentleman at the ball blind, but I can't allow you to delude the Dowager Duchess of Fenmore, of all things and all people. How long do you think it's going to last before she finds you out? The duke will certainly see to it, directly, if for no other reason than to preserve his title. What were you thinking to let yourself be taken for the goddamned Duchess of Fenmore's granddaughter? I won't even ask how you managed to learn the necessary information. By God, you are without a bloody doubt the stupidest, prime-est filching mort I've ever encountered."

She backed away, away from his wrath. Of all the people, she had not expected this from *him*. "I'm not the one who made the claim."

"No, but you didn't refute it. Why, in God's name? Why?"

It took a very long moment for Meggs to absorb all the cutting hurt and shame of his accusation. He thought still, after everything, she was a liar. Not about little things or lour, but—

She lifted up her wobbling chin and made herself speak firmly. "Because it's true."

"God damn it. I told you once, not to even *think* to cozen me, or I'd—"

"It's true," she repeated more strongly as if saying it again could convince her it had truly happened. After all this time. "It's the stupid, God's honest truth. She's my grandmother."

"It can't be true."

"But it is." She subsided onto the bench at the end of his bed. "It's so very strange. I had convinced myself it would never happen. I told myself every day that there was no hope. But I couldn't stop it—the hoping. And now—" She looked at him, willing him to understand. "I thought I would be happy. Or at least gleeful. Finally, finally, she's found us and she's acknowledged us, and we're who we're meant to be. But . . . I dunno. I thought I'd feel . . . different."

"How long have you known?"

She picked up her shoulders and let her hands fall against her sides. "Always."

"Always? Why in the bloody hell didn't you tell me?" His disbelief was rapidly giving way to anger, the raw power becoming unleashed.

"As if you would have believed me. You didn't believe anything else."

He swore, bluntly and fluently, in a way that put the gin men of St. Giles to shame. "And I suppose next you're going to tell me the Tanner really is the heir of the late duke?"

Her answer was quiet. Because, until this very evening, she had never, ever, not even in her sunniest hour, dared to think it could ever become true. "My father was the second son, and took holy orders, but when his elder brother died, he did not want to leave the church. He didn't want to take up the title, even though it was his. Timmy was his only son. He is the duke." An unnerving thought snuck into her brain. "Unless there's something you know and he's . . ."

"No. He is very much alive and well. My good friend Captain Marlowe has the dubious honor of having the Duke of Fenmore as his midshipman on *Defiant*."

She hadn't missed the sarcasm in his tone, but her relief overrode it. She sagged back into the bench. "Thank you."

"Is that all you can say for yourself? My God, Meggs." He ran his hand through his hair in that recognizable gesture of frustration. "It's such a mess. If this is true, we'll have to marry quickly now," he continued almost as if he were talking to himself, prowling back and forth, making plans for a sea battle and not proposing marriage.

"What do you mean, *if?* Haven't you been listening?" Now she *was* going to faint, for real. Her heart had broken open, and all the blood was pouring its heat into the rest of her body, raining needles of pain in her chest, making it impossible to breathe.

"No, we must. There's really no alternative."

"No." Oh, dear God. She was so stupid. She had got it all wrong. She had assumed he cared for her, beyond— Just beyond. She had thought he must love her. He had never said so, but she had assumed it from his caring for her, from his bringing her to his mother, from the way he looked at her when no one else was looking. The possessive way a man looks at a woman he wants for his own. "No." She said it again, and then to get rid of the pain, to share the spite more evenly between them, she added, "My grandmother never need know you fucked me against the wall of your laundry. I do have some discretion, though perhaps not so much as I would have liked."

That piece of ammunition was answered by livid, icy silence.

"You could be pregnant." He stated it bluntly, to shock her, his voice devoid of warmth. "You could be carrying my child. Have you thought of that?"

She found it *was* her turn to be shocked. "Well, what a remarkable sense of timing you have, Captain, to bring that topic up for the first time, now. A little late for you to begin to think of that." She sharpened her sarcasm to a fine, stabbing point. "I didn't hear you say a word about 'your child' weeks ago when you first realized the benefits of sleeping with your employees."

"Meggs." His voice was rigidly controlled. "It wasn't like that, and you know it."

"It was exactly like that. What was I supposed to do?"

"God damn you to hell. You chose, Meggs. You know you chose."

Meggs retreated in the face of this uncomfortable truth. The menace in him was impossible to miss.

"Well, it seems I have another choice to make right now."

She slammed the door behind her so hard it splintered. Just like her heart.

CHAPTER 26

She was gone. Just like that. They took her away the next morning, the Fenmore traveling coach wheeling down the drive with a disdainful spray of gravel, just after dawn. In a hurry to leave.

And he was alone, with his thoughts and his good intentions amounting to naught. Alone, the way he had once thought he wanted to be.

At least until his stepfather looked up from reading his newspaper at the breakfast table and said, "I assume you'll be wanting to use a coach."

"I hadn't thought to return to London. I can travel post to go down to Portsmouth, but—"

"No. To Fenmore." When Hugh didn't immediately respond, Viscount Balfour clarified his point. "You *will* be going to Fenmore. To make your offer."

"I hadn't—"

"Then you should. You will. You will most assuredly spare your mother the indignity of having to tell you to do so. I've ordered the coach for you, for one o'clock. I'm sure you won't want to keep my horses waiting in the cold. The home farm tells me we're due for more snow."

Thus, clad in his best uniform, hat and gloves in hand, he found himself waiting upon the Dowager Duchess of Fenmore. He had asked, upon arrival, if he might speak with Miss Evans, but was instead informed by the butler Her Grace the Dowager Duchess of Fenmore was expecting him. Hugh ignored the fact that his gut was clenched up tighter than a Turk's head knot and went to face the dragon in her lair.

"Captain McAlden, Your Grace." The butler showed him into a cavernous drawing room. His boot heels echoed across the parquet floor. The dowager duchess was alone, seated in a silk-upholstered chair near the blazing hearth. He was glad they kept the place warm. Meggs didn't like to be cold.

"Captain McAlden. Won't you come in?"

"Thank you, Your Grace." Hugh bowed very low over the soft, blue-veined hand that hovered in front of him.

She gestured to the chair across from her and kept to protocol. "To what do I owe the honor, Captain?"

"I wanted to inform you, I have sent communications directly, by express to Portsmouth, and also to the Admiralty, both to your grandson personally and to his commander, Captain Marlowe. I expect we will both hear from them within the fortnight. I also directed Captain Marlowe to inform you, here at Fenmore, of his landing at the earliest possible moment."

"Thank you. Your assistance is much appreciated." She had followed his wandering eyes to the door. "But, I think also, you wished to see my granddaughter?"

"Yes, ma'am. I came to see Miss Evans, that is, ask after her Ladyship's welfare. I imagine it was quite a shock to the young lady to find herself reunited with you after all of these years, and so swiftly removed to a new home."

"Yes, I daresay it was. I know it was for me. And it appears I have you to thank for this unexpected blessing in my life. You have my profound thanks for bringing my darling Trinity Margurite back to me. And dear young Timothy as well, of course, who can now be restored to his rightful place as duke. But I never knew him as a young child. He was a baby when my son . . . died so tragically." She drew herself together visibly, touching the ropes of pearls about her neck for reassurance. "Do you know our sad saga, Captain?"

His mother had told him the outlines of the remarkable story, and he could fill in some of the tale from what Meggs had told him. But it would be impolitic as well as imprudent to dwell on Meggs's prior life in London. "Very little, Your Grace. Only that your son and his wife passed away suddenly, and the children were orphaned and lost to you all these years."

"Yes, that is true. There is, however, much more to the story, but suffice it to say that Trinity's father, my son Arthur John, and his father, the late duke, were estranged. Arthur took orders in the church as second sons often do. All was as it should be until his older brother died. Arthur became the heir, but he did not want to give up his vocation. He and his father clashed. It wouldn't do, you see, for a duke's heir to be a country rector. So the late duke cut him off and cast him from our lives, until such time as he could be brought to see the importance of his place—what he owed his family and his honor, as well as to his conscience. But that never happened. The years carried on by. He had married and had two children on his little income from his livings. I was made to pretend he and his family did not exist. But of course they did, and of course I did what I could under the circumstances to give whatever small assistance I might. Mostly from a distance and secretly." She sighed and dabbed at her eyes. "So many years lost."

Hugh looked away, out the windows into the snowy fields, and waited for the duchess to recover herself. A rector's daughter. He should have known. All those Bible references—*Lot's wife, gone all pillar of salt. I can number all my bones.* And what was the one at the gin shop? *Both the innocent and the wicked he destroys.*

"Oh, she was a little brown wren of a girl, with the brightest eyes, all long braids and long legs." The duchess made a drawn-out gesture with her hands at the memory. "And she's never lost that look, or those bright eyes, else I never would have recognized her. They were gone by the time I got there, you see, Arthur and Margaret. A fever. And the children gone as well. Sent off alone on the public stage, to me, in London. I must have passed them on the road, never knowing. And then, they never could be found. Swallowed into the gaping maw that is London. When I think—"

The dowager closed her eyes against her thoughts. She appeared small and frail, but she pulled her composure back together to continue. "But that is past history. I needs be far more concerned with more recent occurrences. She has been with you for some time, she tells me? Under your protection?"

Hugh answered with as little information as possible. "Yes, Your Grace, she was in residence with my mother, Viscountess Balfour, at her husband's house in Berkley Square and now at Balfour Manor, but she had only recently come into Society."

"That, Captain McAlden, is what my granddaughter tells me is called a very great bouncer. I won't trifle with you, Captain. My granddaughter has been frank with me—exceedingly frank—about where she has been and what she has been doing for the past eight years."

There was that knot in his gut, cinching tighter. "I see."

"Do you? Then I hope that you will be able to shed some further light upon how she came under your *protection*, shall we call it? She said you took her off the streets, and employed her as part of your household in Chelsea, before you took her to your mother."

"Yes, Your Grace," Hugh concurred, careful not to assume Meggs had told her grandmother anything more than the barest of facts, despite the old lady's claims to exceeding frankness.

"But what I want to know, Captain, is why an idle, injured,

half-pay officer of the navy, such as yourself, would want with a pair of young pickpockets from the Cheapside docks? Hmm? Perhaps because you are not as idle as you would like people to think."

He was silent for another long moment, hoping the conversation would turn, but Her Grace was old and she had a seemingly infinite amount of patience. She merely awaited his response with an unwavering eye.

"Perhaps," was all he would allow himself to say.

"You begin to intrigue me. Go on."

"Suffice it to say, I had need of Miss Evans's—Lady Trinity's—talents as a pickpocket."

"In an official capacity? I ask because I should like to know how far the long arm of the law can reach, or if someone, like that revolting Major Rawsthorne, will be back to menace her."

"Official, Your Grace, however secret. But Miss Evans was promised clemency for her assistance to His Majesty's Navy. And I will personally see to it Major Rawsthorne—"

"No," she disagreed. "You'll only try to put a bullet into him, and I daresay you'll succeed. Leave Rawsthorne to Fenmore." She returned to her original question. "That is good to know." She took a deep breath and regarded him anew. "So it was only her . . . shall we say, professional acumen you were interested in?"

Hugh steered very carefully—here was a harbor full of mines. "Yes, Your Grace."

"Hmm," she said again, regarding him in the same steady, mild manner. "And yet you are here. On my doorstep. Or rather, in my drawing room, asking after her *personal* welfare."

Which was to say, he was not fooling anyone with his careful responses. "Indeed, I am here, Your Grace. I realize that Lady Trinity's reputation has been inadvertently called into question as a result of the time she has recently spent in my household, and, as you say, under my protection. I want to extend the protection of my name to her now, and make an offer, a proposal, that she become my wife. Indeed," he said, bowing slightly, "I would deem it the greatest of honors if she would consent to become my wife. It would make me the happiest of men."

"Would it? And yet, you did not propose to her at any time whilst she was in your *care*, or under your *protection*."

The words held a wealth of fuller meaning. It seemed Meggs had been *exceedingly* frank after all. "No, ma'am."

"No, you did not. And now she is an heiress, you suddenly find yourself compelled."

"No, ma'am, Your Grace," he stammered. The collar of his uniform had grown wretchedly tight, and the knot in his gut was twisting higher. God's balls. He had faced down French cannon with more aplomb than this tiny, terrifying woman. "I did not make my offer earlier, as . . . I did not understand Lady Trinity's rightful place in Society."

"Did she not tell you who she was?"

"No, Your Grace." He latched onto the excuse gratefully.

"And you now wish to make an offer for her?"

"Yes, Your Grace."

"I doubt she'll have you. She has said she would not." The cagey old woman narrowed her eyes at him. "Tell me why you became her lover."

Hugh would have dropped his hat except his hands were too numb to move.

"Oh, come now, Captain. I am an old woman, and I have lived and seen a great deal of the world. You needn't prevaricate with me. My granddaughter is a well-made, beautiful, young woman, and you are a well-formed, handsome young man. It is the way of the world." She turned her eyes to him and waited.

"Yes, Your Grace."

The dowager waited, and when he could not find the right

words to speak, she sighed. "Ah. So you became my grand-daughter's lover and yet, when you did so, you did not then offer her marriage? It is no wonder she will not have you."

Put in such an unflattering light, it was no wonder at all. But it hadn't been like that. He needed to remind Meggs of that.

"Yes, well"—the Dowager sighed—"it does you no good to press your suit with me. The dear girl is the one you must convince. Be so kind as to ring for me, will you?" When he had done so, she continued with a sigh. "I find I have little stomach in hearing your rejection, so I believe I will grant you this interview alone. The door will remain open, however. Robinson"—she turned to the august butler who had answered her summons—"please send Lady Trinity Margurite to me."

"Yes, Your Grace." The man bowed and left on silent feet.

"I shall await in the small parlor across the hall. Send my granddaughter to me when you are finished. Robinson will see you out." She rose stiffly and held out her hand for him, although when he had bowed over it very correctly, she surprised him by shaking it. "I do thank you for coming, young man. Good-bye."

"So you have no hopes for my success?"

She looked resigned. "None at all."

"But surely you see that she should marry? I have ruined her, although I take no pride in saying so. Indeed, it is much to my shame, but I know what I owe her, what must be done for the honor of us both."

"Yes, it is much to your shame, but you are incorrect in your supposition that she must marry. She has position and wealth now. Enough to shelter her, even from the Major Rawsthornes of this world, if need be. She need not marry to secure her future or her comfort. And I would not see her wed, even to assuage your honor or your profound, though newfound, guilt." Her dark eyes, so like her granddaughter's, fixed him with a piercing glance. "The world has treated her harshly enough without adding the burden of an unwanted marriage. My grandchildren, especially Trinity, have had a tremendously difficult time in their lives, but she has been fortunate enough to have retained her character to a remarkable degree, and despite her former profession, she is at heart still an honest person."

"I am very much aware of your granddaughter's remarkable character, ma'am."

"In her honesty, she was forthright about the nature of her liaison with you," she continued. "While I may not like such an irregular way of doing things, I am glad, at least for your mother's sake, you've had the sense to present yourself here and do the right thing without being asked, but I fear Trinity will not have you. And I will in no way force her to do so. She *has* been forced to do a great deal too many things in order to survive, and I will not give her any further cause for grief or resentment."

"Yes. I understand." He remembered saying much the same thing to Meggs. "I do not wish to cause her any further grief, either. That is one of the reasons I have come."

"How can that be?" She began her slow promenade toward the drawing room doors. "She has already refused you once by her own account and has asked that she be excused from seeing or meeting you."

"Because she doubts the sincerity of my attachment to her, Your Grace."

The dowager steadied herself with a hand to the back of a chair. "Ah. And have you formed an attachment to her?"

"I have," he assured her.

She merely raised her eyebrows and inclined her head, inviting him to elaborate.

It was difficult, damned uncomfortably difficult, to find the right words for her. "I have had an attachment to her for quite some time. I admire her wit and tenacity, and the strength of her character, and . . . she smells clean and fresh like *hope* . . . I . . ."

He turned away to the window, embarrassed and unsure. He felt like his heart had been ripped open—like he had ripped it open and left it there upon the table, bleeding for her examination. All he could think about was his need to have Meggs back. But he couldn't see his way forward. There was nothing but blindness and pain.

"How extraordinary—"

"Your Grace—Grandmama." Meggs, Lady Trinity, came in unexpectedly, through the adjoining music room, and not through the closed doors to the hall, and he wondered if she had been listening at the doors. It would be the kind of thing his Meggs would have made no bones about doing. And her wide dark eyes were raking over him. Sizing him up. Weighing him out, his Meggs would have said, like an undertaker.

He had meant to go to her directly and take her in his arms, or at the very least take her hands, but she now stood very carefully behind both the table and the chaise, protecting herself from any sort of intimacy.

"My dear." The dowager moved toward her granddaughter and kissed her cheek before she turned to indicate her visitor. "Captain McAlden has called to see you, my dear. I think it best you speak with him alone. I will be in my sitting room should you need me. Robinson will attend you." She took Meggs's hand again and spoke in a low voice. "I hope I need not tell you that you have only to consult your own heart without reference to anything else, my dear. I shall support whatever decision you decide to make." With a final loving pat of her granddaughter's cheek, she made her way from the room.

They were alone. Good God, Hugh felt he had been missing her for days, or weeks even, though it had only been one wretched morning. She looked somehow different already, impeccable and untouchable in the fashionable, embroidered muslin dress some maidservant must have stayed up all night altering to fit. And when she finally broke the awkward silence, her voice was completely changed, as if the last of St. Giles had been scrubbed away with her morning bath.

"My grandmother wished me to see you."

It was not a promising beginning. He took a step or two nearer, and the image of icy perfection melted away to reveal his Meggs. She looked pale and drawn. The shadows under her eyes told him she had not slept last night, either, but she was all but vibrating with nervous energy. Or perhaps just exhaustion. "You look tired."

Up came her first line of defense, the seemingly careless shoulder shrug. "It was a long night. Come to check up on your investment?"

He wasn't prepared for the acid in her tone. "No," he said with some effort, "I came to see you."

"To see me, or to decide what is to be done about me?"

He should have expected the cutting edge of anger in her voice. "No. I came to let your grandmother, and you, know I've written to your brother, his captain, and the Admiralty. I'm sure he will be returned to you very shortly. Patrols in the Channel are able to make port quite frequently. So you don't have to worry about Timmy, at any rate. Though you will anyway."

"Yes, as you say. Thank you." She was tense, her fingers twisting and fidgeting against her skirts as if she had not yet told her hands they no longer needed to work for a living. Or perhaps she had, and they were frightened by the thought of a looming lifetime of inactivity. "Is that all?"

"No. I've missed you." He tried to make his mouth smile, but it felt forced and insincere. He didn't feel like smiling. He felt like roaring at her and tossing her over his shoulder and carrying her out of the house like a prize of war. Like a savage.

"Goodness"—her tone was brittle—"do the floors need mopping?"

"Stop it, Meggs, please. I came to . . ." Take her back, like any man who'd had a lass like her would do if she left him. But he couldn't say that. She wasn't his lass anymore. She was Lady Trinity now, not just Meggs. "I came to tell your grandmother of my proposal of marriage to you. And to make it to you again, in hopefully more pleasing language."

"More pleasing language?" She grew still. Like the sea before a storm, her voice was unsteady with tiny rippling waves. "Is that all you think it's going to take? Pleasing words?"

"No. God's balls. I just can't say the right thing." He felt tired. More tired than he'd ever been in his entire life. He felt like he was sailing against the tide and couldn't make any sea way. "I came to ask if you, Lady Trinity Margurite Evans, would do me the inestimable honor of becoming my wife."

"You know I cannot." She sounded just as weary. And sad. "I cannot. I told you so from the first moment you said we *must* marry. I know you do it only from your misplaced sense of honor."

"Meggs. It's not misplaced! It is right where it belongs."

"Right where it belongs?" she repeated, incredulous. "Please, Captain. Your sense of honor is nothing if not extraordinarily late!"

"Meggs—"

"Don't you Meggs me. You never would have offered for me as *Meggs*, your thief." And now he could hear the hurt in her voice. "Never in a million years! You would have kept me only as long as I served your purposes, as long as I was the right instrument for your 'jobs,' and as soon as you had earned your way back into a command, you would have turned your back on Timmy and me without so much as a fare-thee-well."

"That is not true. Why do you think I kept you with me—" Oh, God. That was wrong.

"Kept?"

"No. God's balls, this is torture. I know I'm an ass in a drawing room, which is why I live the way I do and do the work I do. I knew how to talk to Meggs, but I have no idea how to talk to you now you've become the Duchess of Fenmore's granddaughter."

"I didn't just become her. I always *was*, don't you see? The rest of the world didn't know. But I did. I always remembered. I always knew that I was Trinity Margurite Evans. I always knew that my grandmother was the Duchess of bloody Fenmore. And I knew that she didn't *want* me." Her voice had become strident, filled with unmitigated pain. And loneliness.

"Meggs, that's not true. She said—"

"Yes it is! We were thrown out of her house, Timmy and I, when we went to her after our parents died. They weren't even cold in the ground when the new vicar of Tissington parish bundled us on the public stage for London. But when we got there, to her house on Grosvenor Square, the servants threw us out like garbage into the streets! And I never forgot. I knew every minute of every day I worked the streets. Every time I passed that house, with its knocker down for all these years. I knew every moment I spent in a pawn shop, or adding up my miserable pounds and pence in that office in Thread-needle Street. I knew that moment in your library, when I cracked my skull against your floor, who *I* was. But I don't think I really knew who *you* were, until this very moment. And I must say I liked that man I fought in your library much bet-ter—he was, at the very least, honest."

"He wasn't honest. Because he—I—wanted you even then. Wanted you from the moment you smashed your head on my floor and every minute after. But I'm trying to be honest now, damn it." He couldn't keep a damper on the hot end of his temper.

"Trying?" She swiped at the tears that began to flow freely down her face. "Don't you know? Don't you know I would have done anything for you? Anything you asked. Anything. But now it's too late."

"No. Damn it, Meggs, it's not too late. It can't be. You're confused, and you're hurt, and you don't know who you can trust." This could not be happening. This was not how it was supposed to be. She was supposed to be in his arms, not railing at him like a fishwife.

"I can't trust you. Why would I trust you? Meggs wasn't good enough for you. So let me assure you Trinity Margurite Evans has far too much pride to accept the dubious honor of your rather late offer."

"Is that all this is about, timing?" He wanted to put his hand to his head to hold it together. He felt concussed from all the blows.

"No." She shook her head. "I . . ."

"You can't be thinking straight. I know this has all come as a shock to you. But we really must marry. You're ruined. You must see. You're the granddaughter of the Duchess of Fenmore now, for God's sake. You have to marry."

"Must? On the contrary, as the granddaughter of the Duchess of Fenmore, I finally don't have to do a damned bloody thing I don't want to do. And I don't want you."

"You didn't say that two nights ago. You can't pretend that didn't happen—that we weren't lovers."

"Can't I? I think my fortune will buy me as much virginity as I care to pretend."

"And what about mine? Are you going to buy that back, too?"

He had meant to shock some sense into her, and by God he had. Her hand came up to cover her mouth, and her face went a livid white.

"We were two people together in that bed, Meggs. Two people's lives changed unutterably. Nothing can be the same."

"Nothing is." She turned and ran headlong out of the room and out of his life. The door latch clicked into place with astonishing finality.

CHAPTER 27

He had made a wreck of it. If his life felt shipwrecked, his hopes dashed to pieces, Hugh had only himself to blame. And still he could not stop himself from thinking about her constantly, from hoping and planning, though his logical mind told him it was all in vain.

In such a state, even good news—the best possible news in the circumstances—failed to lift his hopes. A letter came from Admiral Sir Charles Middleton with official news of his honor—he was to be made a knight. Sir Hugh. But in the meantime, the admiral wrote, the country was still at war, and the Admiralty had need of its captains. He would be much obliged if Hugh would resume command of his frigate *Dangerous*, which would be shortly finished with its West Indies cruise.

More promising was the letter from Captain Marlowe. *Defiant* had arrived off Dartmouth, where Marlowe would maintain the boy in his safe keeping until such time as McAlden could be made to shift his sorry, broken-down arse to retrieve him. Hugh siezed the opportunity, damned his pride, and took the letter in hand to Fenmore. He knew it wasn't a good idea. She might not even receive him. But he had to make one last try to see her. To speak to her. To spend a few last moments in her presence. She was like opium—he would have her at any price, any way he could.

He put on his dress uniform, let his guts knot up into a fist, and went. And she consented to see him at once. She walked across the wide, marbled entry foyer and stood not four feet away, curtsying to him. He drank in the sight of her like a man at an island spring, feasting on cool, clear water.

"To what do we owe the honor, Sir Hugh?" Ah. So at least some of his news had already preceded him.

"My Lady." He bowed, though he could not take his eyes from her. Did she look unhappy? Did she look tired? Was she not sleeping at night? Could there be a God, and she had missed him one tenth as much as he missed her?

He made his voice quiet and calm—he would let himself engage in no shouting matches today. "I am come to tell you your brother has reached Dartmouth. His ship put in there two days hence. I thought you would want to know so you could make arrangements to collect him yourself. Although I hold myself still pledged to your grandmother to do that office for her."

"Oh, yes." She let out a rushed sigh of relief. "Thank you. I will let my grandmother know. Or have you . . . ?"

"No. I asked to see you."

"Yes." She nodded. "Thank you."

"You are very welcome. I also came to present you with the receipt of payment for your . . ." He stalled over the most diplomatic way of phrasing. He didn't want another door slammed in his face. "Assistance. Admiral Sir Charles Middleton insisted upon seeing to the payment himself and sends his most profound thanks. And I hope I need not add my own profound and sincere thanks, as well."

She tried a ghost of a smile, though clearly, with her carefully blank face, she was not happy. "You are welcome, sir."

"I made sure the money has been deposited to your account in Threadneedle Street, Miss Evans. I beg your pardon, my Lady. Mr. Levy sends his warmest regards."

"Thank you. Though I've little enough need for the money now, sir."

Every time she said "sir" it was like a fence—a buffer. Or an accusation. "Perhaps not. But you earned it. Honestly. And I pay my debts."

"So you do." She was generous enough to accept his explanation and perhaps to understand his need to say it. "Thank you." She nodded and looked carefully at her shoes while they continued to stand there, the few feet between them an ocean.

And he had still not said what he had come here to say. "I also wanted to apologize."

"Oh?" Her face, which had only been careful and unhappy, now grew guarded and vigilant.

"Yes. This . . . impasse, for lack of a better word, we find ourselves in is entirely my fault. I made grave mistakes, missteps in my conduct, which caused you pain and for which I am deeply sorry." If he had simply asked for her when the thought had first occurred, if he hadn't tried to hedge his bets and see if he could turn her into someone suitable and more acceptable as a wife, she might now already be his. But he would never know.

If he had only trusted her, this small thief who had stolen his heart, the way he had asked her to trust him. If he had trusted his own instincts and his love, he would not be standing in her foyer, begging her to love him. Why couldn't he say all those things? Why did the words pile up inside his chest as if they were going to choke him? And still he was mute.

She spoke quietly, addressing her feet, though her words were for him. "I know you don't really want a wife. You said to marry you would be to condemn your wife to a life of hardship and loneliness. And if you must know, I think I've already had enough of that to last a lifetime."

Ah. With that his hopes were cindered. There was nothing more he could say. But still he tried. "What will you do?"

"Do?" She laughed self-deprecatingly and blew out a huff of air. "As little as possible. For the first time in my life, I find I do not *have* to do anything." And there was Meggs's deceptively casual shrug. "I will sleep late. I will drink chocolate for breakfast. I will walk without any destination in mind." She pretended to be happy with such an empty itinerary while consulting her toes. "I will put my past behind me."

"You'll be bored to death within a week."

He surprised the beginnings of a smile onto her lips. She tilted her head. "Will I?"

Oh, it made him ache for her, that little tilt. "I know so. I know *you*."

She shook her head, stubborn, still resistant, and perhaps a little sad. But at least not angry. "No, you don't. You only know Meggs. Ambitious, worried, hungry, goddamned cold Meggs. She's the only part of me you know."

"Yes." He acknowledged the truth of her words. "Only part of you that you let me know. But Meggs was more than just worried and hungry. She was also extraordinarily loving. And generous. And loyal." He let that sink into her. It was a drop of rain into the ocean that was her. But she had seemed good at absorbing the inconvenient, hurtful truths. The bad facts, she had called them. He had admired that in her. But maybe she was tired of it all—the hard, cold facts.

"It was safer that way. Easier," she admitted.

"Don't know how easy." He smiled a little at her to show her he wasn't trying to antagonize. A man didn't harass a woman into marrying him. Not if he wanted a happy life. And he did. He wanted a happy life. With her. "She had uncharted depths, your Meggs. A man could spend his life sailing in those seas and never find bottom."

"Well. You found my bottom easily enough." Her cheeks

were flushed with her own boldness. But those were the bad facts.

But at least they were talking. And she wasn't running away. She was looking at him now, at least as often as she was looking at her toes. He tried not to be encouraged.

"I reckon so," he agreed. "And you found mine."

"I oughtn't have done. What we did was . . . wrong," she whispered, mortified, as if someone in the empty, echoing hall might hear her.

He stepped nearer and pitched his voice just as low. "What we did, my Meggs, was make love. And it was not wrong. It was *glorious*."

That brought her head up, but only for a moment. "It was not proper."

"It rarely is, Meggs. Not if you do it right."

"There's a danger in giving in to such desires."

He held his ground. "There's just as much danger in not."

"You don't know that," she insisted. "You can't. But all I know is you never would have *done* the things you did with me, or *said* the things"—her face turned scarlet at the memory—"the things you said to me, to a duke's granddaughter."

He couldn't stand the thought of her feeling shame. "Then you don't know me. I never would have done those things, or said those words to *anyone* else, for the simple reason that I never have done those things with, or said any of those things to, anyone else. And I *never* will. Because I never wanted to do what we did—to make love—and to make love the way we did—with anyone but *you*."

She stared at him, afraid to believe him. Afraid to believe in herself.

"Remember that, Meggs, when you're trying to warm yourself by a fire in this cold mausoleum. No matter what you think we did, know that I will never, ever regret it. And I will never, ever stop loving you."

And having finally found the words and said his piece, he jammed his hat upon his head, turned on his heel, and let himself out the front door.

The hall echoed with the same emptiness she felt inside. He was gone. And she had let him go.

Meggs would have gone upstairs to her enormous, luxurious, private room that was big enough to house a family of eight and all their livestock, and thrown herself on the enormous, luxurious bed for a good long cry, but her grandmother called her just as she put her foot upon the first step. And she had never been one for crying much, anyway.

"Trinity, dear." Her grandmother held out her hand and brought Meggs to sit next to her on the chaise. "How was he?"

"He was fine, I suppose." Meggs had never thought about how he *was*. The captain just was . . . himself. Which made no sense. Nothing made much sense anymore.

"What did he want?" The duchess handed her an exquisite porcelain cup of tea. It was mercifully hot.

"Did he have to want anything?"

Grandmother smiled kindly. "But of course. A man like your captain doesn't do anything without a purpose."

"He's not my captain. And he did come to tell me about Timmy. Here is his letter. And he told me about the funds he owed— He came to inform me the full seven hundred fifty pounds I had contracted with him, on behalf of the Admiralty, had been paid to my account in Threadneedle Street."

"Did you accept the money?"

It wasn't much compared to the tens of thousands of pounds her grandmother had told her were her birthright, but it was hers, at least until all the complicated matters of guardianship were sorted out. "I did accept it. I earned it, and he seemed to need to pay it." And, she realized in a brutal moment of insight, he thought she needed him to pay. Funny cove, her captain.

"Ah." Her grandmother invested a wealth of nothing in that statement.

Meggs sighed, too, afraid he was right. Afraid this would be the rest of her life—bored to death with propriety, having tea with her grandmother in this cold mausoleum, listening to her say, "ah" instead of what she meant. "Do you not think I did the right thing?"

"My opinion is neither here nor there. Do *you* think you did the right thing?"

Meggs shook her head and willed herself to keep the heat brewing behind her eyes from becoming tears. "I hardly know."

Grandmother covered the hands Meggs twisted into the material of her dress. "Do you love him *very* much?"

Meggs sniffed back the tears. "Awfully. But it doesn't seem to help."

And so she did have her cry after all, her broken heart leaking with aching pain. But for all the pain, life went on, so she went up to her apartment to bathe her mottled face and recover herself, until the maid, a pale moth of a girl, knocked timidly at the dressing room door.

"My Lady?"

"Yes?" Meggs put down the precious, worn bar of soap and came out of the dressing room.

"Your ladyship, Her Grace the Duchess has sent for you. I was told to fetch you right away, miss. Your ladyship."

"Right away?" Meggs took up a shawl. "Is she all right?"

"In a taking, her woman said. I was to bring you straightaway."

Bloody blue fuck. Meggs ran the whole way—to hell with ladylike decorum. The old lady was the only relative she seemed to have left in the world, and now that she had found her, she would hold on to her for all she was worth. Meggs didn't know what to expect, but when she arrived, the duchess was only wearing out the carpet in her private sitting room.

She held out her hands to Meggs in supplication. "He's disappeared. Oh, my dear, I don't know what to do."

"The captain?"

"The captain? Why should you think of the captain? No, no not Sir Hugh. Charles."

"Cousin Charles? The duke can't just disappear, can he—he's a duke? Or perhaps he can *because* he's a duke."

But the dear old thing really was too upset to find Meggs's attempt at humor amusing. "I can't find him anywhere—he *has* disappeared. I fear the worst."

"Aren't there nearly four hundred people employed on this estate to cater to his every whim? Surely one of them knows where he can be found?"

"I've asked—I've had the staff all looking for him for hours now. A groom says he left in a carriage with no one—not even his man—with him. I tell you, I fear the worst."

"And what is the worst? Surely you don't think some harm has come to him on the roads? Have you sent riders out?" Meggs made for the door. "I'll call the steward or go to the stables and ask—"

"No." Her grandmother grasped at her arm with hard, arthritic fingers. "I spoke to his man. His valet said he was going to the coast, alone. I fear he has gone—gone for the *duke*. For Timothy. To stop him."

Something dark and feral shook loose inside her chest. "What?" Meggs had no idea how loudly she had shouted until Grandmama flinched away, but the old lady held on. "But cousin Charles said he was glad to let Timmy . . . God's balls. I must go— I must—"

"Yes, you must go. Have Lady Trinity's bag packed immediately," she called to her dresser. "Order the traveling coach."

"And I must send a message to Balfour. Captain McAlden must be told. He will help us, I know he will." Of all the people in the world, Hugh McAlden would not fail her. And he would not hesitate to tangle with a duke, no matter the cost. He was that kind of man. The very best.

"Oh, yes. I knew you would know what to do. But you must not delay. Yes. Write your note to him. Here is paper." She led Meggs directly to her escritoire. "I will have it sent directly. But you must go and prepare yourself for travel. Jones, Jones? Where is Jones?"

"Here, Your Grace." Grandmama's dresser was waiting to do her bidding.

And Meggs ran like hell for the stair, because hell had finally opened up under her feet.

The traveling coach pulled away from the steps of Fenmore in a clatter of gravel and harness. As soon as the vehicle had passed down the drive and out of sight, Anne, Dowager Duchess of Fenmore, tucked the lace handkerchief she had only a moment ago been waving tearfully into her cuff and smiled. Around her, all the staff, who had been involved in making the hasty arrangements, smiled back.

"Thank you. Thank you, Robinson. Thank you, Jones, dear. Thank you, one and all.

"You're very welcome, Your Grace."

The duchess took a deep, satisfied breath and headed upstairs. At the first floor, instead of turning for the east wing and her private apartments, she walked quietly toward the ducal suite, where she found her cousin Charles sitting by the fire. Just as he ought. Just as he always was.

The titular duke looked up from his newspaper and asked, "Are they away?"

Anne took the seat across from her late husband's cousin and put her feet up on the hassock. "Yes. Smooth as silk. She never hesitated for a moment."

"Well done. I've poured you a sherry."

"Thank you. You're an absolute lamb. Ah, lovely." She took

a sip of the sherry. "I know I ought to feel guilty, but somehow I don't."

Cousin Charles gave her the look of a longtime friend who can no longer be surprised by character flaws. "No, you wouldn't."

"Well, here's to you, my dear cousin. I must say, you *are* an absolute dear to let me use your name to plant such doubt in the poor girl."

"Not at all. Happy to do my part, my dear. The two of us have been knocking around this big, empty house for far too long with no one else, no heir to share it. It's about time we populated the place with young people, don't you think?"

"I do, my dear cousin, I do. Although if this works, we'll lose her. But I'm convinced it's for the best."

He chuckled. "Pair of old romantics, that's what we are. How long do you think it will take?"

"I hope no time at all. I hope he is holding her hand in that coach as we speak. And as they head down the coast road, I hope she will have her weary head tucked against his strong, supportive shoulder."

"And the duke?"

"Safe, quite safe. His ship came in to Dartmouth two days ago, and he is in the safe company of his captain's family there until Captain McAlden retrieves him."

"Good, good."

They sat in companionable quiet, as they had for so many evenings before.

"Do you think," the duchess asked at last, "she will be *very* angry with me when she finds out we duped her?"

Cousin Charles looked over his spectacles and down the length of his remarkable nose. "*We?* I, myself, plan to remove to London. But with any luck, her captain will keep her occupied."

"Yes, with any luck. But just to be safe, perhaps we ought to have the London house opened. Just in case."

* * *

They were away. The coachman had been given instruc-tions to give his horses their heads and make all speed for the coast, and he was making good with the office. But it didn't seem to lessen Meggs's agitation in the least.

Meggs. Lady Trinity Margurite. Hugh had no idea what to call her. He'd like to call her Mrs. McAlden, but whatever he was to call her, the lass had her face pressed up close to the window on the opposite seat. She was watching every foot of their progress, and when her breath fogged the glass, she let the window down, impervious to the biting wind. Her hands gripped and tugged the sill as if it were she driving the car-riage herself and urging the horses on.

"Lass, come away. We're making good time. The coachman knows his business. He's a professional. It will be hours yet."

"I know." Her eyes were dark and liquid with fear. And anger. He'd have to go carefully.

"I understand." He reached across to pat her hand. Like a friend. Or an uncle. He was going to choke on uncle.

"I can't thank you enough for coming with me. I didn't know who else to ask."

"Of course."

She gripped his fingers tight. "This is all my fault. I've got-ten soft. I wanted this . . . fairy tale, but I should have known better. I should have seen. I should have suspected cousin Charles from the start. Something can *always* go wrong. Even in fairy tales, there are always ogres under the bridge."

"It's trolls. Trolls under the bridge." Hugh kept hold of her hand and shifted across to sit next to her, easing closer, lend-ing her his comfort and support. Anything to be close to her. "Easy now. It will all come out right. Your hands are cold. Come here, I can't watch you worry yourself to death. Come, get warm." He slid the window closed.

She was so tense, she felt brittle. He was a cad to take ad-vantage, to feel triumph when she turned into his coat and held on tight. God, it felt so good to have her in his arms. It felt so right. Just for a while, at least for this little time.

But he couldn't have any more lies or half truths, or even misunderstandings between them. "Meggs, I know what the duchess feared, but I'm not convinced the duke, that is, your cousin Charles, has done anything untoward."

"What do you mean you're not convinced? He's disappeared!"

"Perhaps he went off to see . . . someone else. Perhaps, he has a private life the dowager duchess knows nothing about."

"I can't think so. The two of them seemed as close and cozy as thieves."

"Well. I suppose I'll have to defer to your professional judgment about that."

"Hugh. I'm serious. Please don't make fun of me. Not now."

She was calling him Hugh. He felt his chest expand with hope. "I'm not. But I can't see Lord Charles Evans conspiring against his own flesh and blood. Against his own heir."

"But Timmy's the real duke. Cousin Charles would lose Fenmore to him. He would become *Timmy's* heir."

"But Timmy's only a boy and will need to be taught and educated in his responsibilities for quite some time by your cousin Charles. And neither you nor Timmy, nor certainly the Dowager, are going to toss Lord Charles out of Fenmore. It's his home. And Timmy needs him."

"I don't know. I keep remembering how she didn't want us at all, all those years ago. How we were turned away from her house by that horrible old butler and how she never came to find us."

And here was the root of all her anxiety and fear. It was exactly as she said, she wanted so to believe in her own fairy tale, but she was afraid to do so. He needed to remember his first impression of her—that the years of hard living, hand to mouth, had broken her trust in humanity. And he had not helped. He had broken her trust in him. "But she *was* looking for you. She never stopped looking for you. That's why she was so ready to find you at that damned ball. How can you doubt that she is devoted to you?"

When she shook her head, he carried on. "Meggs. Rest easy. What I do know is that Timmy is fine. He is in the safe keeping of his captain, my friend James Marlowe. Marlowe will not let anyone who isn't you or me take the boy away."

"But the duchess said the duke might try . . ." She pushed off his chest and stared at him, combing his face and eyes for some clue. "But you had already sent those particulars—you or I and no one else—to Captain Marlowe?"

"Yes. Not to cast any aspersions on your cousin Charles, but a twelve year old boy, who is the lost heir to a dukedom, is a very serious matter. I'm not so trusting as to let just anyone take such a boy out of my care. He's my Tanner, too, you know. I care for him, too."

"Oh." She was looking at him in that minute way of hers—weighing him out like an undertaker.

"I do not think there is anything to worry about." He tucked her head back down against his chest. "Your nose is cold, too." He took the opportunity to wrap the free end of his sea cape around her. It felt so good—so right to have her in his arms. To hold her. Hugh closed his eyes and let himself luxuriate in the simple pleasure of her body pressed up tight to his. He wouldn't allow himself to ask for more than this day, this time together.

After a few more miles, she pulled back and asked again, "You're *really* convinced there's no danger? Then what are you doing in this carriage, making hell-for-leather for the coast?"

"Helping you." He reached out slowly to brush a stray lock of hair back under her bonnet.

She went still under his hands, but her eyes never left his face. "Why?"

"Because you asked me to."

She leaned herself back against his chest slowly and lay there, pliant and quiescent for a few moments. He couldn't see her face, but when she spoke, her voice sounded . . . careful. "Why didn't you tell Grandmama your suspicions?"

Hugh took a deep breath to batten down his hatches. "I did."

"Ohh." Her inhale echoed out of her mouth, and she sat bolt upright on the seat. "Do you mean to tell me that sweet little old lady humbugged me? She set this caper up on purpose?"

"It should be a comfort to know you come by your native abilities quite naturally. Must run in the family."

"Why that pattering old goose!" Meggs's astonishment was writ across her gaping face. "I fell for her lies like the greenest gill. Damn me if she didn't run me like a bloody rig. How could I have been so stupid?"

"You're not stupid." He took her hand—her dear, delicate, larcenous, scarred hand—in his and tugged her closer. "Far from it. You let your heart dictate your actions. And Timmy really did need to be fetched home. I'm happy and honored to help you do that. Although I may make him ride on the seat with the driver."

"Are you quite sure?"

"Bloody damn sure. He'll have his sea coat and be warm enough."

"Hugh! Truly? He's safe?"

"Meggs, lass. *I'm what you call a professional.* I sent a dispatch through Admiralty channels immediately, the night of the ball."

She folded back against the seat as if all the stuffing had run out of her. "Of course you did. I should have realized. I haven't thanked you for that, have I?"

"I think you were in a state of shock. And I didn't do it for your thanks."

The carriage grew enormously quiet. "Then why did you do it?"

"Because it was the right thing to do, and because I would do anything I could to make you happy."

"Is that why you're here?"

"I'm here because you asked me. You wanted my help." He looked out the window for a long moment and gathered every ounce of his courage. "You know how I feel, Meggs. I can't say it any plainer. I love you. You know that. But I think what you don't know is why *you* asked for *my* help. Why, when your grandmother told you her story, you sent for me?"

Her face cleared, like the dawning of sunrise. "I knew I could count on you." She said it almost to herself, as if she was just discovering this truth. "Never let me down, not when it mattered."

"I did let you down. I let us both down. But if you'll let me, I would gladly spend the rest of my life making it up to you."

"Will you? Truly? Rest of your life?" Her smile was like the gift of a new day. "And when did you plan to begin that rest of your life."

He pulled her roughly into his arms. "Right bloody now."

"And not a bleeding moment too soon."

He shut up her heathenish cheek with his mouth.

CHAPTER 28

With the half-frozen condition of the roads, it was late in the evening by the time they arrived in Dartmouth. Meggs had fallen asleep for a time against Hugh's shoulder and didn't want to give up the comfort and warmth of his body for the raw chill of the windy quay, where he disembarked to make inquiries and ask all the sailorly things. It made him happy, giving orders and being all naval-like. Meggs elected to stay curled up in the carriage. Out the window, she could see the ship *Defiant*, moored midchannel in the River Dart, its lanterns bobbing like fireflies over the water.

She smelled him first—the pungent, brackish aroma of cloves, the scent cloying up on her tongue—before she registered the steel insistence of the knife at her neck and felt the hand over her mouth, muffling her voice and restricting her breath.

Falconer. Neither escaped to France, nor in the custody of the authorities, damn their incompetent eyes. His appearance there in Dartmouth was so improbable, so ridiculous, she disregarded the healthy, acid kick of fear in her gut and did nothing. The stench of him, so close, was overpowering. And in that moment, before she could muster herself to follow her instinct, he had her.

"You will, of course, be everything sweet and quiet, since you will like to live to see tomorrow."

Too late she tried to scream, to create a disturbance that would bring commotion down upon his head, but the knife was instantly against her windpipe.

"I shouldn't like to leave you here dead, since it will not give me what I need, but slitting your throat can nonetheless be so easily arranged."

And he was dragging her out into the darkness on the far side of the coach, pushing her before him down an alleyway with the same merciless strength he had shown her in London. Out of the corners of her eyes, she saw nets and crab pots stacked against the walls. She thought to kick out at them and leave a path, a trail of destruction and noise, but his hand, gloved in black leather, gouged into her face, and the knife pressed harder at her throat until the edges of her vision began to crowd in. Falconer was not afraid to hurt her. In fact, he would take great pleasure in doing so.

And fear did have a way of sorting out priorities. So she concentrated on staying upright and keeping her hands over his to ease the pressure of the blade at her neck. But soon, he had her down a rotted stair and out of sight into a dark, damp basement somewhere along the waterfront.

"I will let you sit, without the knife at your neck, but the moment you do anything, I will slit you from ear to ear. You'll be no trouble to me dead, so don't think to make any, and still stay alive. You are only valuable to me so long as you make no trouble. Or sound." He eased his cruel grip. "You understand?"

"Silent as the grave—that's me," she croaked, gasping in the dank, stale air.

He made a clucking sound of approval, which sounded suspiciously as if he were sucking on a clove, and maneuvered her back against an upright post, whereupon he twisted her arms painfully behind her back as he tied her wrists together with his cravat. As soon as he had made her secure he came to her side, and mindful of her feet lest she kick him—which she had every bloody intention of doing if he came close enough— he reached around and stuffed a handkerchief into her mouth as a gag.

It was surprisingly effective as such. The heavy scent and taste of cloves, which he must have kept in his pockets, along with the handkerchief, was overpowering enough to make her retch. Jesus God, but he must have one powerful toothache.

He moved away to position himself near a small window set high in the basement wall. In what little light came through the small pane, she could see Falconer looked considerably less than his usual, immaculate self. He was no longer the tidy, serious man of business. He looked hunted, disreputable, and on the run. Clearly, he wasn't used to making do—she would have recommended a visit to a handy rag-trader. And he wasn't used to taking prisoners, no matter his easy hand with cruelty. The gag was easy enough to dispose of. It was the work of only a moment to spit it quietly out and hide it under her feet. But all in all, she felt like the rankest amateur. Caught out flat footed, with nothing but her wits to help her—no picks, no knife, not so much as a comb down her pockets. And even her clever, agile hands were no match for the tight knots in the cravat. Already, her fingers were losing feeling.

As he kept watch out his little window, he amused himself by throwing a knife—a different one, thicker and heavier than the stiletto he had held to her throat—at the wooden beam above her head. It was a more effective deterrent to conversation than the gag.

But the silence weighed on him more heavily than her. Eventually, he spoke.

"Imagine my surprise when I come down to the Devon coast, to Dartmouth to make my usual arrangements to be smuggled back to France, and I see Lord Stoval's former scullery maid rolling down the quay in a ducal traveling coach.

And certainly, you don't look like a scullery maid today. Truly, you fascinate me."

She heard it then, not the accent, which was both precise and unremarkable, but the cadence of his speech. "You're French."

"Ah. Very good. Though it is nothing anyone may not know. London, indeed the whole of England, is filled with *émigrés*, just as Dartmouth is filled with smugglers."

He seemed not to mind that she had removed her gag, so she answered. "But you are not truly an *émigré*."

"Correct. And now, I find I have you, a bargaining chip as it were, to assist me, should I have trouble being returned to France."

And it was there, a sort of loving reverence, when he said the word "France." Here was the zealot. Lord Stoval might have only been in it for the money, but here was the one who paid him. Here was the one who was prepared to do her grievous harm in the name of liberty, equality, and brotherhood.

Bloody Jesus on the cross and all the martyred saints. Something could always go wrong, couldn't it? With a zealot, she didn't like her chances by half.

But then he spoke no more. He did not disturb himself to even ask *why* she was in Dartmouth. Perhaps, like all zealots, he could not conceive of any reason that did not involve himself. Perhaps he didn't care. Or perhaps it simply didn't matter why she was here, only that he could make use of her.

They sat like that—he looking out his sliver of window and she tied to the post. She had slid down the beam to sit upon the floor, but her body grew cramped and then began to go numb, though occasional bouts of pins and needles assailed her arms. She kept herself awake, alternately nursing and accepting the pain of clenching and releasing various muscles in turn, and trying to think up plans of attack and escape.

She had made and discarded several untenable plans when it came to her with clarity and certainty—she did not have to *do* anything. She was not on her own. Hugh would be looking for her. He would come. Any moment he would burst through the door and find her and take her home, because he was just that sort of man—strong and hard, and reliable as granite. Her walking tor. All she had to do was wait and keep herself ready until he did. It brought her a feeling of peaceful calm.

Finally, Falconer liked whatever he saw outside his window and he came to untie her. Meggs made a supreme effort to hold her arms and hands quietly while the blood returned, but the flood of feeling back into her limbs was excruciating.

Falconer pulled her roughly to her feet and began to retie her hands in front of her. "It is time for us to go."

"Us? Why should you need me?"

"You are my insurance, dear girl. Should anyone come looking to interfere with me, I will have you with which to bargain."

"Me? 'Oo's gonna bargain fer me?"

"It is amusing, this scullery character you put on, like that hideous mobcap you left behind you in my office. You are fortunate it amuses me. But do not think I am stupid. Whoever you are, I know it was you who stole the papers and saw to it Stoval was arrested. And whoever brought you here to find me will want you back. It will be up to you how many pieces they find you in."

She tried to laugh. "Me? I'm just his whore. He's already paid as much for me as he's like to, ducks."

Falconer answered her with a vicious backhand across the mouth. Pain exploded and ricocheted around her brain. She had to close her eyes against the echoing agony.

"Again," he instructed. "Do not think me stupid."

So, clever girl that she was, she minded and nodded her understanding, before she asked carefully around her split lip, "Where are you taking me?"

"This will become self-evident."

He dragged her toward the door before all the feeling had

returned to her hands. Meggs tried to fight him, but she was still numb, and her hands were useless. She did manage to kick him, and in retaliation, he cuffed her again, hard. Her face felt blistered with the sting of his hand, and she couldn't stop the feral sound growling out of her throat any more than she could keep from grasping the anger and hatred and fear to put them to better use, the way Nan had taught her. Hugh would come, but there was no reason not to help him when he did.

But Falconer was ready for her. He pushed her up the rickety wooden steps to the cellar door, then shoved her hard against the panel. Pain and anger grew together, twin sisters looking for their revenge.

"And now, before we venture out this door, I will again make my instruction eminently clear."

His leather-gloved hand gripped her throat again and pressed hard, ruthlessly cutting off her wind. She reached up with her tied hands to hang on his wrist and try to pry his hand away. It was to no avail. Blackness hovered at the edge of her vision.

He waved the blade back and forth before her eyes like a deadly snake and said, "You will not make so much as one tiny little peep of sound. Or I will slice your neck open like this—"

Pain ripped across her throat as he cut her. Panic welled and waned in her blood. She staggered in shock, but she managed to keep her feet. It couldn't have been too much then—only a small cut. She was still alive and not yet bleeding to death. But there was pain—and she drew it to her like a succubus, nursing the poison it spread through her.

He brought the blade up again to dance before her eyes, with the crimson droplet of her blood still staining the cutting point. "There, you see what will happen? So you will be quiet, yes? Not one sound."

She nodded as best she could in his vise-like grip, and gritted out, "If that's the way you want it." But she had never been much good at obeying commands, especially when she was frightened. Or angry. And he made her both. So she kept her hands wrapped around the hand at her neck, keeping him from moving it. And at the same time covering her own throat. When he brought the glistening blade around again, she could feel the cutting edge rest, not against her throat but against the flesh below her thumb. He couldn't tell the difference. He would slice open her hand before he got to her throat again. Not an entirely pleasing prospect, to have her hand sliced open again, but one she could deal with far better than a slit throat.

His small mistake gave her strength. She'd serve the bastard up yet. Meggs let the anger and hatred coil through her, letting the boil of rage make her powerful and deadly. She had survived eight years alone on the streets of London on nothing more than her hands and her wits, and they would be more than enough to deal with the likes of this bastard cove. He was like all the rest of them, too sure of himself, too arrogant to figure out what he didn't know.

Well, she knew. She only had to wait for the right moment to serve him up his share of retribution.

She breathed deep through her nose and let the air seethe through her. The alley stank of fish and brine, mud and piss, and she let herself stumble against him, fumbling with her feet close against his as he shoved her along.

He hesitated at the neck of the alley, where the cold clean wind announced their imminent arrival at the quay, looking and listening. Across the cobbles at the harbor's edge a blazing torch revealed one lone waterman in his boat, bobbing against the steps and waiting for fares, but she took a calming breath, closed her eyes, and narrowed her focus to nothing but the man behind her and his hands.

Falconer made his final decision, nodded her in the waterman's direction, and moved. That was when her foot came down with unerring precision upon his instep at the same time she twisted sharply, wrenching back his vulnerable thumb from her neck with one hand while she rammed her strong, sharp elbow as hard as she could into his jaw.

Now, that was going to be one hell of a toothache.

There was a deafening roar of sound and concussion that rang inside her head and knocked her flat against the cobbles. She fell hard into the slime of the gutter at Falconer's feet. Dirt and muddy water filled her open mouth, and every other sensation faded away.

Everything sounded strange and faraway, as if she were underwater and drowning.

Oh, Jesus God. She must have been hit. And she'd never felt a thing. No pain, no anguish. Just a peaceful, quiet feeling of calm. She rolled slowly onto her back, spitting out grit, reaching over her body to find the place where she'd been shot. To stem the inevitable pulsing leak of blood.

Above her head, lights, lanterns, and blazing torches of leaping fire came and turned the night orange and gold. And there was the captain, Hugh, staring down at her, his eyes wide and nearly colorless, looking like God's revenge against murder. Her brother, looking impossibly grown up in his naval blue coat, swam into focus behind him.

The captain knelt down and she saw his mouth move, but she couldn't hear anything. It was as if she were wrapped in a heavy, wet blanket and couldn't move—every feeling muffled and suspended. She must be dying. Oh, sweet Lord, she didn't want to leave him now. Not after all this time, after so many years of pain, hunger, and suffering, and trying to find her way home. She had found her home with him. She belonged with him.

But she was in his arms. He scooped her up and held her tight against his chest for a moment, and she could feel the desperate urgency and anger in the heat and tension radiating off his body in murderous waves. His hand was roaming over her, probing quickly for the fatal wound, and then his mouth came down hard on hers in a furious, possessive kiss.

She clung to his lips, to the heat and life in him. And then he pulled away. And set her on her feet.

Well. She was standing. On her own two feet. Apparently she was not dying after all. Meggs made another, more thorough inventory of her body, which revealed arms, legs, and all the salient bits in between, all present and accounted for and in their proper place.

Two feet away, across the cobbles, Falconer had not fared so well. His head was a tangled mess of blood and bone, and he was most certainly dead. One of the naval men crouching down pulled the loose end of his cloak over his body.

But there was still no sound. She could not hear. She had gone deaf.

"Hugh," she screamed, but no sound came out, only vibration and the feeling of raw heat in her bruised throat. But he must have heard her, because he was there, staring into her face. "I can't hear!"

He took her face in his hands and pulled her to him, kissing her forehead. She covered his hands with her own and stared at his mouth, trying to make the sound come, trying to find something in the buzzing silence.

"I know," he said, but she only knew that because his mouth moved and he nodded at her. And then he pulled her against his chest, and she felt the vibration of his voice through his body.

He said something else, but Meggs had not been able to grasp half of his words. The sounds were still muffled and bleeding together like spoken fog. Still, there were worse things than being deaf—there was being dead—so she had to be thankful. And she had to shout. "Thank you—for coming. I didn't think you'd—"

Now Hugh was shouting, because she could hear some of

what he said, and because the others turned to look at them and then turned just as quickly away.

"I'm sorry, but I had to take the chance."

That she understood, because she saw his mouth make the sounds before he turned her head to examine her ringing ears. And she felt the surging tempo of his heart beating fast beneath his ribs and smelled the acrid, metallic fume of black powder on his hands and coat.

"Did *you* shoot him?" And there, for the first time, were the tinny, high notes of her voice scratching their way through the ringing silence.

"I had to," he growled, the words churning through his chest. "He's a damned French agent, and he had you, he had my wife, with a knife to your throat. I saw the blood—"

"What?" She could not have heard that correctly.

"Your hearing will come back, later, hopefully." He kissed her ear. "I had to take the chance. I had to fire at close range, with the gun right next to your ear, to shoot him because I couldn't take the chance of the ball firing astray and—"

"I'm not your wife." She might have shouted. She wasn't sure. But whatever she was doing, it made him react.

He grabbed her collar and hauled her up close, as if he could grind his desperate will into her. "I'll give you precisely twenty minutes, and not a moment more, to rectify that oversight."

"Twenty minutes? Don't be ridiculous." She *was* shouting now. At the top of her lungs. "I was just almost killed, and I'm covered in dirt and blood. I look awful. And I can't hear a bloody thing. A girl doesn't like to get married like that, see? So don't you dare play the bully boy with me, Captain Hugh McAlden. I want my brother and my grandmother with me. And I want to wear a proper dress, and a proper bonnet, and carry proper flowers. We're getting bloody married at home! In the spring."

He smiled at her. He smiled in that slow, inevitable way

that crinkled up the corners of his eyes and turned those pale
blue chips of ice into nothing but miles of warm ocean. That
smile that made him look young and silly and happy. "That is
a yes, then, isn't it? You did just say you were going to marry
me?"

"I might have done. I can't hear properly, and you need to
work on your style of proposal."

He made his face all solemn, and taking her hands firmly in
his, he knelt down on the wet cobbles before her. She leaned
toward him because with her ears still ringing like the inside
of a church bell, she wasn't sure she would be able to hear him
properly. And she was not going to miss a single word if she
could help it, thank you very much.

"Please, Meggs. I don't want to live without you. I can't. I
can't conceive of my life without you in it. Please, Meggs,
make me happy. Please."

"Thank you, yes. I will. I thought you'd never do it proper-
like. Now, if you please, I'd like you to take me home."

"God's balls, lass, it's miles back to Fenmore. There's an
inn, or we could make it out to Glass Cottage, but—"

"That will do. I don't mean Fenmore. I mean with you. I
don't care where we go, as long as I'm with you. My home is
with you."

"Do you mean that? Truly?"

"Of course I do." Her voice sounded even more affronted
for its tinny timbre. "I'd never have said it otherwise."

"Good." He kissed her again on the forehead, even though
she turned her lips up to his in the hope of something more
substantial. "Because if you want to be with me, to go where I
go, you can't wait until spring. You'll have to marry me right
away and come away with me, for I'm to take command of
Dangerous again, and I want you with me."

"*Dangerous?* Oh, aye, that'd be the one they give you."

"Oh, aye." He gathered her up tighter in his arms. "And

that'll be the one I take *you* aboard. Fair warning to the French."

She laughed, because she had to. Because she couldn't possibly contain all the happiness that was flowing up inside her like champagne out from a bottle. "All right then."

"Then I'll take you, and Timmy, home to Fenmore, long enough only to get married and say your good-byes. And then you'll come away with me."

"And be happy forever?" She was teasing him, she supposed, because it was a ridiculous thing to ask. But even as she joked, she knew she meant it. Because for the first time in a very, very long time, she was completely and unreservedly happy. She wanted to hold on to this moment forever, when she was safe in his arms and sure of his love. And she knew she would do everything in her power to make him happy, as happy as he had made her.

But the captain was an honest man. His face became even more solemn as he looked down into her eyes and answered. "No. We won't always be happy, Meggs, because life isn't like that. You know it as well as I. But we will always be together. We'll weather whatever storms come our way together. And I'll try my damndest to make you happy. Always."

And then he took her face in his hands and kissed her, slow and deep, the way she liked, to remind her he knew exactly what he was talking about.

EPILOGUE

At dawn, Meggs watched from the rail as the green island rose out of the sea like an ancient tortoise. The storms of the gray North Atlantic had given way to warm westerly winds as *Dangerous* sailed across the placid horse latitudes into the lee of the Caribbean. The soft morning breeze wrapped around her as sweetly as a shawl. Blissfully, soothingly warm.

There it was—Jamaica. Her faraway West Indies island. Just as she had imagined it. The profile of the island was low and dark against the lightening sky, and the foaming sea below the bowsprit was warming to a thousand different colors of azure and liquid emerald. There was nothing but sea, sand, and green, green trees. Miles and miles of tall swaying palm trees.

"What is it that has you so enchanted?"

Meggs had thought Hugh was still working quietly with the sailing master and the first lieutenant in his cabin, making their orders for the day and preparing for their arrival to join the West Indies Squadron in Jamaica. But her husband had not only come topside, but had also broken with protocol. He had left the quarterdeck to moor up close behind her and touch her just so—with his hand sliding casually across the small of her back to fetch up innocently along the line of her ribs. He was meant to be all proper ship's captain, carefully solicitous in such a public setting, but his long index finger somehow managed to stroke the underside of her breast, reminding her of what had transpired when they had been alone in the quiet, exploratory dark of the captain's cabin. Wicked, provoking man.

However, he did take care to lower his head and speak directly into her left ear. She had recovered most of the hearing in her right, but sometimes, especially at sea where the breeze snatched words away, it was hard for her to hear clearly. Still, a tin ear was a small enough price to pay for such unspeakable happiness. At the feeling she got when his low words whispered down inside her.

She smiled over her shoulder at him. "Palm trees. I used to dream about palm trees."

"Did you? Then look to your heart's content, but come away astern to do so. You can see your palm trees just as well from the quarterdeck."

"Oh, no thank you. I'd rather stay here, where I don't have to peer around your masts and spars." She turned back to look out over the gleaming water. "It's so very beautiful, isn't it?"

"It is. And the island as well."

She could hear the warmth in his voice. "You're teasing me."

"I am. But you still must come away. You're interfering with the running of my ship here."

"Am I?" She peered at the deck around her, full of little knots of men, seeming to her eye to be going about their naval business just as they always did. "However can I be interfering?"

At her back, Meggs felt his heavy, mock sigh rumble through his chest. "Couldn't you simply allow me to know slightly more than you about the business of my own ship? As you once acknowledged, I am a professional navvy, all trained up for it."

She couldn't resist him when he was self-deprecating and charming, and giving her that teasing, sleepy-eyed, silly smile. "Hmm. But I've learned all this navy business quickly, haven't I, Captain?"

"Oh, aye. I have no doubt you'll be able to pass the exam for lieutenant in no time at the rate you've been going on. But you should remember the first rule of the navy is that you must obey your captain, and come away. The problem, my clever girl, is that with you here at the bowsprit rail, the men can't move forward of the forecastle to use the heads, as they would rather cast themselves overboard than abuse your delicate sensibilities."

"You mean they can't—"

"Get to the business end of their breeches," he finished for her. "Yes."

"Good Lord and all the weeping saints." She turned immediately away from the bow, tugging Hugh's arm in her haste. "Sorry. They're new to me, the delicate sensibilities."

Her husband was making a meal of his laughter, chewing up his smile something fierce to keep his captainly mask in place as he walked her along the length of the deck. "It's quite all right, lass." He leaned close so only she could hear his words. "To tell you the truth, Meggs, I infinitely prefer you without."

"Without delicate sensibilities?"

"Without anything, my Lady Dangerous. Anything at all."

Meggs felt a blush sweep heat across her cheeks despite the cooling breezes. "Lady Dangerous? Is that my new *nom de guerre*? It sounds terribly dashing and romantic."

"Nothing romantic about it. You're more dangerous than a lit fuse."

Meggs smiled up at him and tilted her head, just so he would be defenseless to her brand of rather cheeky charm. "And will you, Captain McAlden, be the one lighting it?"

In answer he smiled. That lovely, silly, happy smile that

crinkled up the corners of his eyes and turned them the color of the warm clear sea. "With a very slow match." He clasped her hand in his and steered her toward the companionway stair. "Handsomely now, my Lady Dangerous. As if we've all the time in the world."

Did you miss the rest of Elizabeth's series?
Go back and read it from the beginning!
It starts with THE PURSUIT OF PLEASURE . . .

"I couldn't help overhearing your conversation." He wanted to steer their chat to his purpose, but the back of her neck was white and long. He'd never noticed that long slide of skin before, so pale against the vivid color of her locks. He'd gone away before she'd been old enough to put up her hair. And nowadays the fashion seemed to be for masses of loose ringlets covering the neck. Trust Lizzie to still sail against the tide.

"Yes, you could." Her breezy voice broke into his thoughts.

"I beg your pardon?"

"Help it. You *could* have helped it, as any polite gentleman *should*, but you obviously chose not to." She didn't even bother to look back at him as she spoke and walked on, but he heard the teasing in her voice. Such intriguing confidence. He could use it to his purpose. She had always been up for a lark.

He caught her elbow and steered her into an unused parlor. She let him guide her easily, without resisting the intimacy or the presumption of the brief contact of his hand against the soft, vulnerable skin of her inner arm, but once through the door she just seemed to dissolve out of his grasp. His empty fingers prickled from the sudden loss. He let her move away and closed the door.

No lamp or candle branch illuminated the room, only the moonlight streaming through the tall casement windows. Lizzie looked like a pale ghost, weightless and hovering in the strange light. He took a step nearer. He needed her to be real, not an illusion. Over the years she'd become a distant but recurring dream, a combination of memory and boyish lust, haunting his sleep.

He had thought of her, or at least the idea of her, almost constantly over the years. She had always been there, in his mind, swimming just below the surface. And he had come tonight in search of her. To banish his ghosts.

She took a sliding step back to lean nonchalantly against the arm of a chair, her pose one of sinuous, bored indifference.

"So what are you doing in Dartmouth? Aren't you meant to be messing about with your boats?"

"Ships," he corrected automatically and then smiled at his foolishness for trying to tell Lizzie anything. "The big ones are ships."

"And they let *you* have one of the *big* ones? Aren't you a bit young for that?" She tucked her chin down to subdue her smile and looked up at him from under her gingery brows. Very mischievous. She was warming to him.

If it was worldliness she wanted, he could readily supply it. He mirrored her smile.

"Hard to imagine, isn't it, Lizzie?" He opened his arms wide, presenting himself for her inspection.

Only she didn't inspect him. Her eyes slid away to inventory the scant furniture in the darkened room. "No one else calls me that anymore."

"Lizzie? Well, I do. I can't imagine you as anything else. And I like it. I like saying it. Lizzie." The name hummed through his mouth like a honeybee sprinkled with nectar. Like a kiss. He moved closer so he could see the emerald color of her eyes, dimmed by the half light, but still brilliant against the white of her skin. He leaned a fraction too close and whispered, "Lizzie. It always sounds somehow . . . naughty."

She turned quickly. Wariness flickered across her mobile face, as if she were suddenly unsure of both herself and him, before it was just as quickly masked.

And yet, she continued to study him surreptitiously, so he held himself still for her perusal. To see if she would finally notice him as a man. He met her eyes and he felt a kick low in his gut. In that moment plans and strategies became unimportant. The only important thing was for Lizzie to see him. It was essential.

But she kept all expression from her face. He was jolted to realize she didn't want him to read her thoughts or mood. She was trying hard to keep *him* from seeing *her*.

It was an unexpected change. The Lizzie he had known as a child had been so wholly passionate about life, she had thrown herself body and soul into each and every moment, each action and adventure. She had not been covered with this veneer of poised nonchalance.

And yet it was only a veneer. He was sure of it. And he was equally sure he could make his way past it. He drew in a measured breath and sent her a slow, melting smile to show, in the course of the past few minutes, he'd most definitely noticed she was a woman.

She gave no outward reaction, and it took Marlowe a long moment to recognize her response: she looked careful. It was a quality he'd never seen in her before.

Finally, after what felt like an infinity, she broke the moment. "You didn't answer. Why are you here? After all these years?"

He chose the most convenient truth. "A funeral. Two weeks ago." A bleak, rain-soaked funeral that couldn't be forgotten. The downpour that April day had chilled him to his very marrow. He went cold just thinking about it, unable to shake the horrible feeling sitting like a lump of cold porridge in his belly. It was wrong, all wrong. Frank couldn't be dead. He shouldn't be dead. And yet he was. They'd found his body, pale and lifeless, washed up cold and unseeing upon the banks of the Dart. Drowned.

At least that was what the local authorities said. But Marlowe knew better. Frank was murdered. And he would prove it.

Lizzie's murmur brought him back. "My condolences, for what they're worth." She ran her palm up and down her other forearm as if she were chilled. Lizzie had never been at ease with open emotion. "Anyone I knew?"

"Lieutenant Francis Palmer."

"Frankie Palmer?" For a moment she was truly affected. Her full lips dropped open in an exhalation. "From down Stoke Fleming way? Didn't you two go off to sea together, all those years ago?"

"Yes, ten years ago." Ten long years. A lifetime.

"Oh. I am sorry." Her voice lost its languid bite.

He looked back and met her eyes. Such sincerity had never been one of Lizzie's strong suits. No, that was wrong. She'd always been sincere, or at least truthful—painfully so as he recalled—but she rarely let her true feelings show.

"Thank you, Lizzie. But I didn't lure you into a temptingly darkened room to bore you with dreary news."

"No, you came to proposition me." The mischievous little smile crept back. Lizzie was never the sort to be intimidated for long. She had always loved to be doing things she ought not.

A heated image of her sinuous white body temptingly entwined in another man's arms rose unbidden in his brain. Good God, what other things had Lizzie been doing over the past few years that she ought not? And with whom?

Marlowe quickly jettisoned the irrational spurt of jealousy. Her more recent past hardly mattered. In fact, some experience on her part might better suit his plans.

"Yes, my proposition. I can give you what you want. A marriage without the man."

For the longest moment she went unnaturally still, then she slid off the chair arm and glided closer to him. So close, he almost backed up. So close, her rose petal of a mouth came but a hairsbreadth from his own. Then she lifted her inquisitive nose and took a bold, suspicious whiff of his breath.

"You've been drinking."

"I have," he admitted without a qualm.

"How much?"

"More than enough for the purpose. And you?"

"Clearly not enough. Not that they'd let me." She turned and walked away. Sauntered really. She was very definitely a saunterer, all loose joints and limbs, as if she'd never paid the least attention to deportment. Very provocative, although he doubted she meant to be. An image of a bright, agile otter, frolicking unconcerned in the calm green of the river Dart, twisting and rolling in the sunlit water, came to mind.

"Drink or no, I meant what I said."

"Are you proposing? Marriage? To me?" She laughed as if it were a joke. She didn't believe him.

"I am."

She eyed him more closely, her gaze narrowing even as one marmalade eyebrow rose in assessment. "Do you have a fatal disease?"

"No."

"Are you engaged to fight a duel?"

"Again, no."

"Condemned to death?" She straightened with a fluid undulation, her spine lifting her head up in surprise as the thought entered her head, all worldliness temporarily obliterated. "Planning a suicide?"

"No and no." It was so hard not to smile. Such a charming combination of concern and cheek. The cheek won out: she gave him that feral, slightly suspicious smile.

"Then how do you plan to arrange it, the 'without the man' portion of the proceedings? I'll want some sort of guarantee. You can't imagine I'm gullible enough to leave your fate, or my own for that matter, to chance."

A low heat flared within him. By God, she really was considering it.

"And yet, Lizzie, I think you may. I am an officer of His Majesty's Royal Navy and am engaged to captain a convoy of prison ships to the Antipodes. I leave only days from now. The last time I was home, in England, was four and a half years ago and then only for a few months to recoup from a near fatal wound. This trip is slated to take at least eight . . . years."

Her face cleared of all traces of impudence. Oh yes, even Lizzie could be led.

"Storms, accidents, and disease provide most of the risk. Don't forget we're still at war with France and Spain. And the Americans don't think too highly of us either. One stray cannonball could do the job quite nicely."

"Is that what did it last time?"

"Last time? I've never been dead before."

The ends of her ripe mouth nipped up. The heat in his gut sailed higher.

"You said you had recovered from a near fatal wound."

"Ah, yes. Grapeshot, actually. In my chest. Didn't go deep enough to kill me, though afterward, the fever nearly did."

Her gaze skimmed over his coat, curious and maybe a little hungry. The heat spread lower, kindling into a flame.

"Do you want to see?" He was being rash, he knew, but he'd done this for her once before, taken off his shirt on a dare. And he wanted to remind her.

And then there's A SENSE OF SIN . . .

The Ravishing Miss Celia Burke. A well-known, and even more well-liked local beauty. She made her serene, graceful way down the short set of stairs into the ballroom as effortlessly as clear water flowed over rocks in a hillside stream. She nodded and smiled in a benign but uninvolved way at all who approached her, but she never stopped to converse. She processed on, following her mother through the parting sea of mere mortals, those lesser human beings who were nothing and nobody to her but playthings.

Aloof, perfect Celia Burke. *Fuck you.*

By God, he would take his revenge and Emily would have justice. Maybe then he could sleep at night.

Maybe then he could learn to live with himself.

But he couldn't exact the kind of revenge one takes on another man—straightforward, violent, and bloody. He couldn't call Miss Burke out on the middle of the dance floor and put a bullet between her eyes or a sword blade between her ribs at dawn.

His justice would have to be more subtle, but no less thorough. And no less ruthless.

"You were the one who insisted we attend this august gathering. So what's it to be, Delacorte?" Commander Hugh

McAlden, friend, naval officer, and resident cynic, prompted again.

McAlden was one of the few people who never addressed Del by his courtesy title, Viscount Darling, as they'd known each other long before he'd come into the bloody title and far too long for Del to give himself airs in front of such an old friend. With such familiarity came ease. With McAlden, Del could afford the luxury of being blunt.

"Dancing or thrashing? The latter, I think."

McAlden's usually grim mouth crooked up in half a smile. "A thrashing, right here in the Marchioness's ballroom? I'd pay good money to see that."

"Would you? Shall we have a private bet, then?"

"Del, I always like it when you've got that look in your eye. I'd like nothing more than a good wager."

"A bet, Colonel Delacorte? What's the wager? I've money to burn these days, thanks to you two." Another naval officer, Lieutenant Ian James, known from their time together when Del had been an officer of His Majesty's Marine Forces aboard the frigate *Resolute*, broke into the conversation from behind.

"A private wager only, James." Del would need to be more circumspect. James was a bit of a puppy, happy and eager, but untried in the more manipulative ways of society. There was no telling what he might let slip. Del had no intention of getting caught in the net he was about to cast. "Save your fortune in prize money for another time."

"A gentleman's bet then, Colonel?"

A *gentleman's* bet. Del felt his mouth curve up in a scornful smile. What he was about to do violated every code of gentlemanly behavior. "No. More of a challenge."

"He's Viscount Darling now, Mr. James." McAlden gave Del a mocking smile. "We have to address him with all the deference he's due."

Unholy glee lit the young man's face. "I had no idea. Congratulations, Colonel. What a bloody fine name. I can hear the ladies now: *my dearest, darling Darling.* How will they resist you?"

Del merely smiled and took another drink. It was true. None of them resisted: high-born ladies, low-living trollops, barmaids, island girls, or senoritas. They never had, bless their lascivious hearts.

And neither would *she,* despite her remote facade. Celia Burke was nothing but a hothouse flower just waiting to be plucked.

"Go on, then. What's your challenge?" McAlden's face housed a dubious smirk as several more navy men, Lieutenants Thomas Gardener and Robert Scott, joined them.

"I propose I can openly court, seduce, and ruin an untried, virtuous woman"—Del paused to give them a moment to remark upon the condition he was about to attach—"without ever once touching her."

McAlden gave a huff of cynical laughter. "Too easy in one sense, too hard in another," he stated flatly.

"How can you possibly ruin someone without touching them?" Ian James protested.

Del felt his mouth twist. He had forgotten what it was like to be that young. While he was only six and twenty, he'd grown older since Emily's death. Vengeance was singularly aging.

"Find us a drink would you, gentlemen? A real drink. None of the lukewarm swill they're passing out on trays." Del pushed the young lieutenants off in the direction of a footman.

"Too easy to ruin a reputation with only a rumor," McAlden repeated in his unhurried, determined way. "You'll have to do better than that."

Trust McAlden to get right to the heart of the matter. Like Del, McAlden had never been young, and he was older in years, as well.

"With your reputation," McAlden continued as they turned

to follow the others, "well deserved, I might add, you'll not get within a sea mile of a virtuous woman."

"That, old man, shows how little you know of women."

"That, my darling Viscount, shows how little you know of their mamas."

"I'd like to keep it that way. Hence the prohibition against touching. I plan on keeping a very safe distance." While he was about the business of revenging himself on Celia Burke, he needed to keep himself safe from being forced into doing the right thing should his godforsaken plan be discovered or go awry. And he simply didn't *want* to touch her. He didn't want to be tainted by so much as the merest brush of her hand.

"Can't seduce, really *seduce*, from a distance. Not even you. Twenty guineas says it can't be done."

"Twenty? An extravagant wager for a flinty, tight-pursed Scotsman like you. Done." Del accepted the challenge with a firm handshake. It sweetened the pot, so to speak.

McAlden perused the crowd. "Shall we pick now? I warn you, Del, this isn't London. There's plenty of virtue to be had in Dartmouth."

"Why not?" Del felt his mouth curve into a lazy smile. The town may have been full of virtue, but he was full of vice. He cared about only one particular woman's virtue.

"You'll want to be careful. Singularly difficult things, women," McAlden offered philosophically. "Can turn a man inside out. Just look at Marlowe."

Del shrugged. "Captain Marlowe married. I do not have anything approaching marriage in mind."

"So you're going to seduce and ruin an innocent without being named or caught? That *is* bloody-minded."

"I didn't say innocent. I said untried. In this case, there is a particular difference." He looked across the room at Celia Burke again. At the virtuous, innocent face she presented to the world. He would strip away that mask until everyone could see the ugly truth behind her immaculately polished, social veneer.

McAlden followed the line of his gaze. "You can't mean— That's Celia Burke!" All trace of jaded amusement disappeared from McAlden's voice. "Jesus, Del, have you completely lost your mind? As well as all moral scruples?"

"Gone squeamish?" Del tossed back the last of his drink. "That's not like you."

"I *know* her. Everyone in Dartmouth knows her. She is Marlowe's wife's most particular friend. You can't go about ruining—*ruining* for God's sake—innocent young women like her. Even *I* know that."

"I said she's *not* innocent."

"Then you must've misjudged her. She's not fair game, Del. Pick someone else. Someone I don't know." McAlden's voice was growing thick.

"No." Darling kept his own voice flat.

McAlden's astonished countenance turned back to look at Miss Burke, half a room away, smiling sweetly in conversation with another young woman. He swore colorfully under his breath. "That's not just bloody-minded, that's suicidal. She's got parents, Del. Attentive parents. Take a good hard look at her mama, Lady Caroline Burke. She's nothing less than the daughter of a duke, and is to all accounts a complete gorgon in her own right. They say she eats fortune hunters, not to mention an assortment of libertines like you, for breakfast. What's more, Miss Burke is a relation of the Marquess of Widcombe, in whose ballroom you are currently *not dancing.* This isn't London. You are a guest here. My guest, and therefore Marlowe's guest. One misstep like that and they'll have your head. Or, more likely, your ballocks. And quite rightly. Pick someone else for your challenge."

"No."

"Delacorte."

"Bugger off, Hugh."

McAlden knew Del well enough to hear the implacable finality in his tone. Hugh shook his head slowly. "God's balls, Del. I didn't think I'd regret so quickly having you to stay." He ran his hand through his short, cropped hair and looked at Del with a dawning of realization. "Christ. You'd already made up your mind before you came here, hadn't you? You came for her."